MINE EYES HAVE SEEN

MINE EYES HAVE SEEN

Land of Promise, Book II

Johnny Sundstrom

Also by the same author and available from Xlibris
Dawn's Early Light and For Spacious Skies

To order additional copies of this book, contact:
Xlibris
1-888-795-4274
www.Xlibris.com
Orders@Xlibris.com
716183

CONTENTS

Part I

HOME

Part II

FAMILY

Part III

JOURNEYS

Part IV

CONNECTIONS

Part V

FLIGHT

This story takes place during the immigrant settlement of southeastern Oregon, and the so-called Nez Perce War of 1877

Dedicated to
My beloved son...

Shiloh Forest Sundstrom
1981-2015

*whose life was taken from us
two nights after
the final draft of this novel was
completed.*

Acknowledgements

*I am very grateful to my immediate family
and my extended family of Arapaho relatives,
whose inspiration and love continue to support me
in my quest for a deeper personal relationship
with this continent, its history, and the inhabitants of
its landscapes for the past many thousands of years.*

*Special thanks and admiration for
Felisa Rogers, writer and blogger,
who proofread this novel and provided
significant assistance in correcting and
editing the text and its time-lines.
She has been a tremendous help.
(All remaining mistakes are the
responsibility of the author.)*

*Cover photo by Alexandra Steinmetz
Author photo by Kate Harnedy*

Foreword

Abraham, Sarah, and Hagar together make up the essential scriptural trio at the foundations of the three largest monotheistic religions in the world today. In the Jewish Torah, the Christian Bible, and the Islamic Quran, the record of these individuals and their relationships serves as the primary source of faith and is at the core of their religious beginnings. These records and traditions are regarded as both sacred and historically significant, and have attained a unique influence and power all their own.

In this trilogy of novels, I have transposed the narrative from ancient times to the period just following our country's War Between the States, and based it on the great migration of immigrant people crossing the continent in search of improved lives for themselves and their descendants, even as the native peoples are being displaced. I have attempted to find ways to echo not only the original story's importance over time, but to demonstrate its plausibility as an essentially human saga by accepting the challenge to tell it in a time and places far removed from its origins. If I have fallen short in my endeavor to demonstrate its relevance and timelessness, I am not embarrassed for having tried. If in the reader's estimation I have either failed or succeeded, you are invited to let me know.

Thank you for your attention, *Johnny Sundstrom*
<siwash@pioneer.net>

Brief Synopsis of Book I

Abe Saunders was wounded in one of the last battles of the War Between the States, in 1865. The first Book of this trilogy recounts his healing, marriage, and an overland wagon journey during the last great wave of pioneering westward migrations. Here were the constant struggles faced in overcoming nature's challenges, the sometimes violent human tensions encountered along the way, and the heartfelt aspirations for a new life among the Indians, ranchers, and miners of the still-untamed frontier.

Abe and his wife, Sarah Beth, leave behind everything familiar they have ever known except one another. Along the Oregon Trail crossing the country they find privacy to be at a premium, and conflict and hardship the norm. Their new marriage and love is often tested, and although Sarah deeply desires to bear a child by the time they will settle in the new land, they have no success in that aspect of their lives together. Challenged by the hostility of some individuals and greatly helped by others, joined part of the time by Abe's adventurous cousin, and seeking the promise of their own land in a place called Jordan Valley, they finally arrive to begin their new life.

They become acquainted with an offshoot of the Indian tribe located some distance to the north of where they end up, and are given a place to stay and build a home. Hawk Man and his relatives need a white man they can trust to occupy the land according to the laws of the USA, so they can continue to use it for their summer camping and hunting, without having those rights taken away. Assisted by their inter-tribal friend Lefty, the newcomers make friends and begin to share the land beyond the edge of any other settlement.

Along the way, they were joined by a young woman, Helga, who has run away from a group who had tried to harm Abe and Sarah Beth, and she quickly becomes a part of their small family. Their relationships with the Indian neighbors become more complicated, and the only apparent resolution results in a change in both roles and possibilities for the three of them. Book II begins at this point.

Prelude

"Mine eyes have seen
the glory of the coming of the Lord,
He is trampling out the vintage
where the grapes of wrath are stored...
His truth is marching on."

- American Battle Hymn (1861)

"Mine eyes have seen
the gory of the coming of their god,
trampling out the plains and rivers
where all our life comes from...
his troops are marching on."

- Lefty's Version (1877)

Part I

HOME

Summer-Fall 1869

CHAPTER 1

Family

That morning, Sarah Beth and Mattie had gone across to Hawk Man's camp. Abe noticed that Helga was washing clothes down beside the creek, not far from their temporary structures. He approached quietly, and scuffed the ground with his foot so as not to scare her. She looked around, and then stood up.

"So you told her," he said.

The young woman looked up at him. "I thought she should know. It was her idea."

"Why didn't you tell me first?"

"I don't know," she said. "Maybe because there's nothing you can do about it. But she could get angry or crazy, and try to make me leave."

Abe tried hard to think of something, anything, he could say.

Helga came closer and pressed herself against him, wrapping him in her arms. "It's ours, yours and mine, isn't it?" She started to cry. "Isn't it?"

He slowly lifted his own arms and held her. "Yes, of course."

They stood there, locked in a seemingly timeless embrace until she said, "I told you I loved you, but I didn't think you believed me." She pulled his head down toward her own, but he eased away from her kiss.

"Yes, but…"

"Mr. Abe, or just Abe, as you taught me to call you, if you turn away from me now, you will never see me or your child again. I promise you that. I love you and I want this to be just our child. Please."

"Of course," he said. He kissed her for the first time since Sarah Beth had returned home from her time away with Hawk Man.

She gently pushed him back and smiled up into his eyes. Neither spoke, and he left quickly, saddled his horse at the stable, and rode off toward the partly finished house. He wanted to complete the installation of the ironwork he got from his neighbor Mike Skinner, brackets that would hold railings for the porch steps, and hinges for the trap door that opened to the cellar.

Helga watched him go, her lips still held motionless in the shape of their kiss. He was so different now that Sarah Beth was back, and now that he knew she was with child, but his kiss was the same as the first time she'd ever felt it. She wasn't afraid he would turn away from her now, it was more that she feared Sarah Beth, who had been her best friend. She wondered what would become of her now that she had done what the wife couldn't do in giving Abe a child, the hope of his future. If Sarah Beth did make her leave or tried take the child from her, Helga knew she would fight, for the child, and for the man. She turned and knelt back down to her laundry work, smiling to herself, now thinking only of this new life within her, thinking only good thoughts for their child.

A short time later, as Helga was hanging the wet clothes on the line, Sarah Beth and Mattie returned from the Indian camp across the way. Mattie had only just learned to ride, and Ginger seemed to suit her fine, an experienced horse understanding this new rider's lack of skill. Helga walked over to assist the older woman down from the saddle.

"Well, Lord have mercy," Mattie said, stumbling a bit as she got to the ground, "I have rode a horse across a river and back. Now isn't that something?"

Sarah Beth laughed and took the reins from Helga and led both horses toward the corral. "More like a creek than a river, I'd say."

"Yes, well all right, but it was still water to ride through. Felt like I was an Israelite crossing Jordan right here in this here Jordan Valley. My, my, my."

Sarah Beth stopped and said, "Helga, maybe you shouldn't be reaching up like that to put the washing on the line. Leave it be and I'll do it as soon as these horses are taken care of."

Mattie laughed and said confidentially to Helga, "Land sakes girl, she's going to worry about you from now on. Now me, I was still pulling a garden plough the week before my first one was born. Probably made it easier." She pushed the kerchief holding her hair into place. "I'd best go get some bread started. That's a nice horse. I appreciate your letting me use her. I think she'll take to me after a bit."

Helga smiled and said, "I think she already likes you. Besides I've got Dandy now, and he's going to take all my horse attention from now on. Isn't he a beauty?" She nodded toward the nearby field and whistled, causing the dark bay horse to raise his head and whinny back to her. "It's like he already knew me when I got him."

Mattie smiled, saying, "A match made in heaven, as they say," and then walked off toward the kitchen shed, thinking about the other match, the one that made a baby with this girl. Where was that match made, in heaven or…? It remained to be seen. She shook her head and ducked through the doorway into the small kitchen.

When the horses were put out, Sarah Beth came inside, and asked Mattie if she needed any help. The woman shook her head and continued the soft song that accompanied her kneading of the bread.

"Then I think I'll ride out and see if Abe needs any help at the house. Mattie, it's going to be so wonderful when it's done, and can you imagine making bread and everything else in that huge kitchen?"

Mattie stopped what she was doing and looked at the young woman. "Not sure I'd call it huge, but it's certainly big enough."

"Oh Mattie, here you're the one calling a creek a river and then telling me what isn't huge. You're so funny sometimes." She turned and ducked out the doorway.

Mattie smiled and went back to kneading the bread, raising the sound of her singing a little, *"Nearer my God to Thee, nearer to Thee..."* As she sang, she thought back on the sad voices of the defeated Confederate troops marching back from the War, singing this new hymn they'd learned somewhere: *"Still all my song shall be, nearer my God, to Thee."*

Abe was inside the house working on a partition when Sarah Beth arrived. She stood quietly, leaning against a doorway, watching him swing the hammer over his head. When he stopped to wipe his face, she spoke softly, not wanting to frighten him, "Hello, my dear. Can I get you some water?"

He turned to face her with a surprised look. "That would be nice."

She went out to where a rain barrel caught the run-off from the half-finished roof. She filled a cup with the dipper and went back inside, holding the cup away until she got a kiss for it. The kiss he gave was done lightly. As he pulled away, she reached up and pulled his head down to hers, kissing him firmly.

"There, that's better, isn't it? Now you can have the water." She held it out to him.

He drank the whole cupful and wiped his mouth. "Sorry," he said, "I guess my mind was on this project."

"Speaking of projects, have you decided how we're going to arrange the bedrooms now that there will be a baby among us?"

"No." He tried to turn back to his work, but she kept him facing her. "No," he said, "I thought I'd let you decide that."

"Oh well, if it's my decision...How much trouble would it be to build another smaller house?"

"What? I don't think it could be done before winter, not when this one isn't finished yet."

"Well then, it's certainly something we'll have to think about, isn't it?" She turned away and began pacing off short distances within the perimeter of the house.

Abe watched her for a moment and went back to his work, then paused. "Well, wait a minute, this was supposed to be Mattie's room, this wall. Should I keep going on it?"

"Of course. Mattie has to have a room, and we do, and now Helga does too.

"What if we just made an attached addition out the back for her? It could be very nice."

"But cold," he said.

"She could use the little stove she has now. It doesn't take much wood."

"Let's think about it. It would take at least another load of lumber and supplies. And maybe we should also ask her."

Sarah Beth turned on her heel and faced him, hands on hips. "So this is how it's going to be from now on? That girl makes the decisions for us now?"

"Sarah Beth, please, that's not what I meant. I just meant that in some ways, we're all in this together now. I'm sorry. But it's very hard for me, just finding out. You have to know that."

"And you think it isn't hard for me?"

"Of course it is, but..."

"But it's my fault. Is that what you're going to say? Well, Mr. Abe, just how was I to know that you would do what I told you to do for once?" She turned and hurried out the doorway. She was mounting her horse by the time he caught up with her.

"Wait. Sarah Beth, please wait. We haven't talked about any of this. We have to."

"Maybe. Maybe so," she said, pulling Morning around, holding him back, "and then again, maybe not." She gave the horse his head and urged him into a gallop in the opposite direction from their home camp.

The sun was lowering toward the horizon and in the glare he could see only her silhouette. He shielded his eyes, thinking about the two kisses, one right after another, and of the two women. What would happen to him? How could he make it work if they couldn't work things out between themselves?

He worked late into the evening of the long day, ignoring his appetite, and trying to exhaust himself beyond the need to keep thinking about the women. By the time he put away his tools, the first star was in the sky and the sunset blue of the western horizon was deepening above the low profile of the hills. This wide open sky held his attention as he finished saddling Bird and stood staring over the saddle, out over this precious land. Its value lay not only in its natural beauty and bounty, and its potential for life and livelihood, but also by now in what it had already cost them, cost them in fighting for it, in disrupted relationships, and the slight sense of foreboding that he couldn't shake off, no matter how hard he worked, no matter how tired he made himself.

He let the reins hang slack on the horse's neck and allowed Bird, this best friend of his, to find the way. Now, here was a female that had never caused him a single problem, a willing worker and a partner through thick and thin. And how many times had she been the one that pulled him through a tough spot, whether with Indians or outlaws or with the weather? He patted her neck and whispered a few words of praise and thanks for this animal, and a special thank you to Lefty, who'd somehow known, clear back in Missouri, how the uniqueness of her one all-white leg would be recognized all the way across the west. He had a sudden desire to see Lefty again, to be able to sit together in the stillness of the early morning. Maybe the man would give him some advice or at least consolation for the mess he'd gotten himself into.

Bird began trotting, even as Abe first smelled the smoke from their cook-fire. He guessed the women might have eaten without him, as that was the usual routine when he worked so late. As he neared the home camp he was surprised to see Sarah Beth standing behind Helga, who was seated on a firewood stump. His wife was brushing the younger woman's hair, and when they both looked up and noticed him, he could tell they were laughing. At him, or at something humorous one of them had said? He waved, and continued on to the corral where he could give Bird a treat, take off her gear, and turn her loose for the night. He looked back and they were still happily talking together. What was that about? The horse gave him no reply as she ate the grain in her bucket.

He was hungry, but almost afraid to join the women or even encounter them at all. It was too strange. The two kisses they'd given him that afternoon, one right after the other, the tension circling around the three of them, and now the happy camaraderie of the two of them, as if nothing was wrong, as if nothing that is, except himself being the one to blame. He let his horse out through the makeshift gate into a large paddock. There was plenty of grass for the night and he would need her early in the morning. He was planning to head over to Mike's and order more custom hinges. For now, he resolved to be just as cheerful and friendly as Sarah Beth and Helga seemed to be.

"Do you want your hair done next?" Sarah Beth called out as he approached and the two women burst into shared laughter.

"Thinking about eating, if there's anything left," he said, as calmly as he could.

"Mattie's got it waiting," Helga said softly.

"Thank you." He went on by them.

When he settled into the bed beside Sarah Beth, she turned away at first, then came close to him, pulling his arms around her. Nothing was said and they were both quickly asleep. Abe's last thoughts were about how different everything was now, but just how much the same as well.

Before daybreak Abe was awakened by the sound of horses and yelling outside of their small room in the shack. He hurriedly pulled on his pants and boots, stuffed in his shirt, and stumbled to the doorway that opened to the darkness outside.

Hawk Man's voice came from horseback a few yards away, "Come, meat, now. Carl, me, you. Come."

"All right. Let me get a light and my horse." He ducked inside, lit a lamp, grabbed a coat and his rifle, and was back outside again, headed for the stable. Whatever plans he had for the day evaporated as he saddled Bird and mounted. As the first glimmer of dawn crept over the far horizon, he urged Bird into motion and followed the sound of the other horses' hoofbeats. In the pink glow from the east, he was able to see Hawk Man ahead of him, riding fast through the scattered boulders and sage. Bird responded to the pace and he let her have her head, knowing she was better at finding her way than he would be at trying to guide her. Even so, Hawk Man was still gaining on him as the light of day increased, and he couldn't help thinking about the silence that had settled over his relationship between his benefactor and himself.

Although he'd been told a few details of the month Sarah Beth spent as Hawk Man's companion, he wasn't sure he knew exactly what had transpired between the two of them. Not to mention that he hadn't yet resolved his own mind to any real judgment regarding his lovemaking with Helga and the revelation of this pregnancy.

A wolf howled nearby, and Bird startled and stumbled. He realized he'd better keep his attention on what he was doing right now, right here, rather than try to define this troubled confusion they'd all gotten themselves involved in. As for him, it was still so new and unclear that he couldn't even begin to decide whether he had sinned with the young woman or had simply followed the path laid out before him by his own wife, perhaps even by God himself. He thought somewhat longingly of what he'd heard about the Roman Church, where a penitent would give himself over to a priest in an act of confession to be judged according to the Law and centuries of tradition and precedent that defined sin and punishment. He had nothing like that.

Up ahead, Hawk Man leaned back and his horse nearly slid to a stop. Abe slowed Bird to a trot as they came closer. The man pointed to an opening in the rock wall that ran along where two low hillsides came together, forming the bottom shape of a V. He gave a shrill whistle that echoed off the rock wall and a single horseman appeared at its opening. It was young Carl and when they joined up, the three men moved slowly into the cul-de-sac canyon, where a small group of elk huddled, boxed in.

Hawk Man gestured for Abe to use his rifle. A young forked-horn bull stood closest to them, and Abe took aim. Just as he was about to fire, Bird sidestepped, startled by something on the ground. Abe

slid off the horse and looked around, but didn't see anything to worry
about. He aimed again and fired. The elk reared up and then stumbled
toward them, gathering speed, beginning a serious charge. Abe was
just about to fire again when the animal went down on its knees and
rolled over, legs thrashing in the sage. Now Carl strung his bow, set
an arrow and rode forward, causing the remaining bunch to gather up
even tighter. He yelled, releasing the arrow just as his horse turned
away from the herd. A large cow elk instantly went down, rose up,
struggled to stay on her feet, stumbled several steps, then fell over.
Hawk Man gave a sign of approval and pulled a long knife from his
waistband. He eased his horse slowly forward and then suddenly
he was off the horse and onto the back of the elk, grabbing its head
and slicing its throat in one quick motion. The animal bucked and
stumbled, and Hawk Man jumped to the ground and walked toward
Abe and Carl, smiling and stooping to wipe the knife on the grass.

Abe had the sudden feeling that this had been some kind of
competition, and that he, with the modern weapon of the white man,
had shown the least amount of skill. Then Hawk Man stopped in front
of him and pointed at the rifle in his hands.

"You must teach me. Is more better than this." He held the knife
out for a moment and then slipped it back into its sheath. "I have only
one old bad gun."

It was now full daylight and the streaks of sunlight from behind
the ridge shone through the morning's rising mist. Carl had reached
the animal he'd killed, and stooped to slice its throat. Then he moved
on and did the same to Abe's. For the next hour or so they labored
together to dress out the carcasses and hack pieces that could be
carried on a horse. Hawk Man motioned Carl to head back to the camp
for more horses to do the packing, and the young man galloped off.

The first flies of the morning began to discover the meat, so the
two men sat down with cedar branches to whisk and protect the piled
up pieces. The sun seemed to leap up and soar above the far ridge, and
the silence of the place was broken by the singing of multiple kinds of
birds and the sound of cattle splashing down along the creek bottom.
Abe found himself wishing that he knew how to ask the Indian man

to tell him about the time he and Sarah Beth spent on their journey north, but he found he lacked both the nerve and the words for such a conversation. He looked up and saw that Hawk Man was studying him, his dark piercing eyes unwavering.

Then he spoke, as if he'd been reading Abe's mind, "Your woman strong for you. And a Dreamer. You now be happy with her and make you good home."

He held up one hand and looked upward. He began to chant in his own language and went on for some time. When he stopped, he leaned forward with his knife and cut two pieces of the heart of the elk he'd killed and offered one to Abe. He held his own above his head, said a few words, placed it in his mouth and chewed, motioning for Abe to do the same. Abe did, and was surprised at the taste of iron and the chewiness of the morsel.

"Thank you for this," he said, and then went on, "Sarah Beth told me you were good to her and I thank you for that." They sat in silence as the sun climbed higher and the heat of the day and flies descended from the now clear blue sky. After some time, they heard hooves pounding toward them and saw a cloud of dust approaching. It was Carl with several horses.

They tied the legs and ribs and lifted the two packs onto the waiting animals. Bird was somewhat skittish and Abe had to keep hold of her reins. When he mounted and took the lead rope of one of the pack animals from Carl, his horse settled right down, as if now she knew what was expected.

The sun was nearly mid-sky when they reached the Indian camp. Hawk Man gestured for Abe to stay on his horse and said, "Take home, is yours."

"But this is almost half of what we got and you have a big family."

"We have much. Get more. You take."

Abe looked around and saw Mary Wolf standing a little ways away, watching them.

Abe called to her, "Tell him it's not fair for me to take so much."

"He won't listen," she said. "Better do as he says. Maybe you can bring some of your women's bread sometime."

"All right." He thanked Hawk Man and rode slowly away. A couple of the children ran beside Bird until they reached the creek and he and the two horses crossed. When he reached his own camp, he suddenly remembered his plans for the day and wondered if he could finish dressing out the elk meat he'd been left with and still get over to Mike's. Perhaps the women could help him. He'd seen the women at Hawk Man's camp come hurrying out to lift pieces of carcass from the pack animals and carry the bundles into the shaded area behind the tipis. It was clearly their work now. But he wasn't sure how Mattie and Sarah Beth would take to a suggestion that they do the same thing. Helga would probably get right to it if he asked, but then she came from a different background, one that he thought of as much more practical for this life out here than that of the two women from city life in Virginia. Then he recalled some of Mattie's stories of the plantation and realized that anyone could pick up this way of life if they wanted to. Who was he to set the standards?

Sure enough, it was Helga who came running to help him throw ropes over a low branch in the shade, and then hold the pack horse while he hoisted the three large pieces of elk up.

"What are we going to do with it? Where did you get it? How are you? Are you all right?"

"Whoa, slow down," he responded. "I'm fine. Hawk Man came and got me before dawn. Carl had located a herd of elk, out by the small canyon where the willow grows. What else did you ask?"

Sarah Beth and Mattie were approaching, as Helga asked again, "What are we going to do with it?"

"Well," nodding to the other two women, "I thought I'd just turn it over to the women-folk like the Indians do." He smiled as he removed Bird's bridle.

Sarah Beth came close and gave him a hug. "I see our great hunter has been busy. Is this all for us?"

"Yes. Hawk Man has most of another smaller animal and the rest of this one. They'll go back for more if they need it, but he did give me a large share."

Mattie came forward to inspect the meat. "Glad I learned about making dried meat. We should get to work before the flies beat us to it." She headed toward kitchen, leaving Abe with Sarah Beth and Helga.

"I've never done this before, but I guess it's time," Sarah Beth said. "What about you, Helga?"

"Mostly just smaller animals, like sheep and pigs, but I think it's all pretty much the same. I'll go help Mattie get some bowls and bags. And knives."

Abe looked down and realized his hands were covered with dried blood. "I best get my hands washed," he said, and started down toward the creek.

"I'm glad you can do this for us. We'll need it for our growing family." She picked up a dried branch and began brushing the flies away from the meat.

When he'd washed as well as he could, he stayed by the creek and watched the women getting organized to do the work he'd brought them. Sarah Beth's comment about their growing family stuck in his mind and he realized he wasn't yet thinking that way. On the way back from the killing of the elk, he had thought about how he probably wouldn't need to butcher one of the half-grown calves, and could let it grow awhile longer while they lived off the elk. That was one thought and the other was his newfound satisfaction in how well his arm was healing and working.

He heard Mattie calling to him and went to where they were beginning to cut the meat off a hind leg. Mattie asked him, "Have you got a saw here, or only at the new house? I'd like to cut some of these bones small enough for soup and stew meat."

"The firewood saw I've got here is too big for that. I'll have to go out and get a smaller one. How soon will you need it?

"Sooner the better with these flies."

As he rode away from the little group of women, he had a surprising realization about how much he was missing Louis with no other men in his daily life. He wondered how it was going with his cousin and his wife and baby. Wouldn't he be surprised if he knew that Abe's hoped-for child was on its way, but not with Sarah Beth. Hard to imagine what the unpredictable mind of his cousin would make out of the situation. Abe remembered now some of the challenges he went through trying to put up with Louis's behavior, but it was always offset by the familiarity and memories of their shared childhoods, shared in terms of both place and time.

Bird wanted to run, but he held her back, reluctant to make this trip any shorter than it could be. It wasn't very often that he had to spend time with all three of what Hawk Man called "his women" at the same time, unless it was for meals. At least they seemed to get along well together. Even though Helga mentioned how worried she was about Sarah Beth's attitude toward her and what happened with Abe, it seemed to him that the two of them were closer than ever.

The new house came into sight and he let Bird go at a gallop the rest of the way. As they came near, he made out something hanging in the main doorway, and waving about in the slight breeze of the early afternoon. Climbing down off the horse, he saw the motion was caused by dozens of large feathers. He slipped the bridle from Bird's nose and let her graze on a patch of grass as he walked toward the mysterious object. When he drew close, he could see a round shape with geometric divisions of brightly-painted color. Feathers were attached to the bottom half of the circle and fluttered and twirled from threads of material. He had seen something like it, though much smaller, suspended from one of the back poles of Hawk Man's tipi. Maybe it was some special object for a dwelling. He was pleased to have found this left here for them; it gave their new home distinction. He smiled as he thought how few homes of any white people anywhere would ever have such.

He hadn't forgotten the purpose of his errand and quickly wrapped his saw in a piece of canvas and went back out, whistling for Bird. She looked at him with a clear message in her eyes that she wasn't ready to leave so soon, but he whistled again and walked to meet her. On the way back to camp, he once again realized that his thoughts about Louis were an expression of his need for more male companionship and help with the work, more than being specific to his cousin. Well, he thought, time would tell. The original idea had been that perhaps Helga would attract a suitor and the fellow would be a welcome addition to their small but growing group. Now, with what had happened, this was fairly unlikely, perhaps even impossible.

Returning to the meat project, he saw Mattie using most of their limited supply of salt to make a brine. Sarah Beth and Helga were cutting large pieces from the haunches and cutting these into strips and roasts. They had about finished what they could do with the hanging sections when Abe walked up with the saw and asked what they needed done.

"We can get a lot more of this off the bone if we have smaller pieces to put on the table," Sarah Beth said. Abe stepped up to the closest hindquarter and began sawing. Helga stood ready to catch the piece that would separate with the cut. Sarah Beth noticed that Mattie needed help moving the large crock of brine and went to help her.

As she was holding the meat steady while he sawed at the bone, Helga sensed their closeness and whispered, "I haven't been alone with you for days."

"I know," he said, "but I don't think it can be helped."

"It could be if you'd make the effort."

Just then the saw cut through the bone and she was almost knocked down by it. Abe dropped the saw and helped lift the meat over to the table under the tree. Sarah Beth came right over and handed a knife to Abe, saying, "This could really use sharpening."

"The stone's in the shed. I'll get it."

As he walked away, Sarah Beth spoke softly to Helga, "Do you two ever talk about what's going on?"

Helga stepped back and looked at her. "No, we don't get to be alone."

"Well, it's a fact of our lives now. Maybe when we're done here the two of you can take a walk or something."

"That would be nice, but I'm not sure he'd want to."

"Well, you can tell him you want to. Or else I will. Mattie and I have been talking and she thinks that if we're all going to have this baby together, we better make a nice enough home for it to come into. If only for the baby's sake."

"That's what I want too," Helga said. "Thank you for thinking about it."

Sarah Beth rolled the hindquarter around to where she could slice into it. "It's not about what I want anymore. It's what I have to live with, we all do. Now where is he with that knife?"

The days were getting longer. After they'd cleaned up from butchering and cooked some of the meat over a small fire, the sun was finally dropping behind the far ridge. Sarah Beth told Mattie that she wanted to show her some of her own mother's belongings she'd brought out after her father passed away. The two of them gathered up the used dishes and utensils and walked off toward their small building.

Helga stirred the coals in the fire pit and asked Abe if she should add more wood or let it go out.

"I don't think we need it, but you can if you want to."

"I want you to take a walk with me," she said.

"Do you think we should?"

"Yes I do," she said. "We've got things to talk about, and Sarah Beth thinks we should too, even though I don't think we need her permission."

Abe was silent, noticing the glow of the sun's last moments of the day lighting her face and making highlights in her hair. He didn't know what to say, or what they would talk about.

She stood suddenly and reached for his hand. "Come. We can do whatever we want." He pushed himself up and looked back toward the little shack-house. Helga was already walking away. He followed.

Once they were out of sight and the twilight was gathering around them, Helga stopped walking ahead of him and turned to wait. "You've made me love you, you know that? Do you really know what you've done to me?"

He looked down at their feet, now just inches from touching. "I'm sorry," he said.

"Oh don't be sorry." Her voice was soft, but carried within it a tone of impatience and maybe even judgment. "You did what you had to do, what she said she wanted you to do, and what I wanted. It's all right. I will do this thing, but I'll tell you something Abe, my dear, dear Abe. This is my baby…Come, let's sit down over there." She took his hand and led him to the edge of an outcropping that overlooked the land across the valley. "This is where I come by myself sometimes. To be alone. To remember how bad my life has been, and to give thanks for how it is now."

"So are you somewhat happy now?"

"Yes, Abe. I'm truly happy now. And I'm going to be the mother of our child…"

They were quiet for a while. The first stars began to appear, and a coyote called out from somewhere behind them and was answered from behind the Indian camp across the way.

"I think you will be a good mother."

"I know I will. But I want you to know this is my baby. I know I keep saying that, and it's yours too if you want it to be, but she will never take it away from me. It's mine."

"What does that mean? Has she said anything like that?"

"Only in the beginning when I first told her. She said that she was pleased I had done what she asked and that now you and she would have a child to take care of."

"She said that?"

"I didn't say anything, but that's when I made up my mind that even if I can't have the father of his child, no one else is going to have my baby…Do you understand?"

He didn't answer right away. And then he said, "I shouldn't think you'd have to worry about anything like that. You will always be the baby's mother."

"Yes, and you will be its father, with or without anyone else. But if I should have to go my own way, if she makes it bad enough I have to leave, nothing will ever stop me from telling this child of its father, of the good man, the handsome man who gave me this child…Abe,

I said I love you…Now I want to tell you that I always will. Nothing can change that…Kiss me."

She slid off the rock she was sitting on and knelt in front of him.

"Kiss me. I miss you all the time." She reached up and took his face in her hands and gently pulled it toward her. Their lips met. Abe pulled back, but she held tightly to his head, pressing their mouths together until he relaxed and began kissing her as well, wrapping his arms around her shoulders.

Finally, she pulled away and said, "See what I mean. No matter what happens we are together in this." She stood and stepped back. "Do you love me at all?" she asked.

He stood up slowly and took her hands in his, raising them to his lips. "Yes, I do, but I don't know how to, how to work it out. I just don't know…"

"Come, we'll go back. Don't think so much," she said, and holding hands they walked slowly back toward their own little homes.

As they walked through the growing darkness, he said, "You've grown up, haven't you?"

"Because of you."

She was walking in front of him and he reached out and touched her on the shoulder. She stopped and turned slightly. Abe drew her into his embrace and held her close. "It's going to be all right," he said. "We are going to have a child. Our child."

She pulled his head down and gave him a quick kiss and then pulled away and walked toward her own shelter.

The next day, Abe discovered that the dog, Happy, must have scattered the pile of bones. As he gathered the bones, he heard the sound of hoof beats coming his way. He dropped the bones and took up his rifle, which was never far from where he was. As the horseman approached, he could see that the man had his hat pulled down, obscuring his face. He didn't recognize the horse and had the anxious feeling that something was about to happen. Then the rider pulled the horse to a stop and jumped off on its far side, away from Abe, who raised the gun and aimed it in that direction. The stranger pulled off his hat and spun toward Abe.

"Hiyo, Big Bear Man, is me!"

Abe dropped the rifle against a pile of boards and ran toward Lefty, laughing at the way the man fooled him into a fearful moment.

"Hey, Lefty, am I glad to see you. Oh my, it's been too long."

"Today is a good day for you, my friend."

"Hello, hello, of course it is. You're here."

"More than that. I bring the papers from the judge and the Indian agent up north." He reached inside his buckskin jacket and pulled out the papers. "Now you are big man here, you are now official sub-agent for this district and lifetime caretaker for this land. It says it here, or something like that. Come let's sit and have a look."

They moved over toward the small tree, but then kept going when they saw the flies on the blood-soaked ground where the elk had hung.

"We have fresh elk," Abe said, "with Hawk Man's help."

"Yes, he told me."

"When did you get here? I didn't know you were coming."

"I come yesterday, when you were hunting."

"Are you alone?"

"My woman, Patsy, and the woman I call mother, Moon Fish. They are here with me. They ask if they can come to visit with your women."

They came to a cluster of boulders and made themselves comfortable. Lefty took out his pouch and tobacco, filling his pipe.

"That would be wonderful. These women work hard, but have only one another for company. Sometimes I worry it's too hard for them."

Lefty lit the tobacco, inhaled deeply and held it up to the four directions. Then he smoked again and handed it to Abe, who inhaled lightly. "For us it is a blessing you are here. Hawk Man say the whites would take this land from his family if you were not. He is thanking you and you will see how he is."

"I don't understand what you said about that legal arrangement."

"Arrangement? I don't know about arrangement, but is here. Look." He pointed to the top page of the papers. "This what it say."

Abe read softly, *"...and shall in perpetuity manage this land, as described herein, in trust for the tribal interests whose ancestral uses of this place for habitation and ceremonies shall be protected. The sub-Agent shall directly serve under the Indian Affairs District of this government of this region until such time as that jurisdiction shall be changed by action of the State or other governance. At such time as a change occurs the authority for the management of this parcel of land shall be legally renewed and safeguarded by the U.S. Government and its authorities within the authorities of such jurisdiction..."*

"What do you think?" Lefty said.

"Sounds good." He turned the pages. "There's more about if a new sub-agent will be required, but it probably isn't any more important than the part I read. This is amazing. I've never heard of such a thing happening." He refolded the papers and handed them back.

"No, you keep them. You are sub-agent Saunders now. You are responsible."

"I can't wait to tell Sarah Beth. She's been so worried about us not having any security on this place, and going ahead building a house, and a family."

"Ahh, she is with child?"

"Uh no, she would like that, but there's something else…I don't know how to say it."

They were quiet. Lefty crumbled the end of the tobacco into the dirt and stared out across the land and Abe looked down at his hands and the papers they held.

Lefty spoke, "My mother has helped your wife. She will have a child. I know this. I have seen this. But you will have to wait. Moon Fish says this medicine takes time, even more time with a young woman than with an older one, and she may have to use it again with your wife to make sure it will be good."

"I am pleased with this way, with this way that Sarah Beth is being helped. I want to believe in it, that it will work for her. But she couldn't wait. When she went away with Hawk Man, she was afraid

I might take his offer and be with Mary Wolf. That's the only way I can understand what happened."

"But you weren't with her. She told me you are very shy, and neither you or she wanted that to happen."

"That's right. But Sarah Beth left her word behind that I and… Helga and I should try to make a baby, because she had given up and said she could never have a child for me."

Lefty looked at Abe and reached out to grasp his arm, the one that had been wounded.

"Ahh, so you see she is becoming Indian woman. That is our way. When a woman cannot make a child, her man will make one with another, and both women will share this one, and the man. She is very wise. Maybe she dreamed it this way. She is a Dreamer and that is what frightened poor Hawk Man. Maybe she dreamed you should go ahead with the young woman, but not Mary Wolf. So it is the young one, yes?"

"Yes."

"Good for you. You are now a full man. And now you will have children with both women and you will be an Indian man here on your own land with us." He threw back his head and gave a long, loud call like a screaming crow. "Good man, my friend."

"Maybe so. But I'm not sure how it's going to work out between them. Sarah Beth can't help being envious if she doesn't have a child, and Helga is set on this one being her own child."

"My friend, now you are truly becoming an Indian. We don't know answers to those questions any better than you do. Men don't understand women, so we tell them how we want it to be. They say yes, they say you are right my good man, and then they do what they want to do anyway. It works best when everyone agrees on everything and then does things their own way. Maybe you watch our Indian women, you can learn much from them. And you are lucky to have the older one, the dark one, here. She will keep the peace. That is how it is. Now, enough of that, tell me about the horse. How is she?"

"Bird is amazing. She knows what she wants and even where I want to go. I don't have to do anything."

"You see," Lefty interrupted, "she is an Indian woman." He laughed.

"Well, I guess that's true," Abe replied. "When I went after those intruders, the ones who claimed this land, I never would have caught them if I didn't let her have her head and race across this rough ground. She seemed to be flying, and she never stumbled. Amazing."

"Best horse we ever had, you and me. I am happy you take care of her. But now I must get back to camp." He stood up and stretched. "Patsy, my woman, will expect me back to help set up the camp. And my mother will want to know about you and your woman."

"My women. Don't you want to say hello to them now? They're out behind that stable-shed still working with the elk meat."

"All right. All of them?"

Abe smiled, "Well they're all together right now. That's when I need another man around."

They walked toward the shed and could hear the women talking as they drew closer. They looked up when the men came around the building, and Sarah Beth dropped the knife and the meat she was handling. She walked toward Lefty, wiping her hands on her apron.

"Oh my," she said, "what a surprise. Welcome to our little home." She extended her hand and Lefty shook it gently. Sarah Beth turned to the others. "Remember Lefty, our dear friend? Oh, you've heard me talk about him so many times."

Lefty tipped his hat, "I hear good of you too. I am happy to see you here on our land. Welcome."

The women said nothing, but smiled in response. Abe tried to cover the silence and any awkwardness by asking Lefty if he had advice for the women in their work with the elk meat.

"Not for me to say," he answered. "For my people, men hunt, women make the food, and don't tell me what they do to make me feel good inside." He rubbed his stomach and smiled. "You will visit with my women and my mother. This one, Sarah Beth, will take you to them. I must go now."

As the two men walked away, Mattie said softly, "Talks and dresses like anybody else. If he wasn't almost as dark as me, I wouldn't know he was an Indian. None of the rest of them act like that?"

Sarah Beth gave a little laugh and said, "Oh no, he's the only one I've seen like that. He lives in two worlds, ours and theirs, and everybody in both seems to have heard of him."

Helga spoke up, "And he gave Bird to Abe?"

"And that horse has saved Abe and us many times."

Mattie said, "We best get back to this meat before the flies carry it all away."

The two men walked slowly after Lefty's horse which was waiting for them down by the little creek. "She's young, that one, but a good woman for you. You lucky man, Indian man with three women to take care of you."

"I know it looks that way, but we haven't got things worked out yet. And I have to take care of all of them, you know."

"I think you do well," Lefty said as he swung up onto his horse. "We will have feast for everybody soon. See you later." He galloped off toward the Indian camp.

Abe went back to ask if the women needed anything else from him and they said not. He saddled Bird and rode off to the new house, once again thinking about how good it would be to have a partner for this work.

When he returned that evening, he was told that Mary Wolf and Patsy had visited, and invited the women to go digging for roots the next day, a kind of root that resembled potatoes. Mattie was the most excited, saying, "I been craving for potatoes since I left Virginia, and I thought I'd never see one again."

Helga had made a stew with elk and dried corn, but said she knew it would be better with potatoes, just like Mattie said.

After they ate, Abe went outside and lit a small fire while the women cleaned up from the day's work and put their knives and the meat away. Mattie excused herself soon after they'd all met around the crackling flames, saying she needed to write a letter and read some Bible.

After a few minutes of silence, Helga was beginning to excuse herself as well, when Sarah Beth asked her to please stay awhile longer, and said, "I think the three of us have to stop pretending things haven't changed around here. They've changed a lot, and since I'm mostly responsible for it, I want to know what I have to do to make things easier for all of us. Helga, you need to say what you expect and need and not be afraid to speak up. I'll try to go along with what you say, but once the baby comes, I want Abe back for myself. I've thought a lot about this. He can be a good father and take care of our needs, but he's still going to be my husband."

Helga stirred the coals at the edge of the fire with a stick and Abe leaned back, looking up at the stars. When neither of them said anything, Sarah Beth spoke up again, asking, "Well Abe, do you have anything to say? Or do you need time to think about it?"

Abe cleared his throat a couple of times, coughed and slid away from the smoke that was blowing in his direction. "I suppose none of us knows how it should be. I think we have to try to be good to each other, and to this child, and then to another child when it comes to Sarah Beth. I think it's a bit like Lefty said about preparing the food. It's the women who do it best, so I hope the two of you can work this out for all of us." He was quiet and neither one of them said anything. He said, "I forgot something in the stable," and stood up and walked quickly away before either of them could speak.

"Helga?"

"I don't know. All I know is that this baby is my baby and his baby, and I want Abe to be with me when I need him for this."

"Helga, that's why I brought it up. If you need him to spend time with you, I have to get used to it. But if I don't like it, please try not to blame me and understand how hard it's going to be for me."

"I will, and I'm sorry for you that you don't have everything you want. Goodnight now, Please, I just have to go."

Sarah Beth watched the young woman walk away, not yet seeing any change in the way she was moving. It would be a while before she showed any effects of the pregnancy in her movements, but for now, it was already clear that Helga's feelings were changing. She also knew her own feelings were very disturbed. She knew that she could start crying at that moment or any other time, because of this new wound in her own heart. It was just so unfair and not right that she should have been forced by her desperation into such a strange and wrong course of action and that God would take what she'd done and turn it into this awful situation. She suddenly felt the emptiness that used to be filled by her father, and though she hadn't thought of him in that way for a while, now the grief came back heavily. If only he were here to help her through this, better yet, even to have made sure nothing like this could ever happen. But now there was nothing for it, nothing else than to bear the sorrow and try to be a friend to Abe's baby's mother. One thing she knew for sure, even as she tried to be generous to both of them, she knew that no matter what, she was going to be more and more lonely as the child's birth came closer, and she was more and more left out of whatever joy it brought to this strange little family.

CHAPTER 2

Neighbors

Moon Fish and an even older woman came two mornings later to see Sarah Beth. They'd walked from the Hawk Man camp. Although it was still early in the day, the heat was already settling into the land and the air. There'd been many days of it now, and the grass was beginning to brown and shrivel. To spread out the impact on forage, Abe and the Indians were moving the herds more often.

Sarah Beth heard the woman calling her and hurried out to meet her. Moon Fish made an introduction to the stranger she called her best friend. "Her name in English is something like Lark Woman, the small bird with the sweet song. She is from south of here, but we see each other as often as we can." Then she spoke to the woman in their language and Sarah Beth only understood when her own name was mentioned.

"I would ask you inside, but it's already so warm. We've been making bread and want to have it baked before the full heat of the day. If you wait in the shade of that small tree, I'll bring some cool tea for you."

"Thank you," Moon Fish said. "And your husband, he is here now?"

"No, he left very early to go to the neighbor man for some metal work for the house. Please," she gestured to the small amount of shade and the stump-stools by the tree.

Back inside the small shed-house she told Mattie who it was outside. "I want you to come out and visit with us. You will like her so much."

"As soon as I can get these loaves rising," Mattie said. "Have you seen Helga this morning?"

"No I haven't, maybe she doesn't feel so well. It happens."

"Lord, don't I know about that. Well, I'll be right out to meet your friends as soon as I'm able. Here are cups for the tea."

Sarah Beth was anxiously looking around the small space for something. "I forgot what I'm looking for."

"Don't worry. Just call for it when you remember. Now go on out and be with your guests. I'll be along."

As it turned out, Moon Fish was mainly interested in whether or not Sarah Beth was feeling any unpleasant after effects of the ceremony she'd been given, and if she and Abe were getting along together all right.

"It sometimes happens that this work we do with our women can make a man somewhat suspicious of his woman, as if she is trying to do something without telling him about it."

"Oh no, it's been awkward, but not because of that. More tea?"

"No thank you. That's good then. He won't mind when we do another part of it now that Lark Woman here to help."

"No, I don't think so, but..." She didn't finish what she was going to say and the two visitors waited politely for her to continue. Moon Fish took out her small pipe and filled it. Just then Helga emerged from her shed and began walking toward the kitchen building. Sarah Beth called to her.

"This is Helga," she said. "You remember Moon Fish, she came with Lefty. And this is her friend, Lark Woman."

Helga smiled and gave a bit of a curtsy. "Yes, I remember. Lefty calls her Mother."

Moon Fish smiled and said, "He is a good son." She lit her pipe, inhaled, and blew the smoke up into the small tree. "You have a nice camp here. And the other woman, she is still with you?"

"Yes, she'll come out soon. She's watching over the bread we're making."

"I'll go do that," Helga said. "Nice to meet you, ma'am," she said to Lark Woman and turned to Moon Fish, "and to see you again." She moved quickly toward the kitchen.

Moon Fish smoked in silence and Lark Woman had yet to say anything, but now she spoke in her own language. Moon Fish translated for Sarah Beth, saying, "She says, that one, she loves you, but she is afraid. Is she your sister?"

"No, no, she came to be with us when she had to run away from some horrible people that were keeping her. Oh, I do hope she's not afraid of me."

Moon Fish translated back and forth again, "Not afraid of you, but of something that might happen because of you."

Sarah Beth asked the older woman whether she should call her Moon Fish or Kate when she introduced her from then on. The woman replied, "I am Moon Fish with my people and others. I am Kate only with you my little sister."

Sarah Beth waited for a long moment before she was able to say, "Remember when I told you what I asked this Helga to do when I left here with Hawk Man?"

"So he wouldn't be with Mary Wolf?"

"Not exactly. More so he would stay with me. I'd given up on having a baby when I went away and I met you, and having the two of them together seemed like an answer for us to have the child."

Moon Fish spoke this to Lark Woman, who answered her. "She says, now this one is with a baby, but you are still not." The two women talked briefly to one another.

Suddenly, Sarah Beth was trying to keep from crying. Then Mattie called from the kitchen's doorway.

"Anything I should bring to you?"

"No, just come yourself."

Both of the visiting women were fascinated by Mattie and her skin color. Moon Fish asked what tribe she was from, and Mattie laughed and said, "Guess I don't rightly know that. Must be from the Africa tribe."

With Sarah Beth's encouragement, she told the two women a short version of her life story, skipping over the worst parts, talking mostly about how wonderful it had been when she found work with this family, with this girl's father and mother. She spoke lovingly about how special a man the father had been to her, and how now she was learning how to be like an Indian woman, and make dried elk meat.

Moon Fish laughed at that, and said, "Now we have a dark-skin Indian woman and two with light skin all together. We are a new kind of tribe." She repeated herself to Lark Woman and they both fell into a laughter that caught up Mattie and Sarah Beth as well.

When the visitors were leaving, because, as they said, it would take them some time to walk back to their camp on their old legs, there had been no further talk of the situation with Helga, Abe, and Sarah Beth. Then, as Moon Fish hugged the younger woman, she said softly. "This will be good for you. Do not be afraid or unhappy. We will make it all good."

The summer was at its high point of heat and dryness, at least that was what Abe was hoping. If it got any worse, he'd probably have to move the cattle somewhere beyond their normal range. So he needed to go away for a couple of days and do some checking into the foothills that lay near the distant mountains. Before he went, though, he thought he'd better go see his neighbor, Mike Skinner, and see if he knew any better place where some unused range might be.

As he saddled up and prepared to ride away, Helga came toward him carrying a small bundle. "Here," she said, "I want you to take this to Mrs. Skinner. It's something I made for her."

"That's nice. What is it?"

"If you're there when she opens it up, you'll see. It's just when I remembered how glad Mr. Skinner was we were here, some women for her to know. I thought I'd make something to welcome her. I know we don't see each other much, but it was something I could do."

"That's good. It's not breakable is it? I can tie it on behind the saddle."

"It's not breakable," she smiled, "and here's your food in case it takes longer than you think it will. Maybe you'll sleep tonight under the stars, alone, instead of with her."

He looked at her, carefully trying to read any signs in her face. "You're upset, aren't you?" he said. "I'm sorry."

"I'm sorry too. I miss you all the time. And now there's a baby that's missing you too."

He busied himself with tying on the bundle, avoiding her looking into his eyes.

"She said we could have time together, so it must be because you don't want it…Abe, are you ashamed? Have you told anybody? I want us to be happy about this child and you make me feel like you think it's shameful, something to hide, to hide from."

"I don't think that. I don't know what I think, but I don't think that."

"Then I think you should tell someone, just to make it more real for you. Tell Mr. Skinner, he'll understand. Please, Abe, soon you'll have to admit it anyway. It's already starting to show on me. See?" She turned sideways and pulled the loose dress tightly around her waist.

"You're right. I'll be better about it."

"Just be the father, that's enough." She stepped closer and quickly put her arms around him, then pulled away and hurried off.

He watched her go toward her own small shed, then mounted Bird and resisted the urge to gallop away, holding the horse to a slow trot.

When he arrived at the Skinner place, Martha was out in front watering plants. She waved as he climbed down and loosely tied Bird to a railing.

"Good morning, Mr. Saunders," she said. "Be even hotter than yesterday, I do believe."

"Very well could be. You can call me Abe if you don't mind."

"Well then, I'm going to be Martha, aren't I? Good."

"Our Helga made this for you. Wanted me to bring it over."

"Oh, what is it?"

"Well, she wouldn't tell me. Said I'd have to wait until you opened it."

The woman untied the string that held a piece of canvas around the object. Then she held up a square of cloth. "It's beautiful," she said, "look." It was a kind of a small quilt, more of a wall hanging, and embroidered on it was the Skinner house and the words, "Welcome" above and "Martha" below the building. "She did this?"

"Yes, she's very good with needle and thread. Taught herself how to make quilts. Good ones too."

"Maybe I could get her to make one for me. I would pay for materials and something for her time."

"I think she'd like that."

"Well, you tell her then. Tell her to have some ideas to show me as soon as she can."

"I'll do that. Mike around?"

"Out back, in his shop like usual. And tell her I said this is so beautiful. I know just where it's going to hang on our empty wall. Perfect." She went into the house.

The man was pounding on something when Abe came into the shop, and when he noticed his visitor he stepped back and gestured at the metal box on the floor in front of him. "Just finishing it up. We need to try it out."

Abe looked it over and asked, "What's it do?"

"Ahh, it's a heater, designed it myself. Small enough for one room, big enough for a shop like this. Said you might need something like that, didn't you?"

"Not sure I said exactly that, but it's a good idea."

"Well, you said you have to add a room or build a separate one for one of the women, maybe more, so I got to thinking. I remembered something I saw at one of those exhibitions back home in Philadelphia. Saves on wood and keeps a fire for a long time, if it works how it's supposed to. So how are you?"

"I'm all right, I guess. Busier and busier. How about you?"

"I'm doing well. Can't tell you what a difference that woman's made around here. Hardly figure how I lived here before."

"Well, that's good. Nice when it works out like that."

"Here," Skinner pulled a flask from a cabinet. "You seem a little down, my friend. What is it?"

Abe turned down the drink and said, "Not much, just some complications with the family, and then I'm pretty worried about the cattle. Wanted to ask you if there's any places to move them to further out this way. Maybe somewhere I haven't been to yet."

"Can't say as I know of any right off, but I'm not using those fields across the creek here. Used to run several head year round. Could handle a few of yours."

"Appreciate that, but if I can I'd like to keep from splitting them up so I don't have to ride all over checking on them. It's just on our place I need to keep them from using up all the grass. Hawk Man needs some for his horses."

Mike took another swallow off the flask and then put it back where it came from. "Maybe you could get the Indians to do a rain dance for us," he chuckled. "Be just what we need. I'll think on it, but first let me show you how this here thing works. See, you can slow the air down here and keep the stovepipe open. Then when it's warm in the room, you can close this part under here and slow it way down without putting it out. At least I think that's what it'll do. Still got a bit to finish up. But it'll sure be ready before that house is."

"This will help," Abe said. "I don't think me and these women can handle being closed in one part of the house during the winter, all of us with nowhere to go."

"Some fellas would think that's great, but I can see it could be a bit difficult, especially when you're the only man. Pretty much outnumbered." He laughed.

Abe realized this was probably as good a time as any to follow Helga's suggestion to tell somebody about their situation, but he found he just couldn't bring himself to do it. Mike was a friend, but there was no telling whether he'd make a joke out of it or feel sorry for him.

"Well, come on over to the house. Martha won't like it if I don't share your company."

"I saw her for a minute. Helga sent something for her."

"All right, you've seen her, but you haven't had any of this new berry pie she's making."

He rubbed his belly. "Getting hard on me to bend over like I used to. Maybe have to go back to my own cooking or get bigger trousers. Come on."

After pie and conversation, as Abe was getting ready to leave, Martha excused herself and went into a back room. She returned with a pillow made with striped material. "Here," she said, "you give this to that girl and tell how wonderful her work looks hanging on our wall. I made this pillow myself back before I came out here. We had our own flock of geese and I learned how to separate out the best down feathers. Tell her I hope it gives her good dreams. And be sure to give my best wishes to your wife and Mattie. I miss visiting with them, but I imagine they're every bit as busy as I am."

"I'll give them your gift and greeting. We should get together soon, all of us."

Martha glanced over at Mike and said, "I forgot to mention Oliver. Should I?"

Mike chuckled, saying, "Well, now you have. Go ahead."

She faced Abe and said quietly, "My brother's on his way here. He was hurt in a mining accident, lost his hand, but now he's doing all right and he needs a place to get himself back together. Says he'll be fit to ride and work again, and asked if we'd put him up and help him find some work. He's funny." She smiled, and went on, "Said he was looking for something he could do single-handed, didn't he, Mike?"

"Sure did, just like him, too. Ollie always did have a sense of humor, always joking. I thought maybe this accident of his might settle that part of him down, but it doesn't seem it has."

"I look forward to meeting him. I've been thinking how much I could use some help on this house building project. Maybe this is an answer. But now, I best get going. See you soon."

"We'll make it happen, maybe a welcome dinner for Ollie when he gets here."

"Sounds like a good plan, Martha."

He was up on Bird, and turned her toward home, calling back, "Thanks for that stove, and for the pillow."

Instead of returning to their small compound, Abe went directly to the new house site. The conversation with Mike Skinner had reminded him that he still hadn't made a decision as to how they were going to make spaces for Helga and Mattie in the overall design of the house, and he was concerned that if he didn't make a decision and propose it, the discussion would just go on and on. Now that he'd seen Skinner's stove, he had a better sense of how the new addition might work with the original house plan.

As he walked around the house and measured two of the unfinished walls, he realized that Mattie and Helga could have separate rooms if he extended both rooms out from just the one side wall. By making a hallway that went past Mattie's space and ended at Helga's door, the older woman could be closer to the main house and its heat, and Helga could have more privacy, more like her own cabin with its own heat, but it would save making a whole separate building. When he and Sarah Beth had talked about this before, they'd both thought the only possibility was to put each room off of its own connection to the rest of the house. His new idea made more sense to him, and he hoped it would be convincing to the others. The challenge of this new plan excited him, and gave him a renewed enthusiasm for the project. Ever since his relationship with Helga had changed, he'd been feeling a reluctance to go on finishing the house. Probably because he was so apprehensive about what it would be like with all of them under the same roof. This way of sharing the space made more sense in terms of privacy for both Sarah Beth and Helga, and he couldn't help but think of Mattie's space between them in military terms, as a "neutral zone." He pounded in a couple of stakes, roughing in the outline of his new idea, caught Bird, and rode off toward the west.

By then afternoon was far enough gone that he needed the rest of day to scout further out toward the foothills, looking for untouched grassland. As it was, he barely got back in time for supper. That evening, as they sat around the small outdoor fire, he described what he'd come up with for the house, and told them about the stove that Mike built and how that made this new plan feasible. There was little comment from the women, with only Sarah Beth asking him to go into a little more detail about where this "wing," as she called it, would be attached to the rest of the house. Abe picked up a stick, smoothed out a bit of the ground, and drew lines in the dirt.

"I see," she said. "I think it's much better than trying to build separate houses, and you're right, it still gives some privacy to Helga, and, of course, the baby. What do you think, Helga?"

The younger woman stood up and moved next to Abe where she could better see the drawing in the dirt. "I'll be fine like that, but I want my own door to the outside."

"I'm sure that can be arranged," Abe said. "Mattie?"

"Long as I've got a bed for these weary bones, I'll be happy." She laughed and got up to take dinner dishes to the shed.

After a long pause, Sarah Beth cleared her throat and said, "Long as the three of us are here right now, I need to tell you that Moon Fish and the Lark Woman are taking me up on the ridge in a few days. She stayed behind for this when Lefty went on his trip to Boise. Said it's the rest of my ceremony. I'm looking forward to it, and now you two can now look forward to some time together, and you don't have to worry about me."

She stood up quickly and hurried to the clothesline to take down the laundry. The breeze blew harder and dark clouds rushed over the hills behind them. Helga came around the fire and passed behind Abe, rubbing her hand slowly across his back and shoulders. Then she, too, went to help gather in the day's laundry, just as distant thunder sounded from the direction of the fast-moving clouds. The touch of her hand stayed as a feeling across Abe's shoulders, but he tried to limit his thoughts to hoping for rain.

With Sarah Beth gone off with the Indian women, Mattie stayed more to herself, saying she wanted Abe and Helga to have some of the privacy they never got. Abe protested, saying that it was all right, she shouldn't have to feel that way. Helga only laughed and said that they should all still have their meals together because Mattie was the best cook of the three.

The first morning, Abe was gone early, first off to check on the cows and keep the herd moving further away, even though the hard rain of the past week had helped the grass recover somewhat. The days were getting noticeably shorter now, and he could feel an urgency from the coolness of these nights. The house was nowhere near ready for occupation, although the kitchen was looking good, and the women were already talking about being able to use it for putting up their vegetables and fruits for winter. They had bought jars and sealing wax, and were looking forward to this welcome supplement to the flour and meat they'd subsisted on the winter before. Martha's garden was, as she put it, overflowing with too much food for her and Mike, and even with her brother coming, they wouldn't need it all.

The real challenge for Abe in finishing the kitchen and the so-called family room would be to transport the glass they'd purchased, which was still at the freight wagon depot in town. Packed in flat zinc and wooden containers, the windows were sealed individually in their own oil baths to cushion them from the hardships of transport. Abe and Sarah Beth had chosen to use a portion of their inheritance from her father for this purpose, to pay for both the glass and its transport. Now he would have to carefully move it from Silver City to their home site. Mike had been a wonderful help in fashioning some special springs that would take some of the lurching and bouncing out of the wagon, and advised Abe to add weight to stabilize it. No matter what all they could do, though, it was going to be a very slow process, and Abe was both anxious and hesitant to make that journey. He decided he'd wait until Sarah Beth returned and was able to accompany him.

On this one particular day, with the cattle settled into some new sage flats, he was ready to begin the addition. He was stretching twine to mark its outline when he heard a horse approaching. It was

Helga, riding Morning with the dog running beside them. She waved and called out to him.

"I hope you need some help. I'm here to work." She slid down off the horse, and unfastened a large bundle tied behind the saddle. The package fell to the ground. "Come and see this," she said. "Hawk Man sent Carl over with it after you left this morning."

Abe came over to stand next to her as she untied the bundle "There," she said, revealing a dark brown hide, nearly black, and shiny in the sunlight. She bent over and rolled it out for him to see. Abe knelt down and ran his hands through the fur.

"Tell me about it. What does it mean?"

Helga knelt down beside him, her hands also rubbing the fur. "He said it's for his friend, Big Bear Man, a rug for your floor. Mary Wolf, who came with Carl, said when the time came it would be for your baby to play on. She said it will protect our home and our children… All of our children. I don't know if she knows…What do you think?"

"They gave it to you, so I don't know. I don't know what to say. It's an honor, for sure. But where will we put it?"

"We'll put it on the floor in front of the fireplace. Haven't you seen that done before?"

"Yes, but I never thought we would have anything like this." He unfolded the hide. "It's huge. Did they say who killed it?"

"She said he has a brother far to the north and it came from him. Hawk Man wanted it for you because now you are the protector of this land. He will bless you and this bearskin when we move into the house. Oh Abe, they care about you so much! They know how important you are, and so do I." She put her arms around his neck and pulled him over onto the bearskin. He struggled for a moment and then relaxed into their embrace.

"I'm just a nobody who can't even take care of himself, let alone others."

"Shhhh." She kissed him once, and then again. "I want you to take care of me. I know you can and how strong you are, and how good…Abe please don't be afraid to show how you feel about us, about the baby…Sometimes I think you want me to run away and leave you and Sarah Beth alone like you were before. Before I came along. I hope that isn't true. I want to please you so much. I want us to love this baby and love each other. Here, feel this." She rolled on her back and pulled up the short dress she wore over a pair of pants she'd made to accommodate her growing waist. She placed his hand on the mound of her belly and rubbed it back and forth, and around and around. "Can you feel that?"

"I feel you. Am I supposed to feel anything else?"

"Not yet. Mattie told me he would start to kick before too long."

"He? How do you know it's a he?"

"Because your first child will be a boy. I just know that. Oh Abe, thank you."

He pushed himself away and started to get up. "Maybe I should get some work done since you're here to help."

She pulled him back and brought his face down to a kiss. "I don't want to let you go," she mumbled, "you're always so busy." Then she pushed him away and straightened her dress and stood up next to him. "What are we doing?"

"Well, I had just started marking out the lines for your addition. It's good you're here. It's hard to do alone. Here." He handed her one end of the twine and walked over to get stakes and a mallet. He looked back at her, smiling, and said, "This is taking care of you, and it really is what I was doing when I was interrupted by you and that bear."

"Yes, mister, what do I do?"

Moon Fish and Lark Woman waited for Sarah Beth near the Indian camp. They'd hung some bundles over the back of one of their horses and Moon Fish handed her a rolled blanket. "Place that in front of you, over the horse's neck," Moon Fish said. "We will ride to those hills where the sun goes down."

The ride took a couple of hours. There was very little talking among them, but Lark Woman sang songs as they rode along. At one point they stopped near a creek bed where the horses could drink, and they sat in the shade and passed around dried meat. Moon Fish took out her pipe.

"I have been thinking about you ever since we met. I call you my little sister, but what I really want is a daughter." She smoked in silence for a long pause. "So I want to ask you if I may adopt you. We can do this at the same time that we make you a stronger woman."

Sarah Beth's mind felt blank at this, and she couldn't think of an answer, couldn't imagine what an answer would be. And what about Mattie?

"It's all right, my young friend, you don't have to say anything now. We will talk more of this before you go into your time alone."

"I just don't know what to say. It would be an honor, but I don't know what it would mean for me, what I would have to do to be worthy..."

Moon Fish translated her words for Lark Woman who covered her face and laughed loudly. "She's laughing because you don't know how to accept this idea. She says when a baby is born, does it ask its mother what it must do to be worthy to be her child? She is a grandmother many times and she says none of her children or grandchildren ever ask her what did they have to do to be hers."

Sarah Beth was embarrassed by this exchange. "What I mean is, I guess, is thank you," she said.

"Good, that's enough. But we must have our fun with you. It is our way." Then Moon Fish said something to her friend that started them laughing again. "I told her that what it really means is that if you are my daughter and Lefty is my son, you can't marry him."

And then she burst out laughing again.

Suddenly both women stopped laughing and stood up, gathering the few things they'd set on the ground. "Time to move along now," Moon Fish said.

When they reached the ridge, they stopped in a small meadow with a rocky spring. From there it was possible to look ahead and see larger mountains above and beyond them. A scattering of willow grew where the water seeped up, and a grove of stunted pines lined the rocky wall.

"This is a place we women have used for ourselves. When the men come here, they go higher up on the mountainside. But this is good for us. We can hobble the horses over that way. There will be enough for them to eat for now. My friend and I will make a small camp here, and we will walk with you a ways further and you will stay there. Tonight, tomorrow, next night, then another day. That last night we bring you back here for food and happiness. Sleep here and go back home in next morning."

Lark Woman was already unpacking the bundles and Moon Fish began stringing a small tent from two pine trees.

"May I help?" Sarah Beth asked.

"Not necessary. You walk around. Make yourself familiar with this place. We will make your place up above us in a little while, then you will have some good food with us and we will take you back there. After we paint you." She turned away and busied herself with the bedding.

Sarah Beth walked to a drop-off point that overlooked the valley below. She could see where the hills came together and thought this must be home. The land seemed to stretch out forever. There was something in this place she hadn't recognized before, a feeling or something in the view or both. Somehow her eyes seemed warm and her cheeks flushed, and yet there was no wind, not even a breeze. She blinked several times and rubbed her eyes with her fingers. This felt good, but things still looked unfamiliar. It was as if there was a kind of warm dust in her eyes, and yet her eyesight seemed sharper than ever. She didn't know if she should ask the women about this and decided that she only would if it didn't go away over the next few days. Then, almost without warning, it seemed she was imagining Abe and Helga seated on some rocks across a small chasm. They were silent and motionless, statues almost, and they seemed to look like they always looked. She couldn't help wondering how and what they were doing without her there to keep them apart. The sight of them here faded away and she was left with the questions that always returned when she thought about Helga and the baby. When she had suggested to them that they be together in the ways of a man and a woman, was she hoping that they would refuse, was she counting on them to treat it all like some kind of game or her own strange revenge for what was happening to her in the arrangement with Hawk Man? How could she not feel betrayed by them? It might have been best if she never returned after telling them to have their way with one another. She had to ask herself if she really thought they would.

She heard Moon Fish calling to her, and she turned away from the beauty of the vista and its strange thoughts and images. "I'm coming."

The next morning, Abe was in the yard of their temporary home when the Skinners and another man rode in. Mike and his wife dismounted, but the stranger stayed mounted until Martha beckoned to him. "Come, Ollie, meet Abe."

The man slid to the ground, holding on to the reins.

"Abe, this is Martha's older brother. Told you he was coming."

Abe held out his hand for a shake, but the man said, "Can't hold the horse and shake your hand at the same time. Apologize." He held up his other arm, which had a metal fixture attached to the stub of his wrist.

"It's all right, Ollie, just drop the reins, that horse won't go anywhere."

The two men shook and glanced into one another's eyes. Martha put her hand on her brother's shoulder and said, "I told you about him, remember. He's looking for some way to help out around here and we thought you might need a hand on your new house. Oh my, there I said it...sorry Ollie." She smiled and looked at her brother.

"Don't pay no mind, sister, that's what I am for sure, a hand. But the one I've still got is a good one. You'll see for yourself if you take a chance on me."

Abe wasn't sure what he could say to this sudden proposal, so he chose his words carefully. "Well, I surely can use help. Don't know how I'll finish the house enough for us to move in before winter. But I really can't afford to pay much. And my wife's not here right now, and I'd want to discuss something like this with her. But let's go sit for a bit." He turned and called toward the kitchen, "Helga, Mattie, we got company here."

Helga stuck her head out, saying, "We'll be right there. Just have to get this batch boiled long enough."

"Oh they're putting up food. I'll go see," Martha said, heading to the shed.

The men sat on the available stumps near the small tree, even though there was little shade at this time of day. Mike pulled out his flask and offered it to Abe, who nodded a negative, and then to Ollie.

"Haven't taken a drink before mid-day since the Good Lord took my hand to be with Him," Ollie said. "But don't drink it all up brother-in-law, that sun's climbing."

"Then I'll wait for you," Mike said, putting the flask back in his vest. "Tell him how you lost it."

"Well, what if he don't want to hear it and what if I don't want to remember?"

"That's fine. I don't need to know," Abe said. "Maybe I should go in and get us some water or coffee."

"The ladies will remember us soon enough. No hurry. But, hell Ollie, I want to hear this story again."

The man raised his stub arm and shook it, "Well, as you can see, you'd have a hard time twisting this arm, but I might as well get it over with. Bound to come out sooner than later…" He paused to roll a cigarette. When he'd gotten it rolled one-handed, and lit, he inhaled deeply, blew out the smoke and shook his arm at the sky. "Good Lord took it," he said. "I only wanted to shake His hand and He pulled the damn thing right off," he laughed and Mike laughed with him. "Of course that was after the cussed thing was mangled all to hell. He was just shaking my hand as a hero. He said, you saved someone's life here, but I can't save that hand, and he just pulled it right off, clean as a whistle. Course it bled some before my partner could tie it off, but what the hell, blood's cheap in a coal mine, guys bleed to death all the time. So that's what happened."

Abe looked at him and didn't say anything, thinking it might be rude or unkind to ask for details, but he certainly was curious. Mike threw a little stick at Ollie and said, "Finish the damn story for the man, before the women come out here."

"All right, sure you want to hear it, Abe is it? Abe, short for Aber-hammer, I'd bet. So, my partner and I was working deep in the shaft in a long flat tunnel, one where they'd laid rails for the little coal wagons. Mostly flat that is. Where we were was at the end of the rails and we were blasting and banging on a wall to extend the tunnel. Sudden-like we heard the noise of one of those wagons coming at us. Now we already had one right there and hadn't filled it yet. Piss-poor amount of coal coming from where we had to dig that day. My partner yelled to get out of the way, but we was in there too narrow to hardly turn around, and he tried to climb out over that wagon we had. He slipped and his leg went down in the coupling that was unhooked and it shut on his foot. I'm trying to get out of there along between the wall and the wagon, being a lot thinner than him, and I'm thinking maybe I can do it, but he's screaming bloody murder like. Screaming 'Jesus, Jeee-suss Christ, Oh Christ, help me help me I'm going to die, don't let me die, Jeeee-sussss!'" Ollie took a final pull on the cigarette and stubbed it out on the ground. "So he's going to die and me with him, that's what I'm thinking, so I grab one of these picks we use down there, like a pry bar on one end and a sideways ax on the other side, and I just raise it up and chop his leg free from his foot. By God, he scrambles but I'm trying to grab his foot for him, don't ask me why, I'll never know, wasn't no good to him or nobody else by then…" He paused as if he didn't want to go on, but then said, "Just thinking about all that 'nough to give me the shits. Damn! So I knew right away I couldn't get his foot loose and just when I went to pull back and climb into the front wagon with him, the other one crashed into it and my hand got jammed against the wall by one of the wheels. They were iron wheels and I felt the whole thing, my hand, just get, well you'd have to say crushed, no other word for it. But that's when the runaway wagon had crashed into us and I was all right in that narrow space between it and the wall. Well, my partner, did I ever say his name was Richard? Nice fellow. Anyway, he was bawling like a baby, guys were running toward us screaming and yelling, and I'm shaking what's left of my hand above my head, trying to think of the words I could use to curse the Good Lord for this entire mess and I felt something grab my hand and yank it off, leaving as pretty a stub as you could ever hope for at a time like that. See?" He held it out. It was now all healed over. "When those fellows got us out of there and was cleaning up, they surely found Richards's foot, but there was no sign of my hand. Nothing, nothing, gone, just flat-out gone." He rubbed his forehead with the stub and smiled. "That's it, all there is to it."

"Except what happened to your hand, you haven't finished that part yet," Mike said as he pulled the flask out.

"Well, I kind of did. See when Jesus come down to answer old Richard's call for help, He saw things were working out as good as they could, and He knew he couldn't do nothing more to help us, so He just shook my hand to congratulate me and His grip was so powerful, Him being the Good Lord and all. He just twisted it loose and must have took it with Him…All I can figure out about that because it never did show up. Oh-oh, here comes the women."

Evening came on when Moon Fish and Lark Woman finished setting up their camp, started a fire, and began cooking. Moon Fish gathered up a deer hide and a handful of painted arrows and beckoned for Sarah Beth to accompany her as she climbed up through the outcroppings behind their camp. They reached a flat spot among the rocks, sheltered by an overhang.

"This is where you'll be. We'll be nearby, and we'll see you once or twice, but we won't be able to talk together until you're done." She stamped on the dry grass between two boulders and laid the hide down. She placed the four arrows in the four directions, beginning west, where the sun was going down behind the ridge. "This is all you need here for your time. We will wait and your spirit will help you find what you're here for. I like you very much, my little sister. You will be a good friend for me. Now we go back down, eat. You first. I am slow."

Lark Woman ladled out bowls of soup made with meat bones and roots, while Moon Fish unwrapped a cloth bundle, and handed out fried bread. She held her piece up and made a prayer to the directions and to the sky.

Lark Woman spoke softly and slowly and Moon Fish translated, "She says you will have time for yourself here. And you must remember your enemies and those who have caused you pain. You must tell them they will not be able to hurt you ever again. Then you must beg Creator for them to have a good heart now, and then you must forget them or they will make it hard for you up here. She says, then you must pray for those you love even if they are no longer alive, and the ones who you want to help with your prayers. She says they will be with you during this time. In the night they will help you, and when you dream do not be afraid. It is for you that these dreams are coming."

She turned to Lark Woman and talked for a while in their language, then spoke again to Sarah Beth, "We will call you Sa-rah now, not use this Beth name now. Lark Woman say Sa-rah is the name how spirits know you. And when we are finished, they may give you another name also. I have told her that you are a Dreamer and she says she was feeling it was this way with you, but she did not know if you knew this about yourself. When you will carry your baby, we will do another kind of ceremony to protect both of you from those who would try to harm you with their own dreams. You have nothing to fear. Now we will paint you and you will leave us when the darkness comes and takes you away. When you are ready, take off your clothing and stand here by this fire now."

Sa-rah did as she was told and Moon Fish draped a cloth around her waist. Lark Woman was mixing powders in the bowls they had eaten from. Moon Fish said, "It is good to have the juice of the meat we were eating with you in the paint."

Lark Woman set the three bowls down by Sa-rah's feet and motioned for her to dip her hands into the white paint. Then she took the young woman's hands by the wrists and made Sa-rah rub her own breasts with the paint. Moon Fish began singing softly as Lark

Woman dipped into the bowl of red paint and made circles around Sa-rah's breasts.

"She says this red paint is to bring your heart into your child's milk, she says this will make you strong and make your milk very good. She says this is why you have been having trouble making a baby, because your breasts were not going to be strong enough to make good milk and your child would have been weak, so the spirits made you wait until you can grow strong again from your journey, from a death happened in your family, maybe your mother, maybe your father, maybe both. She says this red and white are the heat and the light and they make the darkness inside of you go away, and you will make a healthy baby, when it is ready."

Suddenly Lark Woman cried out loudly and began shuffling around the small fire, pushing Sarah Beth out of her way. Moon Fish sang in a clear voice while she beat a rhythm on the cook pot. After circling the fire four times, Lark Woman stopped and knelt down in front of Sa-rah, reached her hands into the bow of blue paint and placed her fingers on the young woman's belly. She moved her hands in a gentle and circular stroking motion, speaking softly.

"She says this is for your baby's first home, in your water. Your baby will live in there and will be always inside you even after being born. Even when baby is outside of you, even when already born, baby will leave something inside you. Will leave its touch inside you. Will leave the shape of hand on inside of you. Like a painting on rock or in cave. Will leave a mark inside you, and you will never be alone again."

Suddenly Lark Woman placed her mouth on Sa-rah's belly and made a sucking sound, then stood up and stumbled off into the nearby brush. They could hear her retching and groaning, and Sa-rah looked to Moon Fish for an explanation.

"She is removing something from you that was in your way, in you, blocking in you. Now go, cover yourself and leave here now. Go quickly up to your place above here. We will come and look on you, but you will not speak to us until we bring you back down here. Go. Be strong. I know you will do well because you are a bringer of blessings. Drink this water and go now." She too disappeared into the brush, her voice rising in a moaning wordless chant.

Sa-rah sipped the water and then swallowed the rest of it down. They'd told her it would be her last until they brought her back down with them. She wrapped herself loosely in the blanket, crossed the clearing, and climbed slowly upwards, shivering from her mix of feelings, although the evening was still warm.

CHAPTER 3

Dream

The second night Sarah Beth was away with the Indian women, Abe couldn't get to sleep inside the small shed they used for both kitchen and bedroom. He found himself wide awake and thinking of several things at once, but always the thoughts kept coming back to Helga and her baby. One moment he would be considering what lumber he'd need for the new part of the house design, and it would end up being about the young woman's need for privacy and for a place to keep an infant. When he tried to think about Sarah Beth and her ceremony with the Indian women, he couldn't help wondering what it would be like if it were successful, and she too, conceived a child for them. When he tried to take his mind off of these things and pray or remember Sarah Beth's father's kindly help and advice, he would come back to the knowledge that whatever came to pass would be much more than the simple fulfillment of his own need for a child with either woman.

He went out and stood under a cloudless, moonless sky. The deep darkness gave added light to the stars and they held his gaze until his neck began to hurt. Then, strangely, he felt someone behind him, and at that moment fingers clasped his neck and began rubbing right where the stiffness was. When he tried to turn around, Helga whispered, "Don't move," and kept kneading into his neck with her knuckles.

"Why aren't you asleep?" he said softly.

"Because you're not."

"How did you know?"

"I've been waiting for you, hoping you would come out, come to me." She moved her hands down onto his shoulders and slowly turned him around. "Kiss me."

Abe hesitated and then did as she asked. Her arms wrapped around him and he remembered how strong she always was. Her mouth was pressed tightly against his own, but she was making sounds that sounded like words. He pulled away and asked, "What are you saying?"

"Nothing really, just that I can't be without you all the time. I need you, I need you. Oh Abe, what can I do? I am hurting inside. And it's not from the baby, it's from you, from not having you beside me, touching me. I'm always so alone, alone, alone!"

"Shhh, let's be quieter. Mattie's sleeping just over there. We can walk this way." He placed his arm around her and led her toward the small creek. The soft gurgling of the water welcomed them. Suddenly Helga stopped and let herself down to the ground as if she'd fallen.

"Are you all right? What?"

"Of course I'm all right." She gave a little laugh. "I'm with you, with my baby's papa, and there's nobody else here." She reached up for his hand, saying, "Sit here."

He slipped to his knees and eased around behind her so her head was leaning back against his chest. He stroked her hair and her face, whispering, "I'm sorry, I'm sorry."

"I don't think you have to be sorry. We just have to do something about all this." She turned and was quickly up on her own knees facing him. "It's like my life started when she went on her trip with Hawk Man, and it ended when she came back. But it started again when I found out I have a baby inside me, but now I'm having such a hard time keeping it from stopping again. I can't do this alone, Abe. I have to have some of you all of the time or all of you some of the time or, I don't know what—I have nowhere to go. Mattie promised me she'll go with me if Sarah Beth makes me leave. But where would a young mother, her baby, and an old black woman go? I know I'm not making any sense and you don't know what to do either, but, oh make me stop. Just kiss me and make me stop, make me stop talking, make me stop thinking."

They kissed and he eased her down next to him into the soft creekside grass. "Sing to me, Helga. Please sing."

They lay on the grassy smoothness, holding one another as she began humming softly in her sweetest voice, and he lay there with her, him thinking she was too good for him, too special and that he was hurting her, hurting her future and taking everything from her and giving nothing in return. Her fingers traced his features and his lips, and her other hand slipped inside his shirt and stroked his chest, sending a tingling sensation the length of his body. She stopped her song and whispered his name several times. He kissed her because he was feeling so sad for her, for them, and for their child inside of her.

"I can't seem to help it," he said. "I can't do anything, anything different, I don't know what to do differently."

"Talk to your friends," she said, "talk to Lefty and Hawk Man. They have wives, they know what it's like. And then maybe you can become a man about all this. Be the man I know you can be, the man I have seen in you…Listen to me, I might sound like someone who knows something, but I don't know any more than you do. I only know that I need to have more of you, or, or none of you. So you have to decide…But not now, not tonight. Just kiss me again, and come to bed with me."

Next morning, Abe left after an early breakfast to get a good start on a long day at the house. The morning was cool and the sky was clearing from the overnight mist. He unsaddled and let Bird find her own way to the grass down by the creek. It felt good to be here by himself, away from the complications of his home life. He was beginning to see just how much having the two women was costing him in worry and concern, with him always waiting for something to go wrong, and with them always acting, around him at least, as if nothing was wrong, when there obviously was something wrong. Sometimes he wished he could just have a private conversation with Mattie and ask her what she thought was really going on. He knew that both Helga and Sarah Beth talked to her, but he had no way of knowing or guessing what those talks were about.

So this morning it was good to focus on sorting through the remaining boards to find the right ones for the sections of wall that needed reinforcing. The house really was coming along quite well, and he was beginning to believe that there would be enough of it roughed in that they could start using it in time for winter. The biggest challenge now was getting the three sleeping rooms closed in and ready for use. He took a short break and walked through the indoor spaces, calculating the amount of work that remained. Suddenly, he thought of a solution to part of the problem. What if he and the two women could share the same room for their beds and night-times? He just as quickly put an end to that line of thinking with a sharp reminder to himself that this was only a man's solution, or at least only an Indian way of solving such a problem. There was no chance that Sarah Beth and Helga would ever accept such an arrangement.

Since he couldn't resolve this issue either by himself or in any other way that he could foresee, he decided the only thing to do was just get busy and get as much finished as possible and see what worked out, or didn't. The women would end up deciding most of these arrangement matters anyway. He knew this was what he should expect and there wasn't much else he could do about it.

Back at the shed, Mattie and Helga were cleaning and laying out trays of what Martha told them were called chokecherries. After drying in the sun, some of the berries might even last almost through the winter. They both looked up to see an approaching rider, Ollie, their new neighbor from down the road. He slid off his horse and went over to help Mattie with the stack of trays.

"Here, let me handle those," he said, as he took them from her with one arm. "Where they going?"

"Over there where Helga is. Those makeshift tables."

She led the way and he followed with the load. Helga passed them going back toward the kitchen. "I'm getting the next batch ready."

So, you've got a lot of these, have you?" he asked.

"We plan to have pies all winter long."

"Well then, I'll plan on being a very good and helpful neighbor. Nothing I like more than good fresh pie."

He stopped by the side of a table and Mattie began taking the trays from the stack, one at a time. "One of the Indian women told us how they dry them and pound them into a kind of paste with other things like meat grease and so forth. Helga and I think we can just do what Martha said, soak and dry them and use them like cherries."

"Wouldn't know about that," Ollie said as she took the last of the trays. "But I got a question for you."

She wiped her hands on her apron and looked up at him. "So?"

"Are there many other colored folks around here, or are you the only one?"

"Well," she started back toward the shack, then stopped and said, "I guess that depends on what you mean by colored. After all, those Indians are colored, just a different shade."

"Uh, that's not quite what I meant..."

Mattie interrupted, "Oh, I know what you mean, you being from the east, and probably the north as well. You probably never knew many of us. Matter of fact, though, far as I'm concerned, white's also a color, so we're all pretty much coloreds, aren't we, Mr. Whatever-your last-name-is?" She started walking again.

"Well, ma'am," he said, catching up with her, "my name is Oliver, Oliver Bentley, but most folks just call me Ollie. Although, I guess if you want, you could call me Whitey." He laughed and then quickly stopped.

"I'll decide what I'm going to call you later. Right now, if you wouldn't mind, I'll take a little more help with this next batch of trays, that is, if you're about earning some pie." She disappeared inside the little building. "Wait there."

He stood waiting, wanting to roll a cigarette, but not sure it would be appropriate. He heard the women's voices and laughter, but couldn't make out what was being said.

Mattie came back out with a half-stack and he held out his hand and said, "I'll get these."

They walked back across the yard, each with a partial load. "You can call me Mattie, and I think I'll call you Mr. Ollie. I like the sound of that, don't you?"

He mumbled yes, stopped and waited for her to lay out the trays she'd carried, and then take his from him. "Surely was nice of Mr. Mike to make up these metal trays for us. We can make cookies on them, or do this, or who knows what else."

"He's a handy man with any kind of metal."

"That he is. Mr. Abe is out at the new house if you're looking for him. Just follow those wheel ruts, take you straight to it. And thank you for your help, sir." She turned, glanced back, and walked away.

"Pleased to help, ma'am," he said softly to her back, and then went after his horse.

He rode out that way, approaching the new building slowly. He gave it a good look-over. He was surprised that it was mostly made of boards rather than logs, and he could see that there'd been some difficult work gone on. It was fairly small, but it looked like there was an addition staked out and started behind it.

"Halloo," he called as he slid off the horse and dropped the reins over a post. He took a small canvas bag from one of his saddlebags and walked toward the back of the house where he heard hammering. The horse shook his head, pulled the reigns loose, and followed him.

Abe looked up from the pile of boards he was sorting through. "Hello…Good to see you."

"You as well. Told you I'd be by, but it took a little longer than I thought. Come to help out if I can."

"Sure, just need to figure out what I can get done with two of us."

"Yeah, I know," Ollie said, "and you're probably thinking more like one-and-a-half because of this." He waved his stump in the air. "But wait until you see what I was waiting on Mike for. Good old Mike." He shook something metal out of the bag. He held it up, saying, "This is it. Wait 'til you see this. Give me a hammer and a spike." He fastened the device to his stumped wrist.

Abe passed a hammer over and set a spike on the top board. "What have you got there?"

"You're not going to believe it. That Mike's a genius. I just told him what I wanted and he figured it out. Took him a bit of time, but watch this."

He reached the device out and picked up the spike, and lined it up between two pincers separated by a spring that he pried open with his one hand. He tapped the nail lightly into the top board. "How about that? Magnet, uses a magnet, and now with a little practice I'll nail good as anyone…And it won't hurt if I miss and hit this here hand-thing—no bloody thumb."

"Pretty amazing."

"You better believe it is. Worth coming all the way out here from Pennsylvania. Now where do I start?"

"I couldn't get these long planks up on the wall very easily by myself. If you can get one end up and hold it, I'll do the other. Then you tack in your end. We'll see how it goes."

By the time they'd done four of the long boards, Abe stopped and said. "Now there's a space for a window here next, so we'll have to cut some of the shorter boards to length."

They worked steadily for a couple of hours, stopping only for drinks of water and for Ollie to have a smoke every so often. During the first break he asked Abe how he'd ended up with such a fine piece of land and Abe began to explain about Hawk Man and his family camp. On their second break, he told the part about the shootout and Ollie said it was a hell of story. When they got back to work, he said he'd sure be looking forward to hearing the rest of it.

The sun climbed and the heat of the day increased. They slowed down some, and then Abe asked Ollie if he'd brought any food for the mid-day. He hadn't and Abe said he didn't have much, but they could share it. Just then they heard the sound of the buggy approaching.

Mattie and Helga were riding in it, and Mattie was holding up a basket.

As they pulled to a stop, she called out, "Hope you fellows haven't eaten yet. We brought you something."

The next afternoon, Abe and Lefty took a ride out toward the low-lying mountains to the west. At one point they stopped in a beautiful sage-filled desert basin and found shade beneath the wall of a small canyon. While they rested, Abe was able to bring up his personal predicament with the man who, after all, was the closest thing he had to a best friend.

"Lefty, you are a good friend. I've known you a long time now, and I'm having some trouble. I love both of these women, and they both want me."

"Life happens, love happens, and Creator always has plans for us. How is the first woman taking this?"

"Lefty, it was her idea. I never would have done this unless I felt myself in a corner, trapped almost by Sarah Beth's demands, and by my guilt for not opposing Hawk Man more and stopping all this before it happened."

"Why did you let it happen?"

"I think it is because when he first offered me the chance to live here, the first time I ever came here and met him, he had me drip some of my blood into the dirt to become part of this place. He said the only real condition was I would have to follow his people's ways. I thought that would be all right, never thinking it would involve anything like trading wives for a time. I did not want to be with Mary Wolf, but he would not back down over Sarah Beth."

"Mary Wolf is very pretty. And she speaks your language. Maybe not too late." Lefty said, smiling. "Unless you are too busy with the ones you now have."

"Too busy is not the problem. I am working hard because I still have to build a house for them and Mattie, and there is still the hunting for meat and the travelling to town for supplies. No, I am always busy with those things, but no more than I would be otherwise. When there is a child, maybe then Helga will need more care from me, and I don't know how Sarah Beth would find that. I just don't know anything anymore, Lefty. I almost want to blame someone for this, maybe even what is wrong to say, maybe I even blame God for this happening."

"Good. That is the right one who to blame. And to give thanks to. Did you not want a child very, very much?"

"Yes, but not this way…I have tried to live a good life, even a godly life. Now look at me. I feel like I am a bad man now."

"My friend, Creator, or what my friends down south say, the One Above the Sky, that is who is responsible, not you, not your wife, not this younger woman, only Creator is responsible. And you are not a bad man, because no one is perfect. This life is just practice."

"What do you mean?"

"My old grandfather, he tell me this life is only practice."

"Practice for what?"

"Oh, he say we don't know."

"Then how did he know that life is just practice?"

"He say we know this because nobody very good at it." He laughed. "You understand?"

"It makes sense, but what our people believe is that we start out bad and have to work to become good."

"How can you look at a baby and say it start out bad? Listen to me now—the souls of the new people are waiting on the other side of the Sky, above the Sky with Creator, waiting to see if they have to come back down here again. This life is hard. They know this. Maybe they do not want to come back. Maybe they do. I don't know. I know I like this hard life good enough."

"I just wish Sarah Beth and I were the ones to have this child."

The stick in Lefty's hands was now stripped bare and the little leaves were piled up in front of him.

"I see you are a strong man. You are my friend." He bent the stick slowly and it didn't break. "You are like this stick, you will not break, but only if you do not feel bad for yourself. Be happy, you will be the father of many, many children and grandchildren and their children. Like this pile of sage leaves. Too many to count. And they will remember you, all of them."

"If what you say is true, it makes me feel good."

"See, you don't have to feel bad, you are not bad. Your priests and missionaries are wrong. We are all good in the beginning, but we make mistakes. Your child is going to be strong and you are a good stick. It is not because of you that this is happening; it is because of the Earth wanting this child. So be happy and let both women take care of you and you take care of them and child. It will be good for all of you. You will see."

"I hope so. I want to be this child's father, to be a good father, I really do."

"Big Bear Man, I say again, Creator want this child, Earth want this child, so you must not regret what you have done and you must be strong for your women and for your children, strong like Bear. That will show your first woman how you are, and she will want a child even more than before and it will happen." He turned and threw the stick into the brush and walked out to where his horse was standing head down in the sun. "We go now. Talk enough. Yes?"

During Sa-rah's second night alone on the mountain, Moon Fish was awakened by terrible screaming from the camp above. As she pulled herself into wakefulness, she thought she heard a mountain lion screaming for its cub. She'd heard that sound a few times, and was always shocked by how much it sounded like a desperate woman in trouble. Now she listened and waited for it to come again, but there was nothing but silence accompanied by the deep darkness of the sky above. "It happens," she said to herself. "Nothing can be done. It happens and the fright caused by whatever approaches that person—it is theirs and cannot be shared or removed." At the same time, she thought, as she pulled the hide close around herself, this one didn't have the experience behind her. What if she couldn't take care of herself? But to help her now would remove what she would gain if she made it through. That was the most important thing. The older woman knew she was having the feelings of a mother not wanting her child to fall and be hurt, but knowing that too much or the wrong kind of help gets in the way of learning. "Nothing to do about it, old woman," she said to herself out loud, and hearing Lark Woman stir on the other side of the small fire-pit, she relaxed her breathing and was soon asleep again.

Even before first light, she was awake and starting the fire. She would make the tea now, to have it ready for Sa-rah when they brought her down. Lark Woman pushed herself up from her bed on the ground and stretched with several deep breaths. Moon Fish told her about the scream in the night and said she was going up there as soon as the first light appeared.

As she climbed up the rocky slope, she was filled with happiness for this young white woman, white like herself, but now becoming one with the earth. Moon Fish stopped climbing and faced the east with its glimmer of a coming day, raised her hands over her head and gave thanks for the night and for the day. She begged the Grandmothers for a blessing for this young woman.

The young woman was huddled against one of the boulders, wrapped in the skin they'd left with her. At first she seemed to be awake, but did not notice the arrival of the other woman.

"Sa-rah, Sa-rah," she said softly, trying not to startle the little sister.

Sa-rah turned quickly to the sound of a voice and seemed to be trying to focus her vision to see who it was. Then, suddenly, she was up, throwing herself into Moon Fish's arms.

"Oh my God, Ohhh, you've come."

Moon Fish clapped her own hand over the young woman's mouth and shook her head, "No," and making a sign over her own mouth to signal that it was not yet time for talking, no words now. Then she took the other's hand in hers and began leading her down the mountainside, carefully supporting her so she wouldn't fall from her weakness.

When they reached the small campfire, Moon Fish gently helped Sa-rah down into a seated position on one of the hides that was rolled into a cushion. Once again she made the motion for silence as Lark Woman poured a cupful of tea.

"Drink, drink all of it," Moon Fish said, "and then go over by those bushes. You must empty yourself of the bad juices, even if you have to use your finger. Hurry now."

Sa-rah did as she was told and found herself retching and heaving as thick mucus emerged from her throat. She retched several times and nearly fell, but then Moon Fish was there to catch her.

"That's good, my little sister. Is good, now you can have a little water, and then some soup we have made for you...Here, take a little more water, but don't try to talk yet. Wait."

The young woman's hair was tangled and she kept trying to smooth it. Her deerskin dress was soiled with sweat and dirt. Moon Fish motioned for her to remove it, and then took her by the hand and led her to a small spring where water gathered in a basin of rocks. She began washing the young woman, using a scrubber, scraping to remove the paints and the grime. She made Sa-rah turn around several times as she washed and then dried her off with a soft piece of cloth. She reached into a bag and brought out a dress made of white cloth with a colored print of flowers. Then she led the young woman back to the fire, sat her down, and served her a bowl of soup.

Sa-rah sat quietly now, breathing deeply of the pleasant steam from the soup. She almost wasn't hungry, but the strong aroma of herbs and meat took care of that and soon she felt as if her appetite was greater than ever. Lark Woman emerged from the brush, went around behind the young woman, and began using her fingers to untangle the matted hair. As soon as she could, she began using a comb. Sa-rah carefully blew on the soup as she took each spoonful into her mouth.

Moon Fish was smoking her pipe and watching the girl while smiling, humming. Sa-rah caught her eye and smiled as well. The terrifying moments on the mountain no longer seemed so horrible; the daylight was filled now with the rising sun's power, and she knew she was going to be all right again. No matter what had happened up there, she was going to be all right, and now the dreams or visions or whatever could be left behind.

When she'd finished the bowl of soup and Lark Woman finished braiding her hair, Moon Fish gave her more water to drink, and said, "Now, you will speak to us. You will tell us of your visitors and your pain, of your dreaming and of your joys."

"Thank you. Thank you for being here for me," she said. "I was so afraid. I was afraid maybe you left me, left me alone. I wanted to come running back down here to see if you were here. I was so afraid, especially in the darkness when many things came and went..."

"You can start with the first night. Better that way."

Sa-rah told them that it took a long time for her to get to sleep that first night. Moon Fish translated for Lark Woman in a soft voice. "And when I did go to sleep I had no dreams and I did not even wake up until the light of day began coming. Then I kind of fell back asleep with my hands over my eyes, and that's when my father came to see me. I told you he died, but I saw him standing there when my eyes were closed and he was still there when I opened them. He was still there. It wasn't a dream, or it didn't seem like a dream. His back was to me and he was facing the light coming into the sky. I called out to him. I got up and walked toward him. Suddenly he turned around and when I went to touch him, he backed quickly away, shaking his head, no, no. Then he held both of his hands up above his head in the way that he used to give a blessing to the people in our church, he looked up into the sky and then he was gone. Just not there. I wanted to follow him, but I couldn't see him anywhere. I started to cry, and I kept crying all that morning, I kept crying for a long time." She took another drink of water.

"It was good that your father came to you. He is also waiting for this child of yours, so he came to help you now. Go on, tell us more when you are ready."

"All day I was hungry and thirsty and sometimes I couldn't think about anything else, but I remembered what you told me and I tried to think about any people who were ever bad to me. There have not been many. A teacher in school when I was very young used to hit me with a stick even if I didn't do anything wrong. I thought about him and prayed for him wherever he is, that he can find peace and that he will never be in my thoughts or dreams again…Is that what I can pray for?"

Moon Fish and Lark Woman both nodded yes, yes.

"The other thing that day—when it got very hot there were ants, many, many ants. They came out of a hole in the dirt near one of the boulders. They were coming and going all day, and when I put my hand down where they were, they went around my hand. They never touched me even though they could have gone right over my hand. They worked all day, very hard, coming and going, but I don't know what they were doing. They would go out with nothing, and come back with tiny grains of sand from somewhere, at least it looked like sand, and some brought back tiny little twigs. I thought they were building something, but I couldn't see anything around or under that rock." She stopped talking for a while, as if waiting for something. "I stood up, sometime in the afternoon, and I walked over to where I could look down across the valley there. I guess I wanted to see if I could see my home, my new home, but there was nothing out there until I saw Hawk Man's horses running across the open place with all the brown grass. I saw his stallion, that beautiful, strong, proud horse. He ran around and around the other horses, keeping them close together. It was like some kind of a dance, and then suddenly they all ran straight, ran away and were gone…Is that important?" she asked.

"We will see," Moon Fish said. "You said you were afraid of things in the night. Do you want to tell us about that now?"

"I don't want to remember it, but also I want to tell you. It was so terrible it makes me afraid of myself."

"That's all right, dear. You are protected now, and from now on."

"When it grew dark, I knew I was not hungry or thirsty anymore. I didn't want anything. I didn't even want to leave that place. I couldn't think of anything I wanted, and I must have fallen asleep without my bedding. Later I woke up because I was so cold and I got the hide and the blanket and made a bed, but I couldn't get back to sleep." She paused, rubbing her eyes with her fingers. "Then it happened. A bright light flashed in front of me and suddenly I saw myself bent over a body in a bed, a regular bed. I could see what was going on.

It was a woman having birth pain, she was giving birth and I was there to help. She was screaming and I was helping, and then I could see that it was Helga, the one who lives with us, the one with Abe's child. I hate myself for urging her to make a child with my own husband...I don't hate her, that's what's strange. I hate myself, but not her...Then she screamed again and again and I saw the baby's head coming and I reached down to help it come out, and it looked like the chord was wrapped around the baby's neck, so I went to remove it, but it wasn't around the neck, it was just in this strange way being pushed out with the head, and, and that's when I did it..." She bent over and began crying, weeping. She started slapping her head with her hands. "That's why I hate myself, because I killed the baby, I wrapped the cord around its neck and I killed Abe's baby; I killed Helga's baby. And then I started screaming myself and I don't know if I was awake or asleep. There was blood on my hands and the baby fell out of her, and I didn't even pick it up. I just kept screaming and tearing at my own stomach with my fingers...And now I hate myself because I know how terrible I am, I know what an evil heart I have." She lay back on the ground, sobbing and moaning. Suddenly she sat up, and said, "But that wasn't the end of it. The Bishop appeared. You hardly know about him, but he was the most evil man I've ever met. He tried so hard to hurt me, and God saved me from him, but now I don't know. He was there and he spoke in a loud voice, saying to me, 'That was well done, now you are as evil as I am. We are equal and I will finally have you as my wife in Hell." She groaned and pulled on her braided hair. Tears fell from her eyes.

"All right, dear," Moon Fish said. "Rest, say nothing now, and rest." As she spoke, Lark Woman moved behind Sa-rah and pushed her forward so she was somewhat bending over her own lap, and the old woman began singing, softly rubbing the younger woman's back, neck, and the sides of her body, gently, gently, singing and pressing lightly, singing, touching and rubbing, singing...

When the woman stopped her singing, Moon Fish said, "Sa-rah, you have done everything you needed to do. You will be safe now. You will have a child of your own. Helga will have her child and you will help her with the birth and it will be good. Now try to rest, even sleep, and then we will talk of these things when you are ready. Know only that you are blessed to have these things happen to you in this way because now you have become a blessing to yourself and to all others."

Sa-rah felt a sudden cramping below her chest and then down into her hips. She bent over, moaning softly. Lark Woman rubbed her lower back and again began the low singing of her song. Moon Fish slid around to sit next to her and asked, "Sa-rah, your pain, what is it?"

"It feels like my time, my time in the month."

"We call that your moon-time," the woman said. "It is good that it did not happen while you were up there. It is good to come now, because it will complete your purification." She reached over to a bag and handed soft moss to Sa-rah. "Can you walk?"

"I think so."

"Then go to the edge over there, behind those rocks, and place this between your legs. Tie it in place with this cord. It will soak up what you release and then we will bury it before we leave here. And we won't be going until you have rested and we all walk down together."

Sarah Beth pushed herself up to a standing position and then did as the woman told her.

When she returned to them, they gave her another bundle of moss to tie in place. They'd made a small bed, and helped her to lie down.

"Try to sleep."

Mattie and Helga returned to their work after taking the food to the men. Helga unhooked the horse from the buggy and gathered some soiled laundry.

"Mattie? Can I ask you something?"

"Of course, my dear."

"I don't know what to do. I'm so unhappy."

"Come, leave the washing. Let's sit for a spell, and you can tell me what it is."

They settled in the meager shade. Helga started to speak, but then stopped, sniffled and cleared her throat. "I love him."

"That's good. You're going to have his child, so it's best that you love him."

"But I can't have his love, so it would be better if I didn't even like him."

Mattie reached over and patted the girl on the shoulder. "Don't even think like that. Believe me. I was forced to have a child with a man who I could never even begin to like the least bit. He was awful, but the owner made me do it."

"But then did you also dislike your baby?"

"Oh no, she was my favorite of all my children. But my heart was always hurting because of how I felt about the man. Believe me, child, it's much better to love your baby's father."

"Even if I can't have him."

"Who says you can't have him? You might have to share him. You will have to share him, and the baby as well, but it's going to be all right once you all get used to it."

"But he won't even look at me."

"Maybe because he also loves you…"

Helga looked down into her hands and tears fell from her eyes. "She won't let him. I know she won't. She tries to be nice to me, but the way she treats him, she seems to be punishing him or something."

"Oh, my little dear, they just haven't worked it out yet. It will take time, and she will have to understand what she's done, and what you two have done, and soon she will be able to do that. Takes time, like any kind of healing does. And I will talk with her. I promise."

"But what if she just gets angry with me? She might even make me leave. I can't go anywhere—I don't have anywhere to go."

"That isn't going to happen," Mattie said as she slowly pushed herself up on her knees, knelt in front of the seated young woman, and put her arms around her. "That isn't going to happen, because if it did, I would go with you…I want this baby to be safe and I want you to be happy with it. Even though she is like my own daughter… If she is wrong, I won't help her in that."

"Oh Mattie, you don't have to do that, it isn't fair to you."

"Don't worry, my sweet child. I know I won't have to do that because it's not going to happen. Now, we should get that work done, don't you think?"

Helga stood up quickly so she could help the older woman to her feet and then they held each other in a strong hug. "Thank you, Mattie. I feel better. I just want to have some time with my baby's father." She turned and went after the laundry.

Sa-rah awoke from her daytime sleep by midafternoon. She looked around anxiously, unable to remember where she was. Then it came back to her. She sat up, rubbed her eyes and stretched her arms and fingers. When she started running her fingers through her hair she found the braid that Lark Woman made. Soon she felt good enough to stand and stretch and twist her neck and back some more. She had the memory of a pleasant dream and she looked around for the two women, eager to tell them about it.

She saw Lark Woman out near the ledge that dropped away into the valley below, and then turned to the sound of small rocks clattering down the slope and saw Moon Fish carrying the things she'd left behind.

"Ah, so you're awake, my little sister. Did you rest well?"

"Yes, very well, and only a good dream this time."

"That's good. I'll call my friend and we can talk some more. Do you want more to eat, or to drink?"

"No, thank you, I feel just right inside now. Maybe a little more water is all."

"It's right there. Take what you want," the woman said, pointing toward a skin bag. She went to get her friend.

When they were settled and comfortable, Lark Woman used a stick to pull a hot rock out of the fire. She sprinkled some leaves on it and then, using a bird wing, she wafted this smoke toward each of them. The herb had a sweet and pungent smell, and the woman showed Sarah Beth how to make motions as if she were washing herself with the smoke. Then Lark Woman sang a short song and put the wing back in her bag.

Moon Fish looked at Sa-rah for a long time, then cleared her throat with a cough and said, "While you were sleeping, you were smiling and you had your hands across your breasts as if you were holding something close to yourself. Do you remember what it was?"

"Oh yes, when I woke up I couldn't wait to tell you. In this dream I had a baby in my arms, and it was my baby, not any other, and then I held it out to Abe and gave it to him and he took it from me. I told him this was our child, his child, and he was happy."

"Good, that is good. I expected something like that. Now, we will tell you what these things mean for you, these things you have seen, these things that frightened you and this one that made you happy. First, we will tell you about those ants. They are the children and the children's children and all the children that will come from you and your husband throughout a long, long time of many generations. This is very good, a message from the Spirit of All We Know...Next, your father coming to you at the beginning of your searching-time. He wanted you to know that you will never be alone. He will always be nearby, just as he was in your life. That is also good for you to know and to keep close to yourself all the time."

Lark Woman interrupted in their own language and spoke for a short while, and then Moon Fish translated for the younger woman, "She says your father also had two women, just as your husband does, and that is known because he raised both of his arms over his head to bless you. He wanted you to know that your husband will always be your man, but you will also do well if you have this other woman with you. She can help when you have your own child."

"May I ask how you knew this?"

"Of course, when you introduced us to the dark woman, you called her your second mother. If your father was only blessing you from himself and the mother who gave you birth, he would only have raised one arm."

Sa-rah looked up into the woman's eyes. "That is true, I just remembered, whenever he gave a blessing in the church when he was the minister, he only raised one hand to bless the people. But how did Lark Woman know this?"

"While you were here sleeping, the two of us went up to the place where you were, and we could feel what was still there from you, and we talked about all that you had told us."

"But what about the horrible things, Helga and her baby...the Bishop?"

Moon Fish took out her small pipe, filled and lit it. She passed it to Sarah Beth. "Take some into your mouth. You do not need to breathe it in all the way, then do like this." She made a cup of her hand, blew into it and them wiped the top of her head.

Sa-rah did as she was told and then handed the pipe back.

"You are a Dreamer-woman and Dreamers have different kinds of power, what comes to them is not always the same. You know that you are the Dreamer because you said you actually saw these things happening in a real way. These were not ordinary dreams, but signs of what will come and what will not come. Many Dreamers have the power to see something in the world of visions and by seeing it, they are making sure it can never happen in what we call the real life. What you saw happening cannot happen now. You cannot and will not harm this new life coming to your man, the girl, and yourself. You have saved the child from harm during birth by having it happen in that power way, so now it cannot happen again. The same with that man who has hurt you so badly, that one you call the Bishop..."

"But I never did what you told me to with him, like you told me to do with those who had harmed me, if they came to me."

"You can do that anytime. You can speak to them and tell them that they can no longer harm you in any way. Now, that you have been through this, they will have to listen and follow your words to them...And the last thing that we have to say, and my little sister, I must tell you that I am surprising myself by how well I can speak in this language of yours and mine. I have not spoken like this in many, many years and now I talk like a woman with a cricket in her mouth, chirrup, chirrup, chirrup, talk, talk...But I will tell you this now. The dream you had lying here just now was only a dream, but it shows that those other things have been got out of you, out of the way, so now you could have a good dream again, a pleasant dream. And this will happen, you will have your baby just like in the dream." She nodded to Lark Woman, who began singing and then finished with a song having a most beautiful melody, a chant with bird sounds, lark sounds…

Ollie came back again the next day and they finished the boards on the west side of the house. He asked where the water would be coming from for the house and if it would need pipes.

"It comes from over by that rock wall, a kind of a natural spring" Abe said. "I've thought about digging out a basin for it and running one of those narrow wooden troughs down to a tank here above the house."

"Got time to show me the spring? I'm curious about how folks dig and make that sort of thing out here. Been drilling and breaking rock most of my life, y'know."

"Sure, we can take a walk up there. It's really not that far."

"Have you heard about that iron pipe they make now?"

"Heard something about it, but you'll see how uneven the ground is up there. Be no way to use straight iron pipes. Hard enough to build it out of wood in short connected sections."

They took a break to eat, and then made the climb to the water source, which was lower now at the end of summer. Ollie immediately began scuffing small rocks out of the shallow basin and trying to remove some larger stones. Abe pitched in and they were able to get down through most of the loose stuff to the bedrock layer.

"Bet that there layer runs on back under that cliff face where the water comes from," Ollie said, using a rock to pound against the wet wall of the stone. "What would be good would be to push back into the wall there and chunk it out so's your storage was mostly in the shade, keep it from evaporating so much." He stopped pounding and squatted down to pick up some of the rock chips he'd made. "You ever hear of that dynamite they got over in Europe now? I mean we've used some explosives back in Pennsylvania, but it was always unpredictable and dangerous. Didn't know how much it would blast or even if it would go off. Nice when it worked, but hell on guys if they got too close and then the damn stuff blowed."

"Don't know much about that sort of thing," Abe said. "But I did hear they were using something like that on the cross-country railroad project, drilling and blowing up boulders too big to move out of their way."

"Yeah, it's a lot safer above ground than in a pit or a tunnel. Well, we don't have any and we don't have a steam drill around here that I know of, except maybe up in those mines by Silver City. Nothing like a man, a hammer, and a sharp iron stake to pound on. Think I'll get ol' Mike to fix me up a tool. Got it in my mind, but never seen one yet. Ought to make this here job a little easier. That's if you don't mind. Hell, be better for you, I'm a much better rock breaker than I am a wood-builder."

"That would be great. I wasn't sure what to do up here, and when I tried to figure how much water our little household would use, it didn't seem like this trickle would be enough to keep three women happy."

Ollie laughed and said, "Women without water is a fierce kind of beast, don't you just know it?

"I do know what you mean. There were times coming across on the wagons when I thought we might have our own kind of war when the water ran out or come close to it. Captain McFarland, our head man, would threaten to stop the whole train and leave us all where we were if those that were hiding some water didn't share it out so we could all make it to the next good water. And the poor animals. One fella tried to make a joke and said you knew it was bad when the oxen started stepping on their own tongues, but it wasn't funny." He paused and thought about those days, then he said, "Think I might head back down to work on the house. You're welcome to stay up here. You might have some more ideas."

"I might at that, and I'll be down shortly."

Abe started down, and then instead of taking the rough pathway, he tried to gauge where the best route for a sluice would be, straight but not too uneven. It felt good to get this part of the project started, good to have Ollie around.

Later in the afternoon, Ollie came down from the spring and said he was going to get Mike to make up some tools for him. He was excited to be doing something he knew about and promised Abe that, one way or another, they would gain a good-sized basin for storage. He asked Abe if there was anything more that still needed the two of them at that time, otherwise he wanted to head back to work on some things with Mike. Abe got him to hold up one end of a beam that would support rafters for Helga's added room, and then the man left. As Abe watched him ride back along the trail, he once again felt the grateful for this man's arrival and the good fortune that would surely make the building easier. Things were beginning to fall into place, and it was only the part between him and the women that was making things so difficult now.

CHAPTER 4

Discovery

One morning, a week or so after Sarah Beth returned from her time away with the older women, she and Abe were working together on the kitchen floor of the new house. He was mixing mortar and pouring it out, as she laid flat rocks into it. When he'd mixed enough for her to finish the job, he went out to the ditch he was digging for the water system. He stopped his digging when he heard a shout and the sound of horse hooves coming near. It was Hawk Man, riding his favorite horse and leading another.

He pulled up to a stop and slid off his mount, saying as he did, "Hello my young friend. Is a good day?"

Abe walked over and replied, "Yes, a very good day. And you? Everything with you all right?"

"Good," the man said, dropping the lead rope of the other horse. "I give this one to you. Name Run Cloud. For you. I take that one." He pointed down to where Bird was grazing. "One name Little Bird. She make colt with my strong horse Lightning, you know. He best horse of all. They make new best horse."

As he tried to think what this would mean, and it made some sense to him, he remembered the first time he'd seen the horse called Lightning, how impressed he'd been, and how nervous and excited Bird was, even at a distance. He had a question in his mind as to who the colt would belong to, but decided that could wait. He would probably be told about the Indian way in these matters.

Just then he heard Sarah Beth calling him from inside the house. Perhaps she hadn't heard the sounds of Hawk Man's arrival. He called back to her, "Hawk Man is here with a horse for me. Come out."

Hawk Man removed a braided leather rope from around his waist and walked down the slope to where Bird was now standing, looking curiously at the other horses. He approached her slowly and then eased one hand up along her neck and over to take the end of the rope from his other hand. He quickly fashioned a knot in the loop and led her back to where Abe stood.

"She will return, and be mother of a great one. We have good son of her, and he have many new one."

Abe decided to bring up his question now, and said, "I'm not sure I want a stallion here. It would be a problem for me if you have Lightning here and I have the son. They might fight."

"Boy horse, I take. Girl horse, you take. Now I go. Hold that one." He gestured at the end of Abe's new horse's rope on the ground. "Keep him good. Is yours now." Then he pulled himself up onto his own horse, and called down, "We need talk. Come my camp.," he said, pointing first at Abe and then at himself. Then he wheeled his horse around and rode off, leading Bird who held back, but then followed obediently. Once again Abe stood still, thinking how this land and this man kept surprising him, first taking his wife, now his horse. He fastened the end of the new horse's rope around a post and moved toward the house.

"Sarah Beth," he called. "I'm coming."

She came out the doorway. "I didn't know who rode up and I couldn't stop what I was doing. I'm sorry if I interrupted you. I saw who it was when he rode away."

"So, why didn't you come out and join us?"

"Abe," she stepped to him and put her arms around his shoulders, "Abe, I still feel very awkward when I think about him or when I see him."

"I thought nothing really happened."

"Nothing, except I lived with him in his tipi and his people thought I was his new woman." She backed away and turned toward the house. "I only want to live with you, here."

"I know," he said.

"Well then, what are you going to do about Helga and your baby? Have you noticed she's been crying a lot lately?"

"No. Why is she crying?"

"I'm sure part of it has to do with her condition. It does that to women, especially at this stage of it. But I think it's also because she's so lonesome...Abe, I know she wants you. She wants you more and more and I don't know what to do about it. And you obviously don't even know what's really going on here."

"I know she would like to spend more time with me. She's said so, but I have this house to get ready for all of us, and..."

"Abe Saunders, that's just an excuse. You are avoiding the issue of who gets you and when, and I want to know as well." With that she tossed her hair and turned away, saying, "I've got my work to finish before everything dries out, and I'm sure you have things to do." She disappeared into the half-finished house saying, "Think about it."

On an afternoon when thunder was rolling far away in the mountains and the air was thick and sultry, Helga walked to the creek and moved slowly upstream along its bank, hoping for cooler air. There was still no hint of rain, just humid air. She pulled up the legs of the pants she'd made for herself and then recently enlarged, took off her shoes and began wading along the edge of the flowing water. There was a boulder that split the stream into two channels flowing on either side of it. She took a seat on it and splashed water up into her face. Looking around to make quite certain that no one was nearby, she removed her lightweight shirt. She was tempted to also remove the thin under-shift as well, but held off on that.

As she rested there and swung her feet back and forth to make splashes and a bit of cool spray, she wished she could have Abe with her sometimes when neither of them had anything that needed to get done. He was always working these days, always busy, seeming to avoid Sarah Beth as much as herself. She knew it was about the house and their need for it to be ready, but still he could take some break times once in a while.

It was too hot on the boulder in the sun, and she was just getting ready to move along, maybe go a little further up the creek, when she heard the sound of singing, beautiful singing, far away. She couldn't make out the words, but she was fascinated and wanted to move closer and hear it better. It was a kind of singing she'd never heard before and as she got closer to the singer, she realized that either there were no real words or she didn't know the language. It had to be one of the Indian women. She stopped in the shade of some willows, up to her knees in the bubbling water, and held her breath, trying hard to hear the song, thinking how much she wished that she could sing that beautifully. Then it stopped.

A minute later Mary Wolf emerged from some brush along the stream, carrying a dripping bundle. The two women stopped and were still as they recognized one another, and then the Indian woman laughed and said, "Hello, you are here."

"Yes, it was so hot and I had finished some work and wanted to be with the water."

"It is a little better here. Very hot day, maybe we have rain later, maybe not."

"Oh I hope so. It can't get any hotter. How are you?"

The woman set down the bundle and rinsed her hands. "I'm well. Working on elk hide from when your man Abe went hunting with Hawk Man. I smell bad."

"Not really. I want to learn how to do that kind of work someday. I like the way the hides turn out so much."

"Lot of work. And you, how are you?"

Helga didn't answer as she tried to think of the best answer, then said, "I'm doing all right, still getting used to all this, this place and this work we do here."

Mary Wolf cupped her hands under her own breasts and said, "You bigger now. Is change, yes?"

"Oh." Helga remembered she was almost naked and quickly covered herself with the shirt she was carrying. "Yes, I guess so."

The other woman smiled and said, "Is good. I no tell others. Is from man Abe?"

Helga knew that her face was flushed now, but in some ways this was what she'd been waiting for, someone to talk to about this thing that was happening to her. Someone to tell, and even though she'd never been with this woman alone together, never spoken with her, she seemed to be kind, and Helga liked her.

"What I want to know," she said, not yet ready to talk about herself and Abe, "is about the song I heard you singing. So beautiful."

Mary Wolf replied, "Oh, it is old song from women who work beside the water. A song to make things clean and to have the water clean itself as well. You could learn it."

"Oh, I don't think so. I like to sing, but I have no mind for words, especially of another language."

The Indian woman laughed, "Is no words, just sounds we make like the water. Like this…" and she began singing softly with a rhythmic sound almost coming from her throat, very much like the sound of a creek bubbling along its course. Then she changed to a kind of trilling and brought a repetitious melody into the song.

Helga listened with her whole being, drawn into the sound of the water, the song, and the day. It was as if something was opening her insides to the world around her and she was losing her own thoughts in a way she'd never felt before. Suddenly, Mary Wolf stopped and clapped her hands once.

"I see maybe you are falling asleep. Maybe you fall over into water."

"Oh no. I was just feeling so opened up to everything. I don't know how to say it, just like my thoughts went away and my body, here where the baby is, like it was opening up."

"That is good for you. Happen more often now. I teach you that one song, but also other song we use for baby and for you, now to help you sleep. You must sleep much, and when light of day keep you awake you will sing to your baby and yourself and be able to rest, grow stronger inside. You will need this. Is what your people call a lullaby, always good for my little ones, and for me. Here please, sit on this grass with your feet in the water."

Helga did as she was told and the woman knelt behind her and began softly humming in very low tones. She placed her hands on the younger woman's shoulders and began kneading those muscles and the neck. Again, Helga felt the soothing strength of the woman's song as it translated into the strength and movement of Mary Wolf's hands as she was gently rocked back and forth to the rhythm of the woman's singing. Her head nodded forward as she felt the hands slowly moving up and down her spine. She found herself trying to stay awake as the drowsiness of the day's heat and the soothing voice combined to bring her to the edge of dreaming.

Mary Wolf gently pulled the younger woman back so her head was resting against her chest, and then she slowly slid her hands down to Helga's belly where she pushed with gentle pressure and slowly circled her fingers in a flowing motion, much like a small whirlpool of some enchanted water. Helga let herself relax completely, and let her mind flow with the singing, and she felt Abe's hands rubbing, rubbing her whole middle, her body slightly tensing to his touch. She knew she was dreaming, but she also knew she was awake. It was both strange and familiar and she heard her own voice humming in unison with the woman whose face was just a little above her own.

The sighing sound of the singing stopped, and the hands lightly pulled away. Helga felt like she was floating above the ground, and she stretched out her arms to reach her fingers into the grass. Then she slowly sat up and curled her backbone forward, breathing out and holding herself in that breathless, empty state for a long moment. She felt the Indian woman standing up behind her and turned to look up at her.

"Thank you," she said. "Thank you so much. I feel like the water, or maybe more like the air, only not so hot anymore."

"It is good. Now you do this for yourself. Remember what you can of song, let your hands be the touch of that sound. You will feel good, you will grow stronger even when you need more rest. I will be able to see you again soon." Then the woman turned and walked into the shrubs that grew above the narrow band of grass where the high water ran in the wintertime.

Helga hardly knew if she could trust herself to stand. Her whole body felt as if it were dissolving into the grass and the water, the air and the sunlight, but she shook out her hair and pushed herself up, first onto her knees, and then slowly to a standing position. To her surprise she wasn't the least bit dizzy or light-headed. She felt balanced and strong now. It was such a good feeling, such a well-being, and not even the heat of the day could disturb the comfortable feeling. The Indian woman, her voice and her hands, had given Helga a new way of looking at herself, her situation, and the world around her. She could accept that she was in love, not only with a person, but with everything around her, No, this love wasn't just with Abe, and it wasn't filled with worries about whether or not he liked her. She was now feeling loved by everything, and wanting to share it all with her baby. She would have to do something special for Mary Wolf, something to show gratitude and happiness for this feeling.

As she walked back down the creek, wading in the pleasant cooling water, she heard a nearby horse fluttering its lips in that characteristic horsy sound. She stood still and listened and then heard the splashing clatter of hooves coming toward her. Around the next bend in the stream and its brushy banks came Abe. He was riding the new horse and looked just as surprised to see her as she was to see him. She clutched her overshirt against her chest, feeling exposed in just the lightweight under-shift. Then she realized she didn't want to hide herself from him. She wanted him to look at her, to look at her and maybe even notice all the ways her body was changing.

"Hello," he said, "didn't think anyone was down here. I was heading over to thank Hawk Man for this horse. He's very well broken.'

"It's a busy day down here," she said, looking up at him. "I only came down to get cooler and I met up with Mary Wolf."

"Is she still here?"

"I don't think so. She was working on a hide or something in the water, and was leaving when I saw her. Why don't you get down and we can sit here for a little while."

The horse finished drinking and shook his head about, flinging water into the air. "I really need to get over there and get back to the house in case Ollie shows up."

Helga shook her head and swung her loose hair about. "What you need to do is stop working all the time and spend some of it with me and your child, but I'll let you go this time."

"I know," he said, "and I will. I promise."

"We'll see. It's easier for you to promise than to do what you say you will. Even Sarah Beth knows that. You're always busy and always running off." She stepped to the side of the horse and placed her hands on his leg, "Abe, I miss you, I really do. We've hardly gotten to know each other and what's happening is very important, at least it is to me."

"I know. I know it is, and I'll make time, I will. I…"

She interrupted him, "Don't promise. Just find ways to do it. Or I'll give up on you." She backed away from him and the horse, wiped tears from her face and hurried away.

"Don't give up on me," he said after her, and then hastened Running Cloud up the bank and toward the Indian camp.

He tied the horse to a sapling near the tipis and waited for someone to notice he was there. A couple of boys came toward him and then ran away. It reminded him of the first time he went near Lefty's camp back in Missouri. Then he heard Hawk Man's voice calling him from the back of one of the tipis. He walked toward it, and saw the man squatting over what appeared to be a hoop of some kind. He was stretching and cutting a piece of hairless skin.

"Hello, my young friend. Sit. I must do this now, is wet for make drum."

"I don't want to bother you. I just came by to see how everything is for you folks. If you need anything, any help."

"We are good. Sun, meat, berries all good now. And you?"

"Things are going well for us too. We are very happy here. I must thank you again for letting us be here. It is a perfect for us. I never could have had this on my own."

"Then is good for you and me. We keep from other whites. They want, but you, me, we keep for us, for Indian people and your family. Your family get bigger be good for them. Yes."

"That's one thing I want to talk with you about, my friend. My family has changed and I'm not sure how to take care of what is new, what is coming to us now."

"Ho, no talk fast. No understand. Should call Mary Wolf for talk." He called out the woman's name. Someone answered. "Oh, say she not here now."

"Just as well," Abe said. "Maybe I talk slow and not use many words."

"I try understand," the man said. He pulled hard on the rawhide strip that held the skin over the hoop. "This drum," he gestured his hand in a circle. "Is like your wheels, but we no have wheels. No use. Only ceremony, drums, children games." Again he gestured in a circle. "You know this?"

"I never thought about it. But I never saw a wheel or a wagon with Indians."

"Is holy, how you say sacred. Not work things, wagons, trains, all you have. For us this," Now he drew the shape of a circle in the dirt. "Belong to Spirit. Not for man to work, only to sing, dance, pray, or play like children. Understand?"

"Yes. But you use guns and other things of the white man. And you are speaking English much better now."

"I have Mary Wolf talk me in your language all time now, in both our way and yours we talk." He smiled and then laughed. "You have her teach you at night, but you no want more woman."

"That's what I want to talk with you about."

"Now you want her?"

"No, no, not that. But I have now, as you would say, more woman."

"The old black one, yes?"

"No, the young one."

Hawk Man stood up holding the drum and said, "Come, I put in sun place. We talk." He hung the drum by a thong from a branch as high up as he could reach. "No dogs get. Come." He led the way into the shade of the cottonwoods. "Cool by creek, but," he shook his head, "bugs. Here good." He squatted, picked up a small branch, and began slowly waving it around his head to deal with flies. Abe did likewise.

"I want to tell you myself. It was not my idea." Abe pointed to his forehead and shook his head negative. He found that using some kind of signs, even if he made them up, seemed to help him communicate with this man and the other Indians. "Was my woman, Sarah Beth. She go away with you. And say to that young one and to me to try make baby."

"Good idea. More children, more good for man when he be old."

"But this is because she does not think she can have a baby herself."

"I know. Moon Fish help. Will have baby, her, you. You will be chief." He laughed and crossed his arms over his chest, taking a deep breath. "Chief Big Bear Man, or maybe Chief Happy Horse. We see. I happy for you."

"But it is not good for me. Two women are one too many."

Hawk Man held up two fingers of each hand and said, "I no understand, two," he wiggled the fingers on his right hand, and said "two," followed by also wiggling the fingers on his left hand, "two more. What means two many?"

"It means one is all a white man has, and I don't know what to do. They are not happy about this. They both want me, all of me. What can I do? What do you do about these things?"

Hawk Man smiled and held the small branch in both hands and broke it in half, then held up both halves fitting back together, and then separated again. "Stick is you. This you to one woman, this you to other woman. They no like this way, they have no stick. One no like, no stick, other no like, no stick. Good? Both like, both have stick."

"My friend, I don't know how to talk to them about these things. They get sad or angry maybe, and I don't want that. I don't want any of this."

"You want children?"

"Oh yes, very much, but why does it have to be this way?"

Hawk Man took his small pipe from the pouch hanging from his waist. "The Way of Mystery we cannot know. You want children, you will be father, one woman, two woman. We smoke for thank Mystery."

When they had finished smoking, Hawk Man motioned for Abe to stand up in front of him. Then he began indicating the parts of Abe's body, saying, "Two eye, two ear, two arm, two hand, two leg, two foot," he paused, then continued, "one head, one heart. One head for think and one heart for life. All you, one man, now two woman. Good way. Come, we eat something."

They sat on hides near the largest tipi. Hawk Man spoke in a low voice, but was immediately answered from inside. Abe could hear the voices and laughter of the women within the structure, but of course he couldn't understand what they might be saying. Then the door covering was pushed back and Mary Wolf appeared with a thick hide pot steaming with meat stew. As she bent over, setting a bowl in front of Abe and filling it, she caught his eyes and gave him a very big, bright smile. He had never been this close to her and couldn't help noticing the whiteness of her teeth as they shone against the bronze of her skin. He smiled back and said "Thank you."

Hawk Man ate without any talk, finished, and wiped out his empty bowl with his fingers. Abe ate slower, but also finished what had been given to him. Just then he saw a face appear at the doorway of the tipi. It was Patsy, Lefty's youngest wife. She too smiled at him and even gave a little wave of her hand before disappearing behind the hanging door cover.

"Is Lefty here?" Abe asked.

"He here soon. Boi-see now, business."

"It'll be good to see him again. Well, thank you for the food and thank the women for me. I should go to my new house and work some more today."

"Is good house? Need good house for three women." Hawk Man smiled and held out his hand to shake with Abe in the white man way. Abe stood and walked off toward Running Cloud. The horse had worn a small path around the tree he'd been tied to, but became very still when the bridle was slipped over his head. Just as he was about to mount up, he heard Mary Wolf saying his name and saw that she was walking toward him, holding out a small bundle.

"Here," she said, "you take to your young woman." He accepted the bundle and was fixing it to the saddle, silently without replying when he heard her go on, "Now I know why you no want me for woman." He looked at her now and she gave another one of those smiles.

"That's not the reason. I didn't want this to happen either, but..." He didn't know what else to say as he felt her hand touch his arm.

"This will be good for you, for her, for Sa-rah. All good. Now you like Indian man. I like you be this." Then she turned and walked quickly away.

Abe mounted the horse and trotted him toward the creek, splashing across it, galloping to the house site. There was already a chill in the late afternoon shade. Fall was coming, and Abe couldn't help but think of how much was left to do before they could be moved into the house.

A few weeks later, on the morning of the fall's first frost, Abe lit a fire of lumber scraps in the stone fireplace. He was pleased with the way the draft pulled the smoke up and out. He walked outside and watched the smoke climb into the bright blue sky. It made him feel good, no matter how unfinished the overall project was. Things were going as well as could be hoped for. Lefty was still visiting Hawk Man across the creek, and Helga's pregnant body was taking on a definite shape. The subtle tensions between the two younger women, and between them and Abe, still surfaced occasionally, but nothing that became a serious problem for anyone. He was now spending a couple of nights a week with each of them and a couple of nights by himself. It had taken some wise intervention from Mattie to help the three of them arrive at a vague kind of schedule. When it became clear to Sarah Beth that some arrangement was necessary to prevent Helga from becoming severely unhappy and perhaps even leaving, Sarah Beth accepted her responsibility in the situation and tried to make the best of it.

As Abe prepared to get started on finishing up the stairs at both the front and back doors of the house, he could hear the distant sound of rocks being pounded. He hadn't realized that Ollie was already at work on the basin up above, digging and building. They had stopped that project for a while, waiting for some rain to show just how the rock wall above it would seep and drain, but Ollie was impatient and for the past two days he'd been going ahead on it, fairly certain he knew what to expect, and promising not to make any changes that couldn't be adjusted later.

The flat rocks that Abe and Sarah Beth gathered for the walkway to the front porch were nicely laid and fit together quite well, though the stones that would support the three-step risers needed more firming up and leveling. Later in the day, when Abe got to that part of the walkway project, he heard Ollie yelling his name and coming closer. When he arrived, Abe stood up and asked the sweating, out-of-breath man what was wrong.

"Nothing wrong, partner" the man panted out. "Nothing wrong at all...I found it, yes indeed I found it! Had a hunch, took a guess, and by God I found it...Oh my God, oh my, my." He slumped onto a pile of lumber and wiped his face with his kerchief. "Abe, I don't even know how to say it, but I found it." He dug into his shirt pocket for a handful of dirt and pebbles. "Abe, man, this is gold!"

Abe could hardly believe what he'd just heard and he stared at Ollie, unable to make any kind of a response as his mind raced through the many possibilities of what this might mean, both the good and the bad.

"Say something, man. What about it? You could be a rich man. Think about it."

"Whoa, slow down." Abe held out his hand and felt the dirt and pebbles fall into it as Ollie dumped the contents. "Let me think for a minute…first of all, this isn't my land, isn't our land." He paused while the impact of the discovery settled into his thinking and he finally said, "Ollie, I can tell how excited you are, but this could be every much as bad a thing as a good thing, for us. I'm trying to sort through it in my mind, but we have to be careful, very careful."

"Yeah, I know. We don't want none of them no-good claim-jumpers out there to take this away from us. I know what you mean."

"Ollie, it's even more serious than that. It might not take more than five minutes for the government to grab this land, kick Hawk Man and his people off, send us packing, and sell it to the highest bidder if they didn't keep it themselves. We got to be careful. First of all, are you sure? And why don't you take me up there and show me what it is?"

"Sure, let me get some water first—throat's dry as a gravel road. Guess I didn't think about much but how good this could be for us. Been waiting my whole life for one stroke of luck, and here it come, and, and now I don't know. First things first. Abe, let's go, I want to show you."

The two men climbed back up through the rocks and the harsh shrubby hillside until they reached the water storage project. Abe was amazed at how much Ollie had accomplished with only one hand and minimal tools. The seeping and trickling water from the rock face had already soaked the planned pond area and was running out through an opening that would be plugged when the digging and removal of the rocks was finished.

"Ollie, this is amazing. Can't believe you've been able to get all this dug and broken away. Never thought you'd be building a cave into the cliff like this."

"Once I got started, just couldn't stop myself. Here, step in there and see if it ain't cooler than anywhere else around."

Abe felt his boots fill with the precious water as he moved into the small shaded cavern. It was cool, and there was even more water dripping from the ceiling of the space than there was off the wall outside. He turned and bent down, filling his cupped hands with the water and letting it drop splashing back into the puddles he was standing in.

"Ollie, gold is one thing, but out here, over the long haul, this water is the real gold. I can just feel it, how important it is. We can make the grass turn green with enough of this water. Now, promise me you won't speak of this to anyone until you and me have a chance to think it out and figure what's worth what. All right?" He held out his hand and they shook.

"Man, I can't tell you how crazy I was feeling when I first found it. Look over here. I was just a-whacking away with my big maul and driving the point of my ax into this here crack in the rock, and all sudden like it just crumbled away and here was this line of soft crumbly stuff and I've seen it once before, down in Nevada when I was working my way up this way. Helped an old guy with his claim and was there the day he struck it. See, here's these ugly-looking little rocks, don't show nothing to give away what they are until you bust them open, then you can see the color. Here, show you."

Ollie dug out a small shovel full of the gravelly mud and rinsed it through his hand in the basin. Then he laid what was left out on a flat rock and tapped lightly with his metal hand, and then a little harder until he'd broken open several of the larger pebbles. These he rinsed some more and then held out to Abe.

"Hard to see there, my man, but it's the real stuff. I just know it."

"How much of this is there, you think?"

"No way to tell, maybe not much. Hell, maybe the whole goddam hillside. Got to dig to find that out."

The sun was dropping toward the tallest ridge and shadows were beginning to crawl across the valley floor. Abe gazed out across the land, noting the small shapes of his cattle far down the way, noticing the thin lines of smoke from the cooking fires of the Indian camp. All of this peacefulness was suddenly threatened in a mind's eye vision of machinery and noise carving into the hillsides and digging for the golden promise of wealth and comfort.

"Ollie, I want you to come on down and stay for supper with us. Don't want the women to know about this yet, at all. We've got to figure what to do and what not to do. But nothing's to stop us from having some good food. Maybe we can talk some more after we've had a little time to digest both our suppers and what's happened here." He started off down the slope then stopped and looked back. "Sorry, forgot to ask if there was anything needed carrying back down?"

"Nope, not that I can think of. And I see your point about this here two-edge sword we got in our hands, but there's got to be some kind of way to keep all this here safe and still make a little off of it."

"Of course. I'm sure we'll come up with something." He turned and started down the rocky path toward the unfinished house. The word opportunity came into his mind like a loud whistle and he remembered Sarah Beth's father's advice and admonition. "When you have a need and it's met by an opportunity matches up with it, that can be the Voice of God giving you the go-ahead. But, be careful, son, it can just as easy be a temptation to grab for something that not only won't meet your need, but will take you on the wrong road to finding God's will in your life." Up until now, it had seemed that his life was a series of these instances where the needs and opportunities came together in the form of blessings and solutions. But maybe this was now an example of the other way, the path of being led astray. He heard Ollie stumble behind him and turned to see if the man was all right.

"Just clumsy," he said, "been up and down this blasted climb too many times today. Damn legs getting soft on me."

"But you're all right? Want to rest?"

"I'm fine, just got to thinking about food instead of where I was putting my feet."

They soon reached the house. Abe put away his tools and they got their horses, rigged up, and mounted.

"Just one thing," Abe said. "Maybe after we eat I can tell you what happened here very soon after we arrived and started to settle.

I had to kill somebody. Don't want that again." Then he turned around the horse he was now calling Cloud and trotted off toward their camp-home.

At first it seemed that no one was around. Then Abe heard laughter coming from down by the stable area. He slid off the horse and beckoned to Ollie to do the same. He said softly, "Wait here." There was a tub used for horse water behind the small structure. That was where the voices were coming from. He moved slowly and eased around the corner of the little building. He was quite surprised, even shocked, to see Sarah Beth and Helga standing in the water of the tub with no clothes on. Mattie was throwing small buckets of water at them and they were washing one another. He turned away quickly and went back around the building, returning to where Ollie was seated on the ground, smoking.

"Sounds like a party," Ollie said.

"Taking baths. Throwing water on each other."

"You have a lot of water at this place?"

"The creek runs right close over there. And they're in a tub I use for the horse water. They must have carried more from the creek. They've got some buckets."

Ollie smiled and said, "Must be quite a sight, them girls and the older one like that."

"The older one is just splashing water on the other two."

"Well, seems like we might best not look like we been looking at them. Better set over in that shadow from the hill while it cools off if it's going to." They moved into the shade. "And you're going to tell me about something that happened here."

"Good a time as any, I guess. Was going to wait until after we ate, but seems that might be awhile now."

Just then Mattie appeared, walking toward them and the outdoor summer kitchen. She stopped when she saw them and called back over her shoulder, "Menfolk hereabouts." Then she came on toward them. "Good day," she said. "We didn't know you were here yet."

"Came down a little early," Abe said. "Want to have Ollie here stay for some supper if that's all right."

"Don't see why not. Just made a big dried meat stew today. Plenty. Going to go stir it." She moved off to the fire pit where a large pot hung from a metal tripod Mike Skinner had fashioned for this use.

"She's pretty handy then, is she?"

"Oh she's a great help, knows a lot. Maybe not so much about living out here this way, but she knows a lot about life and helps keep things straight between the younger women."

"Good to hear. Was she married?

"Not sure you call it that exactly. She was a slave until the War and she came into Sarah Beth's family. Had children. But doesn't seem to have any family since I've known her."

Ollie started rolling another cigarette with his one hand, and said, "Not many women around these parts, white or black, less you count the Indians..." He gave the paper a lick, and lit the tobacco. "So what were you going to tell me about?"

"Well, it happened a few months back…how I got a second wound in this arm. And it has something to do with the situation we're in here with this land, the Indians, who owns it, all of that. When I first started on the house, these two men showed up. Said they had a claim to this land. Wanted to know what I was doing here, what was I thinking building on their land."

Ollie held up his hand, "Just a minute. Horse getting too far away." He walked after his horse, gave a low whistle and then caught up with it. Abe watched as he reached into the saddle bag, then slapped the horse on the rump and came back to sit down. He'd gotten a small bottle of amber liquid, and now opened it and passed over to Abe. "Didn't want this to get too far away if we're telling stories here."

Abe nodded and took a small swallow and passed it back.

"Go on," Ollie said.

"Well, basically they claimed this land, said they had legal right. I told them it belonged to the Indians, and they said not no more. I went into town next chance I got and found out from the clerk of the court they didn't have a claim yet, and that they'd been pretty pushy on him and he didn't like it. He filled in some forms, took money from me and said if need be, my claim just happened to be dated before theirs. The next time I checked in on it, that clerk had been transferred up to Boise and there was a woman who told me that the only way the Indians could claim the land was if the Indian agent up north could assign my rights and theirs in some kind of agreement. Well, it so happened that Sarah Beth was at that time travelling with Hawk Man to a meeting of the chiefs and the government. That's a whole other story why Sarah Beth was going along. Anyway, I got some paperwork done and sent it off after Hawk Man, who'd already left, sent them with that young man Carl. A few days or a week later, two fellows tried to burn the house down, but Mary Wolf and Carl saw the smoke and came quick here, after me." He waved away the bottle and went on. "They told me the smoke was coming from the house. It was hardly started at the time, but there was a lot of lumber stockpiled out there. I saddled Bird and took off with the two of them. When I got to the house, those two men were riding away. The fire wasn't large yet so I yelled at Mary Wolf and Carl to try and deal with it, that I was going after those men."

At that moment, Sarah Beth and Helga came around the stable. They were wearing only blankets and when they saw the men they hurried off laughing, Sarah Beth to the small house structure and Helga to her own quarters.

"Damn man," Ollie said softly, "you got your own woman show."

"This doesn't usually happen." Abe said, trying to hide his embarrassment. "In fact, I've never seen them bathing in the water trough before."

"Must be the heat, or fall coming." Ollie said with a large grin on his face. "Well, go on with the story."

"Oh sure, so one of their horses stumbled and came up lame. The rider jumped off using the horse as a shield and fired at me, so I took off after the one still riding away. I was hoping the one on foot could be taken care of by the others, or at least be kept from running away on foot. I was able to get ahead of the one racing ahead of me when we both went through the big creek at different places. We faced off and shots were fired. I got this wound," he placed his hand on his shoulder. "Not so bad this time as the one from the War. It went through clean, no bones or other stuff, but I was bleeding pretty bad. Turned out when I checked that one, I'd killed him. Somehow I got back on my horse before I passed out, and I made it back to where the others were. Helga was there with her pistol and must have wounded that one so they could disarm him and take his gun. I never did get it straight what exactly happened. When all that was going on, Mary Wolf and Carl managed to put out the fire. The one I shot is buried out there somewhere, and the other one is in prison up near Boise. The reason this matters now…"

Just then Sarah Beth appeared and came over to say hello and to apologize for being so unmannerly before. Ollie said it was all right, he didn't mind a bit. Then she said, "I hope you'll stay for some supper. Mattie's made a lot of a great stew."

"Thank you ma'am, I would be pleased to." Sarah Beth smiled and then walked over to help Mattie with the preparations.

Abe went on, "Let me finish up here. I was about to say that the reason this all matters today is because these were the two who filed a claim on this land and tried to get it away from both the Indians and me. We had to involve the Indian Agent up in Wenatchee as well as the court in Boise to keep it. Of course, when the story of what they'd tried to do came out that helped our case, but I don't think it will be so easy the next time someone wants this land. Especially if it's known that it's worth a lot more than just for grass and cows. That's why I'm thinking we have to be extremely careful how we go about this. Matter of fact, right now I'm almost wishing it'd never happened."

"Well, it has happened, partner, but I think there will be a way to make it work out. And we sure can't let the Indians find out."

"Ollie, that's just what we will do. There's no way we can put their claim in jeopardy without letting Hawk Man in on it, and having him make some decisions."

"Whatever you say, but don't waste this opportunity just cause some Indian don't know what it's worth."

Helga came walking by at that point and Ollie said, "I just heard you're pretty good with a pistol, young lady. I admire that."

"Not really, sir, mostly just lucky I guess." She walked on.

"Cute girl,' he said to Abe. "Looks like she's putting on a little weight being out here."

"Could be," Abe said, "hadn't noticed." He looked more closely at Helga as she joined the other women. It was true she no longer had any narrowing at the waist and was looking well-fed and healthy. He realized he liked that.

During their supper, as they sat in the smudgy smoke of a small fire, trying to avoid the majority of the biting insects that seemed to come in hordes at this time of day, Ollie and Mattie traded questions about one another. Both of them were inclined to make fun of themselves and their humor was in full play.

"Did you play a musical instrument, Miss Mattie?"

"Oh yes, you know us black folk are Jewish so we played the Jew's Harp much as we could. And you Mr. Ollie, I would imagine you play the piano."

"Yes, ma'am, the only one-handed piano-thumper this side of the Mississippi. You ever hear that song 'Johnny One-note'? I'm famous for that number, but I'm Ollie One-note."

"I'm sorry, I never got your last name so I wouldn't know if I've heard of your fame and the glory of your reputation, sir."

"Blanchett, ma'am. And you, do you people have last names or just take yours from whoever owned you?"

"Well, actually, Mr. Blanchett, or as I'll think of it to remember it, Mr. Blank Check…" There was laughter around the fire, and no one laughed as loud or as long as Ollie.

"Good one. Never in all my years of wearing that name have I been called by that handle, Mr. Blank Check. That's a good one, coming from you, Missus Jefferson or Washington or whatever it was."

Sarah Beth chimed in with, "She took Daddy's name when we moved to Missouri. But I don't think I ever knew what it was before that. Just Mattie, our dear, sweet Mattie." She placed her hand over Mattie's.

"Once we were freed, we didn't want to use those old slave names and even though many of us kept the memory of our family name from Africa, we couldn't use those here either. White folks couldn't remember or even pronounce them, so we just got by with first names. I think you folks call it being on a 'first name basis,' don't you?"

Abe said, "Well now that's solved. Mattie I always wondered, but never knew if I should or could ask about your formal name."

Just then Helga spoke up, "I don't have a last name either. At least not one I'd use. They wouldn't ever tell me my mother's name and I sure don't want that Bishop's name they called me by." She paused and then said, "But I certainly want this baby of ours to have a real whole name." There was silence.

Ollie then spoke quietly, "Thought you was looking a bit different around the middle." He looked over at Abe with a questioning glance. Then at Sarah Beth.

"We'll have to talk about that, Helga," she said. "Now, is anyone ready for some berries and sweet cake? I even have cream from the milk Martha sent over with Ollie."

"Sounds good to me," Abe said as Helga and Mattie began clearing away the supper dishes and the pot of stew. Sarah Beth went into the kitchen shed and Mattie brought over another jar of fresh water.

Ollie took a harmonica from his shirt pocket. "There's a secret way to play this old mouth harp one-handed." Then he ran through a couple of series of notes. "You all heard of that Stephen Foster fella, made up a lot of good songs, songs like…" He played some introductory notes and then began singing, *"I dream of Mattie with the dark brown hair, floating like a vision on the soft summer air…"* then he played the rest of the song, tapping time with his foot.

When he stopped, the rest of them were quiet until Helga clapped softly and said, "I so love that kind of a song, a song with a tune that makes my heart want to sing along."

"Well, I know a lot of songs," Ollie said, "and I'd be glad to teach you some of them, maybe with Miss Mattie here as well, or everybody—we could have our own choir. Don't know who'd be the audience, them Indians? Or my sister and Old Mike?"

"Oh, Mr. Ollie, that wouldn't matter. We don't need an audience but I so love the idea of learning new songs. I love singing, I just don't know hardly any songs, except those people's ones from church."

Mattie spoke up, "Helga, I've heard you singing down by the stream when you're washing laundry, some strange songs. And at other times too. You have a beautiful voice."

"Oh you must have heard something Mary Wolf taught me for singing when working in the water. She said it was for washing clothes or a hide or something. It's an Indian song."

"Well, it's beautiful, none the less. Mr. Blanchett can you sing some more of that Jeanie song for us? I like it as well."

"Sure, ma'am, but then you're going to have to sing one of your songs for me." He played some more harmonica notes and then sang a couple of verses of the song:

"I dream of Jeanie with the light brown hair,
Borne, like a vapor, on the summer air,
I see her tripping where the bright streams play,
Happy as the daisies that dance on her way.
Many were the wild notes her merry voice would pour.
Many were the blithe birds that warbled them o'er:
Oh! I dream of Jeanie with the light brown hair,
Floating, like a vapor, on the soft summer air."

As the last notes faded into the gathering darkness, the small group remained silent. The sound of a night hawk calling and a lone coyote howling broke the stillness, but not the mood.

Finally, Ollie said, "I'd best be getting a move on if I'm going to get back here in the morning." He stood and brushed biscuit crumbs off his pants. "Thank you ladies so much for the supper. Best I've had in days, or even longer." He laughed, saying as he turned to go, "You folks sleep well."

Mattie stood up and said, "I'll walk with you to your horse." When they were a ways away from the fire, she took hold of his arm and said, "Bet that was news to you wasn't it, Ollie—I'm going to call you Ollie when we're in private like we are now. I don't think Helga meant to spill it like that."

"Funny thing, Mattie, I'd just said to Abe there before supper that she looked like she was putting on weight."

"Well, she is, and it's a good thing. She's a healthy young thing and she'll do right well, but if you don't mind, I think both Sarah Beth and Abe would prefer to be the ones telling your sister and Mike."

"I imagine there's a story to it, but I don't need to know, and I will keep it to myself." He bent down and caught hold of his horse's halter and then flipped a bridle over its nose. "It's a pleasure to share your company, ma'am."

"Yours as well," Mattie said. "Goodnight."

He tightened the cinch and mounted. "Seeya soon." Then he rode off into the deepening darkness.

Over the next week Abe and Ollie reconfigured their plan for the catch basin at the water source. Ollie said he hadn't found any other fissures like the one where he found the gold and they had somewhat hidden it by pushing small rocks into its opening. Other than the good progress and changes in the water system they didn't really speak of the discovery. Abe could sense some impatience and frustration in the other man, but there was no change in his willingness to continue the work and to keep up his generally cheerful mood. One morning he showed up at their place with a hindquarter of fresh venison, and he was of course invited for the next night's supper. Mattie said she wanted the meat to hang during the cool of the night to tenderize it a bit, and showed Ollie where to so that.

The next day, Abe began building sections of the long wooden trough to bring water down to a storage area just uphill from the house. Ollie knew the formula for creating pressure in a hose, so they were able to convert a watering trough into a holding tank for the water. When it overflowed, the excess would run down to the creek through a ditch alongside where the planned garden would be. It was going to take some expensive iron pipe to turn the angles to bring the main water into the house, but with Mike Skinner's help cutting lengths and threading, and Ollie's engineering skills, the project was moving ahead and would very likely meet their needs.

One morning Ollie didn't show up, but that wasn't too unusual. There were times when Mike Skinner needed his help. Abe was nailing together long pieces of lumber into the three-sided lengths of the trough, which he was calling a flume, although he wasn't positive that was technically the right word for it. As the morning wore on and the work became routine, he was able to think about the things Helga had told him the night before. She was counting the months and predicting when the baby would come, and she told Abe they would have to think of both a boy's name and one for a girl. She liked Isabel for a girl, but was unable to find something that suited her for a boy. Abe begged off having any idea right away, and said there was plenty of time to think about it. Now, as the day grew warmer and the work progressed, he found himself thinking about names.

As he dragged a plank across the yard, he heard a horse approaching and was surprised to see Lefty. The man slid off his horse and came toward Abe with his arms wide and a smile on his face. They embraced, slapping one another on the back and smiling broadly. "Come, come sit, over here. I wish I had some coffee or something, but the water's good. Here." Abe poured out a cupful from a jar he kept in the shade.

"Some house you got here. Big one, huh. For whole family."

"It's really not very big. Just enough."

They were quiet for a while. Abe re-filled Lefty's cup with water, and then asked, "Where have you been?"

"More like, where are you going? I just get here from Boise, and now I must go south. There is big trouble with the Apache people and the Army, and they call for me to do some of the talking for them. Apache good fighters, but they are tired of war and want a good peace. We see what happens. I'll be gone a month or maybe little more."

"That's important work. I wish you well."

"Maybe not so important. Maybe only thing they can agree on is both sides not like this Lefty man, and if they can agree on that, I must have done good." He laughed. "So, Bird's baby colt come next summertime. When yours?"

"I think maybe springtime, month of March maybe. After winter."

"Good. I will be here after that. Come and give your child a good Indian name. Hey, I have good dry meat. You want some to eat with me?"

"That would be good. I have some bread I brought from the women."

They squatted and ate in the shade on one side of the house. Although leaves were already turning from green to yellow, the midday sun was hot like the days of summer, and still drying out the land. As they ate in silence, Abe tried to decide if this was the time to tell Lefty about the discovery. He knew he would have to tell one of the Indians, and he was more comfortable with the idea of it being Lefty than Hawk Man. He still didn't feel he could predict that one's reaction, and although he didn't know Lefty that much better, everything between the two of them had always been straightforward and frankly exchanged. After all, the man had given him one of the most famous horses in the west, and attended his wedding. The only drawback might be if Hawk Man felt slighted because he hadn't been told first. No, the best thing was to tell Lefty, seek his advice, and ask him to keep it quiet until the right time came for Abe to tell Hawk Man himself or when both of them could do it together.

He spoke quietly. "My friend, do you have a little more time, or must you go soon?"

"I think it can wait."

"We might have a problem, but it would be easier to show you than to talk about it."

"All right." Lefty wiped his face on his sleeve, finished the water in his cup and stood up. "Do we go somewhere?"

"Up to the water. Those troughs I was working on when you arrived attach together, and carry it down from up there." He pointed to the top of the rock wall. "In a way I'm glad it's so dry this summer because I can find out if that water is good all year. Here, come this way."

They climbed up the well-worn path. When they reached the top of the incline and came to the cliff wall and its many rivulets of water, Abe watched as Lefty's eyes opened wide as he smiled and said, "Good work, this hole will work good for you. Hard digging." He pointed at the pile of broken boulders and pieces rock. "I am pleased you show me this. It will take care of your needs now. Water come all night, you all day. Good idea."

"Yes, I'm sure it will work. But Lefty, there is something else… Look over here."

Abe moved over a couple of yards to where they'd started the original pond. That basin was now the shallower of the two and fed the larger one. He leaned against the wall with his hand over the split in the rock.

"This crevice, we filled it with some small rock pounded in. Lefty, there is gold in there."

Again Lefty's eyes, which were usually narrowed in a permanent squint, opened wide and Abe could see just how nearly pure black they were. "Gold? How much?"

"We don't know. We didn't go in any further than just the first few feet. It's not a vein, but more like pebbles of dark rock that break open and there's gold inside. I don't know if it's good quality or not, but Ollie has been around the mining business all his life and he's excited. I made him swear to keep this a secret. I have to tell you it makes me afraid," he paused. "If word gets out, the government and everyone else will want this land."

Part II

FAMILY

1869-1872

CHAPTER 5

Moving In

Fall came suddenly after weeks of prolonged summertime type weather. It was preceded by a few frosty nights, but the days were usually warm and dry. One week in early October brought a heavy rain and Abe and Ollie were glad for it as it somewhat replenished the cliff above the water collection site. After Lefty advised Abe that for the time being it would be best to leave well enough alone, neither Abe nor Ollie spoke of the discovery. Lefty had said that of course whatever gold there was belonged to the Indians, but there was no way to trust the government not to revoke their claims to that land. Ollie accepted this verdict only as a temporary status, and was planning to find himself a claim somewhere not too close, so he could appear to be finding gold on that site even if it came from this land, if and when the Indians agreed to it. As he said, "If it don't get me killed, it might be a good thing for all of us, in small amounts."

The house was completely enclosed, with some of the windows boarded up while they waited for more shipments of glass to be delivered to the town. The expense of shipping was higher than that of the materials. The glass was placed between copper sheets that were lead-soldered into flat crates. These were filled with oil of some kind, often from whales or pressed from corn. The oil acted as a shock absorption medium and most of the glass was able to travel safely by wagon from the rail line in Utah. Abe was pleased to end up with the leftover sheets of metal, which could be put to various uses. It was all very expensive, but he and the women saw the benefits of daylight in the house as well worth any price.

During October, Abe and the two younger women spent a lot of time using the horses to drag limbs and logs down from the hillsides for firewood. Helga asked Abe if he remembered the first time they'd ever gotten firewood together and how she'd made a kind of sled to haul it in. He surely did, but said that one of those wouldn't work here where the logs had to be skidded downhill over such rough and rocky ground. Sarah Beth was concerned that the younger woman should be more careful about such hard physical effort since she was nearly halfway through her pregnancy.

Mattie was always busy, working at whatever the season demanded. She'd dried plenty of berries and meat and learned from the Indians how to mix them together into hard patties that could be soaked and softened up later. She was also baking a lot of some kind of biscuit or cracker that could be dried very hard and would last a good ways into the winter. She and Martha and the two younger women were allowed to gather apples from an orchard along the way to the nearby town and Mattie processed the apples into dried slices, cider, and a sweetened sauce that would last in jars sealed with paraffin. During the past month she'd taken several long walks with Ollie. She found herself to be especially appreciative of his humor and stories. However, she tried not to think much about it. It was too unlikely to consider the friendship anything more than just two people in their early fifties, who were surrounded by young folks, who liked to get together to share their views and experiences.

Sarah Beth's final ceremonial occasion with Moon Fish had happened the month before, at the time of Equinox, when the day and night were equal. She was surprised to find that it was a special day for the Indians, much more important than it had ever been in her own growing up years. She was given a song and the permission to use certain herbs for making herself tea and for burning as incense during her times of the month, when she was in what the older woman spoke of as "in the woman-way."

The tea and song and burning herbs were to sustain the medicine aspects of the sweats and dreams she'd received, and to continue the healing that she thought she could feel going on inside her. She felt better in general, but it was still hard to fight off the jealousy she felt toward Helga. It was especially difficult when she saw Helga with Abe, or knew that they were together somewhere. Sarah Beth found Abe no less affectionate or passionate when they did get together to have interludes of deep conversation and physical union, but she often worried he might lose interest in her and find more pleasure and deeper love with Helga, whom she now always called in her own mind, "the other one."

Helga was also anxious at times that she would lose Abe, that as her shape changed and she grew more tired and less able to give him any good company during the few nights they had together, he would find his way back to Sarah Beth in every way. Helga was certain the other woman was waiting for that moment. At times she felt that her only advantage was that she was carrying the child he'd so often said he wanted. She knew that this was her blessing in one way, but she was never sure how Sarah Beth really felt about it all. She found herself hoping and even praying that this "first wife," as she thought of her now, would get pregnant with her own child so there wouldn't be any excuse for favoritism and so they wouldn't have to try to share this one. If she was sure of anything at all, it was that she would never give up this child and no one could take it away from her, as she'd been taken from her own mother.

The first snowfall came in early November while they were moving their things into the part of the new house that could be heated comfortably. Helga's room, farthest from the center of the building, had its own small stove. Mattie's space between the central room and Helga's had some warmth from the fires on both sides. As they set up their rooms, it became clear to Abe that he didn't really know what he was supposed to do. The new double bed was put in the large bedroom next to the kitchen, and Sarah Beth began unpacking her things into a closet and a bureau they'd purchased. She was waiting to see what Abe would do, and if he would finally need to ask.

At one point they were left alone in the house. Sarah Beth, standing in the doorway of the larger bedroom, waited until Abe finished building up the fire in the main fireplace, and then asked, "Where are you going to keep your things?"

He looked up at her and spoke slowly, "I don't have much that doesn't stay down at the stable and shop area."

"And where will you sleep? With your horse?"

He stood up and faced her, "Sarah Beth, I don't know. I'll sleep where I have to, or where I'm welcome." Then he turned and started to leave.

"Well, you're welcome in here with me, anytime. I still need a husband, you know."

"I know, and I never stopped wanting to be that for you."

"Well, I asked Mary Wolf what happens in their camp. She said Hawk Man has his own place at the back of the big tipi, and he usually goes to bed and to sleep first. Then whichever wife wants to go to his bed goes there. Sometimes neither of the women sleep with him."

"Maybe I should have built my own room."

Sarah Beth came toward him and reached her arms around his neck. She pulled his face to hers, kissing him in a long embrace. Then she leaned her head back and said, "Abe, I want my own baby. Do you know that?"

"Yes, I know."

"Before they left for winter, Moon Fish said for me to start trying again, using the calendar of nights and taking certain herbs. She also said for me to make you tea sometimes, made from some kind of tree bark. It will make your seed strong. Besides, I often miss you being next to me, even if I know you are alone and not with her."

He ran his fingers through her hair and looked into her eyes. "Me too. But maybe it can never be the same again."

"Maybe it will be better than the same someday." She kissed him again. "There's room in my closet for some of your things, and there's room in my bed for all of you." Then she turned and went back into that room to continue unpacking her wooden boxes of clothing and other odds and ends.

That night Abe stayed with Sarah Beth for one last night in their old temporary place. It was pretty well emptied out and seemed a little strange.

"This is almost like it was when we first stayed in it. Bare and uncluttered," Sarah Beth said. Abe had just come inside and was brushing fresh snow from his coat. "Guess it won't matter if you track in the outdoors now."

"I wiped my boots off, but I had that same thought. Although I'm not sure what we're going to use this space for now."

"It can be your bachelor house." She smiled to try and make light of the comment. "Abe, it was so much different then. We were filled with the happiness of starting a new life."

"And now?"

"Now we're moving into a new home, but it's all changed."

"Everything?" He took a couple of steps toward her.

She sat down on their old bed and patted the cover beside her. "Well, almost everything. Here, sit. I know I'm different now."

He tossed his coat onto a small barrel they used for a stool and sat beside her, unlacing his boots and kicking them toward the doorway. "Sarah Beth, one thing hasn't changed. I still love you very, very much, if that's what you're worried about."

"Even if I have to share you?"

"Maybe more because you're being so kind to Helga, and to me."

"I do what I can. It isn't easy." She lay back on the bed and stretched her arms over her head. "Kiss me. And tell me if it's still the same."

He turned so he was lying on his side next to her. Their eyes met and held for a long silence. Then he lowered his face and lips to meet hers. Their arms went around each other's necks and they held close and closer. When they came up for air, it was Abe who spoke first,

"It's not the same," he paused to let her eyes ask him what he meant, then he went on, "it's not the same…it's better." He leaned over so he was nearly on top of her. She pushed up on his shoulders and smiled.

"You mean that, or just saying it?"

"Ask me in the morning. Let's get in bed now."

The first snow melted away after a cold week, and was followed by a warm spell that even brought a new green flush to the grass on the valley floor. Abe rounded up the cattle that spent the summer up and down the creeks and in side-canyons and shallow draws. It took him several days to find them all, but he was pleased that only four of the forty or so animals were missing and presumed still wandering or lost to predators. His satisfaction lasted until he took one more ride out and found scattered remains. He could see that the piles of guts and torn skin had been dragged about, most likely by coyotes. It was also apparent that the cows had originally been skinned and gutted by humans, though the thieves had left no tracks in the rocky ground. He did find a broken arrow shaft in a piece of hide.

He cut around the arrow and rode back to their place. He showed Sarah Beth and Helga what he'd found, and then rode on to the Skinner place. When he got there, he found Mike and Ollie out front in conversation with three men Abe had never seen before. He dismounted, threw Cloud Runner's rein over a tree branch, and walked toward the small group.

"Fellas, this is Abe, Abe Saunders. Settled on the place further out," Mike said. "Abe these two are the Patterson brothers and this other one is Ralph Reed. They're from out west of Silver City. Ralph, tell him what you been saying to us."

"Pleased to meet you. Not much to say except that we've lost some cattle. Thinking it's Indians, maybe that bunch that stays out where you seem to be located."

"When did this happen?" Abe asked.

"Last week or so."

"Did either of you tell them when Hawk Man and his bunch pulled out?"

"Nope," Ollie said, "just got here myself and was about to."

"Well, I guess I hadn't told Mike yet, but that whole bunch was gone out of here more than a month ago, back when the first cool nights began. But let me show you something." He walked back to his horse and untied the piece of hide with its embedded broken arrow. "Found this and the rest of the remains of four animals this morning when I was looking for the last of my strays." He held it out and one of the Pattersons took it from him.

"Looks like a Bannock arrow. Your bunch was Nez Perce, weren't they?"

"That's right. Mostly Nez Perce and maybe some Cayuse, but I don't think there's much difference between them. They've got no love for the Bannock."

"Well they're all relatives when they ain't fighting, but I'd agree with you it's probably not the same bunch as your outfit." He handed the skin back to Abe.

"My neighbors said they were headed up to a village," Abe said, "alongside the Snake River where it comes into the Big River."

"I know the place," Reed said. "Lot of cattle between here and there, so's I can't see them grabbing it this far away and hauling it with them. I'd say we've got a small band circling west and south of this country. Hopefully they'll quit us and keep going."

"Tom says they lost several horses at the same time," Mike said. "Abe, you missing any?

"No. We use all ours and keep them close, and there's only a few. I'm not running any out on rangeland. Our Indians had a good-sized herd, but they took them all when they left."

"All right. Well, pleased to meet you. See you again sometime," Reed said. "C'mon boys, Let's go chase down some Bannocks."

All three men shook hands with Mike, and then mounted up and rode off.

After a moment, Mike said, "Sure glad you showed up when you did. They pulled in here a few minutes before you did, and man, they were hot. Hell-bent on killing some Indians, your Indians. I thought yours was gone, but couldn't say for sure that some weren't still around."

"Well, it worked out for now, I guess," Abe said. "Funny thing about it—Hawk Man told me him and his people don't like beef. Don't eat it unless they have to, only when they can't find anything wild."

"How far did these fellows come from?" Ollie asked.

"Might be about fifteen, twenty miles, out past Antelope Lake."

"Not much out there, but seems like they're making it all right."

"Any mountains or high ground that way?"

"Not much more than maybe a prairie dog mound or so." Ollie pulled a flask from his coat pocket and held it out to Abe who took a small sip and passed it to Mike.

Mike drank and then said, "Before I forget, coming up on Thanksgiving. Martha wants you all to come on over here for that. Can you tell your women?"

"I can do that. They'll want to know what to bring and all that."

"Well, they'll probably all see each other before then, if we don't get much more snow. So what you going to do about the livestock losses?"

"I don't know. I brought them in closer now. I've saved a lot of the grass around the new house and up some of the lower draws. Guess I'll keep more of a lookout now."

"Well, if you need help, we'll be here," Ollie said. "Ol' Mike here fixed me up a one-handed rifle. Can't wait to use it."

"I'm hoping they've gone on and it doesn't come to that. Last thing I need is a war on my hands. Anyway, I'll be headed back now. Oh, by the way, Ollie, we've been moving in and I got the water troughs all the way to the house. Mattie says you should come by and have dinner, celebrate with us."

"I'll be sure to do that."

Abe mounted up and rode back toward home. He had a feeling this wasn't the last time something like this raid would happen, but didn't know what he could do about it. Tell the women to stay close, was the most important thing.

He was nearly back to the home place when he saw Happy slinking through the brush. He stopped and called the dog. Then he dismounted when he saw the animal's limping movements. The dog was whining and barely crawling toward him. He saw quills sticking from the dog's face and could see why he was favoring the front foot so much.

"Porcupine, huh dog?"

There wasn't much he could do without pliers, so he stooped down and gently lifted the dog up in front of the saddle. "Hold still," he said to the horse. "Whoa!" He had to work to pull himself up while holding the dog, who struggled as the horse moved about. Once he was in the saddle he was able to clutch the dog close and get the horse moving. He liked this horse, but he was a little skittish with anything new. Abe was glad that Hawk Man had left Bird with him, instead of keeping her with the herd. She was beginning to show some rounding out and he didn't think he should be riding her unless it was necessary, but he did miss her companionship and cooperative temperament.

He thought the women would all be up at the new house, but he heard Helga singing as he neared the old stable. He yelled to her and she quickly came out from behind the building.

"Abe. What's that? Oh no, Happy. What's wrong?" She hurried closer and reached up to help lower the dog to the ground. "Oh, you poor boy, oh. That must hurt so much. Abe, what can we do?"

"I'm getting some pliers. Do we have any alcohol here?"

"We should have, under the sink in the kitchen."

"I'll look. You just try to keep him comfortable. I'll be right back."

With Helga holding Happy down and humming soothing melodies, Abe was able to remove the quills that weren't too deeply embedded. The ones that had pierced through the lips were more work. He propped the dog's mouth open by placing a stick crossways back near his throat, and then pushed each quill through. When those quills were removed and the dog seemed to have given up resisting, perhaps going into some kind of shock, he went to work on the five or six in the front paw. It was nearly dark by the time they were all pulled. Happy was clearly exhausted from the ordeal, as were Helga and Abe.

"Looks like supper's at the new house?"

"Yes. I was just getting some late surviving greens from the old garden to take along with me. They're probably wondering where we are."

"What do you think we should do with Happy now?" Abe asked.

"If we're staying up there, we should take him with us. They took the buggy, but I could wait here with him while you went after it. Or we could put him in one of the stalls and I could come back down here later and be with him. Maybe you could come with me."

"That's possible, but I don't think he'll be calm like this for very long. I didn't get the alcohol yet. Let me get it and at least we can move him into the stall and rinse the wounds." He stood quickly and walked off toward the kitchen structure.

They moved the dog and laid him on an old saddle blanket.

"Did you have a horse?"

"No, I walked. It was still early in the afternoon and I had things to do here. Then this happened."

"We can both ride on Cloud if we take it easy."

They stepped out of the stall and Abe turned to go after the horse. He felt Helga's hand on his arm holding him back.

"Abe, you have to be a stronger man. Either you want to be with me, or if you don't I promise I'm going to leave. I can't take her having it all her way. I'm the one with your baby."

"I'm sorry. I do want to spend more time with you. You deserve it, and I…"

"No excuses. Remember I grew up around many men who had more than one wife. I saw how a strong man could make the women get along and take care of him, and how he took care of them. It was just the way things were. I want that. From you."

She came around to stand in front of him and looked into his eyes. He felt the strength in her arms as they pulled him closer. Then she kissed him and moved one hand up behind his head so he couldn't pull away. With her other hand, she moved one of his hands between them, where their bellies touched.

"Abe, he's starting to move. I don't think you can feel it yet, but I can. He's yours, he's ours, and if we don't act like it now, we never will. Please. She even says it's all right, that she'll understand." She leaned back. "All right. Enough of that now, let's go eat, and then we'll both come back down to check on the dog and we'll just stay down here. Right?"

Abe was quiet, trying to think about this, but he couldn't see how he could say either no or yes to anything anymore. She was right about one thing, she and this child were his responsibility, and if that meant doing things she wanted from him, it was her due. He kissed her again and said, "I'll get the horse. Maybe you'll need to put a pan of water in there for Happy. He'll probably get thirsty soon."

They made the ride to the house slowly, riding double on Cloud. On the way, Abe told her a little about the cows that were killed and the visitors at the Skinner's place.

"They were pretty upset and I'm glad they stopped at Mike's place first, although since Hawk Man and the rest aren't here, there's not much they could have done."

"I hope it doesn't go on," she said into his ear. "And I'm glad you didn't show up when those Indians were doing the killing."

"I guess so, but they might have run off when they saw me."

"Run away from one white man? I don't think so."

"You're probably right."

They were almost to the house when she said, "I think I should go back down and check on Happy after we eat, but remember, I don't want to go by myself." She gave him a squeeze around his waist.

"All right, we'll see. I could just go by myself."

"And stay all night?"

He pulled the horse to a stop, slid off and reached up to help her. He lowered her to the ground and they stood like that for a long moment until she pulled away and disappeared into the house.

Supper began pleasantly. Mattie served up a chicken pie with greens. Then Helga said, "Abe, tell them about the cows."

So he did and went on to describe the encounter with the ranchers from west of town. "I'll bet they go after the Indians. I just hope it doesn't result in any more damage or any run-ins that get out of hand."

Sarah Beth looked at him and said, "Abe, whatever you're thinking, you are not going to get dragged into being in any militia or whatever. You've done enough of that back home, and I won't stand for it."

"Oh, actually, I hadn't even thought of that. I don't think anything like that will happen."

"It won't. You have to be here with your three women now."

"That brings up a point," he said. "You do all need to get some practice with a rifle. Not because of these Indians, but maybe bears, wolves or whatever. We don't know what our new home might attract."

Mattie spoke up, "Well, this is all so interesting and important, I wonder if anyone liked the chicken pie."

They all spoke at once, praising the supper and apologizing for not saying something sooner. Abe was especially enthusiastic, "I didn't even know how hungry I was. And something else, speaking of food, Mike said Martha wants us all to come for Thanksgiving dinner."

"Oh that's nice," Mattie said, "I can't wait to make that squash pie with cinnamon and honey. Is anyone going to town? I think we really need one of those cranker ice cream makers, and a dairy cow."

"Mattie, I haven't seen you so excited for a long time," Sarah Beth said.

"I just love a holiday feast, that's all."

"And there's nobody else at that place you might want to visit with, is there?"

Mattie stood up and began clearing the plates.

"I told you, I just love a holiday."

Just then Abe felt a slight kick from Helga under the table. She was saying, "With all that's going on, we forgot to tell you what happened to Happy. He's going to be all right, but the reason we were late is that he got a nose and paw full of porcupine quills."

Mattie stopped what she was doing and set the plates back down.

"Oh no," she said. "Will he be all right? Doesn't that hurt them real bad?"

"Abe got them all out, we think. He brought Happy in, carrying him on the horse."

"I found him back along the road to Skinner's. Not too far. It could have been worse, and I hope he learned his lesson to stay away from them next time."

He felt Helga's foot nudge him again.

"Helga wants to go back down and check on him, maybe even stay down there. I better go with her."

Mattie picked up her load of dishes, and went into the kitchen.

"I suppose, if you must," Sarah Beth said quietly, then got up and went to her room. The door still wasn't hung on its hinges, but she propped it shut.

"Good for you," Helga whispered to Abe. "I'll get a few things we might need." She left for her part of the house.

Mattie returned, looked at Abe, and said softly, "You don't have to worry about me, son. Long as you take care of the two of them good enough so as they don't squabble."

It was the first time she'd ever called him "son" and he wondered what it meant, what had changed. Then he smiled and said, "I'll try, Mom." He got up and went to catch the horse. Mattie stood still for a moment, looking after him, also smiling.

Abe caught Cloud, got him ready, then heard Helga's door close. He was glad they'd gone ahead and made a separate entrance to the house for her, so she could have more privacy. No one had mentioned that it would do the same for him, should he be using it. He mounted first and helped her up. He felt her settle in behind him as her arms squeezed tightly around his chest.

"Let's go," she said in a loud whisper.

When they got back to the stable, Abe lit a lamp and they went in to see Happy. When he saw it was them he rolled over on his back and made soft whining sounds.

"Looks like he's going to be all right," Abe noted.

"I'm so glad. I was worried. Do you think he can come stay near us by my little place?"

"Don't want him wandering off until we know he's fine for sure."

"You're right. Guess he's doing well enough here." She moved into the stall and bent down beside the dog, scratching his belly. "Now, listen here. You learn your lesson and leave those critters alone, you hear?" The dog wagged his tail while he was still on his back and then rolled over and licked her hand. "I'll be back first thing in the morning. I brought some of the chicken scraps, but maybe he shouldn't eat with his mouth like this. What do you think?"

"I think you're right," Abe said. "Looks like he hasn't even taken any of the water. We'll try to help him eat in the morning."

She came back out to stand beside him, leaning and the stall wall and looking down. "I'm sorry it took this to happen, so we could be together."

Abe didn't reply, but took her hand and led her outside. A half moon was going down toward the west and the brightest of the stars showed their light. "One night when I was lying outside on the ground I tried to find your first initial, H, in the stars, but there were too many of them." He paused.

"Why Mr. Saunders, I didn't know you were such a romantic."

"Not romantic, just curious if they had your name up there."

She turned to him. After a long soft kiss, she said, "Well, thanks for at least looking. Come on." She led him to her shack.

Abe hung the lamp on a hook by the door.

"Do you want me to make a bed so we can sleep out here and you can keep looking for my name?"

"That might be nice. It's pretty crowded in there."

"That's why I'm not moving this bed up to the new house. I'm going to sleep on the floor until you make a proper size bed for us."

"For us?" he mumbled.

"Yes, me and baby," she said and went inside and began passing the bedding out to him.

When it was ready, they lay down, side by side for a few silent minutes. Helga rolled over on top of him and pulled her shirts up to expose her breasts. "Open your mouth," she whispered as she placed the tip of one breast between his lips. "Now you can be my baby, until he comes."

Abe started to resist, but then accepted the nipple and began lightly sucking.

"That feels so good. And we'll have to do a lot of this so they won't be so tender when the little one starts in on me."

Abe tried to say something which was garbled and then he turned his head away. "When does the milk come?"

"I don't know. Sometimes early, sometimes right after I guess. Gracie's almost didn't come at all." She felt his hands rubbing up and down her back and then clasping her waist. She moved a bit with him and rolled off. "Abe I have to tell you something…I am so happy that it's you, that you're the father of my baby, that I ran away. If I stayed with that evil Bishop he would have made me do the same things as Gracie. Make a baby with one of his men. I'd hate that. It has be love to make a good baby, don't you think?"

He propped himself up on his elbows. "I guess so. Do you really love me?"

"Oh yes, more than I ever thought I would."

"Well, I'm sorry I haven't been enough for you. You deserve more. I'll try to be better about all this. I just never expected anything like it, and I don't know how to act most of the time." He eased around so the back of his head was in her lap.

"You'll do fine. Just do whatever I ask." When he started to answer, she pushed her breast back into his mouth, and reached down between his legs. "Just love me," she said.

They made love gently, and slowly, Abe careful not to put his full weight on her, even as she pulled him down tighter against her. When they finished, and lay in the quiet warmth of being pressed together, their beating hearts were even thumping at the same rate. He pulled her over on top of him, and his fingers traced her name on her back. He said, "There. I'm showing the stars how to spell your name."

Next morning, they found Happy leaning up against the stall door, barking for them. They let him out and, except for keeping one paw from touching the ground and constantly licking his lips and drooling, he seemed nearly normal and much improved. Helga offered him the softest piece of chicken skin and he was able to swallow it right down. Abe noticed he'd drank most of the water.

"I think I should stay here with him and when they come back down for another load in the buggy, I'll bring him there," Helga said.

"Good." He leaned over and kissed her. "Thank you for being patient with me."

"If it's going to last, we don't have to hurry," she replied.

On Abe's way back to the new house, he passed Mattie and Sarah Beth in the buggy. Mattie waved, but Sarah Beth kept her eyes fixed on the road. If he thought about it much he knew it would always be that way, and as Cloud picked his way along on a rocky stretch of their road, he tried to imagine how he would feel if it were the other way, remembering how he felt when she was off travelling with Hawk Man. And then he thought about Mattie and what she'd been through with different fathers for her children and not being allowed to raise any of them to grown-ups. There were just so many ways that these things worked out, or didn't. Some were based on cultural traditions, some broke those traditions, and some could only be explained the way Lefty put it, that the Creator and every child had their own plan and needs and they worked together, seeking out the combination of parents and circumstances that allowed each soul to come to earth and have a life. Except for Jesus, he recalled suddenly. That was God going it alone and being both the Father and the Creator. Or was it really that way? Was that really possible? He remembered getting in trouble one time for asking his Sunday teacher how it was possible that all of God could fit inside one man, or was Jesus only one piece of God? The teacher told this to Abe's father, and the boy received a severe lecture on blasphemy.

He stripped the riding gear from the horse and turned him loose. Once back at the house, he found some food to start the day with. Now the main thing he needed to work on next was that bed for Helga, but once again this brought on some anxiety as he imagined Sarah Beth's reaction to him making Helga his priority once again.

Well, he thought, no way around it, and she'll have to get used to it or not. He was feeling stronger about it all this morning and wondered if that was only because of the calm and quiet way he and Helga had taken their pleasure in one another. It would be best to just eat and get to work, he thought, moving quickly so he could get the work started before the women came back and needed his help unloading.

After he'd chewed down some bread and dried meat, he sat near the lumber pile with a board and piece of charcoal and tried to sketch out his idea for a bed. It had to be functional, and he thought it should probably be high enough for her to be able to lay the baby on and dress it or change its messed clothing. At the same time, as Helga got bigger and more awkward the bed couldn't be so high that it would be difficult for her to get in and out of. Then he had a completely unexpected mental picture of Sarah Beth lying in a bed with a baby and realized that depending on when that happened, it might be best to use the same bed again. The one they'd gotten for her wasn't very well made and came from a used furniture store in Silver City. Then he realized she'd probably want her own bed made for her, and tried to shake off those thoughts and get himself to focus on the project at hand.

Once he completed a sketch and wrote down measurements, he set about finding the right boards and was pleased that he had enough to choose from. This part of the pile was left over from some of the better stock mostly used for stairs and shelves. It didn't take long to carefully cut the legs and planks to hold the mattress. He didn't want to make a headboard and footboard without talking to Helga about it, so he figured out how to make these parts separately and attach them later. Maybe he would even create some kind of carved or built design that suggested the blessing he was now counting on for this child. Working on this project made it even clearer there was no looking back now and it was best to hope for the best. Whether he used a symbol or something else, he realized he wanted it to be from the old days of the Bible, and he wondered if he would be able to come up with something within the range of his limited woodworking skills.

As he finished assembling the basic frame, he heard the buggy bouncing over the roadway. Cloud whinnied and Ginger answered—the two horses seemed to have become good friends. The buggy was piled high with Helga's bedding and a couple of trunks that belonged to Sarah Beth and Mattie, pieces of their luggage from Virginia. Helga wasn't on board and he wondered about that, but then Mattie told him that Happy had refused to get on the buggy without a struggle and ran off on three legs. Helga had gone after him, saying he looked able enough to walk the distance with her, but that if she didn't come along fairly soon, he should go after her.

"Well then, let's get these things unloaded," he said, pulling a trunk out and lowering it to the ground.

"Careful with the next one," Sarah Beth said, "I wrapped our paintings in some of the blankets. I was afraid they might get jostled and torn so I drove very slowly and that's why it took so long. Let me help you."

It had taken long enough to unload and store things in the house that Helga was already arriving on foot with Happy. She went straight to her pile of bedding and gathered her arms full, disappearing around the side of the house. Sarah Beth and Abe lifted the trunk she was worried about and cautiously moved it into the main room of the house.

"That will do for now," she said, opening it and feeling down inside. "I don't think anything's been harmed."

Abe went back out to help Mattie and was able to carry her trunk in by himself once she helped him up the short stairway with it.

When he was back outside, he saw Helga waving at him. She smiled and put her hands beside her head in a silent sleeping sign, then blew him a kiss from her fingers, making it clear that she'd seen the bed project and was happy it was happening. He raised his finger to his lips to say, "Don't say anything." Then he went over to Happy to scratch the dog's neck and ask how he was doing. The dog just licked his hand, wagged his tail, and then crawled under a corner of the house.

He wanted to work more on the new bed, but thought maybe that after being away the night before he should be careful and offer to help Sarah Beth with something, or go up and check on the water-basin. Just then he heard her call him from inside.

"Abe, can you come here a minute?"

He found her in the large bedroom, the space they'd planned for the two of them.

"I'm trying to figure out how to better arrange things in this room and I need your opinion. At first I wanted the bed so we could wake up facing the window, but maybe that will be too bright in those early mornings of summer, but if we put it over against that wall, it will stick out too far for my father's wonderful rug to fit. What do you think?"

"I really don't know. Whichever you want?"

"That's no help. You must have some idea."

"What else will there need to be room for?"

She stepped over to him and looked up. "Have you forgotten that we wanted to have room for both of us to sit and read or just talk? That means two nice chairs. And then I keep hoping we'll need room for a baby crib."

"Then maybe it does matter to keep the bed as far out of the way as possible. What about more in the corner?"

"Well, it can't be too close to the wall or whoever gets that side will have trouble getting into bed. And I'd want the crib right next to my side."

"Well, that sounds fine."

"What sounds fine? We haven't decided anything because I don't think you even care."

"Of course I do." He couldn't help taking a step back.

"I'm doing everything I can to put up with all this and with you and her and your baby. All I can, but I need to know and feel that you still care about me, about us. And right now I don't feel that at all. Now go away, yes, go away from me, and when you have something to say to me, about us, I'll be glad to hear it."

He reached out to touch her shoulder with his hand, but she pushed it away.

"Go."

CHAPTER 6

Winter's Ways

The day before Thanksgiving, all three women were working in the new kitchen, preparing for the special dinner with the Skinners. This was the first time they'd tried to do something big and together in the space. Mattie was working on a squash pie, and humming softly. Helga was kneading dough for rolls and loaves, and Sarah Beth was making mincemeat dressing she hoped Martha would be willing to use for the turkey. Abe had reported that Mike knew an older gentleman who was raising a few turkeys from wild stock, and saved one for him every year.

"Can you do that any faster, Helga? I need that space if we're going get this over there this afternoon before Martha dresses the bird."

Helga kept kneading at the same pace. "You know it can't be hurried," she said. "See how she is, Mattie. I told you."

"Oh you told on me, did you? Well, well aren't you the little…"

"Stop it, both of you!" Mattie hit the counter with her rolling pin. "Turning into a couple of magpies and I've about had it. Tomorrow is a special day and if either of you try to spoil it for the rest of us, I'll tell the men to throw you out of there. Land sakes, I will."

"Mattie, she won't listen to anything I say, and I even tried to apologize," Helga said without stopping her work.

"Apologize for what? Sure, you're sorry, but for the wrong reason, and you know it."

"Cats and dogs can't be no worse than the two of you. Now stop it, I say. Am I going to have to be your mama and set you both straight? Well, I will, believe me I will. Now, here's what's going to happen—mark my words carefully. Helga, stop what you're doing and listen, and you young lady, supposedly the older one of the two of you, don't say another word until I'm done. Matter of fact, don't even say anything when I am done. Since you're behaving worse than sisters, you are going to become sisters right here and now. You are going to adopt each other, not as Abe's women, but as sisters. No more trying to figure out who's who and who's in charge.

"We are a family and you are the sisters. For better or for worse, and from now on, I'm your Mama when there's a problem, and believe me I will make you work it out. Is that clear?"

"Who's Abe then, the father?" Sarah Beth asked loudly. Helga covered her mouth to keep from laughing.

"Not at all. You know who your father is, and if he's been watching from up there, I'm sure he's disappointed in you. You can't help what has already happened but, as he said many times, we can make a difference to what is coming. Now smile, make up, and promise to be good to one another. A little argument now and then is healthy, but no more of this angry, cold as ice treatment. I'll be watching both of you, and you certainly don't want to see what happens when I get truly angry, and believe me, I will if I have to." She turned her back on them and went back to mashing the cooked squash.

Helga moved her bread dough over some ways on the counter and said quietly, "I think there's enough room here now."

"Oh, it'll be all right. There's other things I can be doing while I'm waiting. And Helga, I don't want you to not like me anymore. I just want you to know this is never going to be easy. Possible, yes, but easy, no."

Helga held her floury hands up in the air and took a step to give Sarah Beth a hug with her elbows. "I know that, big sister, believe me, I know."

Thanksgiving dawned cold, crisp, and clear. The dying grass was frosted, and ice ringed the buckets and troughs around the place. Mattie was in her room, which was barely finished but gave her some privacy, and she was putting the finishing touches on a dress she'd been working on since the summer. She had it on and was sewing the hem to its correct height by measuring, then sitting and pulling it up onto her knees. She was pleased with the design of her own devising, a full skirt that tightly gathered and belted above her waist, and fell to the top of her dressiest boots. It showed off her figure better than she'd expected. With no other opportunity to show herself off these days, she was glad to at least have this dinner for the occasion of its first use. She hoped it would make her feel as good as she thought it made her look, and that it might collect some attention from the others, especially one.

Abe called from the yard just as she finished the final stitches, and she quickly put away her sewing kit, and brushed her hair down to minimize its tight crowded curls. She spun around once and let the hem stretch out in a bell-shape around her legs, smiled and wished there would be some dancing at the Skinners' place. Then she grabbed her coat and bag and went to help carry food out to the buggy.

When they arrived, Martha was in the final phase of readying the food. The men went outside to sit in the warm light of the sun now crawling past halfway in its trip through the sky. Ollie was in a good mood and wanted to tell Abe and Mike what he'd learned about the big mine out past Silver City. It seemed that the veins of gold they'd been working were playing out and further exploration wasn't turning up much of anything. He was hoping some of the mining equipment would be abandoned if they shut down and he could get some to start out with on a claim he was acquiring over near the border with Idaho.

"I could use a little backing if that comes to pass," he said. "But I promise I wouldn't waste anybody's money. Guaranteed payback whether I find color or not. Got some inheritance coming from my father any time now, and the payback would be the first spending I'd do."

Abe asked if this wasn't all pretty much up in the air until the big mine actually shut.

"Of course, of course, but just want to let you fellas have first shot at investing in me." He laughed and waved his arm with its missing hand in the air. "Gonna call my claim and operation the One-Hand Shuffle, because I'm probably the only man around these parts that can do that, and everybody will know to leave me and my claim alone. Thought about calling it the One-Hand Draw, but that seemed a little threatening." He laughed again. "What do you say, Mike? Don't want to go ahead without you."

"I could be convinced," Mike replied. "Maybe."

"Pretty sure I've picked out a good place. And there's no one else around that area yet."

Martha called from the back door of the kitchen, "We could use a fire in the fireplace for when it starts to get cooler pretty soon."

Ollie and Abe both stood up. Abe said, "Show me where to get the wood."

Ollie took his arm and said "C'mon, plenty over this way. Don't know why I didn't get it brought in before now." The wood was piled and cut to length and they started loading their arms. Ollie continued in a soft voice. "I doubt there's much chance out where this claim's being filed, but it'll cover up for anything else. Know what I mean?"

"I do, and I thought that's where you were going with this, but we haven't heard from Hawk Man and the elders yet. Can't do anything without their knowledge or we could lose all we've built."

"Understood, partner. Fill my arms here."

They carried in two loads apiece and then Sarah Beth called Abe into the parlor.

"Abe, look, isn't this the grandest surprise?" She pulled her dress out of the way and sat down at a three-quarter size piano. "Martha said Mike surprised her with this on her birthday last week. Can you believe it? I thought I'd never see another piano way out here, unless in a saloon." Her fingers lightly stroked the keys and then ran up and down the keyboard with a quick and accurate scale. "She said we can have music after we eat. I wish you'd brought you mouth harp."

"I did. Yesterday when I brought that batch of foodstuffs over here, she showed this to me and said we'd just have to have some singing and music as a part of our feast. I couldn't wait for you to find out. I knew you'd be so happy."

"Oh, I am. And she wants me to come over regularly and give her lessons. Oh," she played a few chords, "it's so wonderful." Then she closed the cover. "Later. We'll save this for later." Then she stood up and gave him a sweet kiss and a bright smile. "Come on, almost time to eat and be merry."

Martha arranged the seating at the big table so that Abe was between the two younger women, Mattie and Ollie were across from them, and she and Mike sat at the ends. Another table was heavily loaded with food and two bottles of wine. Martha asked for quiet and for Abe to give the blessing.

He had a moment of awkwardness when his mind didn't seem to know what to say first, then he started in, "Our dear Heavenly Father, and our Mother this Earth, we give thanks for your grace and for your protection and sustenance here is this wonderful homeland. We give thanks for one another and for the things we have done and can do for each other. Also for this bounteous food and the hands that prepared it. May we always be grateful for what You provide and for the way that our needs are taken care of. In your Name, Amen."

Ollie cheered and raised Mattie's closest hand over their heads. "Good job, young fella. I like that part about the Mother Earth."

Abe looked down at his hands and mumbled, "That's because we're living among the people who really care about that, so I thought I should include it in their honor."

"Of course you should have," Sarah Beth said. "I just wonder why my father never mentioned that in all his prayers."

"Well," Martha said, "who wants what first? Mattie?"

"Oh my, it's all so beautiful. I suppose I just want a little bit of everything. If it all fits on one plate."

"There's plenty, so I imagine there will be more when you're ready for it." She dished up a plate and passed it to Mattie.

"Helga?"

"Oh my, I don't know what I can take. I feel almost full already just looking."

"Tell that little one to move over and make room for his first Thanksgiving Dinner."

Helga seemed to blush and hid her face in her napkin. She wasn't ready for such talk about what was still, to her, too much of a private mystery to be discussed in public.

"I don't know he'd understand yet," she said quietly.

"Well then, here, start with this." The woman handed her a mostly full plate.

Sarah Beth said she could probably eat the whole turkey, but then would be sorry. She helped herself.

"Abe?"

"Everything in moderation, as they say."

Martha filled a plate with heaping portions.

"Ollie?"

"You got a bigger plate, sis? Like a platter?"

"I'll do what I can with this one, but you'll just have to come back for more."

Once she'd served Mike and herself, she sat down and there was quiet around the table as everyone dug into their meal.

When the dinner was over, Martha suggested that they stop and wait awhile for the sweets that would come after. She said, "I've asked Sarah Beth to play some songs for us on our new piano. She agreed. So we'll reconvene in a few minutes. I just love a music evening."

While the women cleared the table and began storing the leftovers, the men went outside so Ollie could smoke his "Thanksgiving cigar."

"Special times, boys. My yearly tradition." He brought out a small flat bottle and handed it to his brother-in-law. "Little after-dinner sipping. Best thing for digestion."

Abe even took a good-sized swallow and said thank you.

Ollie almost finished it off. "There's more where it come from," he said. "Say, boys, what about that Mattie, and me? That's a lot of woman, don't matter what color she is."

"Probably more than you could handle," Mike said.

"Maybe we'll get a chance to see about that."

After a bit of time went by and the whiskey was gone, Ollie stubbed out the cigar and perched it on top of a post. Martha called for them.

Sarah Beth was already playing the piano, and tossing her long hair around to the music. "Oh this is so wonderful. Abe, it's been so long. Remember how I was always playing back home in Virginia?"

Mike pulled a fiddle out and Abe shyly took out his harmonica. Sarah Beth began playing some up-tempo songs from before the War. "Just a little patriotism from when we were still one country. I used to love to go to the park and hear these songs on the 4th of July. Do you know this one?"

Martha joined in with a lovely singing voice and Mattie clapped her hands in time.

Ollie leaned over to her and said, loud enough for everyone to hear, "Think you could teach me how to clap my hand like that?" Then he burst out laughing.

Mike poked him with the fiddle bow, and said, "Behave yourself. There's women present." Then he started up a fiddler's dance tune. Helga somehow knew the words and joined her voice with Martha's humming along. Mattie stood up and began shuffling her feet in time and then moved away from them to get more space and twirled a couple of times, her new dress filling the space around her.

After a few more songs, Sarah Beth changed the mood and began playing a slow ballad from the sad days of the War. Helga smiled and whispered to her, "I know this one. One of the Bishop's women taught it to me when I was little. She got in trouble for that, so I made sure I never forgot it."

"Then sing with me."

Sarah Beth played the introduction again, paused, and looked up at Helga standing next to her, "Now?"

Helga began softly humming as Sarah Beth played as softly as she could. Then Helga clasped her hands in front of her face and sang,

"It's been too long, so long, too long,
My sweetheart is gone.
Will I ever see him again? Too long, too long,
He's been gone.
With his cap and his gun, he said he'd return,
Me and his dog keep waiting and praying.
I miss him, I want him, his dog and I yearn,
Please come back, come back is all I am saying.
So long, too long, come back to my arms..."

When she stopped, Sarah Beth looked up. Helga said, "I never learned anymore of it."

Everyone clapped, and after a few more songs, Mattie sang the popular song from before the War, "The Old Folks at Home":

"Way down upon the Swanee River, Far, far away...
That's where my heart is yearning ever, That's where the old folks stay,
All up and down the whole creation, Sadly I roam,
Still longing for the old plantation, And for the old folks at home..."

She repeated that first verse, and when she finished, there was a long silence, until all at the same time they praised her for her beautiful voice. Then Martha announced it was time for the desserts if someone would help her beat the cream. Abe volunteered and they went to the kitchen. Ollie told Mattie there was something outside he wanted to show her and they bundled up for a walk. Sarah Beth and Mike began working on a couple more tunes they could do together.

As December eased into the New Year, the weather remained dry and cold. They continued to tighten up the new house against the wind, and every day it became more comfortable. Helga was showing her pregnancy more and spending a lot of time in her own space, quilting and resting. Mattie had learned to ride Ginger, and ever since

Thanksgiving she'd been helping Ollie work on his own small house, with him doing the carpentry, and her making such things as curtains. They seemed to have become, at the least, very good friends, and no one was really talking about what else might be developing. With winter cattle chores, gathering wood, and maintaining their water supply, Abe kept himself busy, and was usually worn out by the time the early darkness came along. Sarah Beth continued to work on the inside of the house and handle most of the cooking. She said she was busy creating the "Frontier Diet" for homesteaders and wanderers.

At one point she even told Abe that if he didn't feel comfortable sharing her room most of the time, maybe he could have Mattie's room when she moved in with Ollie. That way the three of them would each have their own bed. "Wouldn't that make this all much simpler?" she asked, and then left the house on some errand without waiting for an answer.

When she returned she brought it up again, "Did you think about what I said?"

"What makes you think Mattie will be moving out?"

"Women can tell certain things. A lonely man and a lonely woman with hardly anyone else around will probably find they have many things in common, don't you think?"

"I suppose so." He was on a ladder, using a pitch and glue compound to fill the rest of the cracks and spaces along where the wall met the ceiling in the big open room.

"Well you should know. Seems like all three of us are pretty lonely these days, even though we're always on top of each another."

"I think we're making the best of it. At least for right now." He came down and moved toward her with his arms open for a hug.

"Oh, excuse me." It was Helga, who immediately went back to her room and closed the door.

Sarah Beth pushed Abe away and said, "There now, that's the problem. We've probably hurt her feelings. Go be with her. I have other things to do."

"So do I."

"Well, you should learn that when I'm all right with the two of you having some time together, you need to take advantage of it. Now go, see what she needs."

He nodded to her and then did as she said. When he knocked softly on Helga's door, she told him she didn't want to see anyone right then.

"Please, I want to talk with you. Just for a little while." There was no answer.

Then she said through the door, "That's what it always is, just a little while, or maybe in a while, or sometimes just nothing, nothing, nothing."

"Helga, please, let me come in. I want to see what you're working on."

There was more silence, and then, "Oh all right. I guess I can't be rude, can I?"

He went in and the room felt cold. There was no fire and no wood beside the stove. "Why don't you have a fire? You'll be chilled."

"I ran out of wood, and my back is sore. I was on my way to get some wood when I guess I interrupted you and her."

"You didn't interrupt anything. Now here…" He picked up a blanket and draped it around her shoulders. "Either wait here while I get some wood and start up the fire, or go out front and stay by that fire while I get this one going."

"I don't want to go out there. And I don't even want your help."

"That's not your choice. I'll be right back."

As he walked through the kitchen to the back door, Sarah Beth asked him how she was.

"Doesn't have a fire or any wood and her back hurts. I'll take care of it." He stepped out to the back porch and got his jacket.

He brought in three armloads of chopped wood from the pile he had cut to length for Helga's small stove. He removed his coat and asked if he could rub her back after he started up the fire.

"If you really want to."

It was a statement that didn't seem to need an answer, so he busied himself with the fire. Once it was burning well, and the wood crackling, he moved on his knees over to the edge of the bed where she was sitting and eased her over into a face-down lying position. He used the heels of his palms to massage the lower back for some time.

"Feels good," she said in a voice muffled by the pillow.

"You're very tight." He kneaded her shoulders. After a while, he let his hands slip between her arms and her ribs, and she turned over to lie facing up and looking into his eyes.

"My breasts hurt most of the time now. They're stretched out, I guess. Rub them too."

He copied her earlier phrasing and said, "If you really want me to," cupping his hands over them and gently squeezing. "They're harder too."

"That's what hurts. Be gentle, but it feels good. I do it myself but it's not the same." She was quiet for a few moments and then moaned softly when he seemed about to stop. "More," she whispered.

He stopped to add more wood to the kindling, and then started to stroke her belly with his hands, reaching under the loose fitting smock she was wearing. "Stop me if it doesn't feel right. I've never done it like this before."

"Where did you learn it then?" she asked.

"I think from my grandmother. She had a lot of pain in her joints and back. I was small, but she said I had healing hands. Sometimes she even wanted me to walk on her back."

"I don't think I'll have you try that on me." She reached up and pulled his face down to hers and kissed him. "Thank you. I want another session, maybe one every day."

"Helga, dear Helga, if..."

"Don't talk about it. Just do what you can for me. I can't be alone so much."

"I know."

"Good, then go, before she has to call for you."

He kissed her again and stroked her hair lying spread out on the pillow. "I'll be back again, soon."

"Go."

He picked up his jacket from the floor and slipped quietly out of the room. It was lightly snowing outside and the new moon, showing through clouds, was already fairly high in the afternoon sky.

Later on in the winter, when Abe was out looking for strays during a blizzard, he came on the bones of a cow that looked freshly killed. Although it was surrounded by wolf and coyote tracks, he couldn't be sure that a human hadn't done it. The eight inches of snow that had fallen in the last twenty-four hours was now blowing and separating into drifts and bare places. The bones were partially covered by snow, in a sheltered area behind some boulders. He didn't like losing any of his stock, but found himself hoping it was a predator kill and not more trouble from Indians or other troublemakers.

He gathered a few long bones to take home for Happy, rolled them in the raincoat he kept behind the saddle, and started for home. This was the only cow missing from his herd. As the horse picked his way through the rocks that stuck up out of the snow, Abe tried not to think about marauders and to just chalk this up to fate. Suddenly Cloud's ears pricked up and then Abe heard a shot. He turned the horse toward the creek and pulled his rifle from its scabbard. The flowing water was mostly covered with a layer of ice, all except a fast current rushing between rocks. The ice cracked under Cloud's hooves as he picked his way across.

When they got close to the camp's area, Abe tied Cloud to a patch of willow and approached the campsite on foot. Now he could smell smoke and hear voices. It sounded like two men in conversation. Friends or enemy, he couldn't tell, but their voices were raised. He moved forward, keeping as low as he could, sheltered by the brushy growth alongside the stream. He heard a sound behind him and looked back the way he'd come. A horse was coming his way, and then he heard a woman's voice call, "Lefty."

Could his friend be here in this weather, this time of year? He decided to take a chance and stood up, moving toward the voices and the fire. He saw two hunched-over shapes dragging something through the snow, toward two Army tents with a fire burning between them. A woman was dragging long pieces of wood from the other direction. Abe held his gun pointing at the ground and waited to be discovered, not wanting to startle these folks.

Suddenly he was grabbed from behind and spun around to look fully into Lefty's eyes and the part of his face showing above the wool scarf he wore.

"Big Bear Man!" He took Abe's hand and shook it once. "My friend."

"I heard a shot."

"Carl also here. He killed deer. We eat good tonight. You bring women."

"We'll try. See if they can get over here in the buggy. And you? Everything all right?"

"Mostly all right. Some things not so good. We talk later. Nothing bad for me right now."

"You need help with the deer or setting up camp?"

"No. Patsy is here, Carl here. You go, come back soon."

They shook hands again and Lefty turned away, going to help the others. Abe rode back across the creek toward the house.

That night Helga and Sarah Beth went with Abe to the Indian camp. Mattie was staying over for two days at the Skinner place, and although she denied any special relationship with Ollie, Martha had informed Sarah Beth that they were spending most of their time together whenever she came for a visit. Mattie had learned to ride quite well and was able to travel back and forth between the two places on her own, in most kinds obf weather.

The meal was pleasant, although it was cold inside the tent. Patsy and Sarah Beth shared news of their two families in a stumbling kind of English, with Helga quietly watching on. No mention was made of the younger woman's pregnancy although it was quite apparent.

Lefty and Abe ate first and then went outside to smoke, Abe accepting the pipe Lefty offered a couple of times. He thought that maybe he was getting used to the sweet sharp taste of Indian smoking mixtures.

When they finished the pipe, Lefty began to talk about the things that were happening in the Wallowa Mountains to the north of Jordan Valley. "There are white men, many coming. They think gold, but not find. Fight with our young men. Our Old Man Joseph is dying, maybe gone now. He passed on that country to his son, whose white man name is also Joseph, for him to be head man. Indians and Agent cannot agree on what Treaty means. White men say it gives right to buy land from Indians because the People own the land and can sell it. White men do survey, say here this your land to one Indian here, one Indian there. Other white men bring alcohol, buy land. Young men want to fight the whites. Old men say no, fighting only get women and children killed."

"It is sad that there is no way to live together," Abe said.

"Two of Indian young men kill three gold miners. Other gold miners kill six Indians. The two Indians are hanged by the Army, no white men hanged. Not good. We left being there now. I don't want this wife, Patsy, to be there now. She is like your younger wife, now making child."

Abe looked up at him. After a long pause, he asked, "And Hawk Man, where is he?"

"He went north to other people near reservation in Idaho. Send Carl with me. He is afraid Carl will fight the whites with young men. Not good."

"And your mother, Moon Fish?"

"She was with illness, stronger now. Send medicine for Sa-rah, she call her. Sa-rah. And you, young friend? How are you?"

"Good. Winter not too hard. We are living in the house. Cows seem all right. But had some killed, other ranchers also lost some butchered. They thought maybe it was Hawk Man's group and came here, but he had been gone for more than a month. They said then it probably was some Bannock raiders."

The women came out of the tent and stood near the fire. Carl had been sitting near the two other men, saying nothing, but listening. He quickly stood up and moved back into the shadows, returning with a small piece of log that he placed behind Helga, motioning for her to sit. She thanked him and sat down and rolled the wood around until it was stable.

"I think we should go, Abe. You can stay if you want to, but Helga and I are tired and the moon will take us to our home."

"Perhaps, I will," he said. "Let me get the horse harnessed."

When they were gone, Lefty asked him to stay for a few more minutes and told Patsy and Carl they could also stay by the fire.

"My friend," he said softly, "who is your God?"

Abe looked away and stared down into the fire. He was quiet for a long moment. The fire snapped, sparked and burnt brightly in changing colors. "I'm not so sure anymore. He keeps changing for me."

Lefty reached over and put his hand on Abe's forearm. "That's good. It's never necessary to be too sure about this Mystery."

"It is easier when you think you know for sure, isn't it?"

Lefty motioned with a sign to Carl who got up and went into one of the tents. He came back and handed a feather to the Indian man. "Eagle carries our prayers. Sometimes we smoke to make prayers and the smoke rises, carrying prayer to eagle high above. Eagle take to highest place and let go higher. We know prayer is heard because we have answer yes or no, our people grow stronger when we have good times or when we have bad times. Now is hard time for us, so we are growing stronger, but we are losing people. We are losing them to sickness, fighting, and now there are two new religions."

"Two?"

"White man's black robes bring their crossed sticks and bleeding God to us. Some of my people think this good for them. Now they are told they will die and go to good place, that heaven place, all other people go to that bad place, burning place." Once again he motioned to Carl who got up and fetched more wood. Patsy brought a kettle of water and put it on the fire.

"That is what I also used to believe," Abe said, "but now I have come to know you and Hawk Man and your families. I have talked of many things with Hawk Man, you, and Mary Wolf. Also my wife has been treated and taught by your good mother, Moon Fish. None of you believe in the Jesus God and Holy Spirit Way. Now I am wondering what kind of a God would send you to what you call the burning place? What kind of God would send anyone who is a good person and never heard of Jesus to this Hell? That is why I am no longer as sure as I was." He paused. "And even back then I wasn't always sure of all of those beliefs."

"You are wise to have questions. Those who are not wise only have answers."

Patsy dropped a handful of herbs into the nearly boiling water and looked at her husband.

She spoke softly in their language and Lefty nodded his head, turned, and spit.

"Now beside black robe teaching, we have our own new believers. They call themselves the Dreamers, but they are not like the old Dreamers, they only have one man who dreams for all of them, and he tells them that one day, not too far off, white man go away and Indians be strong again in our own land. But some of our young men say what he has said is that we must make this happen by getting rid of white men. Other thing this man teach and they believe is that cut into earth is very bad medicine and they will never accept the Agent and Treaty words telling them to plow up earth to make new kinds of food."

"It makes some kind of sense, that part does, if you have always raised or hunted animals. But what will the people eat when there are no more buffalo? Will they have cattle?" Abe thanked Patsy when she handed him a cup of the steaming aromatic tea.

"Those Dreamers don't think about this life so much. I think they want to die soon so they can go to their own good place. But now also want to make the white man go back where he come from. That will bring back buffalo and old ways of being strong while they wait to die and be more happy. I don't like it. And there are those who say that I am now a white man, but one who does not believe in anything. They say I will burn and burn." The fire was slowly dying down and when Carl started to go look for more wood, Lefty stopped him. "We will let our friend go to his home now. We will sleep and when morning comes, we will talk some more."

"I am sorry to hear these things. I don't know what to say to you."

"It is the way of this world." He stood up and held out the feather to Abe, saying, "We need you as our brother now and forever. Take this feather of Eagle and use it when you pray." He paused while Abe accepted the gift, and then went on, "You will tell me of your god, the one you have for yourself. I ask you, but not let you say enough this time. My thoughts were on my own trouble, but I want to know you. Go now, your women need you."

On the ride across the creek and home through the bright moonlight, Abe tried to think of what he could tell his friend he believed in now. Who was his God now? At the moment he was less sure than he'd ever been in his life. Then he remembered one thing Sarah Beth's father told him when he found out they were going to get married. He said, "Your God will bless you because He is your very own God. You must never fight about this, even if you have to listen and maybe even appear to agree with someone about something you don't believe in. God will forgive you and you will become stronger in faith even through your own doubts and those challenges from others."

Doubts and challenges, blessings and gifts, all coming from the Giver of all things, this is what he thought he believed now. But how could he explain it to anyone else? Except to say God is good and cares about us.

Sarah Beth was already sleeping when he came to bed, but he stayed with her anyway. The moonlight filtered in through the material of the curtains and cast a soft area of light around the bed and on her face. She looked so peaceful that he could only stand there and pray silently that this woman who was his first real love could have everything she wanted, and that he could be the man she needed. Then he thought of praying for himself, but wasn't sure what to ask for so he simply gave thanks for all that he had.

The next morning he told both Sarah Beth and Helga that he needed to return to Lefty's camp and asked if they had anything he could take to them.

Helga asked, "Are there more coming or is it only the three of them?"

"I'm not sure. He wants to talk with me some more about problems the Indians are having with the whites and the miners up north of here, also some kind of religious conflict among the Indians themselves."

"Will you tell us about all that, or is it only for men?" Sarah Beth asked.

"I will tell you whatever I can understand about it. It's somewhat confusing to me and I don't feel good asking him too many questions."

Sarah Beth looked over at Helga and smiled and then said, "That's the way we feel about you, isn't it Helga? Don't ask him too many questions."

He tried to laugh with them and then went out to feed the horses. He returned to the kitchen when he'd finished breaking ice out of their water trough. The two women told him he'd have to wait a little longer because they were making honey rolls and needed to bake before he could take them to the neighbors. Just then they heard riders arriving.

It was Ollie and Mattie. They pulled up, and she came down off her horse, one Abe had never seen before, handed him the reins and asked, "The girls inside?"

"Yes, they are." Ollie dismounted and slapped Abe on the back, and they led the horses to the hitching rail. Abe asked about the horse he was leading.

"Got it for her. Needs to have her own horse. Name's Ruckus, but he's gentle as a lamb. She'll be going back and forth more when the weather changes for the better."

"It will change, won't it?"

"Bound to. Whose smoke is that over by the Indian camp?"

"My friend Lefty and his wife. And Hawk Man's son. Guess there's more trouble up north and he's getting away from it."

"I heard they found gold and when a crowd of miners showed up to grub for it, turned out it wasn't much at all. Bet they were madder than hornets. Kind of the opposite of us, huh?"

"Don't get what you mean," Abe said.

"They were looking, but couldn't find any. We weren't looking, but found it anyway."

Abe tied the horse's reins to the rail and stepped back to look it over. "Where'd he come from? Around here?"

"Once she agreed to move in with me, I went looking and found him at the sale in Silver City, so he's local."

"What'd you say?"

"Sale at Silver City."

"No the other part, about you and Mattie?"

"Oh yeah, haven't told anybody yet. That's why we come today. Make it official. I mean, we're not getting hitched or anything, but it'd be a lot more convenient if she didn't have to go back and forth all the time. It's OK, she'll still be here to help them girls when she's needed."

Abe looked at Ollie and thought better of what he was going to say, but then decided it didn't matter anymore—all their friends already knew about the three of them. "I'm more concerned about her helping to keep the peace around here," he said.

"Between the girls?"

"Well, she's a big help, at least to me." Abe smiled and shook his head. "But hey, I guess I should congratulate you. She's a wonderful woman."

"I know that. And I can't believe I'd find anybody clear out here, but here is where we are. Now, before we go inside, I want to tell you what I've done. Got myself a claim across the border into Idaho. Played out ground. Been mined to death already, but who's to say there isn't still a little bit of color left in those desert rock walls?"

"I still haven't heard anything from Hawk Man, what they think about up here."

"That's too bad, but it's no good this time of year anyhow. What I'm doing is just being prepared."

"Well, I hope you don't get disappointed. I won't go against them."

"I understand. Besides, with a woman to take care of, I've got to get some dependable paid work and I think I've got just the ticket. They're building a better road from Silver to Boise and they need some fellas who can handle these new explosives. Well, they're new to out here, but I worked with them for the past seven years, or stuff just like'em."

"I'd like to hear more about it, but maybe we should go in." Abe held open the back door and they could hear the happy chatter and laughter of the women inside. "Anyway, Ollie, congratulations. It's a fine thing, and I'm happy for both of you."

"Good. I think this will be better for everyone."

Later, after they had a bit of a celebration over coffee, tea, and fresh-baked rolls, Ollie and Mattie headed back to the Skinner place. Helga went to her room to gather laundry and Abe got himself ready to go across to visit Lefty.

"Well, I guess we knew that was going to happen," Sarah Beth said.

"I suppose I should have, but I didn't really notice them getting that close."

"That's because you're a man, dear." She adjusted the collar on his coat and leaned back with her arms around his neck. He reached around her waist and held her there.

"You'll miss having her here?" he asked.

"Of course I will, but life is about change, isn't it?"

He pulled her close and kissed her gently at first and then strongly. "As long as this doesn't change," he said.

"Go, so you can come back. Take the rolls. They're wrapped in that cloth on the table."

When he arrived at the camp, Lefty was cleaning a rifle and Patsy was cooking a pot of stew over the fire.

"Halloo, my friend, welcome. I am happy to see you this fine morning."

"And I'm pleased you have come to visit at this time of year—didn't expect it," Abe said.

"We are, as you say, on the move. I will travel south like a snow goose making a late journey without his tribe. I have some people to see in that country. They are waiting for my words that will tell them when it is going to be safe for their young men to come this way again to take back home wives and horses."

"May I ask who these people are, or what people they are?"

"They are called Mescaleros. Whites call them and many others Apa-chee. My friends are trying to be peaceful but it is difficult. They want only the water, the land and mountains they have always had, but the treaties they have signed do not hold off settlers, just as here and in many other places. My friends also have a white man they are close to, who helps them with the Agents. He is much like you, my friend."

"I can only wish there were more of us whites who could come to know you and your people as I do. We are different races, but should never be enemies."

"The Old Man Joseph who was of these Nez Perce, he said we should not fight over the land that is our Mother or about whose god is the stronger Father. And if those are the only things we are fighting about, we should stop fighting and live in peace. Do you agree?"

"Surely that is the way of peace."

"And you? You have come to tell me more of your god?" He finished putting the gun back together and laid it across his knees. "I hope we will not have to fight about what you have to say," he laughed and took out his small pipe. "You take stick and spark from the fire. I want to smoke with you as if it is your own pipe."

Abe did as he was told, and took in some smoke, even allowing a little into his lungs, and then passed the pipe to Lefty.

"As I told you, our smoke and our prayers rise together to the Eagle who carries them above to Creator. As you say," he exhaled, "bless you." The man knocked the ashes from the pipe when they were finished. "So now tell me more of your believing."

"It is hard for me to say in words. Sarah Beth's father was a teacher and a preacher of our God's Word. He taught me that even today God speaks to those who will listen. But not in a loud voice as in the days long ago, not in any voice at all, but rather it happens when we truly need something that is for good, then our God will open the door to provide the place or time on our path that brings us together with the answer to our prayer. This has happened for me many times, so I believe there is a Someone who understands my needs and takes care of me when I can't do something for myself…"

"This is good to hear. What if you ask for bad things to happen to other people or things that are only good for yourself?"

"I don't know. I would probably be afraid to ask for those things."

"Why be afraid?"

"Because the one thing I believe that is evil, is doing hurt and bad things to others, or to wish for those things. I believe what Jesus said when he said, 'Do unto others as you would have them do unto you.'"

Lefty called to Patsy. "Coffee for my friend." Patsy came out of the tent and puts some ground coffee into a pot that was simmering near the edge of the fire. She smiled at Abe and said, "You like?"

"Oh, thank you. And here, I almost forgot." He handed her the bundle of rolls. She went back into the tent and returned with cups and cloth napkins that she used like plates for the rolls.

"I, too, have heard these words of this Jesus. But I think we have a little different way of saying this. I say it is, 'Do unto others as they do unto you.'"

"Yes, it is a little different and I can see why you would follow that way more easily."

"Good bread," Lefty said after breaking off a small piece and feeding it to the fire. "You make this, my friend?"

Abe laughed and said, "I don't think so. I don't know anything about how to make good bread and rolls."

"Same for me," Lefty said as he took a cup of hot coffee. "But she can make the best fried bread in a pan, cooked in grease over the fire. We will make some for you next time we eat together."

"How long do you think you'll be here this time?"

"Not longer, maybe two days if no storm."

"Then I want you to come to our new house to eat with us. Is tomorrow good for you?"

"Is good."

"I will tell the women, and see you then."

Lefty looked at him closely and said, "One more thing. How you call your god, name?"

Abe was standing up and sat back down. "He has three names in our churches, but that is what I am having a hard time with. He is God the Father, God the Son Jesus, and God the Holy Spirit, but He is only one God."

"I see," Lefty held out one of his long braids. "Three together make one."

"Something like that."

"Then who is this one?" He held out his other braid and laughed cheerfully. He pushed himself up off the rock he was sitting on and held out his hand to Abe. "Our Creator likes what you white men call jokes. We try to make Creator laugh, and we Indians are so clumsy and make so many mistakes that this is easy for us."

"Then He must also be laughing very much at the white people."

Lefty let go of Abe's hand and looked into his eyes, saying, "When he is not crying."

CHAPTER 7

Birth

An early warm spell at the end of February melted snow in the mountains, and the larger of the two creeks filled with brown water rushing through and past their place. The sound of its passage could be heard even inside the house and this went on for three or four days. Abe was concerned that a few of his cows might have gotten stranded across the creek from the rest of the herd and he spent hours looking for and counting all that he could find. Just when it seemed certain he was missing two of the females who were expected to give birth around this time, they appeared out of one of the side draws, each accompanied by a sturdy young calf. He was pleased with this and with the apparent good instincts that led them into a sheltered place for their births. He felt relieved that things appeared to be going well enough as spring began its arrival.

Although he stopped short of thinking that all this was any kind of an omen for Helga's birth, he let himself include her in his silent prayer of gratitude for the passage of the winter. When he returned to the house, he found her waiting for him on the deck in front of her room. He went to stand below her, looking up into her kindly eyes. She reached out and picked his hat from his head and tousled his hair. She had placed two chairs on the completed section of the porch and motioned to him.

"Come, sit with me. Sarah Beth has gone to visit Mattie and take some more of her things over to her." He came up the steps and they sat together. The sun was beginning to break through the clouds that seemed to be racing with the swollen creek on their way to elsewhere. "How are your cows? Did you find them?"

"I did. I'm relieved. And they both had calves with them."

"So, 'tis the season." She took his hand and placed it on her rounded belly. "Soon."

"How are you feeling?"

"I'm fine, but I get tired so easily."

He smiled at her and said, "That's as it should be. There's nothing you need to be doing besides getting ready and resting."

"Abe, I have to tell you that your wife is beginning to act like she doesn't want me around. She doesn't say so, but I have to hold my tongue at some of the things she does."

"Like what?"

"Well, I was helping to get Mattie's things together and making that room comfortable for you."

"For me?"

"Yes, the three of us women decided that the best solution to our situation was for you to have a room of your own, and then you could be with either one of us, as needed."

"Whose idea was that?"

"Well, it was Mattie's, but we said we'd try it. It's been so awkward lately and I don't think you should have to sleep on the couch in the big room so often."

"What about when Mattie wants to stay over here some nights?"

"That's when Sarah Beth told me I wasn't going to have you all to myself. Ever. I couldn't help it. I talked back to her and said that if she really wanted you maybe she should show it better."

"What did she say?"

"She said I was only here because she allowed it and if I didn't watch out I'd be out on my own. So I said maybe that would be better than having to put up with her jealousy. Then Mattie came in. She heard us from the next room and made us apologize to each other.

And that's when she came up with the idea of you using her room after she moves out."

"Oh, I see. And what if I don't agree with all of this?"

"Then perhaps you can enjoy your nights alone out with the horses."

"Well, I'm certainly impressed with how you all get along when it comes to deciding my future," he said as he stood up.

"Now don't get upset. We're trying to make the best of these things, for all of us. Here," she said as she leaned toward him, "kiss me." He leaned her way and they embraced with the arm of one of the chairs between them. "Ow. I'm too big to turn like that in this chair. Come be in front of me."

He got to his knees and knelt in front of her with both hands placed on either side of the roundness in front of him. "Won't be much longer, will it?"

"Sarah Beth and Mattie disagreed about that. Mattie said it always takes longer the first time and Sarah Beth was trying to count it out on her fingers. Don't feel bad—neither of them asked me what I thought."

"Want to know what I think?" he asked.

"Of course."

"I think that if you were a cow, I'd say it's a few weeks off, but since it's you, it's right now." He reached around her and gave her a soft squeeze.

"Abe, do you remember when you met the Bishop the first time? You came to our camp that evening for a meal and to talk some kind of business."

"I remember. It made me anxious to come into a strange camp like that. I didn't know what might happen."

"But you don't remember me from that?"

"No, I don't think so."

"I was the girl who brought you your food. I thought you were the most handsome man I'd ever seen." She settled back into her chair, pulling his head to her breasts. "The color of your hair, your sun-browned face. After I handed you your plate of food, I stood behind you and watched the muscles of your back and shoulders move under your shirt while you ate."

"All of that, and I didn't notice?"

"I even got in trouble with the oldest wife for not coming back to our kitchen wagon right away. It was the first time I ever felt how a woman can feel about a man. And it was you."

That evening, as the three of them were having supper together, Sarah Beth also revealed to him the women's plan for his living situation. Helga gave his foot a nudge under the table and let him know with a quick shake of her head that he shouldn't let on he already heard it from her. When Sarah Beth finished explaining the arrangement, she gave credit to Mattie for the offer and the idea, and asked him what he thought of it.

He looked down at his plate, still half-filled with some of the last of the venison from Carl, and mumbled, "It should probably work out."

"Probably?"

"If the two of you can make it work, it will," he replied to her.

"Well, Helga, I suppose that's as enthusiastic an agreement as we're going to get from him. Abe, we've agreed to try to do our best, especially with the baby coming so soon. There is something else I need to say to both of you, and it's not really about the three of us. But maybe it could wait until another time."

Helga touched Sarah Beth's hand and said, "What is it? You seem sad all of a sudden."

"I had one of my dreams. This time it was about Moon Fish. She was ill and called out for me to come to her."

Abe swallowed his food and cleared his throat to say, "Lefty told me she'd been sick, but she got better, so I didn't tell you. So you wouldn't worry."

"I don't think this dream is about the past. I think it's about now. I told Mattie and she said that Martha and Mike might be heading north after the winter storms are past, but before the snow melts in the mountains and fills the rivers. I think they wouldn't mind taking me."

"But you promised to be here for the baby," Helga said, looking alarmed.

"Of course. I won't go anywhere until after you've had the baby, settled into each other, and you've recovered. Mattie said she'll stay here often and do cooking for a couple of days at a time. My problem would be finding Moon Fish. That part wasn't in the dream."

Abe said, "You'll just have to dream some more."

Helga looked from one to the other of them and said, "I don't know if this will help, but I was talking with Carl when they were here and he said his father and his family were spending the winter near where the Snake River meets the bigger river. Idaho, but not too far from here."

Abe spoke up and said, "Next time I see Mike, I'll ask him what route he'd be taking and if they could take you there and bring you home again, if they go."

"That would be good," Sarah Beth said. "I don't really want to go away, but maybe it would also be best for the three of you...and I am worried about her. She's been so good to me."

Now Abe reached across the table so he could take her hand and Helga's, and said, "I feel like praying." The two women clasped hands.

"Our Father in heaven and our Mother here beneath us, we humbly ask your guidance and protection at this time of change for us and our growing family. Be with those who have allowed us to live on this land and may be losing their own homes, and guide us in the season ahead of us. I ask you to bless both of these women who have been so good to me, and to bring this new life safely among us. Amen."

They sat in stillness for some time and then Sarah Beth said, "One more thing. Moon Fish says she thinks of me as her little sister, but I think of her more as my mother. She doesn't call me by the name Sarah Beth. She calls me Sa-rah, and I think that's what I want to be called from now on, at least by those who are close to me. Would that be all right with the two of you?"

Helga smiled and leaned closer to her, "What did you say, Sa-rah?"

They all had a laugh that broke the tension, and then Abe said, "I'll try to remember, but it may take some getting used to." He paused, and then said, "I've known this Sarah Beth person for so long now." He stood up and collected the used plates from their places, and started to carry them over to the sink.

"Oh my, Helga, will you look at that? Am I seeing things? You don't think he's going to wash them too, do you?"

Abe stopped and turned to face them. "Thought I could use some practice if I have to take over this household when you're gone and Helga's busy."

Helga began having pains in the middle of March. The weather was changeable, but no longer very cold. Winds blew from one direction one day and from somewhere else the next. Sa-rah was washing baskets full of laundry that had accumulated over the winter, bedding and the like, and hanging it out to dry in the wind. More calves were born and so far Abe was pleased with how healthy they seemed. He began talking about building pens so he could have options about which cows were kept together and which separated. Ollie came by several times to see about the water system, and Abe reminded him that they were still waiting for some kind of sign from the Indians regarding any more digging.

"I haven't forgotten," Ollie said, laughing. "But you ought to see what I could do up there with a few pounds of these explosives I'm using on the new roadway."

"Probably send pieces of rock all the way down here and break our precious windows."

"Don't think I could shoot stuff that far, but don't worry—I'm a lot more curious than greedy about what's up there."

Since Abe was using the room that had been Mattie's and it was next to Helga's space, they slept with their doors open so he could hear her if she called for him in the night. She was having more difficulty sleeping, restless enough to cry out sometimes without being aware of needing anything. Rather than have to get up to see if she did need something, he moved a pad in next to her bed and was able to get some sleep there on the floor.

Sa-rah seemed to be in good spirits about it all, but was spending more and more of her daytimes over with Martha and Mattie. She told Abe she was really enjoying the piano lessons and the three of them singing together.

One evening when Sa-rah and Abe were taking a walk together, she told him she'd been working on some of the choir pieces from when she sang at her father's churches. "A three-person choir is interesting because it's more complicated than a simple trio. Abe, you should come sometimes. We need another voice or two."

Abe smiled, "I think you'd be disappointed in my singing. Even the cows object if I try a tune or two on them."

"Well, we'll see. I've never heard a fiddle do church music, so maybe we'll expand our songbook to include Mike's kind of music. Maybe even some dance tunes. You could learn to be a caller and play your harmonica as well."

"And what does Mattie do?"

"Oh my, the other afternoon we were trying to get her to join in with us and she said she'd rather play a harp than sing. Martha asked her what kind of harp and she said the kind the angels use, so she would be ready for Heaven. We all laughed and laughed as she made all the motions with her arms and legs of playing a huge invisible instrument."

"Helga will be ready to join you before too long," he said.

"Yes, I suppose. She does have a lovely voice, but let's not talk about that now. I just want to hold your hand and watch the moon rising above our beautiful home. Beautiful, isn't it?"

They sat down on the dry grass and leaned back against a boulder. She was humming a song that reminded him of their days back in Virginia. She looked up and saw him nodding his head in time with her voice. They kissed and with no other warning they lay together and partially disrobed to make the other kind of music they'd always shared since they'd married. It had now been some time since Abe made love with either of the women in his life, and he nearly forgot to be more gentle with Sa-rah because they were on the ground. She whispered to be careful with her. He took a deep breath and then another, and said he was doing his best, but she was moving so strong with him that he couldn't slow down…

When they got back to the house, Helga was pacing up and down in the big room. She tried to smile at the two of them, but winced instead. Sa-rah rushed to her side and held her from falling as she bent over and cried out.

"Come, let's get you back to your bed. Abe, bring me that heavy cloth to put under her, and then heat some water, not hot, just warm. There you go," she said the Helga. "That's good, strong. We'll have to see how close together they're coming."

Helga collapsed onto her bed and then had to struggle to get back up again as Abe and Sa-rah arranged the heavy blanket where she would lie. "This is to catch the water," Sa-rah said. "We don't want you to have to lie in a puddle after it breaks loose."

The contractions came and went, but they were still irregular. Abe built up the fire—more to have something useful to do than for its heat. After it was going well enough and the water was warm, but not hot, he went back to Helga's room and looked in. She had her head turned away from the doorway and Sa-rah made a quiet sign with her finger and lips. Abe signed back that he was going to go outside for a few minutes, and whispered for her to call him if she needed anything.

It was dark outside now and the moon was part of the way up the sky. He went down to the new half-finished barn he was attaching to the shed he'd built when they first stared on this site. It was his tools and material storage, but he'd also turned it into a small shop where he could repair harnesses and other things. Most of all though, it was where he'd been able to work on the small cradle he'd just finished in time. Now he picked it up and carried it into the front room of the house, avoiding Helga's entrance and the open door to her room. He didn't think the baby would be put in a cradle for a while, but he wanted Helga to see it.

He could hear the soothing sound of Sarah Beth's voice between the moaning and outcries. He was still thinking of her as Sarah Beth. It was going to be hard to get this new name into his mind. For now it felt like he would always think of her with the name he first knew her by.

"Abe, can you come in here?"

He quickly moved to the open door of that room, but didn't look inside out of modesty or shyness perhaps. "Yes."

"She wants you and I need to go out for a minute."

"All right." He passed her as she left the room and he went in and sat on the chair next to the bed. Helga gave a muffled cry and he took her hand in his. She instantly turned to look, and tried to smile even as she cried out with another pain.

"Abe," she moaned his name. "Stay with me."

"I will," he said. "Can I do anything for you?"

"Another pillow behind my back would help."

He placed one under her back as she arched up from the bed, one leg kicking and thrashing against the bed. She was groaning and saying the word grace, over and over. He leaned close to try and make out what it was she trying to say.

"I'm stronger than Grace," she said, and repeated it several times. Sa-rah returned and went to the other side of the bed.

"What does she want?"

Abe said, "She asked for another pillow under her back, and now she's been saying something about grace. Maybe it's a prayer."

"I think she's talking to or about that other girl she and I helped to give birth. That one at the Bishop's compound."

"I'd forgotten that," he said. "I just thought she was saying something like she is stronger than grace, maybe than God's grace."

Helga looked at him and said clearly, "I need all God's grace I can get, but when I helped Sarah, Sa-rah, to deliver that baby, that girl was so weak I don't know how…" and then she screamed.

Sa-rah went to the foot of the bed and pushed the covering blanket above Helga's legs. It had gotten all tangled in the struggles. She looked at Abe and said softly, "Nothing you haven't seen before."

"Not with a baby coming, I never have."

They looked at one another and both of them seemed to want to say something, but neither did. Then Sa-rah said, "You need to learn about this in case there's no one else around when I have our baby…Now go and get something to eat. This is still going to take some time."

He nodded and backed away, saying to Helga, "Stay strong, I'll be right back."

Helga nodded to him and then gave a long soft moan as Sa-rah massaged her belly with long downward strokes.

He found some leftover meat in the porch cooler that had one compartment for ice and another for food. It wouldn't be much longer before he wouldn't be able to find any more ice, no matter how far up the little creek tributaries he climbed. He fitted the bread and meat together and went outside to sit on a stump. Clouds were drifting and the moon was at its mid-point in the arch of the sky. That meant the baby's birthday would be the next day instead of this one. He thought of his mother and her birthday being right around this time of year. When he was little he was always able to find some early spring flowers to gather into a bundle for her. This memory led him to wonder what his own birth was like and how hard she had to struggle, how much pain she went through to bring him into the world. And then he thought about all of the other women of the world…and all the female animals…and then his mind jumped to the awesomeness of the number of stars visible through breaks in the cloud cover, how many there were everywhere. Then somehow it all seemed to be the same number, the women and animals who'd given birth in the whole history of the earth, and the number of stars in the sky, a number close to infinity that could never be calculated. He used his sleeve to wipe the meat's greasiness from his mouth, and with one last look at the sky, went back into the house.

Sa-rah asked Abe to watch over Helga again while she took a short nap. "I have a feeling this will still be going on come morning and by then I can't be falling asleep. Call me if anything changes.

Try to get her to sleep if possible. She needs to save her strength." She gently pushed him out of her way and went to her own room.

Abe pulled the chair closer to the bed so he could be next to it. Helga was breathing hard, but the pains seemed to have subsided somewhat. He thought she might even be napping now. He could still hardly believe this was happening, that what he'd wanted so much for these past couple of years was actually happening, but in no way like he'd thought it would. And yet, if he applied the good Reverend's formula of real needs being matched by divinely arranged opportunity, he would have to accept that this was right in line with that. His need for a child was being answered, but in such a strange and different way than any of the three of them could ever have imagined. Just then, Helga stirred, moaned and then relaxed again. The most unlikely thing about it all was Sarah Beth's role in making it happen this way when it was what she'd been wanting so much for herself. Was she only making this sacrifice in order to please him, and was her own heart regretting or even resenting what she'd felt she had to do?

He found himself dozing and woke with a start when his head rolled to one side. Helga reached out for his hand and brought it to her belly. "It's not where it was," she said. "It used to be bigger here, so it's happening. He's moving down." Her face twisted into a grimace and she moaned louder than she had for quite a while. "Here he comes again." She was beginning to sweat again, so Abe went for a damp cloth. On the way back he saw a fan on a shelf, part of a small collection of items Sarah Beth had placed there, and he took it down. He gently wiped her face and then began fanning her.

"Oh, that feels so good. I'd ask you to close my door and open the window, but I'm afraid I might get a chill. But close the door so it won't get any warmer in—" Then she screamed, long and loudly. Sarah Beth came into the room.

"Why was the door closed?" she asked.

"Helga didn't want it to get any warmer in here. Maybe I should just let the fire go out."

"No, because she'll get cold again anyway. It's best to just shut the door like you had it." She closed it again and went to Helga's side.

Another scream.

"It seems to be coming faster than I thought it would. Was she resting while I was gone?"

"Yes, almost peaceful except for some moaning."

"That's good. Sometimes a woman will just stop for a short time and be able to rest. That's usually close to the end." Another scream, and thrashing of the legs. "Abe, see if you can hold her legs down. It's not good for her to be twisting her body so much. Here, let me in front of you and you reach around me and hold onto her feet."

They stayed like that through three more contractions, each one harder than the last. Helga tried to push herself up on her elbows and shouted at them, "I can't do this anymore." She tried to kick, but Abe held on. "I can't do this anymore!"

Sa-rah said over her shoulder, "It's coming. Oh, I hope it comes quickly."

"How can you tell?"

"She's as wide open as she can get and I think I see the top of the head. Quick, get me more water in that basin, warm water."

He hurried out to the fireplace where a large kettle on the hearth held warm water.

"Here," he said.

She took a cloth and dipped it, then cleaned between Helga's legs. "Grab hold again," she said to Abe.

With Helga's next spasm the three of them were locked together, Abe holding on to the feet as hard as he could, Sa-rah in between, bent over and struggling to help hold the thighs apart, and Helga screaming, "I'm sorry, I'm sorry, I'm sorry…"

"I see the head," Sa-rah said, "the top of the head." Then almost immediately there was another long thrashing about, and her saying, "Push Helga, Push!" Then the struggle subsided.

"Abe, it won't seem to come, I'm trying to make room, I'm trying, but a few more of those and we'll have to do something else…"

"Is this what happened with that girl at the Bishop's?" Abe asked.

"No, we had to push hers from above because it wasn't coming down enough."

Helga moaned loudly and then kicked one of her feet free from Abe's grip. It knocked Sa-rah in the head and she screamed again. Abe grabbed for and caught the loose foot. "Are you all right?" he asked. Sa-rah was shaking her head yes and now kneeling on the floor and reaching between Helga's legs, trying to ease the tissue back around the head.

"If I can only get my fingers inside without tearing..."

There was a short silence and then Helga's back arched up off the bed as her feet and legs stiffened straight out. Sa-rah struggled to get a better position, saying, "Push," over and over again. Helga was trying to sit up. "No, stay down. Abe, go hold her shoulders down. Whatever it takes."

Another longer, struggling spasm, but no sound other than hoarse gasping came from Helga with this one.

"Now push again, not so hard this time...There, there, I have it. It's coming...Oh my God, the cord, the cord..." The baby's cord was wrapped once around its neck, but Sa-rah was able to quickly slip it over the head and let it loosen. Now she pulled gently, gently. "Push, Helga, but not hard, just squeeze your belly. All right, her it comes."

And then the baby slid out into the world with its arms waving and sounds of choking. Sa-rah quickly wrapped it in a small, soft, waiting blanket. She held the head back slightly and sucked from its mouth and nose, spitting the mucous aside, then repeated it.

The baby gave a cry and Helga sat up, reaching her arms toward it. Sa-rah unwrapped the little one and peeked in saying, "Boy." Then wrapped him again, handing the bundle to Helga who lay back and cradled the new life on her chest.

"Abe, bring me the lamp from the other room, the bright one."

He went for the lamp and when he came back Sa-rah had the baby held in one arm and was holding up the cord with the other hand. It was still pulsing. "We'll wait until it stops completely," she said. "Here, the light."

He moved it toward her. "What are you looking for?"

"I think he's a little blue in coloring…but not bad." She whispered to Abe, "Sometimes when the cord is around the neck, the baby has difficulty while still breathing from the mother. Makes them a little blue, but this is not bad at all. He'll be all right."

Helga shook her head, as if to clear her senses, wiped her face with her hands and reached for the baby again. "He looks blue. Sarah, Sa-rah, is he all right? Ohhh, please God."

"I'm sure he's all right, Helga. This happens sometimes and it's no cause for worry."

"Thank you, thank you. Oh God, I'm so happy, so happy. Abe look! Look at him, look. It's our son, your son."

Abe set the lamp on the small table next to the bed and leaned forward to look closely at this little one, this little miracle. Sar-ah waited quietly, her fingers on the cord, waiting for it to completely stop pulsing. She was refusing to let her own thoughts come into her mind, trying to see this as if it were any other birth she'd served at. But inside she knew she was weeping with the sorrow of the deepest loneliness she'd ever felt. The three of them, now all joined as one, on the outside, but in her heart it felt like nothing less than the final loss of her husband. He was no longer hers no matter what he might say or how she might change it in the future. Her dream from the vigil returned to her, vividly casting up the picture of the alternative, a slight tug on the cord, leaving it tight around the baby's neck while she cut its connection from the mother…

"No," she heard herself say so loudly that Abe and Helga both turned to look at her. She struggled to control herself and explain. "I was just thinking that it was too soon to cut his cord and I guess I was thinking out loud. Here," she said softly, "let me wipe him off while you hold him. Then we'll want to cover both of you. It's not that warm in here." She was glad to have something to do at this moment.

When everything had been cleaned away and Helga was dozing off, Sa-rah took the baby in her own arms and once again listened carefully to the infant's breathing. There seemed to be no congestion and the breaths, while coming more rapidly than her own, were softly regular and quite normal. She looked back at Helga who was now sleeping. A mother, she thought, already a mother at such a young age. The baby made a sound and she rocked back and forth with him, shifting her weight from one foot to the other. She carefully moved to sit in the one chair in the room, wondering for a moment where Abe had gone, then remembering he'd taken the afterbirth and soiled linen outside. He said he would wait and bury the placenta somewhere and now set the cloths and clothing to soak. Sa-rah also wondered where Mattie was, since she'd promised to come by to see if they needed any help.

The baby lay pressed to her breasts and the small breaths rose and fell within him at about twice the rate of her own. The feeling of this new life was unlike anything she'd ever felt and her own body seemed to make slight shudders in rhythm with this one's movements. He was so new, so free from anything in this life, a blank book filled only with its blank pages and the unknown future of all its times yet to come. She realized that at every other birth she attended, the baby was quickly taken from her, if she held it at all, and then turned over to the new mother or the doctor or midwife. This rare moment, these moments, of new life and living, and the first responses of an infant to being surrounded by air and light, by touch and even sounds, were more precious than any other on this earth. She felt as if she was the only thing in the world for this one right now, and that he was all she could know and feel at this moment. Suddenly she was overcome by a wave of love that took her off guard and nearly carried her away from herself. This was the baby of her husband's dreams, but this little one was also her gift to him and to God. No more did she feel the pain of loss and of confusion about what was happening. There was no way to blame or criticize anyone at this moment, especially herself. A song came into her mind and eased out through her softest voice. A lullaby calling on the angels to watch over us, and praising the great Maker of our souls. For the first time in a long time, she felt that God was truly taking care of her, and this small child was the greatest gift she'd ever been given and that she had ever given.

Helga stirred in her fitful sleep, moaning and twisting her head on the pillows. Sa-rah sang a little louder and reached out with one hand to stroke the other woman's bare arm. The baby gave a cry and then whimpered for a short time. Helga stirred again and then woke up, reaching around herself, touching the bedclothes with both hands.

"My baby, where's my baby?"

"Here, Helga, he's right here." She leaned forward on the chair and held out the small body, placing him in his mother's arms. "He's so beautiful, so fine," she said.

"What do I do now?"

"Nothing. The two of you need to rest, nothing else. When you want something to eat, it will be here for you. When he wants something, he will let you know by reaching for your breasts and making sounds. But that doesn't need to happen for a while." She stood up. "How do you feel? Are you in any pain?"

"It hurts down there, but I guess it would have to, wouldn't it? I've never had so much pain in my life. Sarah Beth, Sa-rah, I didn't think I could do it. I was so afraid I couldn't do it."

"Well, you did, and you did it very well. I'm going to step out right now, just for a moment, but I'll be right back. Try to fall asleep again."

"Sa-rah, thank you so much. This is all because of you…And I love you."

"I love you too, Helga." She straightened out the covers and turned away, wiping the fresh tears from her cheeks and going out into the other room.

A couple of days passed in the aftermath of the birth and its blessings. Abe and the child found each other's company to be calming and almost familiar. The blueness had faded in the first few hours and the little one showed he had strong lungs when he cried loudly for his mother and her milk. Helga seemed to be recovering fairly quickly and Sa-rah continued to show that she felt this whole thing much more as a blessing than a burden.

On the third day, when the three of them and the baby all happened to be in Helga's room together, Helga asked what the "fancy name for blue" was.

Sa-rah and Abe looked at each other questioningly. "I'm not sure what you mean," Abe said. Sa-rah nodded her agreement with him.

"One time I saw a beautiful deep blue necklace on a woman in a store. I was very young, but I've never forgotten it. The stone had a name, but also its color had another name. I want this baby to have that name."

"Of the stone, or of the color?" Sa-rah asked.

"Of the color."

"Maybe Ollie knows what you're talking about. They should be here a little later this afternoon. Said they'd be by when you were ready to see people. I thought it would be all right."

"Oh Abe, I can't wait to see Mattie and have her see this baby. She was so good to me when I was all afraid and I didn't want it to happen. But she told me that God wanted this baby or He wouldn't have gone to so much trouble for it."

There was a short silence and then both Abe and Sa-rah said they had things to do and nearly bumped into one another leaving the room.

When Mattie and Ollie arrived, the woman went straight inside to see Helga and the baby. Ollie stayed out with Abe and offered a drink of whiskey in celebration. Abe took it and then passed it back. "We have a question for you," he said to his guest.

"And what might that be, my young friend, Papa?"

"Helga wants to know the name of a dark blue stone, used in jewelry. And the name of its color, which I guess is different."

"Well, have another taste while I rattle my thoughts and try to come up with an answer."

Abe took another swallow and felt the liquid burning in his chest. Never one to drink alcohol on his own, it was sometimes pleasant when he was with either Mike or Ollie.

"I'd guess she's talking about that one they call lapis. Something they had in Egypt and foreign places. Never heard of any being found in the country. As far as the name of its color, I never heard it called anything but lapis. It's a deep blue and you can't see through it. Why does she want to know?"

"Helga says she wants to name the baby after that color. He was a little blue when he was born. It went away pretty quickly and he seems perfectly normal, at least to Sarah Beth. By the way, on the subject of names, while you're thinking, Sarah Beth wants to be called 'Sa-rah' from now on. Something to do with how Moon Fish named her."

"Well, I doubt the girl's thinking of 'ultramarine' as a name for a child, and the only other thing I can think of is 'indigo.' It's a real deep blue and they use it for lots of things—again mostly in foreign countries. I'll have to get used to this Sa-rah name. Want another swig?"

"No thanks. Maybe we should join the ladies."

They stood up and Ollie held out his hand. Abe took it and they shook. "Congratulations, young man. I guess you found a way to get this thing done."

"Wasn't me exactly," Abe said.

"Well, I hope it was you. Ain't nobody else been around here, except me and the Indians, and it sure wasn't this old bastard." He clapped Abe on the back and they went inside.

Near the fireplace, Mattie was seated on the easy chair holding the baby. The soft cooing of her voice brought a quiet to the room and its people. Sa-rah was pouring coffee in some cups and tea in others. A plate of sweet biscuits sat on the table. Helga was lying on the bed-like couch that was placed against the wall opposite the fire. A peaceful smile played across her lips.

Abe waited for someone else to say something, but when no one did, he went ahead and spoke, "Helga, Ollie here says that the color of the deep blue stone you remember might be indigo. The stones are called lapis."

"Yes," the young woman said, sitting up. "That's it! I want him to be named that, Indigo. Can we?"

"It seems to be your choice, but why?" he asked.

"Because one time I saw that color again on the wall of a church. It wasn't a Mormon church and I don't know what kind it was. Someone said it was 'royal blue,' but the woman I was with said, no, it was really indigo. I loved the color and the name. I asked if I could have a dress that color and the woman said only if I became a queen." She lay back against the pillows behind her. "If I can name him that, Abe, you should choose his other name…after someone you really admire."

Sa-rah was simply watching all of this, and her expression showed very little of what she might be feeling. Then she spoke quietly and asked, "Will he have a family name?"

"You mean like Saunders?" Helga asked.

"Well, it could also be yours," Sa-rah said.

"But I don't have one. They never told me what it was."

Sa-rah chose this moment to pass out the cups of coffee and tea, "Well, in any case this is a very special moment, one that we all will always remember." When everyone had either tea or coffee depending on their preference, she moved around and offered the pastries.

"We should make a toast to little Indigo," Ollie said.

"Not until Abe gives him another name, a proud name. Please Abe," Helga said, reaching for his hand. Mattie continued her lulling melody and the baby remained asleep.

Abe cleared his throat, paused, and then started to speak. "This is almost too important for me to choose anything. It makes me wonder how anyone can ever choose a name for someone else. A name is something that has to last a lifetime."

"But once it's chosen, it will seem to be the right name for all time." It was Mattie speaking for the first time. "I know I didn't get to name my first couple of children and their names never seemed right for them, but the one I did get to name fit perfectly."

"What was it, Mattie?" Sa-rah asked.

"David, David Bentley. As long as he was with me, we called him Davy." She sniffed a little and said, "He was such a good baby. But let's not think about that now." The infant in her arms was stirring. "This little fella wants this name business to be done with so he can have something to eat, no matter what he gets called."

Helga looked up at Abe and just nodded. "Please think of something."

"All right," he said. "If it's all right, think it should be an American name because we're here helping settle the frontier. And for me it's important to bring together the two sides in the terrible War we've all been through, so what about 'Jefferson' for his second name? After Thomas Jefferson and Jefferson Davis. Two of my heroes."

At first no one said anything, and then Sa-rah smiled and clapped her hands together. "It sounds perfect to me."

Ollie raised his half-empty cup of coffee in the air and said, "I hereby offer this drink of honor to the boy to be known as Indigo Jefferson, and even though I'm not no minister, I think that will do it."

"Why Ollie," Mattie said, "that was wonderful, but what about God?"

"Oh He's here, don't you worry about him. And Helga, I'm sorry if I butted in."

"No that was fine. I just want Sa-rah to give him a blessing since she brought him into this world and helped me so much. Please Sa-rah."

"Well, I'll try. Let's all hold hands and bow our heads…Dear Father in Heaven, we ask your blessing on this child, this new life who shall be known as Indigo Jefferson, and on all his deeds. Protect him and guide him and may he be healthy and strong, bright and shining with Your spirit showing through him all the days of his life. In our Lord's Name, Amen."

"Thank you." Helga said and then reached out for her son. "Time for him to eat now." She stood weakly and as she started to step toward the privacy of her own room, Abe put his arm around her and helped.

Three days later, Ollie's foot was blown off in an accident with explosives when he was at work on the new road. Mike Skinner rode over to find Abe. He explained what he knew, but it wasn't really clear, just a terrible accident. Ollie was now in the small medical facility in Silver City and the doctor was trying to save as much of his leg as possible. Mattie was beside herself with grief. They were hoping to get Ollie home as soon as possible, but they would need to borrow the buggy.

"Of course you can. Maybe I should come along. Just in case there's need for some extra help," Abe said.

"That would be good, if you can," Mike replied. "I'll come back for you and the buggy as soon as we get definite word. Maybe if it weren't too much trouble, Sarah Beth could ride over and sit with Mattie for a bit."

"I'll tell her right away."

Skinner climbed back on his horse and rode off. Abe walked slowly toward the house. He was thinking how hard this would be on Mattie, and because of that on Sa-rah as well. He wished he didn't have to tell her, especially since he didn't know any of the details.

"Sa-rah," he called from the porch. "Could you please come out here?"

She came and he took her in his arms. She looked up at him questioning, "What is it?"

He finally spoke, saying, "Ollie's been hurt. Accident with the explosives. He may have lost his foot."

"My God, how, oh this is terrible, how?" She stepped back from him, shaking her head.

"I don't know any more than that. Mike was just here with the news and that's all he could say. He asked to use the buggy and said he'd come back when they got told they come after him. He's in that little hospital place in Silver City."

Sa-rah was crying and still shaking her head, "No, no, no...but I have to go to Mattie. This will be so hard for her. Finally some happiness and now this. Oh, Abe, ever since father died, and until she and Ollie got together, she's been so sad."

"I guess I hadn't noticed."

"Well, she loved being here with us and was getting used to the country, but she wasn't very happy and she was so lonely. One time she told me, 'You all have somebody, even if you have to share. I don't.' That's what she said, and now this."

"Do you want to go to her now?"

"Of course. Can you saddle my horse, or should I take the buggy to them?"

"If you take the buggy and they take it, how will you get home?"

"It doesn't matter. I'll just ride." She turned and went quickly into the house. She was still crying and nearly pushed Helga out of the way at the doorway.

"What's wrong with her?" Helga asked.

"Ollie's been hurt. On the job where he's working. Mike said his foot got blown off."

"Oh my God." She sat slowly down on a chair. "He was just here, with the baby and getting its name. I was thinking of him as the godfather. He gave us the name."

"I know. This is going to be hard on everyone, but especially Mattie."

"Oh, poor Mattie." Indigo began crying so Helga covered up and gave him her breast. "What can we do to help?"

"Mike asked for the buggy when they go to pick him up. I might go along to see if they need any help getting him home, and Sarah, I mean Sa-rah, may go along because of Mattie. Do you think you could stay here by yourself? It might be overnight."

"I won't be by myself, you know. There's two of me now. But I'd be fine."

When they picked Ollie up, he was sedated with opiates, but seemed to be in fairly good spirits, considering the seriousness of his accident.

"Same as my hand," he said. "Couldn't find nothing of the foot either. Smithereens!"

"Ollie, Ollie, Ollie, oh my poor man," Mattie was kneeling by the side of the low bed he was lying in. "You'll be all right, I know you will, we'll be all right, we will."

He reached out for her and brought her head to his chest. "Sure we will. Not like it hasn't happened before. "Hey Mike, life's expensive, didn't you say that once? But I'm getting off cheap, only a hand and a foot—it's not costing me a whole arm and a leg." He laughed hard, but then winced from the jarring motion.

The doctor came in and gave some medicinals and instructions to Mike. He said that it would be couple of weeks before the dressings could be removed completely, although they should be changed every few days, especially if the wound was draining any.

"Always wondered why they called you fellas 'sawbones.' Guess I know now," Ollie laughed, and then went on, "Seriously, Doc, I appreciate what you done. Come and see me out on the ranch if you care to."

"Sir, it would be a pleasure to get to know you better. Some of the things you mentioned while I had you unconscious were pretty interesting, not to mention the colorful language."

"Colorful! You hear that Mattie? I can talk colored." He started to try and get up.

Mattie took him by the arm, "Shush, you crazy man. Now lie there and behave or we'll leave you here and you can hop home when you're ready. Won't we, Mike?" She sounded harsh, but was looking at him with all of the tenderness of her heart and the relief she was feeling now that she'd found him to be alive and growing stronger.

Abe had been quietly standing in the background, with Sa-rah by his side. When the doctor pointed to a stretcher leaning against the wall, he reached for it and opened it on the floor beside the bed. It was of military issue and he was familiar with its workings.

"Come on now, partner. You're going to have to help us get you onto this thing and then hold still while we carry you out to the buggy. Mattie you walk along one side, and Sa-rah the other. When we get to the buggy, we'll have to all lift together to get him up and over the back. All right, let's lift."

As they picked up the stretcher and jostled it to get better grips, Ollie groaned and then waved his good hand, "Onward, my hearties. Into the breach, whatever that is..."

CHAPTER 8

Another One

Sa-rah awoke with joy. The dream she was remembering was of a family reunion where there were dozens of people attending, and most of them were related and descendants of Abe and herself. It wasn't clear to her if it was the Dreamer type of dream that meant it would have some impact on herself and others, but it was enough to give her great feelings of happiness. As the day went on, she realized that she was becoming less anxious, both about the prospect of her own childlessness, and about the role of Helga and Indigo in their lives.

The boy was two years old now, and growing fast into a strong and somewhat wild child. His hair had come in reddish-brown and was quite thick and bushy. Sa-rah would have trimmed it by now, but Helga seemed to like it the way it was. During the time the boy was nursing, and learning to walk and talk, there was little tension between herself and the younger woman. In some ways, having the boy as her main responsibility and full-time companion made Helga less dependent on Abe and abler to be her own person. Though this did not result in Sa-rah getting more time and attention from Abe, it did make her less concerned about the future and about the way things were working out for the three of them.

She had finished her special treatments with Moon Fish just after the baby was born. There was no guarantee that it was working to make her more fertile, but she did feel stronger, her female rhythms were more regular, and the pains she had felt before lessened and were more tolerable. Both things were signs that the older woman said were associated with the work they'd been doing for her. Moon Fish had gone through a rather serious illness, of unknown causes. She had not come to their shared land with Hawk Man either of the past two summers, as it would have been too hard for her to travel. So Sa-rah had visited her village twice during that past year, and she kept hoping to have one of those powerful dreams, about the woman and her illness, and possibly be given a cure. So far there were none.

Abe's herd was growing and seemed to thrive in this country. Since there were no other landowners to the west of their place, he'd been able to expand the range for his animals and even required a young helper at certain times of the year. When Carl was around, he provided the needed assistance, but if he wasn't, there was a young fellow on the road to town whose parents had settled there soon after Abe and his family had arrived in the valley. His name was Edward and he was already planning to build his own herd and was eager to learn everything he could from Abe and any other ranchers.

When Ollie was able to move around on his crutches and had gained most of his strength back, he and Mattie took an extended trip back to Pennsylvania and Virginia. Sa-rah was concerned for them being a mixed race couple, but Mattie dismissed the issue by saying that Ollie would just have to be dressed as a wealthy man and she would be happy to act as his maid and nurse. Before they left on their journey they put on a little show for the rest of their folks in which they acted out these roles. The comedy involved in the two of them falling over each other to be completely different toward one another than they usually were. This provided a great evening of fun for their two families, following a wonderful send-off dinner prepared by Martha and Sa-rah, with help from Helga.

One thing that made their trip more feasible and gave Ollie the confidence to attempt it was the device Mike created to substitute for his missing foot. It had a built-in boot and hardly resembled one of the usual prostheses that so many veterans of the War were using. Ollie simply had to strap the device on just below his knee and he was ready to go. "Never did like tying damn laces with only one hand," he said. "Now there's just one boot to tie up, and I've got two different set-ups."

Mike was going to take them to the stage stop in Silver City on his wagon. He was making a quick trip for more metal for his latest project, some railings for a church being built not too far away. Just before they were loading themselves onto the wagon, Ollie took Abe aside for a short conversation.

"You know, I haven't brought it up because I couldn't do anything about it. But by the time I get back here, I should be able to ride and climb hills, so I wonder if you're still going to have that talk with the Indian." He gestured down the valley toward the hillside behind Abe's house where the water supply was located.

"No, I haven't. But I'll bring it up if it doesn't seem out of line."

"That's all I'm asking."

"You've heard about the killings up north when the miners tried to kick the Indians off their land, haven't you?"

"Yeah, I did, but we're not that kind. Just want a little bit of it for important things. Making it easier on the women and all."

"I'll see what I can find out. Don't want to appear impatient."

"Yeah," Ollie said, putting his arm around Abe's shoulders, "not waiting any longer than two years for an answer might seem a little impatient, I guess," he laughed, "to an Indian."

They walked to the wagon and everyone said their goodbyes, waving as they moved on down the road.

"This baby is going to miss his Grandma Mattie, that's for sure." Helga set the boy down and watched as he tried to run after a chicken in the yard. "I only hope they don't decide to stay back there."

"I don't think there's any chance of that. Do you, Abe?" Sa-rah asked.

"No, from what I've heard both of them say, getting their own place out here somewhere is what they want. And it won't have to be a big place either. They're both getting along in years to where they won't be doing too much hard work."

"I hope they don't find a place too far away," Sa-rah said.

Helga had been listening while staying close to little Indigo. "Maybe we should start looking for something while they're gone."

"Not a bad idea," he paused. "But right now, if it's all right with the two of you, I want to scout some land out further than I've had the cows up until now. And I might stay out there overnight."

Sa-rah tossed her hair and went up the steps to the house, "Good, we'll have a girls' night with our baby boy here."

It was still snowing in April and the cows were wandering further and further from the home place. There was no point in trying to herd them back, they would just leave again, but Abe was worried about hungry wolves and possibly Indians just as hungry. He thought of having the young man, Edwin, stay out with them, but it wasn't something he thought he could ask. Then one day Edwin himself suggested it.

"I could stay out there for a few days at a time, then come back for supplies. I think I'd like that. Besides, I'd be learning about the habits of the cows and how they take care of themselves."

"But you would also be with them?" Abe asked.

"Oh yes, but they wouldn't have to know I was around, except at night when I'd be close to them."

"Well, I suppose we can try it. See how you like it. But there's no way I can pay you anything much for all that time."

"Can you pay me with a cow sometime?"

"That I can do."

"All right, then it's a deal." The young man stuck out his hand and shook with Abe. "I'll be back in the morning, ready to go."

The arrangement they made was that Edwin would report back in to Abe every fourth day, spend a night at his parents' place, and then head out again the next day. In the meantime, Abe would have time to build a set of corrals for sorting and holding cattle, for branding if that became necessary, and for doctoring sick animals. He was thinking of using the kind of arrangement he'd seen back in Wyoming at old man Bradford's place when he'd had to replace an ox on the trail. That thought led him to wonder how those folks were getting along. When he met them, they certainly seemed to know what they were doing, and to be doing well enough with the income from selling both to the Army and the wagon trains. Now that the emigrant trains were no longer moving like they used to, with more and more freight traveling by train, they must have found some other ways to make their living.

As far as Abe being able to make a living, he and Sa-rah were both aware that the income they'd received from her father was dwindling and wouldn't be around that much longer. He figured that it would be another two years with the cattle before he would have enough to make a useful contribution to their expenses. Helga would occasionally bring in some small amounts for her quilts, but with the baby she didn't have much time for that. Sa-rah worried about these things more than the other two, but she herself didn't have any income to add to the family's needs.

So once again he found himself thinking about Ollie's discovery, wondering just how much reality there was to it, and whether or not it was a real "find" that could be tapped into for some time. Neither Hawk Man nor Lefty had mentioned it when they were on the land the past summer, and Abe didn't feel comfortable about bringing it up himself. As he'd told Ollie, the conflicts going on up north seemed to be directed more toward the invasive miners than against settlers or ranchers. As far as he knew, this area had been peaceful, with the exception of fights between some of the whites themselves over property claims. Hopefully none of the trouble in the Wallowas was headed their way.

With May came a burst of grass growth accompanying the warming and lengthening of the days. Sunrises came early and golden, and the sun's setting often brought with it rosy-pinks and long fingers of clouds stretching toward them from the west, then disappearing overnight. It had been over a month since they'd seen any rain, but the ground still held moisture from the late snows, and the creeks ran full from melting at higher elevations. Birdsongs filled the air at certain times of day, and their horses seemed frisky and full of energy, as if looking for some work to do.

During the past winter, Abe had built a sled for Indigo. The boy could pull it himself if the snow wasn't too deep. The success of this project gave him the idea to work on a small child-drawn cart for when spring came, and he did have it ready about the time little Indigo began to really run. Abe showed him the buggy and how the horses were hooked up to it, and then the small cart and how the boy could be harnessed into its staves. The first time the youngster tried to pull it, he got tangled up and took a fall, and screamed loudly, which brought both his mother and Sa-rah rushing outside.

Abe picked him up and checked him over. He found no cuts or scrapes, and the boy was immediately ready to try again. This time, to the applause of the women and the cheers of his father, he made a complete circuit of the flat area between the house and the stable. Then he undid the harnessing and climbed into the cart and began calling for his Da-da to pull him around. Helga and Sa-rah clapped loudly, and went back in to their kitchen work, and Abe played at being the horse for a good long time. Finally, he pulled to a stop by the bench beneath the one tree in their slowly developing yard. This was his favorite and most restful spot for just sitting and looking out across the land, or for trying to think out some problem or other. As he rested, he watched as Indigo began gathering up sticks and loading them into the cart. The boy then pulled it over to the house where a remnant pile of the past winter's wood lay scattered about. He was all business as he unloaded his cargo and then yelled back to his father.

"Da-da, me work. Like you."

Abe clapped his hands together, and gave a short cheer, thinking that this was the way things were supposed to work. No wonder he'd been so eager to have a child these past years. As he watched the boy bringing the cart back over to where he was sitting, he wondered if perhaps there was a way to train Happy to pull the cart with Indigo driving. What a sight that would make. Moments like these filled his heart with a kind of happiness he didn't remember from any other experience. It was similar to, but not the same, as the love he felt for Sa-rah in their first years, when they were crossing the country, before his involvement with Helga and the complexity it brought on. But now, here was all the benefit of that and the feelings that went with the boy's place in their lives. He knew he wouldn't trade this for anything in the world, no matter how difficult it made things sometimes.

Just then they both heard Helga calling from the porch. It was time for the boy's nap. Abe got up and went to take Indigo's hand and walk with him to his mother.

"I don't wanna nap, Mama.'

"Well, you need to, and Da-da has some other things to do, don't you?"

Abe nodded yes and lifted the boy up the steps. Then he reached out and took Helga's hand in his own and gave it a soft kiss. "See you both later."

One day Abe realized that Edwin, his young man, was overdue and he set out looking for him. It took half a day's ride to find the cattle, but there was no sign of his helper. He urged Cloud into a ground-eating lope and criss-crossed the grazing area, growing more concerned as he covered more and more of that end of the valley. Then quite some ways away in the shadow of the ridge, he saw a horse that nickered at the sight of them. It looked like Edwin's mount. Abe slapped his horse lightly and sent him running in that direction. When he got close to the other horse, he found it saddled and dragging its reins, tripping as it moved away from the strange rider and horse.

Abe pulled up and dismounted, walking slowly up on the other horse until he was able to grab one of the trailing reins. He tied it to a low-growing shrub and went back to Cloud. He scanned the hills on either side of the valley. Then he felt a sinking feeling in his belly as he saw four or five vultures circling above a gentle slope that climbed into a field of boulders. He led his horse in that direction and drew his rifle out of its scabbard. It could be a carcass that wolves were returning to, or any other kind of death, but he didn't want to take any chances. He drew close to the boulders, hunkered down behind one, and hollered out to who or what ever might be there.

"Halloo. Anyone, halloo!"

His yell was answered by a pistol shot, and he ducked even lower.

"Who is it there? Edwin, is that you?" He saw a piece of cloth on a stick rise above a rock some fifty yards away. He dropped Cloud's reins and stayed low as he circled around through the boulders until he was up behind where he'd seen the makeshift flag. He slowly stood up with his rifle ready and asked again "Edwin, is it you?"

The flag waved and Abe moved slowly toward it. After a few steps, he saw the form of a man curled up in the sparse shade of a scraggly juniper. The arm of the body was waving weakly in his direction. He hurried the last few steps, reached the twisted shape of the man, and recognized Edwin's face. Below the chin was a bloody rag the young man held against his neck. His pistol was held loosely in his other hand and he began shedding tears. No sound came from his throat, but his eyes were blinking fast and he dropped his gun and reached out for Abe's arm, drawing it toward the wound of his throat. He made a gasping sound, but still no words came out. Abe carefully removed the stained and smelly rag made of the young man's shirt, trying not to disturb the slashed tissue and start the bleeding again. It wasn't a deep wound, but it was swollen and Edwin's breathing was rasping and difficult.

Abe pulled his knife and cut a sleeve from his own shirt and wrapped it around the young man's neck. He put Edwin's hand back in place, holding the cloth, and stood. "I'll be right back, go get your horse, and take you home. Stay still."

Edwin managed to croak out the word "water," and Abe said, "We'll try some."

He hurried back to the young man's horse and led it as close as he could, tying it next to where Cloud still stood. Suddenly, he could smell a foul odor on the slight breeze. He didn't want to waste any time, but wanted to know what it was since that was most likely what the vultures were attracted to, and what had helped him find the young man among these rocks. He didn't have to go far to find the stinking pile of guts and cow hooves that were scattered among some of the rocks. He knew he couldn't take any more time to investigate and would have to wait for an explanation. He hurried back to Edwin with the canteen, holding it to his cracked lips and slowly dripping some of the water into his mouth. Abe wasn't sure this was such a good idea if the wound went very deep, but he also had no idea how long his helper had been without water.

He took the water away from Edwin's mouth, saying, "Not too much. More later." Then he tried to help him to stand. They slowly staggered toward the horses, with Abe struggling to support Edwin, and trying hard to keep from falling on the sharp rocks. They made it to the horses, stopped for a while to get their breathing to more normal. Abe then did his best to boost Edwin up until one foot found the stirrup. With more effort on his part and weak movements on the part of the young man, they managed to get him mounted and Abe lashed him into the saddle. He looked up to see if there was any sign of bleeding coming through the bandage and was relieved to see none. He took hold of the horse's reins and led it slowly down onto the flat land below where he'd found the hurt man. He caught Cloud, mounted, and the two horses began walking back toward the home-site. The breeze increased and a few clouds were forming to the north. Perhaps it would rain later, but it wasn't likely to come before they reached shelter, even at such a slow pace.

When they reached the house Abe hollered for help and Helga appeared right away. Together they carefully lifted the semi-conscious young man down off his horse, but it was hard to do without some jarring and groaning. Helga was silent while Abe helped Edwin up the few steps and eased him into the house. They had come in the back door so he could be settled into the kitchen and given some kind of treatment. Abe was still completely unsure as to how serious the wound was and what its effects were.

Helga, who'd been patiently silent, finally spoke up softly, "Abe, what? What happened to him? Is he all right? Can we do something? What do you need? Hot water? What?"

"Whoa, slow down. Yes to the hot water and clean cloths. I don't know what happened. Even when he's mostly conscious, he can't speak. If he hadn't had his pistol, I might not have found him. And now that I think of it, I never saw his rifle...Here, help me pull off his boots, hopefully we can make him more comfortable. I don't want to lay him down yet. Once saw a man in the infirmary nearly choke to death, bleeding from a bullet in his neck. So get me some things to put under his feet, and another chair I can sit on when I uncover the cut."

Just then Sa-rah and Indigo came into the house, the boy immediately running up to his father to show off a small fish he'd just caught.

"Careful son, this man's hurt. Stay back."

"What happened Abe? It's Edwin!"

"I don't know. Slash on his neck, can't talk. I'm going to clean it up best I can without starting it to bleed, and then I think we need to get a doctor out here."

"Martha was a nurse, she told me she did emergency care. Should I ride for her to help?"

"Good, unless you know more about what to do here than me."

"I don't think so. I've never been at one of those emergency births. I'll go. Indigo, you stay out of your Papa's way. This is very serious here now. This man is hurt badly and he needs us to be quiet." She bent over Abe, looked at Edwin's pale and contorted face, then turned away. She gave Abe a quick caress, and said, "I'll be back as soon as possible."

Abe heard her voice, but not her words as she said something to Helga on her way out of the house. He was slowly loosening Edwin's grip on the shirt-sleeve and trying not to disturb anything else. Just then Helga brought heated water and a soaked piece of cloth. He used it to soften the stuck shirt-sleeve for removal. What was revealed was a deep cut about four inches long that went from the back of the jaw down to near the middle of the throat. Raw flesh showed beneath the slashed skin. From what Abe could see, nothing vital was sliced or chopped away.

The young man woke suddenly when Abe tried to soften and wipe the caked blood away. He touched Abe's hand and then let him go on with it. He moaned s little, but held very still. Helga hovered nearby and kept more clean cloths ready.

"I wish I'd learned how to sew wounds like this," Abe said. "I think that's about all a doctor could do now."

"If we can wait until Martha gets here, she may know what else we could do, and maybe I can do the stitching. I'm pretty good with quilts, but I've never done anything like this before."

"We'd need some very thin, strong thread."

"We've got that cat gut fishing line you brought home for Indigo. It might work."

"Have you got a thin curved needle?"

"I'll go get what I have. You can see. Maybe Martha will think to bring something."

She handed him another fresh cloth and hurried to her own part of the house. She was quickly back with her sewing kit, selecting two needles from it. "I'll get the fishing line too and maybe we should boil all of this."

"I just wish we had a sedative for him. Whatever we do is really going to hurt and we can't let him struggle if we try to go through with this."

"Mattie told me once that she had some kind of opiate for when she got those terrible headaches. Maybe she left some here. She did leave some things in case we needed them, herbs and whatever."

"Well, look if you can, there's not really anything we can do until they get back. Where's Indigo?"

"Oh, thanks. I better look after him for a minute. He was in the chicken yard."

Edwin was unconscious again, but this time it seemed more like he was sleeping than the paleness, sweat, and fluttering eyelids of before. Abe seriously wished the young man could talk to say what had happened.

When Martha arrived she helped rinse the area with an alcohol solution, and then, working with Abe to hold Edwin steady and still, they were able to assist Helga while she inserted several stitches to bring the two sides of the wound together. Part way through the process, Abe noticed that the young man had bitten his lower lip hard enough to cause some bleeding. He reached in his pocket and brought out a small piece of wood he'd been carving on for Indigo, and stuck it in Edwin's mouth. There was an instant grinding sound.

A week went by before they were able to move Edwin to his parents' ranch in the buggy, and although the ride was hard on him, he was able to communicate that was what he wanted. He still couldn't talk, but by means of hand-signs and short written notes, he was able to let Abe know that he'd come on a small group of Indians butchering out a cow. When he tried to run them off, a man mounted on horseback was able to knock him from his horse. Another Indian got his rifle and another cut his throat. He'd used his pistol to run them off. It turned out later on when he could speak again and describe what all occurred, that none of them seemed to know how to make his rifle work, and didn't know he had the pistol until he'd acted dead from the throat wound, and then shot one of them in the belly. They'd ridden away as fast as they could, taking their wounded companion with them. The assailants also left most of the dead cow's carcass, which the wolves finished off over the next two nights, filling their bellies and perhaps not even noticing Edwin hunkered down behind the boulders.

When Abe visited him at home a week later, there was no sign of infection. He drove the young man to town and was gratified when the doctor said that their treatment, and Helga's sewing job, was as good as what he himself could have accomplished.

In the meantime, Abe gathered the cattle and brought the herd closer to the house. This meant that each day he needed to herd them further away for forage, guard them for a while, and then take a chance that something might happen while he went back to take care of other chores. Helga and Sa-rah worried for his safety, but he assured them that he stayed out in the open and took no chances. Sa-rah even offered to ride with him if he would let her, but he said it wasn't necessary, and she was too valuable tending the garden and helping Helga with the child.

One day there was a problem with their water supply. It was dirty and running slowly, barely enough to fill the washtubs for laundry. Abe climbed up toward the pool and the spring and found a small tree somehow uprooted in the damp ground around the pond, and fallen across the trough, plugging it and backing it up. The water flowing past the obstruction was filled with dirt and small pebbles. He went back for a saw and other tools, and was almost to the house when he caught sight of black painted buggy with a white canvas top. He'd never seen it before and was immediately curious as to its owners and their business.

He approached the house slowly, from the back side, and stopped when he could make out voices around the corner. He thought he could recognize the man's voice, but a woman was speaking so softly he couldn't make out who it was or what she was saying. Sa-rah laughed at something that was said, so he showed himself. The people in the yard were the doctor from town and a woman he'd never seen.

Abe tipped his hat and walked toward the small group consisting of the visitors, Sa-rah and Helga. He didn't see the boy anywhere, but maybe it was naptime. "Hello," he said. "How are you?"

"Doing well, Mr. Saunders. I have a new assistant. Miss Carla Watkins. I thought I'd show her some of the country. Never been out this far myself."

"Well, welcome. It's getting hot, but we've got some chairs around to the side of the house where it's shaded this time of day."

"I'll get something cool for us to drink," Sa-rah said on her way into the house.

"I was just telling this lady here," he smiled at Helga, "that I learned something from her stitchery on the young man. I'd never seen quite that technique of overlapping and knotting before, certainly not in a medical situation. But it surely did the job. Matter of fact, when the young man came back to have them removed, I was nearly unable to loosen the stitches enough to cut the threads loose. And that was strong thread, wasn't it?"

Helga hung back and was looking down most of the time the man was talking. "It was for fishing with," she said quietly.

"Well, perhaps I'll have to get myself some of that. We get some pretty serious gunshot wounds out in these parts, and it might work better than what I get from back east."

Abe noticed that this man was more talkative than most westerners he'd met, and wondered what the doctor's background was. More than that, though, he was curious about the silent woman who remained standing next to Helga while the others took chairs, leaving two unoccupied.

"You're welcome to sit," he said to the woman.

"That's all right. This suits me, and my new friend here is also standing."

Helga smiled at her and said, "I'll be right back. Should help Sa-rah bring out the drinks."

Abe couldn't remember the doctor's name, but thought it might seem rude to ask, so he smiled and just said, "Where did you come to these wild parts from?"

"Connecticut. When I finished my medical training, I had a yearning to see the wide open spaces as they were called back there. Found this place almost by accident and didn't see any reason to leave. The only thing missing for me out here were an assistant and a wife." He reached his hand out toward Miss Watkins, and she smiled as she took it in her own. "Might have found them both in one package with this lovely lady."

Miss Watkins spoke up, "He doesn't know what he's in for if that's his plan."

Sa-rah and Helga returned with a small serving table, a pitcher of tea, and glasses. "I'm sorry we don't have a way to chill our drinks. I keep the tea in the little creek, but that's not like the iced drinks I've had in town."

"I'm sure this will be just fine," the doctor said, raising his glass and saying, "May our acquaintance deepen with time and with the blessings coming to this household." He took a large swallow and set his glass on the small table. "Well Mrs. Sa-rah, have you let him in on it yet?"

"No, no, this isn't the time for that." She seemed flustered and blushed.

"Well, well, I see. I'll just say that your neighbor down this road told myself and Miss Watkins that you're an excellent midwife. We can quite possibly use your help in that field. Carla here is also a midwife and will be taking on most of that responsibility in the Silver City area. Perhaps even as far out of town as your place here at the end of the road, should that be needed." He smiled and emptied his glass. "Well, thank you all for your gracious hospitality. I suppose we'd best be heading back now if we're going to arrive by dark. You have a wonderful place here. Best wishes." He stood and offered his hand to Abe. The two men shook and then walked toward the buggy, followed by the womenfolk.

When they were gone, Abe returned to his work on the water system and got it clean flowing well again. When he finished, he climbed the rest of the way up to where the spring came out of the rock wall and formed the collecting pond. Everything seemed in order in that part of the system and he sat for a while to rest and think about the meaning of what was located here. The temptation to use the gold to make their lives more secure, as well as for Mattie and the newly wounded Ollie, was strong and made a certain kind of sense. What was also strong in him was the fear of the possibilities the gold could unleash. Lefty's story of the bloodshed further north when gold was discovered, or thought to be discovered, on Indian land, was enough to make him want to avoid all of the consequences of their discovery, both the good and the bad. The only thing that made sense at this point was just to continue waiting until Hawk Man and the others gave some kind of direction or made some decisions that he and his family would have to follow. He watched the sun sinking lower in the west, and the peaceful sound of the slow running water as it splashed into the small reservoir seemed an invitation for him to stay and accept the gift of the peacefulness of this place. He stood up, shook off that feeling and headed down to the family.

Early in the month of June when the fields were filled with dots of color from the thousands of blooming wildflowers, Edwin came to visit and to thank the family for, as he put it, saving his life. Or, as Abe replied, they owed him for risking his life. He brought with him a rope and cattle halter in expectation that if he hadn't earned the cow promised him for his work, he was ready to take it back to his parents' ranch and either work off or pay for the balance. Abe assured him that the debt was paid in full and he could even have his choice, although he recommended one that hadn't calved yet, if the young man could take his time moving her to where he wanted her to end up. Helga was the one who noticed the bandana around Edwin's neck and asked if he was hiding the scar or just being careful to keep it protected.

"It's pretty well healed up now, thanks to you. Want to have a look?"

"I would," she said.

He carefully removed the scarf and folded down his collar. The gash had left a long white line in the otherwise darker area of his neck. As Helga leaned over to look closely, he chuckled and said he was hoping she'd signed her work like an artist would, but didn't see anything like that. She laughed and said it would have taken too long and he was hard enough to hold down as it was. Abe agreed and reminded him of the carved stick that he'd chewed to sawdust.

When he and the young man had picked out a pregnant cow and gotten her adjusted to being led by a rope, they stopped once more by the house. Sa-rah came out onto the porch.

"You're looking a lot better than the last time I saw you," she said.

"Thanks, ma'am. I feel a lot better."

"Well, thank you for what you did for us. We haven't seen any sign of those Indian rustlers, you must have put quite a fear into them."

"Well, here's hoping they stay away. Good day, then. I'd best move myself and Bossie here along toward her new home."

"Take care of yourself, and come back any time. We'd be glad to see you, and feed you." She turned and went back inside.

Abe said he had only one question, and that was whether anyone in town asked him about the incident, not just casually, but from an investigative kind of way.

"No sir, the sheriff asked me if I was going to go after them, and did I want help, but other than that, there was nothing beyond a little curiosity about what happened. By the time I could talk again, it seemed pretty much forgotten."

"Well, I'd appreciate it if you'd let me know if you get any kind of official inquiries."

"I surely will. And thanks for the cow and saving me. I don't think I'd have lasted much longer if you hadn't showed up," he said, mounting his horse.

"Nothing you wouldn't have done for me in the same fix," Abe said as he reached up and shook the young man's hand.

Not long after that Sa-rah and Helga took a trip to town, leaving Indigo and Abe to take care of things. "Now you two be sure and bring in the laundry if there's a thunderstorm."

"We will, won't we boy?"

The women rode away in the buggy, planning to fill it with supplies for preserving. Abe set off for the corral to get hold of Ginger and set her up for a riding lesson for the boy. His first.

"Come along, son. Best we do this while the ladies are gone. You on a horse might worry them a bit."

"Da-da, can I have my horse for me?"

"You mean your own horse?"

"Yes, yes, my horsie."

"We'll see about that, maybe not yet, but certainly someday."

The boy gave a shout and ran on ahead to the corral, climbing the fence to perch on the topmost rail.

The riding lesson went well and when they finished, Abe gave the boy high praise, "Son, you're a natural."

"Papa, what's a natch-ral?"

Abe laughed and said, "It means you ride like you already know how, like you were born knowing how."

"Was I born here?"

"Yes, you were. Right in your Mom's bed."

"Then I'm a natch-ral here 'cause I was born here."

"That's right. And don't ever forget it."

Chased by the dog, Happy, the boy ran off and jumped into the swing Abe had made for him only recently.

When the women came home the next day, they were all smiles and laughter when they saw Abe and the boy.

"And how did the two of you get along without us to take care of you?" Sa-rah asked even before she climbed down from the buggy seat.

"We did just fine, didn't we boy?" he said as he handed Indigo up to Helga.

Later that evening when they'd finished their hastily-made supper, Sa-rah and Helga kept exchanging looks and making Abe more curious all the time. Finally, he just had to ask, "What is going on with the two of you?"

"Oh nothing," Helga answered first.

"That's right. Nothing out of the ordinary." Sa-rah said.

"Well it certainly seems out of the ordinary to me. Ever since you got home."

"Well, shall we tell him," Helga whispered loudly, "or make him wait?"

"I'll have to tell him, I suppose, but not until the time is right." With that, Sa-rah got up and cleared the dishes from their meal. Helga followed her to the kitchen, and Sa-rah came back in alone. She eased Abe's chair back from the table and then sat on his lap with her arms around his neck. She kissed him and then began laughing again.

Abe couldn't help being a little perturbed, and started to push her away. "I really don't know what's going on with you, and I'm not sure I even like it."

"Abe," she said, "we have two items of news to share with you. So settle back and I'll try to let you in on our secret, but first of all we got a letter from Mattie."

"Oh, great. How are they doing?"

"She and Ollie are both doing well, having a very nice time, but they both say they're missing us and this place so much. Mattie quoted some of Ollie's comments on the 'stinking cities and their rude citizens,' and she said she wouldn't provide accurate quotations because the language he used was so coarse. Her words."

"So they're coming back. Did they say when?"

"As soon as Ollie's new leg is ready. They have a new way of making them and he's apparently quite excited about it."

"Good…And the other item?"

"I don't know whether or not to have Helga come back in or not. It involves her as well."

Abe started bouncing her on his knees, saying, "Just tell me. Or I'll dump you off me."

"All right, all right." She paused and then went on, "Abe, we're going to have another baby. That's the news."

He threw up his hands, and smiled broadly, then a strange look came across his face. "We? You mean Helga?"

"No, no, no…You and me. We're going to have a baby, our own baby."

Abe pushed her off his lap and stood up quickly, then grabbed her around the waist and began spinning around the room, shouting, "Yes, Yes, YES!"

Helga appeared at the kitchen doorway, clapping her hands and chanting some nonsense words. Abe finally set Sa-rah down on her own two feet, and took her face in his hands. "How? And how do you know? Oh my." He sat back down in his chair. "Can't believe this. You two better not be fooling with me or I'll never speak to either of you again."

"It's true," Helga said. "Abe it's true. Isn't this wonderful?"

"Unbelievable. How do you know?

"I went to that doctor over a month ago, when we were in town and you went out to check on those cows in the stockyards. I knew you'd be busy for a while, so I took a chance and I told him I thought I might be. He just talks so much, I almost didn't get away in time to meet you when you got done, but I didn't want you to know until it was for sure."

"She didn't even tell me, so don't feel bad," Helga said softly.

"Then what?" Abe asked.

"Then when he got his new assistant, that Carla woman, I liked her immediately and felt I could trust her so I went to see her this morning before we left town. She is so nice, and she said it was one hundred and one per cent for sure. Oh, that's why we couldn't stop laughing. I am so happy, for you, for me, for this baby," she patted her midsection. "Now I'll finally get to know what it's all about. I'll get to feel everything."

Helga wiped off the table and then took off her apron, saying, "I think I better leave the two of you alone right now. Maybe you should take a nice long walk together."

Abe and Sa-rah hardly heard what she said as they just kept looking into one another's eyes. After a long moment, they did get up, go out, and take a walk as the moon was just rising over the valley.

Part III

JOURNEYS

1874

CHAPTER 9

News

The new baby turned a year old on New Year's Day 1874. They named him Isaiah because Abe felt that it would be strange if parents named Abraham and Sarah had a child named Isaac, but he really wanted to invoke the blessedness of the story behind those biblical ancestors with a name that at least suggested the connection. Isaiah, with its first initial and second letter being the same, served the purpose.

Abe was pleased that, coincidentally, Helga's choice of Indigo gave him the same first initial as both Isaiah and the biblical Abraham's sons. At age four, Indigo was growing into a strong boy who always wanted to be outdoors, regardless of the weather. He had become a competent fisher, and was learning to hunt birds with a slingshot and a bow and arrow that Lefty made for him. Abe was often confronted with the need to impress on the boy that hunting should be limited to the purposes of food and protection from predators. Although Abe and his son hardly ever argued, the youngster did resort to reactions of silence and what Sa-rah referred to as his "sulking" ways. He would leave the family home for hours at a time when he felt he'd been wrongly disciplined. In these instances, it never took too long for him to either get hungry or forget the source of his injured feelings and return home.

Isaiah, on the other hand, was a quiet and even-tempered infant. Sometimes Sa-rah worried that the boy seemed too quiet and calm to be normal, and that maybe there was something wrong with him. Abe usually replied that she should be happy for this and not worry about something that was a kind of gift both from the baby and from God.

As for his own worries, Abe was mostly concerned about the relationship within their family, between Helga and Sa-rah, and between the two boys. There were times when hard work or severe weather seemed to increase the stress on the two women and separately they might each complain that the other was possessive, either of the space within the house or of Abe himself. Fortunately for him, Mattie was a regular visitor—when one of his two partners was upset, they were able to express their frustration or anger to a usually neutral and understanding woman they both knew they could trust.

Ollie had become amazingly mobile on his replacement leg and spent as much time helping Abe with maintenance around their place as he did at the Skinner place, where he and Mattie lived. He'd received a monetary settlement because he'd been working on a government contract when the explosion caused his injury. It was determined that the cause was a faulty mixture of chemicals in the explosive itself and the authorities forced the manufacturer to pay compensation. This financial windfall eased his short-terms worries about supporting Mattie and himself, and he only mentioned the gold issue once, right after they returned from the east. Abe's answer, that there'd been no messages or comments from the Indians, seemed to satisfy him, at least for the time being. He didn't think he was able to make the climb now as it was. Perhaps when Abe improved the rough trail.

Sa-rah was as happy as she could ever imagine herself being. Now all the waiting and trying seemed to have been nothing more than a prelude to this fulfillment of their dreams and prayers. She was even inspired to begin creating a song of praise and thanks for this happiness. Her only problems were the ones that had been there since she first brought Helga and Abe together. Though this caused difficulty and tension in the household at times, she hoped they could grow used to it. The only new source of worry was the difference in size and age between the two little boys. Twice Sa-rah had reprimanded Indigo for being too rough with his little brother, and the second time it was serious enough that she spoke to Helga, asking to help make sure it didn't happen again. Of course she knew it would, but it just meant being more watchful and aware of the possibility. On the other hand, the older boy was quite enamored with the baby and spent a lot of time playing gently and happily with him on the big bear rug in front of the fireplace.

Three weeks after the New Year and the little birthday party they had for Isaiah, a blizzard hit hard. When the snow finally stopped falling, the wind worked to build countless drifts across the lowland portion of their valley. As soon as he could move around on horseback, Abe was working all day and awake almost all night, searching for his cattle and trying to herd them up into sheltered areas and draws among the low ridges that formed the borders of their ranch's useful land. He was relieved that the storm came before any calves were born. Even so, the deep drifts and freezing weather were hard on the pregnant cows that made up most of his herd.

He had heard no news from Lefty or any of the rest of the Hawk Man group and it was hard wondering what might be happening in the ongoing conflicts up north. He could only hope for the best for his friends, and wait for some kind of news. The thing that bothered him the most was the insecure basis on which he and his family were occupying the land. Although this arrangement was worked out with the full knowledge and cooperation of the regional Indian Agent, he could be gone tomorrow or replaced any day. Also, the raiding parties could return at any time.

Edwin was married now to a neighbor girl, and he still worked for Abe on occasion. They were trying hard to build up their herds to be in position to take advantage of the emerging markets to the east. It was rumored that a spur of the railroad was to be built that would connect the main line of the Union Pacific and its transporting capabilities to the country along the Snake River, and that Boise might even become a livestock hub. Even if that didn't happen, the new settlers coming into the territory would require larger and more productive cattle operations.

One early evening when the snow was mostly blown away and the trails and roads were opening up, a rider appeared with a message from Louis, Abe's cousin. The man was riding from New Mexico to the Washington territory. Abe welcomed the man, who said his name was "Samuel Burnett, call me Sam." He took the reins and led the horse over to the side of the stable, out of the wind. Sam pulled off his gear and hung the saddle on a railing, and then undid the bedroll and a small pack from the rigging. "Could use a night's rest if you didn't mind. This here would be fine, better than what I've been having." He gestured to the shop area where Abe did some blacksmithing and harness repair.

"If that's enough for you, you're welcome to it. It's warmed up some, but it's all right if you want to start up a fire in the forge there. First, though, let's get you some supper. It's about time for it."

"Appreciate that and won't turn you down."

"How's Louis doing?" Abe asked.

"He sent a letter to you. It's here in my pack." The man rummaged through the bag and came up with a waxed wrapper containing papers. He handed it to Abe. "If you don't mind, I'll just settle my horse, but I could use to buy some oats off you if you've got any."

"Tether him out by that boulder so he doesn't get tangled. The grain is in that barrel. Take what you need for tonight and I'll send some on with you when you go. You're a friend of Louis's, least I can do is put you up and send you off in good shape. Come to the house when you're ready."

Abe turned and went to the house, his mind turning over this development, coming out of nowhere. It'd been a long time since he'd heard from his cousin and he hurried in to read the letter. He sat down next to a lamp and opened the packet.

"Abe, we're about to eat. Are you ready?"

"Got a visitor. Some stranger Louis sent. Brought me a letter. I told him to come in for supper. Need an extra place at the table." He unfolded the two sheets of paper.

Dear Cuz,

Surprise. It's me. Haven't wrote to you. Been busy and lately I've been in a little hot water, you'd have to say. Maria and me moved down here to a border town where I got myself roped into being a deputy to the Sheriff. At least that's what I was for awhile. This here is one mean town. We're on the so-called USA side of the border and there's another town on the other side of the river. Two towns, but one just as evil as the other. I was sent out to arrest the son of a damn important fella in these parts. The son had taken up with a young woman who was already married and when he killed her husband, Sheriff sent me and some volunteers to bring him in. We caught up with him and he surrendered pretty quick like, but then he jumped me and grabbed my gun. I no more expected that cowardly kid to do that than for hell to freeze over, but we got to struggling and my so-called helpers just stood there until I had to kill the kid.

Turned out the sheriff was owing the father some big money and was only a lawman because that kid's Dad was backing him for it. They took away my badge and got those boys that was with me to say I didn't have to kill the kid, but did it anyway. Put me away in prison for two years. Maria went ahead and had our second baby, another sweet girl-child, before they put me away.

Well, here's what it is. They're going to release me here in a month, and they told me I best get gone quick because the kid's brother swore to get me once I'm on the loose again. Turns out that family has plenty of enemies around here and I've some boys that say they'll get me out of here safe, but once I'm past Santa Fe I best keep going north and don't look back. I trust them like I trust the man bringing you this message. But what I need from you is the biggest thing I could ever ask. I need you to meet me in Santa Fe where the federal marshal has guaranteed me a safe passage to the Utah territory border. Maybe you got some Mormon friends there can help us out. Cuz, my life isn't worth dirt around here and I never wanted to ask you for more than you've already done for me over and over again, but I got no one else. Maria doesn't want to come north again, but I try to keep telling her we don't have a choice. I will be in Santa Fe after the 15 of March. The marshal said he'd keep me in the jail until I could get out of town safe. Please come there and we'll make things even when I can help you out someday.

Your Cuz, Louis
p.s. You can trust the man who brings you this message. He's using the name Sam.

Abe sat still, then folded the letter and unfolded it to read it again. Sa-rah came into the room and stood beside him, placing her arm across his shoulders.

"What's that? And who's here?"

"It's a letter from Louis, brought by a man who's still outside at the stable. Says his name's Sam Burnett. Louis says to trust him."

"Strange to hear from Louis after all this time. Is he all right?"

"Hard to say. He's been in a bit of trouble. We'll talk about it later. I want to read it again before I can talk about it."

"All right, but now I'm very curious. Anyway, Helga went out to bring in some more wood. We wouldn't make it through the night with what we had inside."

"I'll go get some more, she shouldn't have to do it. I just got delayed by this visitor."

He put the letter away in a drawer of his desk and went back outside.

"Helga, that's enough for you. I'll get the rest."

"I don't mind. It's good for me once in a while."

"Well, you might have to be doing more of this. I might have to go away for a bit."

"What? At this time of year? Why? Where?"

"We'll talk about it later. Nothing's definite so don't get worried."

She turned and went toward the door of the house with a large armload of wood.

"And we have a visitor tonight. Someone who knows my cousin, Louis."

"Really. Any news?"

"We'll talk about it later."

After dinner and some conversation, Sam excused himself, and said, "I do appreciate a home cooked meal like this one. So good. Thank you. But I'm pretty beat from a couple of days of hard riding so I think I'll turn in and see you folks in the morning."

Abe stood to go out with him, and asked how early he'd have to be leaving.

"Not in so much of a hurry anymore. We are in Oregon, aren't we?"

"Yes, we are, sure are."

"I'll probably take a little time to rest that horse of mine, if you-all don't mind. I don't want to be a bother to you."

"That's fine," Abe said, letting the man out the door. "Got everything you need?"

"Sure do. Thanks again ladies."

Abe closed the door behind him and came back to sit at the table. Indigo and the baby were sleeping and for a long moment the only sound was the crackling of the fire.

"Tell us," Sa-rah said. "What's going on?"

"It's a bit confusing. Seems Louis was hired as a deputy marshal in some border town and got himself crosswise with a young man who was wanted for murder. The man took Louis by surprise and ended up dead. Turned out it was the son of the most powerful man around those parts, so they threw Louis in prison for a couple of years. Now he's getting out, but that family will be after him for revenge. Near as I can figure out my cousin has some kind of safe passage out of New Mexico, protection from the territorial marshal or whomever. But he has to get out while he can."

"What about Maria?" Sa-rah asked.

"She had another daughter and she doesn't want to come north again."

"Where is he now?"

"I'm not sure. Maybe in jail for his own safety until he can get on his way. Probably coming this way."

There was a long silence, and then Sa-rah said, "Well we can't have everyone we know coming here. We're lucky to be here ourselves."

"I realize that, Sa-rah. But he is my cousin and he might need to be somewhere for a short time until he can get himself settled."

Helga got up and began taking away the supper dishes. Sa-rah followed her to the kitchen. Abe pulled out the letter again, wondering what the two of them would have to say if he decided he had to ride to his cousin's assistance. He slowly read over the part with Louis's request, and decided to try and not think any more about it until he could talk to Sam, and find out how serious it was. If Louis's life really was at stake, he knew he'd have no choice but to make his family his priority, all of his family, all of it that was left.

He slept alone that night after being as honest with both women as he could without coming out saying exactly what might be necessary. He was awake before daylight, but not before this man Sam, who was sitting near a small fire in the forge with a hot pot of coffee.

"Travel equipped, I see."

"Can't get started so good without a cup of this black juice. Enough for two, but only got the one cup."

Abe pulled up a nail keg and sat across from the man. "It's all right. I'll make some soon enough inside. Louis said I should trust you. Care to tell me how you and him met?

"Prison. I was in for collecting some unbranded cattle running loose near the border. Not even sure which side they was on."

"How's that against the law?"

"Not against the law, against the Big Man in those parts. Same one as got Louis put up."

"Sounds like he pretty much runs that part of the country."

"Some say he's Mexican, some say he's an Englishman. Most folks just call him the Texican. Say he come from San Antonio after Independence back in the '30s. Had enough of a start-up to buy all the good land that had any water."

"And Louis had to get cross-wise with him?"

"I don't know much about how it came about, but I do know some about Louis. Him and somebody like that Senor Rojado just seem hell-bent to have to settle it between themselves, something's bound to happen."

Abe was quiet and then pulled a tin cup off the shelf, wiped it out with his shirtsleeve and said, "Might take a bit if you'll come on in and I can pay you back inside."

"Be all right."

"How's Louis now?"

"Restless as hell. I'm a bit worried about him being jailed for his own protection, not having any time of his own left to serve, not knowing how long. Helps a man get through it if he has some idea of his time and can at least count the days. Hope he don't crack under it."

"He asks me to come and kind of escort him away from there."

"He doesn't have anyone else. I can't go back to that territory. Jumped my parole. That's why I'm headed back to Montana. Hoping they'll take me back on."

"When would you have to be there for that?"

"Not 'till spring, but got nowhere else."

Abe stood up. "Women and kids ought to be up and at it by now. Let's go in and have that next cup of coffee. Oh, and let's not say anything about him wanting me to come after him, not yet at least."

Later that morning, Abe talked Sam into staying over at least another night and they saddled up and went out to check and move some of the cattle. When they found what Abe was looking for and herded that bunch up to higher ground where the sun had melted almost all of the snow, they took a break and dismounted near the top of a rise overlooking a good part of the shallow valley.

Abe had noticed the scar that ran across the man's head when he took off his hat to wipe some sweat that had formed in spite of the cool temperature. "Can't help notice that scar there. Close call for you."

"Yes sir, it was. But I was one of the lucky ones."

"War?"

"Yes, sir. Right near the end of it, too. Damn near died for nothing."

Abe flexed his elbow and said, "Got this one at Appomattox, last day of that fight."

Sam looked at Abe and then spoke slowly, "Don't know if I should say this, but hearing your talk makes me think you was Confederate side. Me, I'm Union. But you know what? From what I see, it don't make a goddamn bit of difference now. Nobody won, everybody lost."

"I won't disagree with you. Maybe that's why fellas like us end up out here."

"Could be."

They rode back to the home place. While they were turning out the horses, Abe asked the question that was on his mind, "Let's say I went after Louis. You look like you can handle cattle. Think I could get you to stay here and mind my stock and family while I was gone?"

"How long?"

"I don't know. How long would it take me to get there and back with him?"

"Probably three weeks hard riding down there, more coming back with his kids, if they was to come, and his wife."

"Once I got him into Utah, maybe I could come on back ahead."

"Could be."

"What about it?"

"Seems to me, you'd have to ask your woman, or women."

"I just feel like I've got to go."

Later that night, when Sam had gone back to the shed and Helga to bed, Abe told Sa-rah he needed to talk with her. She was nursing Isaiah and rocking gently in a the chair by the fire. He pulled up a stool and sat next to her.

"That's a handsome boy you've got there."

"Takes after his Papa, don't you think?"

"More likely his Mama."

"What do you need to talk about?"

"Louis is in trouble."

"I know. You said that, but what kind?"

"He had to kill someone in the line of duty as a deputy marshal. But that fella's family got him convicted of the killing. He did some prison time and got released, but his life is in danger from that family. He's holed up in jail under protection of the territorial marshal until he can get safe passage out of there."

"That man finds more ways to get himself in trouble. What does he want from you now?"

"Wants me to come get him and escort him out of New Mexico, with the marshal's help."

"Abe, you can't possibly go away, not now."

"I know…but I kind of have to. I can't let him die, or rot in jail to stay alive."

"Oh, of course, and what about us?"

"I talked to this man Sam. Louis said he's to be trusted and he doesn't have to be in Montana until late spring."

"And you'll just run off and leave two children and two women with a stranger." She stood up. "He's asleep now, and I will be soon. Sorry Abe, but you just sleep alone and think about how you have absolutely no sense of responsibility." She walked to her room mumbling, "I can't believe it, just can't believe him…"

In the week that followed, a false spring melted the remaining snow, the creeks filled with rushing brown water, and the sky turned the kind of blue that only pure moving air at high altitudes can give. Sam stayed on and was politely received by Sa-rah and Helga. Mattie came to visit and was curious about his past as a Union soldier, but he didn't want to talk much about that and turned the conversation back on her by asking questions about her experience as a slave. He showed himself to be a competent cattleman and took on a few responsibilities that freed Abe to work on an addition to the house, an indoor laundry and food storage area. Helga was non-committal about the idea of Abe going off after Louis, although she did say that she understood his feeling of obligation to family since she herself didn't have anyone like that and wished there was somebody she could call a relative.

Indigo was at a stage where he was demanding his own horse. Abe was giving him lessons in riding and caring for the other animals, but neither of the women thought the boy was ready to ride anywhere alone; they knew that once he had that opportunity there was no telling where his adventurous spirit would take him. Abe quietly assured Helga and Sa-rah that he would not give in to the boy's request until they could all agree that he would obey limits that they established as to where and when he could be gone from them.

Indigo's demands were motivated by the friendship he'd developed with a couple of the boys from Hawk Man's family who were only slightly older than himself and who were allowed to have, if not ownership of a horse, access to horses and the freedom to wander about as long as they returned to the camp by nightfall.

"Why Dada, and why not?" Indigo stamped his foot on the porch. "All my friends have their own horses."

"How many friends do you have, son?"

"Lots and lots, and they all have horses."

"Did you know I'm going to have to go away for a while?"

"Mama told me. She told me I'm going to have to help take care of everything. So I need a horse or I can't help."

"Sam is going to stay here with you all, and sometimes you can ride with him when he is doing the work with the cows."

"I should do cow work. I'm your son."

"You are my son and you can help with the cows, but it will take two of you sometimes, and I'm trusting you to be a good hand at this.

And when I get back we'll see about getting you a horse. But if I were you, I'd wait until Hawk Man returns this summer. He has the best horses—don't you think so? Now run and tell Sam I need to see him."

Abe had a long conversation with Sam about the route and possible problems on the way to Santa Fe. The day before he'd told Sa-rah and Helga that he had to go and go soon in order to be back in time for the late spring work of clearing rock from new pastures and beginning the construction of a real barn. Helga received the news silently and nodded her agreement with his plans. Sa-rah made what she knew was a futile protest and then quietly agreed that she understood he thought he had to do this, but that she didn't think it was that necessary "to always be jumping to Louis's rescue when he gets himself in trouble."

He set the date of his departure for one week. Sa-rah's last effort to change his plans was to urge him to take Edwin with him for safety and company. It was a good idea, but not practical since Abe knew the young man was in for a busy season ahead. His father was ill and, though recovering from what was supposed to be pneumonia, too weak to do his own work. Besides, Abe told her, this was the time the young man was seriously going to increase his own herd and begin filling contract orders from new settlers.

The day he left the sun was shining bright and what seemed to be the last clouds of the winter blew away east, leaving a nearly transparent sky and a very warm day. He was riding Cloud and leading Bird, who carried a small amount of packed goods. He was going to leave through Silver City and head toward Boise, turning off to take the most direct route south. That would take him first to Salt Lake and then east through the corner of the Colorado territory and into New Mexico. He hoped the trip south wouldn't take more than three weeks with good weather and the strength and good health of his horses.

The days went by in an uninterrupted fashion with the kind of weather that he would have asked for if he thought it ever made any difference to pray for any one type. He soon reached the vicinity of Salt Lake and passed around its rapidly expanding settlement, and then took a more easterly heading. He'd met several other travelers along the way and ridden with them for short distances and was feeling confident that he could reach Santa Fe in good time. The problem was how to transport Maria and the two children back this way. The more he thought about it, he decided it wasn't his problem. Outfitting Louis and his family with a wagon once they were out of the dangers of New Mexico would allow him to hurry on ahead and get back home much sooner than Louis. From the talk he'd been hearing along the way, the Indians of the sometimes risky western Colorado area were behaving. Travelers reported there was little danger, given the numbers of white folks and freight moving along these routes.

The horses were holding up well and some days they managed more than forty miles. His plan was to cut across Utah to the settlement of Grand Junction and then make his way south into the New Mexico territory. As he passed through northern Utah, he'd been concerned that some chance meeting with the Bishop's people could cause complications, but nothing like that happened. Matter of fact, he almost wished that he could have taken the time to drop by and visit the Judge who'd been so understanding and helpful when he and his small family escaped the Bishop's enclave.

Thinking about that whole experience just reinforced something he learned from Doctor Randall, Sa-rah's minister father. In explaining some of his conflicts within the hierarchy of his own church and its larger organization, he'd told Abe that there was never any doubt in his mind that the character of a man can remain unchanged even by his professed faith in God. He'd gone on to say that some of the most devout worshipers and ministers of the Word of God were also the most judgmental, intolerant, and dogmatic. He talked about the time his own congregants tried to censure him for praying for peace instead of asking God for victory over the Union forces in the War. Then again, after the War, when his denomination split over the issue of Negro preachers being consecrated in northern churches, he was finally driven out of the position he'd held for his daughter's entire life. Although he understood the passion such issues generated in the aftermath of the War, he still held to his own faith in a God of tolerance and justice, and was rewarded when he was accepted by a very open and compatible congregation in Missouri.

Abe's conclusion from these teachings and his father-in-law's experience confirmed his own instincts that carried him along with the diversity of human relationships he'd experienced as a youth, as a soldier, and as a husband and now a father. While he didn't fully believe in evil as a birthright of the human race, he was more comfortable with the idea that self-interest and a narrow allegiance to one's own family, community, or even nation was often the cause of what turned out to be quite "evil" behavior toward others who were different or from different places and walks of life. He was even now especially thankful for the experience he'd gained by being beholden to Hawk Man and his people. Though he could see in his Indian friends a somewhat less than noble or holy attitude toward all people, they were most often simply reacting to the treatment they were receiving from the immigrant, invading, newcomers. Of all the people he'd met in his life, three men stood out as both the best and the most real examples of human character. These were, of course, the Reverend Doctor Randall, Jefferson Davis, his wartime president, and Lefty the Indian who'd done so much for him.

Davis had appeared to Abe as a man whose anguish in the face of terrible responsibility for the death and mayhem of a losing cause often made him unapproachable and filled him with a stoicism that masked his deep despair. There was one incident when the President had called for Lieutenant Saunders, his young aide, and asked him to take a seat on a camp stool so he could speak with him.

"Son, I address you a representative of the generation whose lives and futures my own generation has foreclosed and perhaps completely ruined. And yet, I do not ask your forgiveness nor your approval. I only ask that when and if anyone ever asks you about that man, that failed leader you served in those terrible times, I only ask that you report that he knew what he was doing and he knew the costs of a struggle that could not be won, but that above all, he knew in his heart that no matter the cost to his people and himself, an honorable defeat was far better than any form of capitulation and a failure to resist the tyranny of man no matter where and when it exists." He'd stood then and placed one hand on the young man's shoulder. "Son, know this and perhaps this alone: when they hate me and they hate my name, when both the losers and the winners revile me; know that perhaps my only achievement was to prevent an even worse and more devastating cataclysm for the ideal of freedom. Go now, and God bless you."

As Abe rode along through the sagebrush emptiness of his easterly heading, these words and the quaking voice of a man at the edge of his emotional reserves echoed in his mind. And he thought that history so often fails to acknowledge the losers and their nobility, and to recognize that when a man places a cause and a mission above his own interests, then he has made some kind of peace with his purpose in this life. This might be as close as he had ever come to this kind of choice. To some it might appear that he had turned his back on his women and his children in favor of his last remaining blood relative. He was risking serious failure should some misfortune befall either them or himself. The choice was a challenge to his own sense of loyalty and the pitfalls of responsibility.

It was midday and he was about to stop to eat and let the two horses graze the patchy winter-brown grass along the wagon trail he was now taking toward Colorado. His mind had moved on from the reflections on Jefferson Davis and he was beginning to compare that president's expressions of conscience with those of his friend Lefty, a man who seemed to be striving to live in two worlds at once without failing either. Just then, as if on some kind of a signal, Bird stumbled and he heard the clatter of a loose shoe. He slid down from the saddle and picked up the hoof. There didn't seem to be any damage other than to the worn shoe now dangling from two bent nails. He'd hoped to make some more miles before stopping to get new ones, but this and the wear on the shoes he and Mike had put on before he left testified both to their good work and to the rigors of the trails he'd been travelling. The rocky surface of the country he was passing through was hard on the horses, as well as their shoes.

The first thing he needed to do was switch horses and gear and ride Cloud until he could find a smith or at least a shop he himself could use. Just then he saw a small sign fastened to a cottonwood tree growing out of the bank of the creek alongside the road. It said "Town – 6 miles" with no name of the town or indication of what size or kind it was. But it was his best chance and a relief to know he wasn't too far from possible help.

They moved slowly as the terrain climbed toward a low line of hills in the eastern distance. He supposed they might be the foothills of the Rocky Mountains, but wasn't sure. Finally, after almost two hours of holding to a pace to accommodate the shoeless Bird, they came to a crest in the trail's climb and a junction with a well-travelled wagon-road. A wide valley stretched below, with a river and a collection of buildings. As he eased his horses down the road he could see smoke coming from a building that looked like a sawmill, and several small herds of cattle spread out along the river. He thought he might already be in Colorado, but had no way of knowing. Then around a bend in the road another sign announced he was on the road to Durango, and that he was about to enter the town of Blessing, Utah.

The vista before him was as pretty a piece of landscape as he could remember and he remembered that he'd not stopped for a meal break, either for him or the horses. A few minutes would suffice for the three of them, so he climbed down from Cloud's back and led him off to a grassy area with just the beginning of new spring growth. He pulled the bridles and got his own small bag of foodstuffs from the saddlebag. As he sliced bread and cheese he wondered whether the town's name came from the desire for good fortune or from it having already received its "blessing." Since he was still in Utah, there was little doubt that he would find Mormons in the settlement, and he could only hope that they were of the friendly sort. He thought of Sarah Beth and the terrible experience she'd gone through where they'd first settled. He shook off the memory. He wouldn't allow it to spoil the beauty and peace of this quite special scene.

The first building on the edge of town turned out to be a smithy with a sign over its wide open door proclaiming, "Caldwell's

Horseshoe and Ironworks Foundry." A big title for such a small operation, Abe thought, but he felt fortunate and glad to see it. He looped Cloud's rein over the hitch-rail and led Bird into the building's shadow.

"Anyone here?" he called.

A voice came from the dimness at the back of the space in front of him, "Course there is. Door's open, isn't it?"

While this reception was neither pleasant or hostile, Abe decided to be as careful and diplomatic as he could be and replied, "I'm just pleased to find such a good-looking establishment out here and I'm in need of some service for my horses."

A young man with a long flowing moustache came out of the back of the shop and stuck out his hand for Abe to shake. "Guess you might have come to the right place since this is the only place, but because it is the only place I might not be able to get to your needs as fast as you might want. Everybody's always in a hurry seems to be. At least the strangers that come through. I'm Ben Caldwell. You?"

"Abe Saunders, from up Oregon way."

"That horse walk all that way?" He walked around Bird.

"Yes, except when we were trying to cover ground faster when we could."

"That white leg is kinda strange. Never seen a horse like it."

"Given to me by a friend back in Missouri."

"You do get around then, don't you? How about your other horse?"

"Needs the same, all four."

"Can't be done with all that until sometime tomorrow, but you're welcome to make a camp out back here. I'll do what I can to get you moving again. There's some hay back there, cost added, but they'll eat it. Tie'em out, though. There's a small place serves food," he gestured with his chin. "Now, I'm busy. Fixing a plow the man needs yesterday."

The next morning Abe was awakened by a boot toe nudging his shoulder. "I'm taking that white leg horse. Fix her up first. Coffee in the shop."

Abe pulled himself up to sitting and watched the man lead Bird away. He'd had some trouble getting to sleep, but when he did it was deep and satisfying. Now if he could only wake up. He heard the sound of a whistle and machinery starting up. Must be the mill, he thought.

When he arrived at the shop and peered into the gloom at the back, with its flickering flames from the forge and sounds of metal on metal clanging, he was surprised to see the silhouetted form of a woman holding Bird's halter rope and stroking the horse's neck. He walked forward and cleared his throat so as not to startle either the person or the animal.

The woman turned to him and said, "I think I know this horse, and if it is the horse I think it is, I must know you. Are you Abe? Mr. Abe?"

"Yes ma'am, I'm called Abe. And you? I can't see you in this darkness."

"Grace. My name is Grace and if it's really you, I am so glad to see you...Oh, tell me, tell me, how is Sarah Beth?"

"Grace? Would you be the one who she helped to have a baby?"

"Yes, yes. Little Rachel. She's almost growed up already, well, almost. Your wife saved her life and mine, and I thought I would never get to thank her."

"I guess we all had to leave there pretty quickly. Here, I'll hold the horse." Caldwell had moved around to change sides and work on another foot. He hadn't said a word, but Abe could tell that he was efficient at his work.

"They took me away from there. I could hardly travel, but I was so happy to leave. Oh, I came out to get the coffee pot. I'll be right back. Don't go away."

By the time she returned, the smith had finished another foot and was taking a short break to lean pieces of metal against the furnace.

"Plow parts," he said. "So you knew my wife?"

"Barely. We were on a wagon train together and stayed at the same place for a while."

"Don't have to keep it from me. I know the story, or most of it."
He rolled a cigarette. "Best thing that ever happened to me was when
that sonofabitch kicked her out after damn near killing her."

"He tried something similar with my wife. Tried to force her to
marry him while I was gone to look for land out in Oregon."

"Then it was your wife. Like Gracie said, saved her life, she
tells me."

They were both quiet with their own thoughts while Caldwell
smoked. Bird pulled on the rope, but Abe settled her down. "You
ever want to help me kill that Bishop fellow, let me know." Then he
went behind Bird, grabbed his tools and tapped one of her hind legs.
She lifted her foot.

Grace came back, this time with coffee and a little girl. "Mr. Abe,
this is Rachel Sarah. I hope it's all right I gave her that name because I
was so grateful. Sarah Beth is the kindest, best woman I ever met and
Rachel and I both love her for what she did for us. Don't we, Rachel?"

"Who is she, Mama?"

"You know, I told you. The woman who helped you be born." She
patted the girl and stroked her hair. "Say hello and thank you to Mr.
Abe. It's a miracle he found us here after all this time."

"Hello, Mr. Abe. Thank you. Now can I go play with Esther?"

"Run along, but come back soon. We'll invite Mr. Abe to eat our
midday with us."

When she was gone, Abe said, "Beautiful child."

"And we have two more, don't we Charles?"

The man under the horse grunted a "yes."

"I do want you to stay for a meal with us. Charles told me you seem
to be in a hurry so we won't keep you. I'll go fix something now."

As he moved around to the last of Bird's feet, the man stood up
and looked Abe in the eye. "It's hard having another man's child to
love, but by God, that little girl is ours and nobody can say different."

"How did you meet Grace, if you don't mind my asking?"

"I got a brother up Provo way. He's still in the Church. Me I quit
when I heard what that bastard did to her. I don't care what they say

about him being just one of the bad apples. I'm never gonna believe in any Church that lets him run peoples' lives. No, sir."

"Your brother?"

"Franklin Caldwell, runs a bank nowadays. They brought her to his Church, nearly dead and the baby as well. Him and his wife took them in and cared for them. She healed up pretty good and we met up the next Christmas. Been together since, and I'll keep her, and keep her safe until their 'Latter Days' come to pass. You might as well catch up that other horse. This one will stand for me while I finish up."

Abe was blinded by the bright sunlight outside the shop. As he went after Cloud, he realized he'd never let himself fully feel his anger toward the Bishop. He'd been angry of course, but he'd never thought about hating the man like this Caldwell obviously did. But even now that he'd encountered this kind of loathing, Abe felt more pity than hate for that worn-out and vicious old Bishop. On the other hand, how many peoples' lives had he abused and ruined using his church-granted power? It was a riddle in his mind now, and, as he caught up Cloud, he knew that these questions about evil and hatred, abuse and pity wouldn't go away. It was a miracle that he found them, and, as Grace said, in more ways than one.

Charles finished Cloud's feet and some other work. Abe went down the town's single street and purchased supplies for the next leg of his trip. During the midday meal, Grace brought out a smaller child, a boy, and introduced him to Abe as Charles Anthony, nearly a year-and-a-half old and walking and starting to talk.

She said, "I was so afraid after the trouble I had with Rachel and everything that I couldn't have another baby, and Charles was so good about it. But I knew he wanted one of his own and…"

"Every child you have and will ever have is mine, right wife?"

"Of course, but this baby named Charles is very special to all of us and Rachel loves him so much, don't you honey?"

"Yes, Mama. Can I take him now so you can eat?"

"Of course. Thank you. Just don't let him run away."

"Mama, he can't run."

"I know, dear."

The three adults ate in silence for a few minutes, Abe particularly enjoying the home-cooked meal of cornbread, stew, and early spring greens. The main thing he was missing while traveling, besides his family, was the food Sa-rah and Helga cooked for him.

"Where you be headed, if you don't mind saying?" Charles asked.

"Santa Fe. Got a cousin there needs some help."

"Still some ways to go. Which way you taking?"

"Head east from here then turn south, I guess."

"Save time and horses if you go south from here and take what's called the Indian Road. No Indians to speak of anymore, but it's the way they used to get from down south to the Salt Lake. There's mountains, but nothing your animals can't handle. By the way, those are both fine horses. Never seen one with a white leg marked like that. Man gave him to you must have been a good friend."

"He gave me the horse when we first met. Said I would need her to help me get where I was going. Since then everywhere I've been seems like somebody recognizes that horse and asks about how I came by her. Even had some Indians thinking I'd stolen her from him."

"Just gave her to you?"

"Said there was something special about me and about her that belonged together."

They were quiet for a moment, then Grace said, "What about you and Sarah Beth? Do you have any children? I know she very much wanted one."

"Yes, we do, finally had a little boy about the same age as yours there. Name's Isaiah."

She clapped her hands together, "I'm so happy for you."

For a moment, Abe considered telling her about Helga's child, remembering that Grace had to have known the girl, but he quickly decided that wouldn't be easy to explain without making Sa-rah seem a little strange, even to someone of Grace's background.

Soon after the meal he saddled up and tried to pay Charles for the work. The man refused any money and said they owed him for Rachel, and for his wife's blessed work with the birth. Then he showed Abe where the suggested road took off into the hills to the south and wished him well. Abe mounted up on Cloud and rode off out of the small town. He looked back several times and saw that the small family group was still standing in front of the shop and waving to him. He couldn't wait to tell Sa-rah about this unexpected and wonderful encounter.

CHAPTER 10

Break Up

Four weeks after Abe left for New Mexico, Sam still remained a mystery to the two women. Both tried to engage him in conversation many times, but he simply responded with polite and short sentences; if they asked a question about him, he quickly changed the subject to work on the ranch. He'd gone several times over to the Skinner place to visit with Mike and Ollie, needing some repair or another. Only once did he venture to town, and that was, as far as Sa-rah and Helga could figure out, just for supplies for the animals and some bare necessities for himself. Calves were being born and he was often out overnight with the herd, making sure that no problems cost them any losses.

Helga continued her sewing projects, completing two small quilts and one for a full-size bed. The one store in town that catered particularly to the needs of women, selling such things as hair brushes and fabric, was willing to take her work and display it for a time. If it didn't sell, they forwarded it to another shop in Boise.

Sa-rah was already digging in the garden and planning to expand it this year. She enlisted Sam's help in moving manure from the stable to the garden area and was beginning to work it into the soil. Sam also worked on the placement of a low wall of rocks that she hoped would keep Happy the dog from running through and disrupting her rows and plants. She was surprised at how many of the rocks came out of the ground where she was digging the expansion, but once they were removed and made a part of the wall, good soil remained.

The boys seemed to be well and thriving as the weather turned warmer and they could spend more time outdoors. Indigo, especially, was everywhere making hiding places, gathering sticks with his little cart, and even splashing in the near-freezing water of the smaller creek. His mother specifically warned him that she better not catch him close to the dangerous flow of the larger stream. Isaiah was learning to shuffle along and was almost running. He tried to keep up with Indigo when he could, but the older boy would tease him to follow and then run away. He was also getting more curious about the area around the house and wandering away from Sa-rah's sight if he could. The rock wall provided a barrier to keep him nearby, an unexpected benefit of Sam's good work as a builder: the wall was firm and the little boy was unable to dislodge the rocks. Sa-rah and Helga often found him pushing loose dirt into shapes and bumps and couldn't imagine quite what he thought he was doing. He would then pile pebbles on top of the dirt piles and call for them to come and see what he'd done.

"Maybe he watched Sam build the wall and is trying to do something like that," Sa-rah said to Helga one day.

"When I was little back where I was growing up, we had these animals that lived in the ground and were called moles. Maybe he's being like them, making those little hills," Helga replied.

"But he's never seen a mole hill."

"Maybe he's got mole instincts." They both laughed and for a few days they called him Little Mole, but even though he didn't know what it meant, he didn't seem to like it.

At first, after Abe left, Sam wouldn't eat with them in the house, but he would accept the food and eat out in the space he'd fixed up for himself at one end of the workshop. After a while, though, he would come in and eat at the table, pass the time in near silence, and then leave when he was finished, after making a short grateful speech and perhaps telling them what his plans were for the next day. He always asked if there was anything they needed him to do for them, and would promptly take care of it.

One evening at supper, he said, "Should be headed back by now. Hope so, because I'm going to have to head north before long."

Sa-rah gave Helga a questioning look, and then said, "If you need to be leaving, I'm sure we'll be all right here now. I don't expect more hard weather and we can check up on those last two or three cows yet to give birth. Don't you think so, Helga?"

"Oh yes. We'll be fine, and Ollie and Mike can come over for anything out of the ordinary."

"Well, we'll see. I don't want to leave before I have to. It's been good here. Might still be snow up in Montana." Then he thanked them once again for feeding him and went out.

"Such a strange man," Sa-rah said.

"Just very private, I suppose. Unless maybe something really bad happened to him."

"Abe said he got that scar in the War. Maybe he almost died from the wound and hasn't recovered some part of who he is. I've heard of that kind of thing." Sa-rah reached down and lifted Isaiah, who was trying to climb into her lap.

"Perhaps Louis will know more and can tell us when he gets here."

"Oh, Helga. I know I shouldn't even say this, but every time Louis comes around or gets ahold of Abe, it seems like there's some kind of trouble comes with him."

"I know what you mean, but he seems to have such a good heart and he very much admires Abe, you can tell that."

"Well, we'll just have to wait and see this time. I hope they return soon. I'd rather not be here alone without Sam, but we have no right to hold him up. He's done so much for us."

Several days passed before Sam brought up the possibility of his leaving again. He found Sa-rah working in the garden, walked up to the wall near where she was, removed his hat and said, "Ma'am, I think I'm going to have to move on next couple of days. This here warm spell is going to fill the rivers between here and where I'm headed, so it's time I was on my way. I surely have appreciated your kindness and the good treatment. I wish you and your husband the best and maybe when I come this way again, I'd be allowed to stop in?"

It was the longest speech Sa-rah ever heard from him and it took her a moment to respond.

"Sam, I hope you know how much help you've been and how much it meant to our family to have you here to rely on while Abe was away. And of course, you're always welcome." She gave him a smile and went on, "Matter of fact if we hear you went through this area and didn't stop, we'd probably be very upset with you."

"Thank you, ma'am. Now I'll get back to it. I've got quite a bit left to do before I'd feel comfortable leaving it all behind." He backed away, and went off toward the barn.

A few minutes later she heard him galloping away out toward where the cattle were grazing, and she realized that she better take that ride with him before he left and see what had to be done, and what might come unexpectedly. Helga might need to go out there as well, so either of them could handle the chore and any problems. She felt a kind of sadness at this news, although she'd always known it would come. Part of it was just her loneliness for Abe, but a part was also her curiosity about the man and his past. All they really knew was that he'd met Louis in prison when he was serving a sentence for alleged cattle rustling. Well, she thought, most of the people in the west these days had some kind of reason for being here, and they often had good reason not to explain themselves and their personal history. That was one of the things that made the west so different from where she'd grown up, where everyone knew all there was to know about everyone else's family background and most everything else. And that was even true about newcomers in a place like Virginia. It didn't take long for a person's past to be found out and passed around.

Later, when she told Helga, she expected similar regret to see the man go, but she was surprised by the revelation that Sam had talked to Helga a bit and told her that he'd lost his family to an Indian raid in western New Mexico.

"He had a wife and baby girl and a young boy and they were killed when some of what he called the 'Common-chees,' or something like that, set the house on fire when he had to be away for a few days. He said that was why he tried to stay here as long as possible, hoping Abe would return, but now he just had to go or maybe lose his job for the year."

"He told you all that?"

"Well, not exactly all at once. I just got more and more curious and I kept at him until he finally told me those things. I'm sure there's a lot more he didn't say, but I was kind of being a bit of a pest about it all."

"We'll see what Louis knows when he gets here. You know I was wondering earlier just how many people live out here that have secrets or things they'll never talk about. Even how many people aren't using their real names, the ones they were born with."

Helga covered her mouth with her hands and still couldn't help laughing out loud, "You mean like Sa-rah instead of Sarah Beth?"

Sa-rah was washing dishes in the kitchen sink and threw a wet dish-rag at Helga. Helga picked it up and threw it back. Suddenly they were tussling and trying to throw each other down on the floor, but they were both laughing so hard that they just ended up sitting sprawled on the floor with their arms around each other.

"You know you're a horrible person, don't you?" Sa-rah said between fits of laughter.

"Oh, if you say so, Madam Perfect."

Just then Indigo came running in and said, "Mama, Auntie, Isaiah's hurt, hurry."

They both jumped up and went running out. The baby was screaming and tangled up in a rope. He was trying to walk, but kept falling down. Sa-rah quickly untangled him from the rope and held him close while she spoke loudly at Indigo.

"What happened? What did you do?"

The boy was crying and could hardly talk between sobs. Helga knelt beside him and wiped at his tears with her sleeve, saying. "It's all right. He's all right now. But what happened?"

"We–were–play cow and me–catch–him-cow."

Sa-rah spoke in a low but threatening tone as she told the boy that he better never ever let anything like that happen again. As she walked away, she looked back and added, "You could have choked him to death." And then she took Isaiah in to the house, trying to soothe him and calm herself.

Helga gathered up the rope and coiled it neatly. "Do you understand what she said?"

The boy looked down at his feet. "Sorry. Sorry. Sorry."

"Do you understand?"

"What be death, Mama?"

"Oh, that's hard to understand, for you, for anybody…Death is when someone or an animal or a bird stops living, stops breathing."

"Why?"

"Because they get really sick, or they get hurt real bad, then they're dead, they're not alive anymore."

"Isaiah not hurt bad, fall down on rope. Not bad."

"I know that, and your Auntie knows that too. But he could have been hurt much worse."

"But I help him. Not hurt bad."

"Yes, you helped him, but you were the one that got him tangled in the rope. It's good that you helped him, but you should not play with ropes like that."

"I sorry. No more Isaiah play cow."

"Good, now go find something else to do. Here…" she hugged him and watched him run to the corral where he found their dog. Helga turned and went into the house.

Sa-rah was sitting in the big chair and Isaiah looked like he was napping. She got up slowly, trying not to disturb him and set him down on the small day-bed by the window. Then she motioned for Helga to come into the kitchen.

"Did you tell him what he did?" she spoke in a low but harsh voice.

"Yes."

"Did you punish him?"

"He is very, very sorry."

"Did you punish him?"

Helga raised her eyes to look directly at Sa-rah. "He feels bad enough. It won't happen again. I promise you."

"How can you promise anything with that wild child? We never know what he's going to be up to next." Her voice was rising. "He's a danger to Isaiah and to himself. I don't know what to do about him."

"I don't think he means any harm and he's learning how to be more careful," Helga said softly. "I'll make sure he knows he has to be more gentle and careful with his little brother."

Abe made good time from Charles and Grace's small town to the New Mexico Territory, and down an open road to Santa Fe. He was pleased with the time he'd made and was looking forward to a quick return. Although he and the horses were equally worn out, he put them in a livery stable for feed and rest while he kept moving on to the business he came for. The main jail was at the south edge of the town. He had no trouble finding it, but its doors were locked and there didn't seem to be anyone there. He knocked as loudly as he could and finally a prisoner hollered through a barred window.

"Down at the marshal's office. Nobody here but us jailbirds," he said with a crazy laugh. "Where's that?" Abe hollered back. There was no answer.

He turned and wandered back into town until he found a barber shop at the near end of the main street. He went in. The barber was shaving someone and two other men were either waiting their turn or just visiting.

The barber looked up from his work and asked, "Need something, stranger?"

"Yes sir. I'd like to find the marshal, talk to him about my cousin."

"Most days at this time he'd probably be taking a snooze in one of the cells down the road there, but today I imagine he's in court along with a lot of other folks."

"Where's the court?"

"Keep going back up this street and take a left where you see some pretty good-sized trees. That'll be it."

"Thank you, sir."

He backed out the door and as he turned to walk away, he overheard one of the men saying, "Sure hope for his sake it ain't his cousin on trial."

Abe walked quickly in the direction that had been described. Under the two large trees there was a small crowd that seemed to be overflow from the building or maybe just folks having their mid-day meal with blankets spread out on the ground. The windows of the first floor of the building were all open, as the day was what he thought must be unseasonably warm. He heard the rhythmic sound of a gavel on wood, and a loud voice, but not loud enough for him to hear the words. He edged his way through the crowd and tried to get to the front steps. When he could go no further he asked the man next to him what was going on.

"You don't know? Biggest trial we've ever had. And it's a woman on trial, Mexican. She killed her two brothers when they came after her, trying to take her back across the border. Pretty woman too, but mixed up with one of the big families down south of Albuquerque."

Just then there was a stirring toward the front of the standing room only folks in front of Abe. A couple of men were dragging a woman through the crowd and out of the building. They both wore badges and suddenly Abe was able to recognize one of them as his cousin. As the two passed by him with the struggling woman, they were only a couple feet away, but the noise of the crowd drowned out his attempt to get Louis's attention. He pushed his way back from the building and got himself to where he thought they would pass by. Then he heard a booming voice from the direction of the courthouse steps.

"You-all dis-perse by order to the law of the Territory of New Mexico and the authority of a federal law officer. That's me, Marshal Winthrop C. Henderson. Now be gone! Get! Court is adjourned for the day. NOW MOVE!"

People backed away from the steps and the building, mumbling and grumbling but obeying the order just the same. Louis and the other man now had the woman lashed to the trunk of one of the trees and the marshal was striding toward her and pushing folks out of his way. Abe moved closer to that tree by following in the wake of the giant of a man who was serving as the law and looking very much like he could back it up. He stopped right in front of the woman who was now shrieking angry words in Spanish at him.

"Señora or señorita, as the case may be. You've less than one more chance to keep from being buried alive with only your pretty little nose sticking out of the ground. You think I'm lying, try me. Now shut down your screaming and listen to me. And listen good. If you ever spit in anyone's face again during this trial, you will be put away for so long that your teeth will fall out, your hair turn white, and your eyes go dark. Contempt, that's what it is, contempt of court and contempt of humanity." Then he ducked just as she spit at him. "You owe me now. I saved you by ducking, so don't try it again or I'll stuff this snot rag of mine between them pretty lips and wait for you to choke on it." He whipped a wrinkled kerchief out of his pants pocket and waved it in front of her face. "Boys, tie her feet and hands and I'll just carry Mrs. Rojado back to the jail."

The two men wrapped her arms and legs in rope. She unleashed another flurry of Spanish words, but much softer this time, as if she was speaking only to the marshal. The last words were in English and Abe heard them. She said softly, "You have nothing between your legs that no woman would ever want." She was quiet for a long moment until the tying was done and the marshal stepped up and hoisted her over his shoulder.

As they passed by Abe, he heard the man say, "You try to bite me and I'll knock your teeth out and call it self-defense. C'mon boys."

Abe followed along some ways behind the three men and the trussed-up woman, but close enough to hear her saying, "You know your mother was my father's whore, you know that, you Mexican bastard..." The marshal swatted her butt, which was hanging over his shoulder.

As they neared the jail, Abe called out to his cousin, "Louis."

His cousin spun around and his mouth dropped open, "Cuz? What the Hell. CUZ!"

Abe caught up with him and they grabbed each other's arms.

"C'mon Deputy. Got to get this done now," the marshal said.

"Come with us," Louis said to Abe as the other man unlocked the doors of the prison. When Abe tried to follow inside, the man started to stop him, but at a word from Louis he was allowed inside. The doors slammed shut and were once again locked. The marshal continued down a hallway while Louis moved ahead of him and opened a cell door, so the woman could be dumped inside.

"Leave her tied for a few minutes. Do her good." He backed out of the cell and motioned for the other man, with the keys, to shut and lock the heavy steel door. "And who's this fella?"

"My cousin, marshal. Told you he'd come after me."

"Yes, you did. Too bad you couldn't let him know those boys that were after you are both dead now. Let's have a drink." He reached into a drawer and sat behind the large desk. "Clarence, bring us some glasses. We got to welcome this man came all this way."

Drinks were poured and downed. Abe refused another, and resisted the urge to ask questions about the scene at the courthouse, thinking he would have to wait until he and Louis were alone. Then the marshal leaned across the desk. "Biggest mess I've ever had to deal with," he said. "Ever. Should've hung her when we first caught her. Damn." He downed his second drink and poured himself another, offering again to Abe, "You sure?" Abe nodded yes. The man took a sip of his own. "Ever had mezcal before?" Abe shook his head no. "Best goddamn stuff ever made to heal a man's broken heart or cheer the soul of a dead man..."

Louis stepped a bit closer and said, "Marshal, think me and my Cuz could have a little time to catch up, him just now getting here and all?"

"Be fine with me. Nothing more's gonna happen today." Just then they heard a long shrill shriek from the cell where they'd left the woman. "Except her screaming and carrying on. Best help me untie her before you take off. Bring this cousin along. He should have a proper introduction to the hussy that saved your life."

All four of the men proceeded down the corridor to the cell. The man called Clarence unlocked the heavy door and swung it open. The woman sat against the far wall, smiling. "You forget me, my brother. How can you forget me like that?" Then she rattled off a string of Spanish words and struggled to push herself up onto the small cot by the wall. "Help me, you bastards."

The marshal pushed past the jailer and Louis and went to her side. "I should hang you from a hook on the wall. Now hold still and stay that way or one of these boots is gonna find your belly and stomp you." He bent over and untied the rope around her legs. She quickly gathered them under her and pushed herself up to a standing position, holding out her arms. He untied the rope above her wrists and when she tried to take a swing at him, he grabbed her by the shoulders, spun her around, and forced her face down onto the cot.

"Elena, you must be calm and quiet, and you must act like a lady or you will have the terrible accident that happens to people when they are in prison and attack those who are trying to take care of them. You understand."

There was a muffled sound from the blanket. The marshal relaxed his hold on her and she turned herself into a sitting position, straightening her long, black hair and politely said, "Gentlemen, I would like a glass of water, *por favor.*"

"Clarence, get her some water." The marshal gestured and the man left.

"Elena, you know my Deputy, Louis. You know him very well, don't you? He is grateful to you for saving his life from the Rojado boys. Say thank you, Louis."

"Yes ma'am, señorita. I am much obliged and thoroughly grateful for what you did."

The woman didn't reply. Instead she pointed to Abe, who was still standing in the hallway. "Who is the handsome one?"

Louis answered, "That's my cousin, Abe. He came to visit me, to see how I'm doing."

"Step in here so I see you," she said. Abe stepped to the doorway. "Yes, he is a good man, maybe the only one in this town, maybe in all of this New Mexico. I like you, Mister, because you do not look like this monster or your cousin. You may sit beside me and we will talk about our plans for this life…"

Clarence came into the cell and handed a tall glass of water to the marshal, who gave it to the woman.

"That's enough, Elena. We'll leave you now."

"Yes, my dear brother. I am sure you have much more drinking to do. Abe, come back and see me."

The men left the cell and walked back to the office. She was singing as they left and the sound followed them. She had a beautiful voice.

Louis and Abe went to a small place that seemed to serve more food than drinks and sat in a quiet corner.

"Glad you came, Cuz, but I'm sorry to cause you all that trouble."

"Your letter, Sam, it all sounded pretty bad. What's going on?"

"I'll tell you when we've ordered some food. Margarita," he called out to a woman serving food. They ordered and then sat in silence for a long moment.

"Tell me, are you all right? What happened here? Where's Maria? Are you coming with me? And what is all this between the marshal and that woman?"

"Good questions, Cuz. I'll try to answer, but it's damn complicated, as you can probably tell from the goings on. I'll do my best to make it clear as I can…" Coffee arrived, and Louis didn't put anything in it, but stirred it slowly with his spoon. "First, I got a question for you. How's Sam?"

"Sam is great. Doesn't say much and wouldn't talk about himself, except to say he was Union and thinks both sides lost the War. Said he met you when he was in prison for stealing cows that were running wild with no brands."

"He's a loner, more so since the Comanches burned out his place, his wife, his son, and his daughter. At the time he was away in Las Cruces. Some say he was drunk. After the fire, he kind of went crazy and stayed out in the desert for many months. But he's right about those cattle. They were just mavericks and didn't belong to anyone. Problem was Señor Rojado claimed them and had him put away. Same old bastard that had the son that tried to kill me. Elena, the famous Elena, the woman in jail over here, was his mistress. Turns out what I didn't know when I was first taken on by Henderson as a deputy was that him and her had the same mother, and you might be noticing they kind of hate each other."

Food arrived.

"Eat, Cuz, you look like you're missing Sarah Beth's cooking pretty bad. Anyway, Elena got into it with Rojado's sons over something or everything, and she sent for her brothers down in Old Mexico. They come and shot the two Rojado boys and took off back toward the border, but then they found out she was living and loving with the old man, and that they weren't married. They figured their family name was dishonored, so they tried to take her back home with them. That's when things got real crazy. I can't say for sure what happened exactly because by then I was transferred from Albuquerque jail because my time was all served, but, like my letter said, Marshal Henderson was kind enough to put me up here in Santa Fe until you got here. So I still haven't got the story straight, but I don't think anyone has, that's what this trial over here is all about. Keep eating, Cuz, there's more where that come from."

Abe sat back while the woman refilled his cup of coffee and removed his empty plate. Louis asked her to bring their best piece of pie. "Let me interrupt to say one more thing about Sam. He stayed with Sarah Beth and Helga and our two boys, running my cattle and watching out for them. I've got to hurry back because he'd got to clear out for a Montana job he's got."

"We'll get to all that part in a minute, Cuz, I just don't want to lose the rope I've got on this story half way through…" He pulled out a flask and poured a shot into his coffee. "Cuz? No? Didn't think so. I went most of that time in jail without a drink, had to pay high for those jailers to bring it in and I was pretty near broke trying to support Maria…Anyway, they say those brothers of her sneaked into the old man's ranch house at night and tried to take her. Old Man Rojado woke up and started shooting in the dark and nailed one of them. Elena grabbed that one's gun and killed the other one. The old man was hit in the neck, but he's all right, just can't talk—told you it was crazy. Marshal showed up the next morning after the doctor came back to town from patching up Rojado, and told him what was happening. There he found the wounded old man, a screaming woman and two bodies. Follow me so far, Cuz?"

"I think so."

"Well, he told Elena he was going to take her back, put her in protective custody, case more of her brothers showed up. She threatened to kill him if he tried, said 'What's another brother to me. I kill you all.' He come back and let me out of the jail and put my badge back on me and said we were going to bring her in one way or another, but he wanted me to just go out there, stay out of sight and follow her if she tried to leave. He was pretty sure she wouldn't leave the old man, wounded and all. So I did, and after two days Señor and Elena got on a buggy and headed for town. I went around them and got to the marshal, who set up a surprise roadblock and had me ride out and meet up with them. I was supposed to ride along with them until we got to the trap. Everything would have gone off as the marshal planned it except Rojado got it in his head that I had been loving on his woman and was trying to steal her now and he pulled a gun on me. My luck was good that day and she knocked it out of his hand, picked it up, and then pointed it at me. She said 'Keep going, Mister, you going to make sure we are safe to the doctor or I kill you too.' I tell you Cuz, she is something else. I almost wish the old man was right that I was loving on her, almost be worth getting killed over," he laughed, but then was quiet for a long time. Abe watched him without saying anything.

"Was the pie good? Best pie in this town. Most of these Mexicans got no idea how to make a pie, but this place does. So, I guess you're wondering about Maria and the girls. How about we just put this on my bill here and take a walk over to the square. Be nice out there now there's a breeze come up and nobody to bother us. I'm happy to see you, Cuz. It's been almost more than I could handle."

They walked down the cart and horse-filled street and turned into the main square. It took up a large area in front of what would be a very small cathedral in Europe, but was the largest building Abe had yet seen since coming west. They found a vacant stone bench in the shade of a bushy kind of tree he didn't recognize.

"It's a little hard for me to talk about. Especially since you've come so far and done all this for me. I just got to hope you're not angry. Can't expect Sarah Beth not to hold it against me, but Cuz, I can't go back with you. You might think you come all this way for nothing, but I have to tell you it's the best thing anyone's ever done for me. Absolutely."

Louis paused and waved to a young couple walking by.

"Go on."

"Well, it's like this," Louis paused again. "I'd just as soon go with you, go back up north there, maybe partner up and make something of ourselves. But I can't. Not unless I leave her. I might even get away with the two girls, but she won't move north, not a mile, not an inch. After I was let loose in Albuquerque, and then the marshal put me back in here for my own safe-keeping, she came to see me. When I told her you was going to come after us, she broke down crying and then started screaming at me, like they do, like that one over there right now. Cuz, that Spanish is a screaming language, at least in some women. When I could get her to slow down and listen, I tried to tell her how good it would be for us and she went crazy again, just screaming their word for 'salt' over and over again." He stopped to roll a cigarette. "Trying not to smoke so much, but it's handy when some subjects come up and this is one of them."

Abe waited, and then he said, "So far not much I've heard or found out about this country down here makes much sense. Don't think I could live here."

"Well, that's the truth, but I got kind of used to these folks, crazy as they are. Now, I'd be one happy cowboy if I could pack out of here. I had some pretty bad luck in these parts. But I've had some pretty good luck with my bad luck, if you know what I mean. I mean, just like this Elena's brothers killing the two men who were sworn to kill me. That's the good luck in a pretty bad situation. What's crazy about it is why'd she kill them two, her own brothers? Wasn't for me, that's sure. But it goes to show what can happen and can't nobody figure it out except the court, and I don't think even the judge can do that. Besides, she must have more brothers or cousins or whatever across the border and if he hangs her, they'll kill him sure. See what I mean?"

"Sort of, but what's the salt all about?"

"Oh, right, back to that, back to Maria. She's from further south, you know. She gets scared, bad scared, every time it snows. It was especially bad when we spent that winter in Montana. Wouldn't go out in it, just pulled a quilt over her head and moaned and cried. She didn't even have a word for it, for that snow. Called it salt in her language, frozen salt, and then she'd go from angry to scared and talk so fast it took me many times hearing the same thing over and over again to figure it out. I tried to keep telling her it wasn't salt, it was snow, but she kept saying that the whole Salt Lake we went by on our way up to your place was made out of frozen salt when it went down the rivers and melted. And the kicker in the whole thing is she was sure that if she stayed out in it she'd get covered up with all that frozen salt and die like a damn statue. She even said she saw statues in paintings of churches that were made out of white stone, 'See, they turned into stone when they froze'....Cuz, I even tried to joke her out of it saying those were statues of Mother Mary, and they were Jesus' own Mother's way of sayin' it was all right to be turned white by the snow, but she come back at me saying that how did I know those statues weren't Mother Mary but some poor woman who got frozen by the salt. Cuz, I love that woman, she's been all good to me, and the two girls love her and they're the sweetest things I'll ever know. Once I save up some dough working for the marshal, we'll probably head south like she wants to. Until then, the marshal guarantees me protection. He's put it out that if anybody harms me, he'll personally hang them by their thumbs, and when their thumbs pull off, he'll tie 'em back upside down and hang 'em until their toes fall off too. Then he says it'll get worse after that until they beg him to kill them. He's something when he's mad."

There was a long pause between them while they each thought about Louis's story and what it meant for their futures. Abe stood up and stretched and then turned to look down at his cousin.

"I know how you feel about your girls, Louis, I've got two boys now myself."

"That's right, you did say so, but I just went on talking about me and all this. How'd you get her to have babies? Thought it wasn't working so good. Man, I'm happy for you."

"It didn't quite happen like normal. It's true Sarah Beth, now she calls herself Sa-rah, got some Indian medicine and treatment. She had a baby boy a year ago last New Year's. But before that, well, it's strange, kind of hard for me to explain or even think about."

"Go ahead, Cuz, unless you need a drink first. We can get ourselves something at that cantina back there."

"No, that won't help, I'm afraid. It's just that she gave up trying to have a child with me, and felt like it was all her fault. So when she had to go away with that Indian, Hawk Man, and I'll have to explain that, too, I guess, but anyway when she left on a trip with them, she left myself and Helga alone with Mattie. Left us there with orders to both of us to get together and try to make a baby for our family. Strangest thing I ever heard of, but I guess it kind of put a spell on us, her leaving us like that, and we kind of couldn't help ourselves, and Helga got pregnant and we got a boy, turned four years old now since I left home. What do you think of that for strange?"

Louis didn't reply. He rolled another cigarette and kept looking out of the side of his eyes at Abe. Finally after a couple of puffs, he held out his hand to shake, "Cuz, it must take some kind of a powerful God-fearing man like yourself to pull that off."

"Almost felt like I didn't have anything to do with it. Just happened that way. And you know Sarah Beth when she gets something in her head. Course now she got proved wrong, now she's had a baby, either because it was time for it or the Indian medicine and ceremony worked, guess we'll never know."

"What do you call the boys?"

"Helga's was born a little blue, cord got tangled, but he's fine now. So she wanted him named for that color, calls him Indigo. Our baby, mine and Sarah Beth's, we call Isaiah."

"That's good news, Cuz. If anybody ever deserved to have a child it's you and now you already got two."

"Funny how much I miss them. To be honest, I think it's harder being away from those boys more than it is from their mothers, but maybe it's just a different kind of missing."

"Are you angry at me, 'cause of how things worked out?"

"No, wasn't your fault. When a man has to fear for his life, he has to try anything that might save him. You had a right to call on me. I'm just happy for you that I wasn't needed. And now I just want to get back home fast as I can."

"What way'd you come?"

"Headed east this side of Salt Lake, into Colorado country, ran into someone we knew on the wagon train. They told me a kind of short cut down to here."

"That's all right when there's a chance of snow or Indians, but now it should be all right from both to head west from here, then north and cut out of Utah to Nevada Territory. Follow the railroad to where you can get north to your place, you know that one road, right?"

"Yes, but someone told me the Indians out west of here might be worked up."

"I doubt it. Besides, you've got that horse of yours. They probably know your friend Lefty. That always worked before."

"How much will it save?"

"Three, four, five days, maybe more. Depends on you and your horses. It's how me and Maria come down from your place. We hit some snow, but it wasn't this time of year."

"Guess I can try it. Where can I get my horses checked? Shoes might be loose on one. Don't want trouble on the way if I can help it."

"Abe, Cuz, you are going to be all right because you just done a huge good turn for me, and the Old Man in charge up there is gonna take care of you all the way."

Abe was ready to leave by daylight the next morning, after spending the evening with Louis and the marshal. They took him by the jail one more time, saying Elena was asking for him. When they got there, the marshal yelled back to her that they'd brought the stranger.

"*El hombre guapo*, that one?"

Louis translated, "She asked if it was the good-looking one, the handsome man."

Abe backed away, and said, "Maybe I should just be going. Need to start early."

The marshal laughed and took him by the arm, "Won't let her hurt you, son, just give her a little happiness. Hell, she might not live much longer if the judge has any balls. We'll be right behind you."

They took him down the corridor and opened the woman's cell door. Louis gave Abe a nudge and urged him in the doorway. The woman was lounging on her cot, back against the wall. She smiled and waved the marshal and Louis away. They closed the door, after saying they'd be watching. Elena got up slowly and stood with hands on hips, her feet spread apart.

"You got a woman, Guapo?"

"I do," he said, wondering what this was all about.

"She pretty?" She took a step toward him.

"Yes." He stepped back against the door and then slid sideways, thinking not to block the view of the others in case she tried to attack him.

"She is far away?"

"Yes."

"Then she will not know you kiss me. I kiss good."

She moved quickly and used her body to push him against the wall, reaching both arms around his neck. Before he could react she'd locked her lips on his and was pushing against him even harder with her breasts and hips. She put one hand on his forehead and pushed his head back, looking up into his eyes.

"*Señor, gracias.* When they hang me you will be the last man I ever kissed and I will think of you as I die. Is good for you, *mi hombre*, my kiss?"

Abe had no idea what to say, or how to sort out the feelings that raced through his mind. His heart was even beating fast and he couldn't say what he wanted at the moment.

"One more, *mi hombre*, this one, you kiss me, please, please, por favor..."

Her fingers caressed his face and his lips and he felt himself slowly bending to her touch. His lips and then his mouth felt hers and it was as if he were being swallowed or inhaled. She moaned softly and then suddenly pushed back away, her hand covering her mouth.

"Leave me. Now, I want you too much. They will pay. If they kill me they will pay, but I will have you in my heart, *Señor.*" Then she threw herself on the cot, face down, and she began sobbing and slapping her hand against the wall.

The marshal threw open the door and motioned for Abe to get out. The man stood there for a moment, looking down at Elena's heaving body, and mumbled loud enough for Abe to hear, "I hope you will escape..."

The grass was tinged with the green of new growth. More birds were in the sky and fields, and the dirt in the garden space felt warm to the touch. Since Sam left, Ollie was a regular visitor, still talking about the trip east, and how glad he was that he didn't live there anymore. He helped move manure out of the barn to the garden, and it was something of a miracle how well his replaced leg worked. He'd gotten a few new parts on the trip and Mike found a way to make the hinge part stiff enough not to collapse, but flexible enough to bend when Ollie wanted it to.

Lefty and Carl arrived and set up camp across the creek. They were traveling from somewhere in Utah back to the home territory of Hawk Man and Carl's people. Lefty gave Sa-rah a yellow scarf and a pouch from Moon Fish. He said she would know what to do with the contents of the small bag. He then told Sa-rah and Helga that they would be staying only a few nights and that they didn't need anything; he would be pleased to trade some dried meat for any of their good bread. When Sa-rah asked him about his wife, Patsy, he smiled and said she was doing well, another baby on the way. Since they were talking about wives, she went on and asked Carl about his wife, not knowing for sure whether he had one or not. The young man's face seemed to darken and he turned away, walking quickly to stand by his horse with his back to the small group who had been visiting with each other.

Lefty spoke softly, saying, "He no longer has his wife. She got a sickness we have no medicine for and she has gone. There are others who have been sick that same way. Moon Fish says it cannot be cured with our medicine and the missionaries and soldiers say they don't have enough for the Indians. It is one more problem between our peoples. I want it not to be true." He paused and then spoke in a different tone of voice, "Now tell me why I do not see my friend? Where is he today?"

Helga and Sa-rah both started to explain about Abe's whereabouts, and Helga stopped speaking first. When Lefty heard about Louis and the sudden journey, he said he was disappointed that he hadn't crossed paths with Abe, as they had likely been somewhere close to one another in the past few weeks. With that, he said they would be going to see what their camp might need before darkness fell, and he and Carl rode off.

A while later, when the two women were both in the house beginning to prepare supper and put away the day's laundry, they heard screaming from the yard. They exchanged frightened looks and both ran out the door, nearly colliding. They were in time to see Indigo sliding down the trunk of the one large tree and dropping his bow as he ran as fast as he could toward the brushy boulders on the hillside behind the house. Isaiah was still screaming and when they got to him they found blood flowing from a cut above his forehead. Sa-rah yanked him up into her arms as Helga tried to hold out her apron to cover the bleeding. Sa-rah slapped her hand away and ran to the house. As she climbed the steps she turned and screamed at the other woman, "Go find your little killer!"

Helga turned and went toward the hillside where she'd last seen the boy. On her way she nearly stumbled over a straight branch at the spot where they'd found the baby. As she kicked it out of her way she saw that one end of it was roughly hacked into a point, making it into a kind of spear. She gasped and then ran into the brush calling Indigo's name. She was still looking when dusk began to fall over the shallow valley below her. She sank to her knees and stared at the scrapes and scratches on her hands. How far could he have gone? Where could he be? Why, oh why wasn't Abe here to help? They would have no chance to explain anything to Sa-rah in her fury. And what was there to explain? It was clear to her that her son was up in the tree and had thrown a spear at his baby brother. Why? Was he really a bad child?

Just then she heard rocks falling up the hill above her. She caught a glimpse of Indigo trying to scramble up the rocky face and she crashed through the brush in pursuit. He seemed to have seen her and was trying even harder to climb the wall, but the loose and breaking rock face was shredding under his feet. Then he fell and she lost sight of him, but could now hear his muffled sobbing.

"Indigo, stop, wait for me, stop right there. I only want to talk."

There was no answer. She called out again. Nothing but the sound of the sliding stones. Suddenly she heard, "Maa-Maa! Snake, MaMa!"

"Get away slowly," she yelled back. "Slowly." She angled across the ground until she caught sight of him. He was doing as she'd told him, backing slowly away from a gray shape on the flat top of a rock. She broke a dead branch from a scrubby tree and gripped it with both hands. Taking small steps, she edged closer. As the coiled snake raised its head and rattled loudly, she brought the branch down on its body with all her strength. The wood shattered, but the snake writhed. Grapping a sharp rock, she smashed its head. Then she nearly fell against Indigo as she wrapped her arms around him.

The boy began crying silently, his small body heaving as he buried his face against his mother's shoulder and neck. Helga was crying too, and together they rocked back and forth as the sound of a fresh wind echoed the sounds of their fear and relief mixed together. After a while, she kissed him on the top of his head and pushed him back a little, still holding him in her outstretched arms.

"Are you all right? You're not bit, are you?"

The boy shook his head no, but then pointed down at the gash on his knee. It was bleeding, but not badly. She pulled her shirt over her head and tied a sleeve tightly over the wound, then wrapped the rest of the shirt around his waist.

"Come along," she said, partially holding him up so he could walk alongside her.

When he'd stopped crying and they were near the bottom of the hillside, they heard the sound of the buggy and horse pulling away from the stable. Helga could only hope that it didn't mean the baby was hurt worse than she'd thought. It made sense that Sa-rah would go to Mattie and Martha for help, and she probably didn't think she could wait for Helga to return.

"Mama, I only played with him," Indigo said as he reached up to pull on her bare arm.

"I not try to hit him, try to miss him." Helga looked down at him and from the look of pleading in his eyes, she couldn't help but believe him. "I almost fall from tree and my arm throw stick. It hurt baby Isaiah. I sorry, so sorry, not try to hurt..."

"All right, son. I believe you, but we'll have to tell Isaiah's mother the truth and hope she believes it." She held him up again and they walked to the house, climbing the steps carefully.

Tacked to the door was a piece of paper with a note. It read:

You and your evil child must be gone
from here when I return. Go away now.
Leave forever!

CHAPTER 11

Homecoming

When Abe arrived, nobody was at the house. The buggy and Ginger were gone, and Helga's horse was missing. He took his time unsaddling Bird and unpacking Cloud, hoping someone from his family would show up. He hid the presents he'd brought and walked down to the creek to wash the dust and grime of travel from his hands and face. As he stood and looked around the place he was filled with gratitude and needed to pray thanks for the safety of his journey and the beauty of this home.

He walked slowly back up to the house and opened the door, calling inside. No answer. Inside, the house was changed and the orderliness he'd been used to wasn't so apparent. It almost looked as if someone had left in a hurry. He walked past Sa-rah's room and saw that it hadn't changed. His own space looked as if no one had been in there he whole time he was gone, but it was Helga's room at the end of the hall that gave him the biggest surprise. It looked ransacked. He stood in the doorway and let his eyes move across the piles of bedding and clothes on the floor and on the bed he'd built. Something had happened and there was no sign that Helga was still using this space. He turned away quickly and went out the back of the house to look for a sign of cooking smoke from the Indian camp. Nothing there either.

He began to worry and now wished that he hadn't been in such a hurry when he passed by the Skinners' place without stopping. They would have been able to tell him something, and one or both of the women might even have been there. Although his horses were tired, he quickly caught Cloud and saddled up, then rode across to Hawk Man's camp. It was clear that the group wasn't there and hadn't been there yet for their summertime visit. He turned the horse away and galloped him back down the road to the Skinners.

When he rode into their yard, he saw Mattie sitting in a hammock seat a tree. He dismounted and hurried over to her.

"Mattie, hello. I'm back."

"I see that Mr. Abe, and you're looking well for a man who's been gone so long. How was your trip?"

"It went well, but didn't turn out like I expected it to. Louis didn't need me after all. By the time I got there, things had worked themselves out and he stayed on down there in that part of the country. But Mattie, what's happened here? No one's at our place, and, and…" He didn't know quite how to explain what it seemed like to him at home.

"Oh my, you don't know anything, do you? I'm so sorry, Mr. Abe, so sorry to be the one to have to tell. Oh, I don't know what to say…" she paused, and then motioned for him to sit on a log stool. "Sit and listen. I'm so sorry. I tried to stop it, but I couldn't."

"What, is everyone all right? Are they hurt? Are they…"

"No, no, everyone is well. It's just that, well, Helga's had to leave."

"Leave, but why, leave to go where?"

"I don't know everything that happened and I still can't believe it, but Sarah Beth made Helga and Indigo leave, about three weeks ago."

"Why, where'd they go? Where is she?"

Mattie set her sewing in her lap and took a soft kerchief out of her sleeve. She blew her nose and wiped her eyes. "Makes me tear up when I think about it. Sorry, Mr. Abe. The baby, Isaiah got hurt. We haven't heard Helga's side of the story, but the little one was hit in the head and cut in the scalp. You know how those things bleed. Sarah Beth showed up here driving the buggy like a madwoman, which she was. I've never seen her so angry all the years I've known her...My, it's certainly getting warm today, must be summer, do you need some water or something to drink, Mr. Abe?"

"No Mattie, just go on."

"She was saying all kinds of things while Martha and I were trying to see how badly hurt the baby was. It wasn't so bad, just like I say, those wounds just bleed so bad they scare anyone. But we got it to stop bleeding and Martha knew something that worked better than stitches, said she learned it from her mother who was a nurse in the War. She put salve on the cut and then took strands of hair from either side, pulled them together and tied a knot. It took about ten of those and the poor baby screamed at every one, but his mama held him tight and we made it through. Then Martha melted some wax and pressed it on the knots. Sometimes I think that woman is a miracle woman, all the things she knows how to do."

"If that was three weeks ago, how is he now?"

"Why just this morning they cut the knots away and the cut can hardly be noticed, it's so healed up, Mr. Abe. Nothing to worry about now."

"Where's Helga, and Indigo?"

"Don't rightly know. Far as I could get out of Sarah Beth, who says she doesn't even want to mention 'that girl' again, was that she must have gone off with your friend Lefty and the young man that was travelling with him, the one I met before."

"Carl?"

"Yes that's it. They happened to be passing by, headed back to their home north of here, and I guess they took her with them."

Abe put his face in his hands and sat motionless for some time. Finally, he looked up and said, "Mattie, what can I do?"

"Help me up and come with me." They walked slowly toward the small house she shared with Ollie. When they got there, he asked her where the man was. "Took Mike with to go look at that claim of his. Now he says even if it doesn't have any gold in it, maybe there's something else worth his time. He wanted Mike to drive him over in the wagon and take a look. I don't know about that man. Now he wants to bring back some kind of rocks he found to use for our pathway right in front here."

She motioned for Abe to have a seat while she went inside. He looked at the flowers that were just beginning to bloom. It was a nice touch and he thought how now he and Sa-rah might not have Helga's help in the garden and on other projects. What would it be like from now on if he couldn't straighten this out? Not only would he miss his oldest boy terribly, but he knew that his feelings for Helga had also grown over the past few years. Not having her company and her ideas would be a great loss.

Mattie returned carrying a roll of heavy paper. She sat down beside him and unrolled it to show him a charcoal sketch of a young man or older boy. It was very realistic and well-done.

"This was my second son. We had an old man on the plantation who could draw good and I begged him to make pictures of my children while they were still with me. I never knew when they would be taken away and sold, but this is the only one he completed before he went blind. This is Daniel. What you can't see in this drawing is his hands. One of them doesn't have a top part of the little finger. His older brother, Thomas, used to scare him all the time. They played together real good when they were youngsters, but as they grew up to be about ten and twelve years, something changed and Thomas began tormenting his brother whenever he thought he could get away with it. One day he dared his little brother to take a small ax they'd found laying around somewhere and chop off the top joint of his little finger. He promised Daniel that he, Thomas, would chop off his own fingertip next. Daniel told me later that he refused and wouldn't do it until his brother called him a girl and a mama's boy and said he would never be a man if he couldn't take the pain and that if he did it everybody would be proud of him, and so forth, on and on. So Daniel pretended he was going to do it and swung the ax over his head a couple of times and brought it down next to his finger, which he'd set on a block of wood. Thomas laughed and said he missed on purpose and Daniel got angry and swung the ax at Thomas. It was sharp, belonged to one of the men, and it cut Thomas when he tried to protect himself. When Thomas started bleeding, Daniel was so frightened that he went ahead and chopped off his own little finger. Part of it, anyway, and they both came running to find me, both screaming and bleeding."

"How bad was it? For both of them?"

"They healed up, at least the hurt parts, but then they became such good friends no one could believe they could have ever argued about anything. But it goes to show just how bad young brothers can be to each other."

"You think that could happen with my boys? The becoming friends part?"

"Mr. Abe, what I think doesn't matter. It's what Sarah Beth thinks and she's just sure as can be that if Helga and her boy stay around here, that boy will end up killing her son, on purpose or by accident. It doesn't matter what I could say, and that's why she told me she made them leave. She never had any brothers, sisters either, for that matter, so she's just so afraid right now and I don't know what to tell you to do…Maybe just be gentle with her and wait this out a little, like waiting for a storm to pass. She'll come to her senses, I hope she will."

"Thanks, Mattie. Where is she now?"

"She's gone off to town with Martha. They might make it back tonight, more likely tomorrow mid-day. Mr. Abe, there's not a lot any of us can do to change what's happened. We just have to pray for peace and loving kindness to prevail. I know I'm praying for that."

"Well, thanks again, Mattie. That surely is a handsome son in that picture. What happened to him, if I might ask?"

"He was a good boy and grew up to be a fine young man, so I'm told. Ran away from his owner during the War and got killed fighting for the Union Army. Thomas is a preacher in Georgia, last I heard. Has his own Negro church and found out where I was after the War and has written me a couple of letters."

"Mattie, if you're all right here alone, I think I'll go back to our place and try to sort some of all this out. It's been strange couple of months for me, what with that trip and now this. Maybe it's all a part of God's plan, but I sure can't see why?"

"It's not for us to know sometimes, Mr. Abe. But believe on the Lord and He shall make you whole."

By daylight the next morning he was locating and rounding up his cattle and pushing the herd back toward the home place. From what he could see, Sam had done good job with the new calves and there seemed to be a full count. One of the older cows, a spotted one, was missing, but he couldn't remember well enough to know if there were one or more others missing like that. As for how they looked, he couldn't have been more pleased with the way they'd come through the winter. If anything, he was surprised and wished he could personally thank the man who had helped out. He realized he'd forgotten to ask Mattie when Sam left for Montana.

The herd seemed content with the fresh green he'd brought them to, and he figured they would stay put for a while. He actually wanted them closer, where he could check them often and hear any sounds of wolf or coyote. The one or two cougars in the area wouldn't make any sound to alert him, but they would tend not to come in too close to people.

By midday, he was back at the house and fixing a late morning meal when he heard horses whinnying and the sound of the buggy arriving. He pulled the frying pan off the stove and hurried out into the yard. Sa-rah was climbing down. She saw him and called out his name, grabbed the baby and ran toward him. They met in the open yard and she held out his son to him. He took the boy in one arm and pulled her close to himself with the other.

"Abe, Abe, oh, I'm so glad to see you, oh, you've been gone so long. Look at him, hasn't he grown? Oh, I've missed you."

He pulled her even closer and bent down to kiss. The little boy in his arms began struggling and reaching for his mother. "Maybe he doesn't remember me," Abe said handing him over to her.

"Of course he does." She turned the child to face his father. "See, Isaiah, It's your Dada." He hid his face in his mother's hair. "He'll remember and get over his shyness. Where's Louis?"

They started walking toward the house. "It's kind of a strange story, but he's all right. Just didn't come back with me, this time."

"This time? Well, I'm not letting you go after him again. It was so long."

"About the same as when you went back for your father, don't you think?"

"I don't know." They went into the house. "It seemed much longer." She set the boy on the bearskin on the floor. "He loves Lefty's bearskin," she said. "You were cooking?"

"Haven't eaten yet today. Moving the cattle in closer," he said. "You poor man. Here let me fix up what you started."

She stopped and pulled him to her, kissing him and running her hands up and down his back. Then she pulled away and went to the stove. "Mattie says she talked to you."

"I went over to see her yesterday afternoon."

"And she told you what's happened?"

"Somewhat, I suppose. She might have left things out. Like when did Sam leave?"

"It was a while ago. He wanted to get across the rivers before the snow melted into them. I have to tell you, I don't know what we would have done without him. He was so helpful."

"That's good. At least that part of Louis's plan worked out."

"Oh, I know, what happened anyway?"

"It's complicated. I'll tell you later. Just say that Louis has about as much chance of getting out of scrapes as he has of getting into them. He's all right, far as I know, but it could have turned out much worse. But Sa-rah it's what happened here that I'm worried about."

"Sit down and eat. I'll nurse your son and put him down for his nap and we'll talk about all that."

Sa-rah's story was very close to what he's heard from Mattie, with added emphasis on what a threat she thought Indigo was becoming, and the added part about the time he roped the baby and she thought he almost strangled him. When Abe asked where Helga was, Sa-rah didn't answer for quite a long time.

Then she stood up and started pacing back and forth. "You might not like what I did, and I so wish you'd been here to help with all this. I can't believe it had to happen right while you were gone. When I was getting us ready to drive off to Skinners' place, I was so upset I didn't even know what I was doing. I was able to stop the bleeding out of his head by pressing and pressing on it, fighting him all the time. He was screaming and kicking. I know it was so painful for him. It wasn't until I came back two days later that I remembered I scribbled a note and left it on the door telling her to be gone when I got back. Oh, Abe I really meant it. I was so frightened for our son." She stopped and stood still. "And who knows what could have happened the next time? I stayed away so she could have time to leave. She left a huge mess in her room, but didn't harm anything else. Lefty and Carl were passing through, did Mattie tell you that part?"

"Yes, she did, said she thought that's where Helga went."

She sat down next to him and put his arm around her shoulders as she began to cry.

"There, now. You did what you thought was right."

"Abe, there was nothing else I could do. What else could I have done?" her sobbing grew until she was shaking. He was trying to hold her still and was mumbling comforting words. She slowed her breathing and wiped her eyes on the sleeve of his shirt, then said, "Abe, you need someone to do your laundry."

"Couldn't do much of that on the trails I've been on."

"And here I am crying like a baby, and you've been through such a hard time. Was it terrible? Any storms?"

"No, but I have a surprise for you." She smiled up at him, and held out her hands. "No it's not a gift, just some news. An amazing coincidence. It made me remember what your father said about coincidences, that they show us God's sense of humor. Anyway, I ran into that young woman, Grace, the one from the Bishop's people. She's doing well."

"Grace, oh my. How could that happen? Where?"

"A small town on near the pass between Utah and Colorado. Bird threw a shoe, and I needed a smith to fix that one, and really all of the horses' feet. Turned out she's married to a good man and he ran the smithy in that little town. Such a coincidence."

"Her baby? Did it live, is she all right?"

"Her little girl, Rachel, is a beauty and so sweet. Talks very well."

"And the Bishop, the Church, is she still involved?

"She's married to what I guess you'd call an ex-Mormon, name's Charles. He doesn't have any use for the Church and hates the Bishop because of what's heard from Grace. It kind of ironic that they live in that town, it's called 'Blessing' and they certainly do feel blessed. Have another child, a baby boy named Charles after his father."

"Oh, I'm so happy to hear this, I've thought about her so many times, thinking the worst, but this is wonderful. Did you stay with them, see them again on the way back?"

"Stayed over one night so he could do Cloud's shoes in the morning. Didn't come back the same way. Louis told me about a faster route."

"That's just such good news. Makes me almost forget our troubles." She stood up and straightened out her clothing.

"Our troubles?" Abe asked.

"Oh I do sometimes feel terrible about Helga, but Abe, do you realize this is the first time we've ever been alone, just us in our own home."

He stood up beside her, and pulled her into a hug, "Then we'll have to enjoy it, because I don't think it can last too very long."

"Abe, I don't know if I can ever be with Helga again. I feel guilty, but I feel so right about it at the same time. I know it's your son, but we have Isaiah now, and we have to take care of our own part of this family."

"We'll see," he said. "Whatever happens, I'm not going away like that again. It's not good for you and Isaiah, or for me. It's not good for anybody."

The baby cried from his crib and Sa-rah went to him.

"I'll be back later. I have to unload some things and I want to put my horses out on the best feed I can find. They've been so good and so hungry most of the time."

That evening, after their supper, Sa-rah played the piano and Abe dozed in the comfort of his own favorite chair. It was warm enough not to need a fire and the moonlight shone through one of the large windows. He thought about the old saying, "no place like home" and found himself nodding his head in agreement and in time with the notes of the piano. A short time later he felt Sa-rah's hand on his shoulder and he shook himself awake.

She said, "Come to bed, my tired man. I'll rub your shoulders and your neck. You deserve to rest and be taken care of now you're home, now you're back with your own family."

Rather than putting him back to sleep, the rhythmic hands of his wife both soothed and awakened him. She pulled herself up over him. He was lying face down and she straddled him in order to press down harder as she worked the muscles of his back. She was thinking of the nights along the long trail, the times they'd made their connection under the wagon, silently coupling with the unexpected feelings that always came over her when she was filled with Abe's love and strength. Now she was feeling this again and realizing that all that time sharing him with Helga, she'd never felt the freedom to release herself and her feeling, to make soothing sounds and even more sounds that she could feel wanting to come forth from her depths and from her heart. This was her man, and now, once again, he was with her and with her only. Strangely, when she made the other woman and child leave, she had never once had any thought of this part of it. It was truly the mother in her that rose out of her insides and would have attacked both of them if they hadn't left at that time. It had nothing of the competing urges she'd often felt, and the hard, hard loneliness that swept over her and kept her awake imaging the two of them, Abe and his young lover, together...

Abe moaned softly and then rolled beneath her until he could look up into her smiling face. He pulled his arms out from between her legs and reached up to stroke her hair which was hanging down around him. His hands moved lower to her breasts and it was as if he'd never touched them before. She tossed her head and arched her back as he pushed her upright and massaged what he now shared with their son. She gave soft cries in time with his hands squeezing and releasing, and she pulled her nightgown up and over her head. She slid down until he was inside of her and she collapsed onto his chest, kissing him everywhere she could reach with her lips without dislodging him from her warm and throbbing center...

She remained lying on him in the stillness that followed as he fell quickly asleep. As she eased off and aligned herself with his familiar form, familiar yet strange due to all that time away, she couldn't help wondering if she could be enough for him now. How would he feel about Helga, and did he really love her? Sa-rah knew in her own heart that she could never go back to the way things had been since Helga's pregnancy. No, it would be one or the other of them from now on and she tried to feel confident in her place in Abe's heart, in his life. How could it be otherwise, now that they had their own child, now that they didn't need anyone else to complete their family, unless it would be another child or more. She fell asleep thinking of a new baby girl, and how careful she would be to make sure that Isaiah never felt any need to frighten or upset her.

One of the reasons for Lefty and Carl's journey that spring was to bring back some excellent horses the Pauites owed Lefty for helping solve their problems with the government and the Mormons. While the solution that was worked out satisfied none of the parties completely, all had come to see that it was still the only outcome that could end the fighting and assure water and game to both Indians and settlers. The government gave Lefty a payment in gold coins, and the Mormons paid with a promise of some cattle from some of their people who lived closer to where Lefty's family stayed. The Indians gave him three of their best horses.

When Helga came riding into the camp with her boy on the horse in front of her, it was clear to Lefty that she'd been crying, and perhaps still was. She slid off the horse, took the boy down, and let him hide behind her.

"Mr. Lefty," she said, her voice catching in her throat, "she said I have to leave, now. I can't be there, even if she changed her mind.

I'm afraid of how angry she is. Mr. Abe is gone, you know that, been gone a long time to help his cousin. Oh please, can I stay with you? Only tonight until I can gather my things and leave here tomorrow. I'm sorry I have to ask this, but I have no one else and you're Mr. Abe's best friend that I know of."

Lefty motioned to her to come with him and he led the way to the fire, where a leg of venison roasted. "Sit." He pointed to a small stump that was still rooted in the ground, but had been leveled off at chair height. "We are now to eat. You will eat with us and then we will talk."

Helga nodded and brought Indigo around to sit on her lap. A strong breeze blew through the fresh green leaves in the treetops along the creek that flowed beside the camp. She realized that she brought no bedding with her, only extra clothing for her and the boy. Then she noticed that Carl was unrolling a buffalo hide and fixing it into a kind of a bed. He straightened it out and reached under to clear away any sticks or rocks. Looking around she could see two other hides similarly arranged, but further away from the fire. As far as she could tell, the young man hadn't looked her way even once since she'd ridden up on them. His eyes always seemed to be looking down or out into the distance.

The meat was tasty and Indigo was so hungry that she felt she had to tell him to slow down, or stop, but Lefty assured her there was plenty and it was good to see a young boy eat his fill. Helga also felt her own hunger, but was more restrained about the meal, although she didn't refuse a second large piece of the roast Lefty carved from the bone suspended over the slow-burning fire. Darkness began edging its way across the open land of the small valley and the steep-sided hill was already in shadow. The sky filled with streaks of color, which quickly vanished until even the high-above clouds lost their lighting. Indigo nodded against her and seemed ready to fall asleep. Lefty pointed to the bed that Carl had fashioned and gestured for her to take the boy to it.

"You can put him there. Is where you will sleep tonight."

She settled Indigo under the heavy hide and waited for him to sleep, and then she moved back to her seat by the fire, which Carl was stoking back up into flames.

"I want to thank you. I'm not myself right now. I'm going to be all right. I just wish Abe was here. That would help everything."

"You want to say about what is happening? Or no. Is all right. You are my friend's woman, mother of his oldest son. You are safe here with us. We will leave in the morning, but you will have to know what you are going to do. You may come with us until Big Bear Man returns and can come after you. We have horses to take you. Is Sarah Beth there at the home place now, or will she be in the morning?"

"No, not there now, and I don't think she'll come back until I've had time to leave. Oh, it's all so terrible, and I don't want to make it a problem for you. We will be all right once we know where we can go and stay."

"Come with us. As you say, you have nowhere else. My elder woman, Moon Fish, is not well all the time anymore and she can use some help from a younger woman. We will know when your man has returned and we will send message for him to come and see you when you are with us. Is best for now."

"Thank you. I would want to be here when he returns, but there is no way to know when that will be and I know I can't be here now with her."

"This happens. We also see this in our homes and families. One wife and the other wife must be apart for a time. It happens and we will pray for you and Sarah Beth to be together again. I think it is what my friend would want. Now, let's sleep to be ready for the journey we will take for the next few days."

"Thank you again," she said, standing and walking into the brush near where her horse was grazing. By moonlight, she took the bridle and small pack of clothes from his back and brushed his mane with her fingers. She looked to the east where the moon was rising above the ridge and felt herself releaseing a prayer of thanks for this help and of fear for what was coming, "Oh God," she thought, "please take care of us." Then she paused in the bushes to relieve herself, and took her bag back to where she lay down with Indigo and tried not to think about the events of that day.

The next morning Lefty sent Carl over to scout the house and told him to see if Sarah Beth had returned. He returned quickly and said that there was no one there, so Lefty sent him and Helga and the boy back to gather up what she needed to take with her while he secured their camp so that it would be available the next time it was needed. By midday they were on their way north, the two men and their horses and a pack animal for their gear, and Helga on her horse, and her load packed on one of Lefty's new ones, with Indigo riding in front of the pack. He was thrilled to be on a horse by himself and was acting much older than he was. Helga couldn't help laughing for the first time since the altercation with Sa-rah, because the boy was acting so important and grown-up.

The men might have traveled faster without Helga and the boy, but Lefty seemed content with the pace they maintained over the two days it took to reach the crossing of the Snake River. Although the water was moving somewhat slowly and it was not yet at the flow height of the spring thaw, there were always some difficulties to be faced in the effort, and for that reason, Lefty had Carl take Indigo and used a leather strap to secure the boy. The two men kept the horses in a tight bunch as they entered the water and Lefty called for Helga to come along. Part of the way across, the current pushed one of the free horses into a tangled mass of cottonwood roots. Lefty yelled to Carl to stay downstream of the hazard with the other animals and to keep moving with Helga and the boy while he went after the stray. There was a sand bar just below the surface of the water midway, and they were able to pause with the horses knee-deep in the water. They could see that Lefty was having trouble dislodging the horse because its mane was tangled in the roots. The frightened animal reared and thrashed.

Carl yelled, asking if Lefty needed help, but the man apparently couldn't hear him. Helga waved at Carl, hollering for him to go on ahead with the rest of the horses and the boy. Then she wheeled her horse around and headed back for Lefty. Just as she came near to the scene of the struggle, the man managed to loop the end of a rope around the root that was trapping the horse. Helga made her horse move up alongside of him and he was able to hand the coil of rope to her and motion for her to back away. As she did that, the rope put tension on the root and Lefty was able to slide from the back of his own horse to the back of the twisting, frightened caught horse. He grabbed his knife from his belt and slashed at the long tangled hanks of hair, freeing the horse. The animal reared back and then submerged with Lefty still hanging on. He yelled for Helga to throw the rope, caught it, and then cut it from the tree. He reached out as far as possible, got a loop over the horse's nose, and began tugging him away from the root mass, forcing him back the way they'd come. In a matter of moments, Lefty and Helga and the three horses were on the sand bar and then the whole group pushed on across the rest of the river.

When they reached the other side, Indigo was screaming and waving for his mother. Helga took him in her arms and began trying to comfort him, while Lefty and Carl led their own horses up away from the water, into the woods that lined its banks. They unloaded the pack animals and then set about making a temporary campsite.

Helga walked slowly up to where they were and set the boy down on the sandy ground beside their pile of wet belongings. She began spreading clothing out to dry, but had some difficulty as Indigo wouldn't let go of her leg. She kept patting him on the head and telling him that everything was all right. He finally caught his breath enough to be able to speak.

"Ma-ma, that horse," he said pointing to the one that was trapped in the river, "that horse was scared, was he?"

"Yes, he was very frightened."

"I want that horse because he is same me."

"How is that?" Helga stopped what she was doing and knelt down beside him.

"I don't like that river. Same as horse, I don't like."

She hugged him and then said, "It's good to be afraid of some things, like rivers, but it's also good to be brave when you have to face those things. Before you were born, your father had to save a girl from a big river. He is very brave, your father." She hugged him again and said, "We'll have to see about a horse for you sometime soon."

Indigo pointed at a wet and shaking horse standing somewhat apart from the rest of the animals. "That one, Ma-ma."

When they'd finished eating the soup Carl made from dried meat and wild turnips, Lefty looked at the young boy. "How's this boy now?" he said, addressing his question to Indigo. "You are a strong boy. You were able to keep Carl on his horse, weren't you?" He laughed and said, "Isn't that right, Carl?"

The young man didn't say anything, but nodded his head in agreement.

Lefty went on, "We'll have to get you a good name, young boy. You are very brave, and you must have your own horse someday when you are big enough."

Indigo pointed toward the group of horses grazing in a small meadow clearing. "That one," he said, indicating the rescued horse, now dry and eating.

"We see about that." Then he looked straight at Helga, and said, "You also, must have good name. What you did was a strong thing. I am happy to know you and you are also very brave like your son, and you help me save horse. I will call you, 'River Horse Woman' and that name we use in our camps, for you with our people. We will have ceremony soon."

The next day they arrived at a semi-permanent village near the place where the Big Fish River met the Snake. From above the valley they could see smoke from several fires climbing in narrow threads to the clouds above.

"Is my village," Lefty said. "Moon Fish stay here, you stay here now." Indigo was still riding the horse he'd started the trip with, and now it started moving down the trail to the lowland. "Wait for us, young one," the man said loudly, and then laughed, turning to Helga to say, "He is going to be a leader. See?"

The days went by quickly, what with all the late springtime work that needed doing. They planted the garden and Abe worked on a new cistern. The year before they'd almost run out of water trying to keep both the vegetables and the household supplied. He also moved the growing herd of cattle more often while waiting for the best of the grass growing season to get ahead of their appetites.

Isaiah was walking and even trying to run, so he fell down a lot and his loud cries could be heard often in the otherwise still air of their clearing. Happy was now his constant companion and playmate. It wasn't clear to Sa-rah whether or not he missed or even remembered Indigo, although she sometimes found him talking to a homemade toy in his own language, talking as if it were another person. This was the only thing that made her feel bad about Helga's leaving, but she cleared those thoughts from her mind by reminding herself that the other boy was a threat to her son.

She and Mattie were spending more time together than before. Ollie was gone some of the time, working for a surveyor out past where his claim was located. He drove the wagon with the tools and supplies for the other man and was learning quite a bit about the skills required for that job. Mattie confided that she wished he was home more of the time so they could finish some of the work on their little house. Sa-rah offered Abe's help, but Mattie turned it down, saying that wouldn't be right until he'd finished the work on their own house first.

One day when it was time to butcher a steer, Ollie showed up to lend a hand. "Got need for a one-armed outlaw? I can skin an animal with my teeth, throw the guts over my shoulder and cut that fella into pieces faster than you can get yourself hungry for the first bite."

"Ollie, I always believe half of what you say."

"Then you're a bit of a fool. I, myself, only believe a third of it." He laughed and pulled out a knife and a sharpening stone. "Where is it?" he asked.

"I've got a new corral out back there. He's waiting for us."

Within a couple of hours, they finished the job of quartering the animal and the pieces were hanging in the combination cold cellar and storm shelter. When they had cleaned up, they sat to rest under the tree, which had grown quite a bit since the previous summer. Ollie pulled out the flask that seemed to always be with him, and offered it to Abe, who took a swallow and passed it back. Ollie took a long time sipping and wrinkling up his nose in pleasure for the familiar but welcome sensation.

"Just can't get along very far without my helper here. You wouldn't know about it, but every once in a while either my missing hand or the blown-off foot starts either itching or throbbing. Swear to god. Strangest thing, that is. Damn thing wants my attention to scratch it or stomp on the ground or something. The only thing that prevents such shenanigans is this friend in a bottle."

"Sounds like a medical answer to me."

"You bet it is, young fella, and for more things than that." The two of them sat quietly for a time as birds squawked and bickered nearby. Then Ollie spoke quietly, "You ever miss them, the others? You ever wonder how they're doing?"

Abe bent down and wiped some blood off of his boot and then dragged his hand through the dust at his feet. "Surely do. I'm of half a mind to go off looking for them, just to make sure they're all right."

"Well, you said they went off with that Lefty, the Indian fella. He'll take care of them."

"Oh, I know he'll do what he can. It's just if there's trouble up that way, more killing could get out of hand. And who knows what would happen to a white woman and child if they were found in that camp by the whites."

"Think about it a lot, don't you? Here have another taste of the medicine."

Abe took another swallow and gave it back, "Thanks, I guess."

"Another subject, my young friend. Ever since I lost this piece of leg, I know I've been no good for climbing anywhere, so's I wouldn't expect you to still think about me in concern with our little discovery," he said, nodding in the direction of the low ridge where the water came from. "But if it ever comes around, with them Indians letting it happen, you let me know. I'll give you all the pointers you need to make it work out for you."

"Well, if that ever happened I'd sure consider you still being a partner. I wouldn't even have known it's there if it weren't for you."

"Appreciate that, my young friend, but that's not something I'd ever hold you to. Main thing now for you is to make sure nobody else trips over it. Them bastards are all over this country now, hunting for any damn thing. Keep your eyes out, friend, they'd just as easy come down from up top there as not."

"Thanks for the warning. I think I'd hear them yelling when they fell. No way to come down that rock face without coming down awful hard. It's all loose as can be."

"Well, just keep your eyes and ears open. Matter of fact, if it's clearly a part of this here Indian land, I'd advise you to file a claim, a mining claim on that part of it up there…It's easier than a homestead claim, and they might not look too closely at whatever other legal stuff is associated with it here. Matter of fact, I'll get the legal description of it for you from where I'm working now. They've got maps in that office of everywhere around here."

"I'd appreciate having that information. Sounds like it might be a good idea, even if just to protect our water supply from anyone else."

"Good. Hey, I've got to get a move on. Woman's waiting for me and I don't like to make her wait too long."

"Let's grab you some of that meat and send it back to her."

"How about we do that once it's hung for awhile? Wouldn't be wanting to eat it right away anyhow."

Later when he was thinking about the conversation with Ollie, he realized he hadn't told Sa-rah about that discovery, and that it was one of the few things he'd ever kept from her. Well, other than the personal details of the times he spent with Helga and the things they talked about. Then, as he was saddling Bird for a short ride out to check some of the cattle with young calves, he had the sudden thought about the woman in Albuquerque, the one in Louis's jail, Elena. That was certainly something he wouldn't be discussing with his wife. A few minutes later, as he rode out toward the setting sun, the picture of the angry, fiery woman came back into his mind, along with the memory of those last minutes they were alone together in the cell. Although he'd thought about it many times before, especially while riding the lonely trail home, he now felt some of the same intensity he'd experienced in those totally unexpected instants. He remembered the kiss, the confusion of feelings he'd felt toward the woman, and the way she pressed herself against him and seemed to take his whole body into herself for that long strange moment they were alone and intertwined.

What if he'd stayed? He immediately tried to rid himself of such a thought. Here he was with one wonderful woman right in his home, and another with whom he would most likely be reunited, and he was finding himself thinking as if he were a solitary young man with an appetite for the unusual and impossible. It was hard enough to stay close to Sa-rah and Helga without losing touch with one or the other of them, or even sometimes with himself. And he had to tell himself that he loved these women, differently perhaps, but with real honest feelings for them both, but now with the situation like it was, he was once again wondering why it had to happen to him.

Just then he heard the sound of a calf bawling some distance away. He urged the horse into a gallop and headed in the direction of the cries. After a ways, he pulled to a stop to listen again. It was much closer now and just off to his left toward the hillside. Now he also heard the sound of a grown cow answering the calf. The rising ground was almost too rocky for his horse, so he jumped down and hurried toward the animal. He found the calf with one leg wedged into a crack between two large rocks. It could have either fallen into the crack or walked forward into it and become too panicky to back out again. He moved carefully so as not to cause more struggle, but he had to jump down to grab it around its middle in order to free the caught leg. When he pulled it out from between the two rocks, he was relieved to see the leg wasn't cut open, and didn't appear to be broken. By this time the mother cow was standing only a few yards away, but unwilling or too smart to try moving up through the sharp rocks. Abe helped the calf by carefully picking up its legs one at a time and putting them back down until the calf reached flat ground and trotted, limping, to its mother, and immediately began sucking milk. Abe wondered how long it had been caught up like that, but there was no way to tell now—the calf would be nursing with the same energy whether it had been one hour or all day.

He let them have a moment of reunion, but eventually began waving his arms and urging them back down to the valley floor. Now he could see the rest the herd out toward the creek and he got this one and her calf moving toward them before he mounted Bird again. He tried to go back to what he'd been thinking about, but Elena's image seemed to have slipped out of his mind, at least as far as being able to remember at that moment what she looked like. The intensity of the kiss must have had something to do with her predicament and the possibility that she was facing death by hanging. He hoped it hadn't turned out that way. But what would it be like to face death with no one to share the fear and the anger that came with it? Now, thinking about it, he was almost glad it had been him, that he'd been there, been there for her to grab onto in her time of facing the awfulness of the unknown and the terror of what could happen in the next day or two. He decided he'd have to write to Louis and find out what happened. He should write anyway, just to let his cousin know he made it home safely. As he thought about the letter he also decided that he wouldn't mention to rift between Sa-rah and Helga. Who could say that it wouldn't be all in the past by the next time he saw Louis. But he did want to know what happened to the woman. Even though he knew he'd never see her again, he knew that he would never forget her or the way she hung onto him, then pushed herself away, saying "I want you too much." It was surely one of the strangest things that had ever happened to him, and now he had to struggle with his own feelings to forget about her, to think of himself as not in a trap between two women, but as the most fortunate man alive to have two women and two children, and to be strong and free to live here where he wanted to be. Enough of worrying about the future, enough of letting circumstances keep him from giving thanks and listening for the Voice of God in all that he did and all that came his way...He realized he was praying and startled Bird when he slapped her neck with the reins and gave out a loud whoop that echoed across the valley.

CHAPTER 12

Visit

Abe had heard nothing from Helga and Indigo. He thought about them most days and often wished he could just take off and go find them, just to see that they were doing well or at least all right. Although he didn't mention this to his wife, he knew that she was serious when she'd told him she didn't want him leaving again, leaving her and the growing child who was requiring more and more care as he gained his running legs and a hefty interest in exploration. One of the two of them needed to be nearby, looking out for him whenever he was awake. Abe sometimes thought the task would be easier if his older son were around to keep track of Isaiah, but again, it was something he knew better than to mention to Sa-rah.

Then one day she brought up the subject in an odd way. She told him that she'd had a dream about Moon Fish, and that it was the first time she'd had any kind of a powerful dreaming experience since he was away on his trip south. Now she told him that she'd had almost a waking dream of him with another woman, that he was a prisoner and that woman came to him to try to help him escape. When he asked why she hadn't told him about it, she said she just wasn't able to decide if it was real "dreaming" and he needed help, or just some kind of loneliness turning into jealousy. She said she'd been somewhat ashamed of the dream; and when she'd started to tell it to

Helga, the younger woman just laughed and said she had nothing to worry about, that Abe would come back to them as soon as he could and probably wouldn't even notice any other women because he was such a shy man.

Abe tried not to let his expression change with this news. He waited until he thought she was finished and changed the subject, "But what was this about Moon Fish now? Was that last night?"

"The night before," she said. "I wanted to let it stay with me for a day before talking about it. Lefty once told me that if a Dreamer talks too soon about a dream then it will lose its power."

"Well, you can wait to tell me then, if you should. I am curious, though."

"I think it's all right, and remember he also said that a dreamer and their man or woman partner are connected in this way. Even though you don't have the dreams, you are part of where they come from. I didn't understand it then, and I still don't think I can understand much, but when I wake up from one of these, I always feel like I was in someone else's dream, someone close to me, and who else would that be but you?"

"I don't know. I hardly ever remember my dreams."

"Maybe that's because you're busy having mine. I know it doesn't make sense, but then none of it really does…so I'll just tell you about this one."

Just then they heard a loud cry from Indigo, who'd disappeared around the side of the house while they were talking. They both moved quickly to go to him. He was sitting on the ground and pointing to the garden. At first they didn't see anything, and then Abe saw the quick movement of a shadowy shape that stopped and turned to look at them. It was a large rabbit.

"It's a rabbit. Can you say rabbit?" he said to the little boy.

"Abbit? Abbit?"

"Yes," his mother said, "rabbit. And we have to get it out of our garden before it eats all the small plants I worked so hard over."

Abe stooped down and threw a rock in the direction of the animal. It jumped into the air and disappeared in the brushy edge.

"Abbit. Abbit."

"Yes, Rabbit. And we'll have to catch it and get rid of it or we won't have a garden," Sa-rah said, bending down and picking him up.

"Maybe we should weave a brush fence around the garden. Even if we got this one, there's bound to more."

Sa-rah looked at him and said, "So much work, but if we don't do something, we won't have much food come next fall and winter."

"I saw a fence like the kind I'm thinking of and it can be made from all those willows downstream toward the Skinner place."

"How high do you think it has to be?"

"I doubt they'll jump over it," he said. "So not too high." He reached out and took Isaiah from her, and threw him up in the air and caught him a couple of times. "But I'll bet it won't keep this 'abbit' in or out."

Later when the boy was napping, Abe brought up the dreaming subject again. "Can't you make someone else have a dream?"

"It's happened a few times, but I don't know how to make it happen."

"Remember what you said you did to Hawk Man? Maybe it just has to be something you really want to see happen, and it turns into someone's dream."

"Maybe I should practice on you," she laughed, "Let's see, what do I want you to do for me around here?"

"I was actually thinking about Moon Fish. I know you wouldn't want me to go after her, and maybe she can't travel, but who knows, if you put your mind to it she might be able to come to be with us here."

"Well, it is the time they usually come and it's strange they aren't here. I can try, but I think I shouldn't just make it about her, but ask for anyone to bring us word of what's going on with them all...You know, it's kind of like prayer, I think. I have to be really clear about what it is and then make a strong request to myself..."

"And then if it's supposed to happen, it does. It's similar to your father's explanation of God's Voice coming to us is when an opportunity really matches something we need and ask for and it's up to us to take it..."

"I hadn't thought of that, but it is kind of like that. Are you going to be hungry soon? I'd like some of that roast deer tonight if you'll get it from the cellar."

The older woman awoke feeling there was something she'd forgotten to do. This wasn't that unusual as her memory was weakening with the passage of years. She often didn't want to bother trying to remember things if they didn't come to her the first time she had a thought about something from the past, but didn't remember the details. On this particular morning, she also realized that she was alone in her cabin for the first time since the young woman came to stay with her over a month ago. She'd been such a help, but now she was going with some of the people to a different summer encampment than their usual spot. With all the trouble of late between the gold-seekers and the Indians, Hawk Man was reluctant to leave their home territory in the hands of only a few families. Two miners had been killed over in the Bitterroot Mountains. That was some distance from their village, but word traveled fast. The possibility of white man revenge was as likely as not.

Moon Fish was saddened by the story that the young woman Helga told about the incidents with Sa-rah…Just then, there it was, the memory she'd lost on waking. It was another dream and it was a dream of the other young woman, Sa-rah, and her husband and child. It was the second time this dream and another like it had come to her, and she sat up in the bed to try to think harder about this. These days it was all too easy to just lay back and fall asleep again, but today she wanted to be awake, first to recapture these dreamings, and second to see what she would have to do for herself now and to arrange for another helper if she was going to need that.

She eased up from the low bed and its buffalo hide mattress, and slipped her feet into the warm moccasins with the fur inside. She stood up and shuffled across to the small stove Lefty brought her and lit the shavings of pitch that Helga had left is readiness for this fire, a kind of good-bye present. Moon Fish's shoulder hurt again this morning, but not so bad that she couldn't put a few larger pieces of wood over the kindling and place the kettle of water on the stove. Even though it was turning into the hottest time of the year, a cup of her own tea was a comfort that eased the stiffness of the first movements of her day.

Now, about these dreams, she thought. In both of them, Sa-rah and her baby were trying to swim the big river, but couldn't make it all the way across. While they weren't in any danger, neither could they make any progress against the currents in the middle of the wide channel. When they made their way back to the other side, she could see that Sa-rah had pulled off her long outer skirt and tied it to a small tree by the riverbank. She had to bend the tree to fasten it; when she let go, the sapling sprang back up and the skirt fluttered in the breeze as if it were completely dry, waving like a flag, even though it had been wet only moments before.

The child ran away from the river and climbed up among the boulders that marked the boundary of where the high-water floods would reach. He stood on one of the rocks and began singing in a voice she could hear above the sound of the river, and he was singing about a grandmother.

"Oh Grandmother, Oh Grandmother have you forgotten
Grandmother, have you forgotten my name, have you?
I am waiting to see you again, I want you to give me my name,
Oh Grandmother, Grandmother, don't please don't forget me,
Please don't forget to give me my name..."

She knew that Sa-rah had the power of a Dreamer, but she was surprised that the young woman could send a message through someone else, especially a child. She remembered she was making tea for herself and shook the dried leaves into the boiling water. Lefty would have to be told about this. It was good that he was nearby and she could get word to him. He would know what to do.

She poured a cupful of the hot tea through a piece of cloth and carried it out to the porch. It pleased her to be able to sit with the mountains in the distance and the sounds of this branch of the Imnaha

River singing the song of the fast-moving waters and telling her of its journey from snow-topped mountain peaks to bring her this news of the warm weather melting the winter into summer. She cradled the warm cup in her hands and felt its heat soak into her stiffened hands, bringing some relief from the pain of waking and beginning to move them again for another day.

She thought back on the conversations she'd had with the younger woman, this Helga, who was mother to that Abe's first son. If she could have changed anything, she might have wished that Sa-rah was the first to give him a son, but she knew that there were reasons above and beyond her understanding, or anyone's for that matter, why there must be two of them from this one man. She also knew from her own experience as a child of whites, brought up with the whispered assignment of blame for what she had come to learn was what they called adultery. Funny word for it, she thought, makes it sound like it's only for adults to do, but doesn't make it sound like a bad thing. As a child and as a girl coming into womanhood, she was warned about this and other sins, and when it came time for her to begin receiving suitors and for her parents to begin making suggestions as to which of the young men were preferable to others, she was also reminded again that there would be only one choice. Her mother would often say in a whisper, "You can only have one of them, so we shall help you to choose well."

Then when she was almost ready to decide between two of the young men in the vicinity of her parents' homestead, an Indian raid burned her home and killed her parents. She was taken captive and sold to Lefty's father to replace a wife who'd recently died, leaving behind two sons, Lefty and an older brother. The woman whose white woman name was Kate became Moon Fish and found herself taking charge of a family that included the boy, Left hand Crow, or Lefty as he became known across the west. In spite of his special fondness for this young white woman, her Indian husband, being a powerful and wealthy man, was unable to avoid taking on two more wives to assist in the management of his camp and to bring him more children. Now, here she was an adopted grandmother to the children of two young white women, what her father would have called headstrong fillies. It was strange how the memories and particularly the memory of white man language would come back to her when she was thinking of her past. Whenever she thought or talked of her adopted Indian people, it was always in the native tongue.

"Fillies." Wherever that word came from, it was what she was called as a young woman because she had not yet been married or had children. Now, these two were both with a man and each had a child, but she couldn't help thinking of them as young horses pulling away from each other, but tied together by a single rope. Neither had any preparation for sharing a man. After all, it was a "sin" in their way. But here they were, and she was probably the only person who could go between them and try to make things better. She stood up and gave a long warbling call into the air. Soon a young boy appeared from the trail that led away from her clearing to the next cabin. She motioned for him to come closer.

In Indian she said, "Tell your uncle Lefty I want to see him."

The man showed up that evening when she was napping. He woke her gently, and then went to wait on the porch while she brought herself back from the mystery world of sleep. Ever since he was a boy, she'd told him we don't have to know where we go when we are sleeping, but we have to be careful when we come back to this awake-time world that we do it slow enough to make sure we bring our whole self back and not leave anything behind. She went to sit with him and they sat quietly while evening songs of the birds filled nearby woods. The sound of the river blended in a softness that welcomed the stars as they appeared one by one in the darkening sky above.

"You have news?" he asked in their Indian language, knowing that she wouldn't have called for him if it wasn't of some importance.

"Yes, my son. A Dream message. From Sa-rah. She had her child. Abe's new son sang to me how he wants his name. I think that means she wants to see me."

"Her son, you say. How big was this son in your Dream?"

"Same as this Indigo, Helga's boy."

"Strange. Sa-rah's boy is still a baby."

"But a baby couldn't sing me to come there."

"And you," he said as he took her hand in his own, "what do you want?"

"I want to see her again. To see this baby. To see what she says happened with her and this Helga. To see Abe. I want all that before I leave this life."

Lefty was quiet for a moment, and then said, "I say the boy in the Dream means you will live at least until he is that much grown. And he will be able to thank you for his name. But the rest of it is this woman saying she cannot come see you, so she wants you to come to her."

"In the Dream she and the boy try two times to swim the big river. Both times they have to go back to their side," the woman said. "This means to me, she wants to come but cannot. Same as you say. So what do I do? I can no longer ride a horse."

"Give me a few days, my mother, and we will see what comes of this. Maybe I, too, will have a Dream message. I have some things to do here and then we will see what is possible."

"That is good, my son. Come back soon. And send someone to help me a little bit now that the young woman is not here. It is harder for me without her."

He took her hands in his own and kissed them, and stood up, looking down at her silver hair. Then he reached out with both hands open and held them just above her head. "Bless me, mother. I return soon."

She sang a few words softly in a low voice and then said in white man talk, "Go and return."

In three days, she heard the sound of a horse approaching, but it was without a rider and pulling a small wagon, what is called a buggy. Lefty was riding alongside the horse with a lead rope connected to its headgear. "My mother," he called out. "Look what I have found for you."

She came out onto the porch and gave a big smile at the sight of the small wagon. "For me?" She laughed. "I don't remember how to drive one."

"Easy. Watch." He climbed into the seat and flicked the tip of a slender whip to graze the horse's rump. The animal trotted around in a big circle as Lefty guided it with the reins. Then he pulled the horse to a stop and then started again. "See. No problem. Besides I will be with you. This is how we go to visit."

"Where did you get this?"

"From that new doctor in the town. I let him use Hawk Man's wagon to move things from Fort Boise where he was living. You like this?"

"It's nice. Looks good like new."

"Probably is. He is a young man. New here. From somewhere else. We can leave day after tomorrow."

"I will be ready."

Their journey was without incident, although they had to rest often for the woman. When they were almost there, they stopped first at the Skinner place to find out how things were with everyone. Martha had never met Moon Fish, or Kate, as she introduced herself.

"I've heard so much good about you from Sarah Beth," Martha said.

"Thank you. Are they at home?"

"Oh yes, they hardly go anywhere. Mattie, her step-mother, is over there now, staying and helping out some. My husband and Ollie, my brother, are gone for the day. Will you get down and have some tea or coffee?"

Lefty climbed down off his horse and bowed slightly to her. "Thank you, but I think we should keep going until we can stop. My mother here is very tired from this travelling."

"Well, I'm sure they'll be glad to see you. None of us get many visitors out here, and your people didn't even come this year. At least not yet."

"No, and they probably will not, not the usual families. There is some trouble up home. They are all right, but too much taking care of things there."

"Well, maybe we will get to visit with you while you're here." She looked at Moon Fish and said, "It is not often that I can meet a wise woman, as I know you are."

"Thank you. We shall see you again." The older woman snapped the whip gently and the horse turned and went back to the roadway. Lefty waved and mounted his horse.

When they arrived at Abe's house, Mattie was hanging laundry and the little boy was playing around her feet. A dog began barking as they pulled in and Sa-rah appeared in the doorway on the porch. She wiped her hands and covered her mouth as she gave a short shout of surprise. She ran down the steps to the buggy, and reached up to take the older woman's hands in her own.

"Oh my, oh, oh, it's you. I'm so glad to see you. Please, let me help you down. You must be so tired. You must come inside." She helped Moon Fish down from the buggy seat and steadied her as she gained her balance. The older woman was clearly very tired and stiffened up.

Mattie and Isaiah came around the corner of the house just as Lefty led the horses to a railing. He stopped as the boy hid behind the woman's skirts and waited until he peeked out.

"You're a big boy now. Good for you," he said. "Good day to you, ma'am. I am known as Lefty, a friend of Mr. Abe."

"I know who you are. I remember. He will be very happy to see you."

As soon as Moon Fish was settled and resting, Lefty went across the creek to check on the old campsite and to wait for Abe to return from his work with the cattle. The camp looked good, ready for people, and it gave the man a kind of unhappy feeling. The families had such good times in this place and now they weren't here and the times weren't what they had been. He had a sense of foreboding that maybe things would never be the way they were again. So much change.

He made a small fire and burned some herbs, lighting his pipe and offering it to the directions. He said a simple prayer for his family and people back to the north and asked for his mother to be given the strength to revive here and grow stronger again. It had been a hard trip for her. Although she never complained, he could see that it was taking much out of her and her weariness was obvious as was the strength of her spirit which kept her moving and trying to be cheerful. He also blessed the land he stood upon and asked for the safety and wellness of his friend and this family. He thought back to his conversation a few days ago with the younger of Abe's two women. She told him she very much wanted to see and be with Abe, and that her child missed him very much. But she also said that she was not ready, and perhaps never would be, to live with Sa-rah.

He said he would talk with his friend and see if there wasn't something they could do to make this hurting stop and be healed. His mother was the one who could do the most if anyone could. For now, he was glad to be here and looked forward to visiting with his friend. And just then he heard a horse splashing through the creek. It surely wasn't anyone trying to sneak up on him, so it must be Big Bear Man. He quickly lay down and covered himself with loose branches. He peered out from this sparse shelter and watched as Abe rode into the clearing, stared at the horse and searched around. He climbed down and began walking slowly around camp area.

He called out, "Lefty, where are you? They told me you were here."

Lefty waited until his back was turned and then with great stealth he eased out of his hiding place, moved over to a bare spot, and sat down, looking very much as though he'd been there all along. He coughed and smiled when Abe spun around.

"Where? Where'd you come from?" he said. "You weren't there just now." He reached down for lefty's hand, pulling him up and laughing. "You're becoming more powerful, my friend. Appearing out of nowhere." They clasped each other's shoulders and laughed together.

"Good to see you, blind man. I was there all the time."

"You were not." Again they laughed and slapped each other's shoulders. "What are you doing here this time?"

"I bring my mother to see Sarah Beth. I bring message from Hawk Man, and message from the young woman, Helga. But all that is for later. And you? How are you?"

"Doing well. Grass good. Many calves. Building some corrals so I can separate and sort the cattle. But tell me how it is with you and your people. We hear rumors of troubles."

"Is true. Many fights between white settlers and our people. Young men angry. Whites want more land. Army not want to fight anybody, but tell Indians to stay away from good land and to stay in mountains. But not good for horses. Need grass." He paused. "Army strange. They want horses, but do not want Indians to have land to raise horses for them." He filled his small pipe, cradling it in the palm of one hand. "We will smoke other pipe later, for prayers. Now, just this little one for being happy to see you and me together again." He lit the pipe, puffed a few times and offered it to the sky and the earth, then passed it to Abe.

Abe held it carefully and offered smoke from its bowl to the air. He waved his hand through the thread of it as it climbed skyward and made as if to brush it on himself as he'd seen done. "I am grateful to be here. It is good."

"Any strangers come around about the land? Any government? Hawk Man worries."

"No, no sign of anything like that."

"So, my friend, how was your journey to New Mexico Territory? Did you go that far?"

"I did. It was good to travel that way. But when I got there, my cousin Louis was all right. He didn't need my help as things worked out for him…But it is strange down there. Wild people. Louis is a deputy marshal and gets involved with fights and killing. I worry for him."

Lefty took in several more puffs, offered the pipe again to Abe who passed it up, and then he emptied it onto the ground and rubbed the hot ashes into the dirt. "Too many poor people who have nothing to live with and some very rich people who have everything. They are all Mexicans. I try my best to keep the Indians away from there, away from the towns and the Mexicans. Always trouble when that happens."

"And the Americans. Seems to me they try to control everything and they will only make it worse for themselves. The country is beautiful, but I was not sorry to leave quickly."

"And when you returned? The young woman was gone?"

"Yes. How is she?"

"We will talk about that. She told me to tell you she wants to see you."

"But I don't know how that can happen, unless she comes back here."

"We will talk. Now, take me to see your cattle. I want to see this land once again."

Isaiah fell asleep for his afternoon nap soon after the visitors arrived. Moon Fish also dozed off while Sa-rah began getting things ready for a welcoming supper, vegetables fresh from the garden and salted meat from the underground room. While she was cutting the meat and placing it in a pot of boiling water, the older woman appeared in the doorway. She stood there quietly and waited to be noticed.

"Oh, I didn't see you there. Did you get a nice rest?"

"I rest a great deal these days. It is what I do best now." She smiled and took a seat at the table. "Can I be of help?"

"No thank you. I have it almost all ready. I hope those two men don't stay away too long."

They were quiet together for a while as Sa-rah finished her preparations. Then Kate broke the silence by asking, "Do you know where your other young woman is?"

"No. I thought she might be with you."

"She was. Now gone to another village with Hawk Man and his families. She is lonely for this place. She stayed with me, helped me, was good to me. But now she goes to help those ones build a new village where it is safer. Too many whites where they have been living in the winter times. Too much trouble."

"Is she all right? Is she safe, she and the boy?" Alarm sounded in Sa-rah's voice.

"She will be as safe as any of them. I hope they don't try to fight anyone. Some of the young men have no more patience and that is the danger."

Moon Fish slept in Helga's room, which Sarah Beth had straightened up for potential visitors. Lefty rode back to the old campsite and said he wanted to sleep there, but would be back in the morning. Sa-rah and Abe went to their room and stayed awake for a long time talking about the surprising way in which Moon Fish received the message that she was wanted by them, and about how weak she seemed. Abe related what Lefty had told him about the conflicts breaking out between the people and the settlers and miners.

"Did Moon Fish say anything to you about how she's feeling?" Abe asked.

"All she would say was that getting old is hard work. Don't let anyone fool you she said even if you have less to do it gets harder and you get slower. Then she smiled and told me not to worry, that I have a long time before that happens to me…She asked if we were going to want another baby. I told her we were so grateful for Isaiah, and thankful for her wonderful help, that we hadn't thought about that yet. She told me our next child would come when I stop nursing unless I take some kind of herbs."

They were quiet for a time. Then Abe asked her, "You must have thought about it once or twice. Yes?"

She rolled over toward him and pressed her body against his. "I think about this." She kissed him. "And this makes me think about that."

"I think about you and me and our boy, and I think about more children someday, but now I also have to worry about my other son who may be in danger."

Sa-rah pulled away a little bit, but then said, "I know. Believe me or not, I think about them a lot, and I miss Helga and Indigo. I miss them, but I can't change my mind about what I've done."

"Let's not talk about all that right now." Abe touched her hair and then let his hand move down her shoulders and across her breasts. "Remember how quiet we had to be under the wagon on the trail. Do you remember how to be that way with a guest in the nearby room?"

She answered by reaching in under his nightshirt and stroking his chest, whispering her love and kissing his eyes and face and mouth. They eased into their lovemaking and kept their silence and moved slowly so the bed wouldn't shake. When they were complete with one another, they lay for a long time, breathing softly and slowly dozing into the night.

Next morning, after eating a large breakfast that Sa-rah put together while Moon Fish watched her, Abe and Lefty saddled up and rode away. They were headed to the water source above the headquarters buildings. Lefty had asked if he could see and feel the place where the water came from, where the "medicine metal" was discovered.

They hobbled the horses and began climbing the rough slope to the cliff above them. When they got up to the pond, Lefty set down his small pack and knelt at the edge of the rock and mud structure that held the water. He scooped up several handfuls of water, one after another, and poured it over his head, and each shoulder, then rubbed some into his shirt at his belly. He bent forward and drank.

"Ahh, good water," he said. He stood up, looking around and taking in the extent of the pond basin and the wall of rock and the seeping water and running streams that fed it. Then he backed away and found a place with room for both he and Abe to sit. He removed his larger pipe bag from the pack and beckoned for Abe to join him.

"Good water and all year round, at least it has been."

"Good." Lefty emptied some smoking mixture into one hand and then began filling the pipe's bowl, raising each pinch of the herbs into the air and singing softly. When he'd filled the bowl he held the pipe out to Abe. "I want you to tell me what it is you need, what it is you want. About the women, about the land and about this medicine metal. Then we will pray for you. But first I want you to know that I am praying for my mother, and for you and your family. That way our prayers will twist together as they climb into the sky and the heaven above. This smoke will carry them and make them powerful, because we will not be asking for ourselves, but for those who need us and depend on us. And there is no hurry, you have time to think how to say these things in very few words."

Far off a hawk screamed as it dove for some kind of prey. Abe sat quietly, holding the pipe and listening to the sound of the water falling and dripping into the pond. He thought of himself and his past, of the ways that he'd worshipped and prayed during his life, of the ways of prayer he'd seen and come to know, both the strange ones and those more familiar. The memory of Dr. Randall, Sa-rah's father, came to him and he acknowledged to himself just how much he owed the man, both for taking him in and for giving his daughter. And how much she loved him...He felt almost like crying for a moment... what she'd gone through, left behind, put up with, struggling to build a home out of nothing here on the frontier, and how she went through so much to finally be blessed with the birth of their son. She would do anything, even give her own life to protect him, and maybe another, others to come. But there was also Helga, the one who was now gone, but who loved him as much and in a different way, almost a kind of adoring of him. Hopefully, oh how much he hoped for this, perhaps Moon Fish could help resolve this circumstance and all of its distance and hurt.

He looked up from his hands and glanced over at his friend, Lefty, this man who never seemed to want anything for himself, who was always giving, always helping, and who seemed to know what everyone else needed and how to get it, if possible. Now, here on this land, the two of them together, so far from the Missouri riverbank where they first met, so far in time and in space and in what had happened to each of them in that time and across that space. This land, now, as a home, as a gift and a responsibility, a blessing, and yes, a kind of a burden that seemed to be more and more his to bear. And the gold, the gold...Please help us know what and how to do with the appearance of this strangeness that was to be either a great gift or a great temptation that could lead to its own kinds of disaster. Why and what was this mysterious discovery meant to show him?

Abe stopped his thoughts and looked up into the blue sky with its small scurrying clouds, and he realized for a moment that he already had everything he needed and that his most heartfelt prayer would be one of gratefulness and not one of beseeching.

"My friend," he said, softly, "I think that all is well with me. There are things I don't understand or don't know what to do about, but they will take care of themselves or be taken care of. I only ask for the happiness and protection over those I am close to, those I am responsible for and to. I know that may not be what you said I should pray for, but it is enough for me now."

"A good prayer, my friend. Here, we will smoke together for that prayer." He struck a match and held it out to the bowl of the pipe Abe was now holding out to him, then he bowed his head as Abe puffed on the stem to get the mixture to light. Abe passed the pipe to Lefty, wondering what they would do next.

Lefty held the pipe up in front of himself and turned it in a circle, pausing to lift its stem straight up at west, north, east and south, above and then touching the earth with the bottom of the bowl. Then he puffed smoke and took some into himself. He blew it skyward and said, "Hear this man. He is a good man and he has a family and is here very much alone taking care of this land for our people. Bless him and his women, his children and his animals. He is a good man and You need him, and we need him. Take care of him and answer the prayers of his heart." He handed the pipe to Abe, exhaled into his hands, and "washed" his head and upper body with motions of his hands.

Abe prayed, "Dear God above, bless this man, his mother, his wives and his family. He is a giver of blessing so I pray for him to be blessed in all that he does for You and for his people and for my family. Give his mother the strength to do the work that she is here in this world to complete, and let me say thank you for all that he has done for my family and for me. I ask a special blessing for his

People as they face these struggles and conflicts over their homeland. Protect them in the lives and their homes. A-men."

He passed the pipe back to Lefty. It had gone out, so Lefty lit it again. They smoked and passed and smoked and passed until the coal lost its glow and the pipe was finished. Lefty picked up a handful of dirt four times and rubbed each handful along the stem and around the bowl. He said, "I'm cleaning it off with this dirt." He laughed. "White man call things dirty when he doesn't like them. Indians wash things clean with dirt. We are so different, but the time will come when there will be no more difference. Either there will be no more white people, or no more Indians, or we will all be together so no one can tell the two from one another. Who knows, my friend?" He separated the bowl from the stem and repacked the pieces into the leather bag. "Now about this treasure."

"Ollie, you know him, Mattie's man and the Skinners' relative. He was a miner back east where he came from. Lost his hand underground in a mining accident. Now he lost his lower leg from the knee down working on that new road. I told you he's the one found it up here, but now he can't make the climb on his replacement leg. And he told me we should put a claim on this area, before someone else or some company does. He says they're after everything these days."

"We know all about that up where we are. What do you think?"

"Don't know exactly. Could protect us from trespass and strangers blowing open this place for the gold. At the same time, it could draw attention to it and bring it anyway. How good is our claim on all this from the government, the Indian law?"

"Supposed to be protected, but no law protects Indians. That's what we're finding out." Lefty gave a bitter laugh. "The gun is the only law anymore."

"So what can we do? What do Hawk Man and the elders want me to do?"

"We never told very many, only Joseph, and another one, Looking Glass. They don't want anything done to make attention, but they say it won't be long before all land is taken away. You are a white man. But you live here because it is Indian land, but only by laws that are far away, and the men who make laws are always changing places, changing who's in charge. Perhaps, if we hurry, you have to buy it from the government with our permission because is not possible for homestead land. We make it that way in one treaty. Use some of this shiny metal to pay for the land, but keep it secret where it comes from. Give Hawk Man a long-time right to come here, hunt here, just as it is now, but it will be your land with the law."

"Your people will allow that?"

"Do we have choice? It will either be you, or someone else will take it from us." He smiled and went on, "and we know you." Then he spoke seriously, "And we trust you because we smoke together, is more strong than paper and ink. And because Hawk Man tells me you make your blood go in this land."

"I would be pleased to do this with you, with your relatives, but I don't even know how to get the gold out and Ollie can't help. This idea is good, but it can't work."

"You are still a white man, my friend. It will work out if it needs to, for us and for you. What is above this rock wall? I don't know, do you?"

"Never been up there, but it looks like a man could go around down the valley and maybe get up on top."

"If you could get your friend up there that way, I'm sure he could lower himself down to here. Then he should be able to make it back downhill from here. We go see." Lefty stood up and shouldered his buckskin pack, looking up the rock wall. "Not too far down from up there."

They rode out the valley until it narrowed and that ridge lowered its shape toward them. There was a kind of a notch in the rocks and some trees growing in a narrow canyon. Lefty urged his horse in that direction and they began climbing a gradual incline that wound its way between two walls of broken rock. The horses moved carefully through spilled boulders and gravel. They emerged on a level area of grass and short, twisted trees. It looked as though springtime meltwater would find its way down from the nearby heights and was the cause of the trail they'd climbed. They rode through the stunted, scattered pine trees until they were suddenly surprised by a narrow cleft in the ground. It was only a few feet wide and went away from them in both directions. Lefty's horse stooped short and wouldn't move forward.

Abe pulled up alongside his friend. "What do you think?"

"Maybe water down in there, maybe your water." He dismounted and dropped his horse's reins. He picked up a couple of rocks and went to kneel beside the opening in the ground. Abe joined him. One rock dropped from his hand held out over the shadowy opening. They heard it hit once on the rock wall and then splash.

"Come," Lefty said, standing, "We see."

They walked quickly toward where the cut of the crevice ended near the edge of the land. Suddenly the valley below them was visible and they could even see the house down there. Lefty dropped another rock, but this time there was no splash and it struck bottom only a short way down. They both squatted at the edge, and then Lefty lay down and inched his way to where he could look down over the rock face.

"Close," he said, "not far down. Your water."

"Is the rock wall solid or broken up?"

"Looks solid with places to step down. Use rope from up here. Easy to get down."

"Then that's why we don't want to file a mining claim," Abe said. "Anyone found out about it, they could come in this way and we'd never know they were here."

"You know, your friend, he probably knows how to rig some kind of way to get himself down there. You hook a rope onto that horse Bird and she can do the work. Done that kind of thing before. One time, I was sneaking around in an enemy camp and found a good young woman to steal. Got chased and had to lower myself down a cliff, then loosen the rope and yell for her to leave and meet me at the river. That horse was waiting when I got there. Still had the rope."

Abe looked at him skeptically, then laughed and asked, "And what happened to the young woman?"

"She was waiting at the river."

The man was still lying near the edge so Abe grabbed his feet and lifted as if to drop him over the side. "Don't need a rope or a horse, you'll land in that water down there."

Lefty kicked and worked out of his boots so that Abe was left holding on to them. Lefty jumped up and somehow got behind Abe and grabbed him in a bear hug. "Now, who's going swimming?"

"I'll toss these boots down that hole if you don't let me go."

"Not my boots! Anything but my boots." He let go and Abe turned and handed them to him. Laughing.

"Should throw them down there anyway, and then take your horse too."

"Don't think so, my friend, that horse owes me his life and he'd probably bite into that hairy head of yours and scalp you alive if you tried anything like that."

"All right, all right. We should head back. This been a good ride so far. He slapped Lefty on the back. Lefty was still pulling on the second boot and fell over.

"Don't give up, do you? Maybe I'll be the one does the scalping."

They laughed together and mounted up, headed back the way they came.

"It's nice up here," Lefty said.

That evening, when Moon Fish had gone to bed, Lefty said he should leave as soon as he could due to the troubles back in their home country. He worried Moon Fish needed more rest before she could take the trip back north. Sa-rah immediately suggested that she stay with them, then looked over at Abe to see if he would agree or not.

"I'm sorry, dear. I didn't talk about this with you, but it has been on my mind."

"I think it's a good thing," he said.

"I will say that I thought about that, but I'm not sure she will agree," Lefty said. "We'll have to ask her in the morning."

Moon Fish was pleased at the idea, but was concerned about what might happen to her cabin and her belongings if she wasn't there to protect them. Lefty assured her that those things would be looked after, and said she would be safer here anyway. She laughed and told them that she still remembered how to fight, she was just a little slower now.

The morning Lefty headed back north, he took Abe aside for as he said, "a short talk." They walked down past the stable and found a place to sit on an unused firewood log. "My friend," he said, handing Abe a small carved stick with circles cut into the bark, "I was talking with your other woman before I came here. She is sad, maybe angry, but she told me to tell you that she keeps you in her heart. The boy is growing strong, running after the bigger boys and wrestling with them even when he gets hurt."

Abe smiled, though he felt a pain inside.

Lefty continued, "We have many such times like this among our people. Even when the women are blood sisters. But this time, for you, it is not between the women, not fighting over the man and who gets what, but is about the children. This is more difficult because they can be angry for their children, not selfish for themselves, so they feel very much they are right. She say it is not the boy's fault. He is not a bad boy. He want to play and be with his little brother, but he have to learn to be not so hard at playing. He will learn from the big boys what it is to be the little one and he will learn to take care of his little brother." He pulled out the small pipe he carried in a pocket of his jacket and held it without lighting it. "You think this is so?"

"I do. Indigo is somewhat wild in his play. He wants to grow up fast so he can have his own horse, his own weapons. So he can hunt and ride like a man. He is impatient, but he is not a mean boy, only rough."

"This what that one say too, but this one here, your Sa-rah, I like that new name, she is afraid, afraid something will happen to her son she wanted so badly." He paused and lit the pipe, offering it to Abe, who puffed on it once and handed it back, gesturing that he wanted no more. "I know she feels bad that she cannot have other one here," he said, "but she is sure it is a danger. And that one knows that. But what can she do? Only you can make it fixed. But even I don't know how you could do that. So, we have problem now. A woman with no other family will not be able to live our way without a man to help her through the winter. And we are making new village, even more hard. So she say to me, what can she do about this? I cannot take her in my lodge, is full. My women like her, but don't want another one, one who they don't know how she will be in hard times of the year."

"If I had another house nearby, but even the neighbors don't have room for anyone else, and especially a young boy as well," Abe shook his head sadly.

"There is a man who could take care of her. He lost his own wife to sickness. You know him, Hawk Man's son. He is alone, but is strong and other young women will want him soon when his time of sadness is passed."

"Carl. Yes, I know him. Has he said anything to you about this?"

"No, but I have seen him look at her and he has made a bow and arrows for the boy."

Abe stood up suddenly and took a couple of paces away from the log, then he turned and said, "She is in my heart as well. The boy is my first son. I can't just let them go. I don't know what to do, but I want them with me again."

"Would you give up this one, Sa-rah and the little boy for that?"

Abe thought for a moment, "They won't leave, they have nowhere to go. And even if I left to be with the other two, she could not make it here without me or another man." His thoughts were whirling inside him now. "Not even Ollie and Mattie could make a difference; it would only be harder. No, I want to be here, I want to be with them, but then I can't have the other two." He sat back down and put his head in his hands. "I can't help feeling these things. I want them to be friends, to take care of one another."

Lefty knocked the ash out of the pipe, and said, "I will tell her what you say. Not everything, but that you still want her. Maybe Carl will take care of her without making her his wife. That has happened sometimes, but the man usually also has wife as well as the woman he is taking care of as a not-wife. We shall see."

Abe held the stick up in the air and said softly, "Tell Carl I would be grateful for his help in this, but I am not ready to give her to any other man. Tell him to take care of my son and I will repay him somehow. Tell him…no, only say, I said I cannot stand in the way…"

"I will say what I think they need to hear from me, from you. Winter has its own ways of making things clear, my friend. We never know what the cold wind will bring, we only know it is our life to live and we must survive each test, of weather, and of this thing the white man calls love. Remember, no one is very good at living this life. That's what we are here to learn."

Lefty took off an hour later, driving the doctor's wagon with his horse tied behind. He took some of their salted and dried beef after Abe assured him they had plenty. Lefty said they had no idea how much "that little old woman can eat." She shushed him and they had a heartfelt goodbye.

Several days went by until Abe could meet with Ollie and plan their attempt to get the man back to the site of their discovery. Lefty was right about Ollie's abilities. He was able to convince Abe that he was willing to take any risks and was excited to get going on the project. Once they got what they needed packed up, they started out, left some things at the foot of the trail to the pond, and then headed up above. It was still midmorning when they arrived at the crevice.

"I can make it down there pretty easy," Ollie said, looking down into the dim space below. "Only got one leg to get in my way. Question's gonna be, how hard is it to get out above our water-wall? But looks to me like there's some light coming in down there. Must be a hole in that wall we can't see from down there."

"If it's not too high up the wall, we can hang this pulley and use this long rope for you to slide down," Abe said. "Problem is…Once we've got you down by the pond, can you get down the hill on your own, back down there?" he pointed to the valley's floor and the trail to the house.

"I can get down if I have to slide on my goddamn butt. It's climbing up I can't do."

Once they had everything ready, it all went fairly smoothly. Lefty had been right about Bird, she seemed to know exactly what to do as

Abe held on to her reins and asked her to back toward the edge of the deep spot with Ollie's weight pulling against her rigging.

Ollie got a little impatient waiting the hour it took Abe to get back down and around, and make the climb up to their catch-basin, and yelled some things at the younger man when he saw him climbing the trail. Abe was surprised to see Ollie so close above him when he got there, and he saw that the man already had the pulley fastened to a sturdy outcropping. The plan was for Ollie to lash the rope around his waist and thread it through the pulley. Then Abe would pull the rope to its full length and use his own weight, easing slowly toward the cliff and lowering the other man's weight. It was all working well until Abe tripped and was then dragged across the rough rocks toward the pond. Ollie hit the water with a splash and they both had a good laugh and took a rest to eat before they got on to the work they'd come to do.

Abe had packed Ollie's cane and replacement leg on his back when he came up, and he handed them to the man. Then he pulled out their tools. Ollie showed him the crack in the rocks that held the crumbly rock soil mixture and Abe began hacking away at it. The dislodged dirt and rock fell onto a blanket they'd brought along for that purpose. After a few minutes Ollie held up his hand and stopped Abe from going any further. He got down on his good knee and began pawing through the materials on the cloth.

"Get me that bucket with some water in it," he said.

Abe brought back the bucket. Ollie picked up some mud and rock from the blanket and dropped it into the water. He swirled it around, let it settle, and then slowly poured the dark water off onto the cloth. Then he moved over to a dry part of the blanket and dumped out the residue in the bottom of the bucket. He sifted through it with his fingers.

"There," he said, "and there, and there. There's the color son, the beautiful color of the most precious metal in the world. Yeeeee-HAAAH." Abe knelt down beside him and could make out small flakes of the shining material.

He slapped Ollie on the back, and said, "You did it, partner."

Part IV

CONNECTIONS

Fall 1874-Winter 1877

CHAPTER 13

Separation

Mary Wolf was teaching Helga to work the softness into an elk's hide when Lefty arrived. She stopped what she was doing and called out to him in their language. He swung down off his horse and unloaded two bags hanging from the saddle.

"Hallo, good women. I bring you white man food and material for dresses. Also for Patsy I bring a blanket, but do not say that to her. How is everyone here?"

Helga stood now, not answering but asking her own question, "How are they? Abe?"

"They are well. They are having a good season. I left Moon Fish with them. She was not so well, but I am thinking she will grow stronger there."

"And the little boy?"

"He is talking and learning to run, fall down and get up. They sent some things of yours for you. They are here somewhere. But where is Hawk Man? Is there any bad trouble?" He spoke briefly to Mary Wolf in their language. She answered and he smiled. "Good, is not so bad. I worry."

He looked at Helga, "She say we not at war yet. Things better." He pushed the bags closer to them and said he would go to find his family.

As he was leaving, Helga came after him. She caught his arm by the elbow. "Did he say anything, anything about his son, about me?"

The man looked down into her eyes, "He say you are both in his heart. But he cannot leave where he is. We must try to find a way for everyone. I do not know. He does not know what to do. But he does not want you to stop being his woman."

"But if he can't come and see me and I can't go there…What do we do?"

"I don't know, but we will talk more of these things. I will also talk with my woman, Patsy. She is very wise in these things. Have you talked this with Mary Wolf?"

"Only a little."

"She is also wise. And Moon Fish is with Sa-rah. Maybe they will find a way. I go now, but I will see you again later, soon." He placed his hand on her shoulder. "Pray." He climbed on his horse and was gone down the forest trail.

Helga wondered where Indigo was and then remembered he was picking berries. He was away from her more and more, and it wasn't easy for her to get used to. She sat back down and went to work kneading and twisting her side of the hide. Mary Wolf reached out and touched her hand.

"You can talk to me when you feel so alone. I know it is not easy for you."

"Thank you, but I don't even know what to say. Maybe I was hoping Lefty would come back and say everything was all right and I could go back home now. But he didn't say that. I guess nothing changed there, with her. She is still angry."

"You never told me why you had to leave. She did not want other woman with her man?"

"No, I don't think that's it. Maybe part of it, but it was really about my son, our son. He is big beside her baby. He is always moving and making games of hunting and running. He was a little too rough on the baby. He didn't hurt him, but she thought he would. She said he was a bad boy, a danger to her baby and we must leave."

"What did the man Abe say?"

"He was away for many weeks. He went south to help his cousin. I have not seen him since when he left at the end of winter. Ohhh." She tried not to cry, not to let her tears show as she wiped her face with her greasy hands.

They were quiet for a while, then Helga sniffled at her tears, cleared her throat, and said softly, "He would not have let this happen, but I could not stay there with her anger. I thought she would hate me and even hurt me, and Lefty said I could come away with him. So…"

"So you are here now, we will take care of you, and someday, not too long from now, we will find a way for you."

"But winter will come and I have no home and everyone has full lodges and I would only be a burden to anyone who helps me. I will have to leave here, but I don't know where to go. Maybe to a town, to where there are white people's churches. Sometimes they help people."

"Better you not think about that now. Our lives are not our own. The Spirit will say about this. We only must be patient. My mother told me about this work we are doing: 'No one ever made hide soft in a hurry.' Now, think about good things. You are a good woman and what you need will be take care of."

When the leaves of trees along the river began falling, and the nights turned crisp and chill, Helga and Indigo were given a small lodge made of skins. The boy was eager to take on responsibility for dragging tree branches for their cooking and heating needs. Carl gave him a small saw, and the boy quickly learned to use it. Then he wanted to learn how to keep it sharp. This meant a trip to the trading post with Carl to choose a sharpening file. Indigo had never seen so many amazing tools. He was fascinated by the small animal traps he saw hanging from the roof beams, and asked Carl how he could get some.

The man at the post was known for being friendly to the Indians and had even learned a little of their language. Carl asked him how much the traps would cost, but the sum was more than they could afford. Indigo was disappointed and tried to be a little man about it, but the trader could see how sad he was.

"Tell you what I'll do, young fella. I'll let you have two of these here traps, the size that's good for putting down holes in the ground or along the small streams. You can pay for them with what you catch and skin. Bring me the skins, good ones, and I'll let you know when you've paid me enough for these traps. Rabbits don't count. I want muskrats, big gophers and anything with skin thick enough to be sewed together to make a small fur blanket. What do you think about that?"

Indigo looked up at Carl, his eyes shining with excitement, "Can I please?"

Carl asked the man to explain in Indian so he could be sure he understood, and then he nodded to tell the boy it would be all right. Then he said the boy would need a knife to skin the animals. He pointed to a small folding knife in a glass case and asked, "How?"

"Same cost as the traps," the man said, and then repeated it in Indian. "You'll have to work hard, young fella, but with winter coming on, it's a good time."

He reached up with a short broom handle and unhooked two of the traps, and let Indigo remove them from the stick. Carl went over to the tools on a shelf and picked out a file. He held out the coins Helga had given him and the trader took a few, then got the knife out of the case and handed it to the boy, saying "Now remember, if you lose it you still have to pay for it."

Indigo tucked the knife deep into his pocket and slung the two traps over his shoulder. He grabbed Carl's sleeve and pulled him toward the door. The man called after him, "Do you know how to set those?"

"Yes, my Papa showed me." Then he kept going out the door to where their horses were tied, still pulling Carl by the sleeve.

As they were leaving the store, the man mumbled to himself, "First time I ever seen a red-headed Indian kid."

Over the next few weeks, Indigo and Helga kept busy helping others prepare for the coming winter and being helped in turn. She completed the work on two elk hides to have for their own bedding. One was supplied by Carl and the other came from Hawk Man or someone who owed it to him. The boy helped his mother find and peel the right-sized willow sticks to construct bed platforms to keep them up off the ground. The things Lefty had brought from home included a couple of blankets and these she planned to use on top of a hide she could lie on and fold over herself. The smaller one could do the same for Indigo. When they finished the beds, she stepped back and clapped her hands together.

"It's going to be perfect," she said, lying down.

Indigo watched her roll over a couple of times and said, "Mama, it's good. Now can I go and look at my traps?"

"Yes, but be back in time to make the fire for me to cook on. Don't be gone until dark."

Later, as darkness began to filter down through the tree limbs and the sky was filled with bright colors toward the west, she went ahead and began collecting enough wood to last through the evening. She was somewhat worried, although her boy often stayed away longer than she thought was safe. She got the fire going and was beginning to cook a stew when she heard his voice outside the tipi. He didn't exactly sound like himself and she called for him to come inside.

When he came through the low door opening and pulled the covering back in place, he turned with his head down and quickly put something behind his back. He sat down on a small stump that was his to use as a stool, but still he would not look up at her.

"What's wrong with you?" she asked.

"Nothing."

"Yes, there is. Let me see you."

He slowly raised his head to where she could see his face in the firelight. There was blood on his mouth and cheek and she hurried to his side. "What happened? Tell me what happened. Are you all right? Does it hurt?"

"It's not bad, Mama. I'm sorry I came back late."

"Well, don't worry about that now. Here, let me wash your face." She reached for a strip of cloth, dipped it in a bucket of water and began cleaning away the drying bloodstains. He squirmed and tried to push her hand away. "Let me do this," she said. "It has to be done. Then you're going to tell me what happened to you."

Just then her cooking pot began to boil and she had to move to push it to the edge of the fire. She stirred it with a stick and came back to finish cleaning the boy's face.

"Now, tell me, did you fall or what?"

"Mama. I'm all right. Don't want to talk about that."

"Well, you will talk about it. I need to know." She scooted over and added some chopped roots to the pot, then came back to kneel beside him. She gently took his head in one hand and cradled it against her shoulder. She felt his body shudder and he began crying again. "There, there, you're going to be all better soon. Was it your nose that was bleeding?"

He nodded his head up and down without removing it from her comforting hands and the hollow of her shoulder. After a long moment, he sat up straight and looked into her eyes. "Mama, they didn't get my little beaver. They tried to take it, but I got it back. It's mine. They try to take it. That man will give me more for this than for other ones."

"Who? Who are they?"

"Mama, when I went to look in my trap, I heard a voice. I was very quiet and went close. It was two boys and they had the little beaver from my trap. They were laughing and holding it up. One boy got the tail in his teeth and let it hang from his mouth. That's when I went to them. I was swinging a stick and I hit them. Two of them. I hit them and one of them held me and the other one hit me in the face with my little beaver. The head hit my nose. I feel blood and taste blood and I fight, get away into water. Get rocks from water and throw hard at them. They laugh. I hit one hard with rock and he bend over and other one start throwing sticks at me. I go under water and swim away. When I come up on other side of creek, they are leaving. I hide. When they are gone I go back and get my little beaver and my trap and come home." He stopped to catch his breath and then nestled against her again. "I'm sorry, Mama. I come back late, not help you. I'm sorry."

She stood up and handed him the wash-rag. "Here hold this over your face, over your nose so it won't start bleeding again. I'll finish making the bread and put it in the pot. We'll have a late supper."

Later that evening, as they were squatting to eat next to the pot of stew, Helga pulled the iron pan of bread from between the hot rocks where it baked. She unwrapped the cloth that had been wet enough to keep the loaf from scorching. Then they heard a loud scratching outside the tipi, alongside the door.

"It's me, Lefty."

"Come in," Helga said. The man ducked through the low opening, replaced the covering and sat where she motioned him to take a place on a rolled up hide. "You will eat?"

"Yes, thank you. Did the boy trap the meat?"

"Not this time. It's dry elk from Carl." She stirred the coals and made the fire brighter by adding small sticks.

"Boy," Lefty said, "what happened? Looks like you got your nose caught in one of your traps. Big nose now."

Indigo looked away and his mother answered, "He was in a fight with some boys he found taking a small beaver from one of his traps. He fought them. They ran off. Right, son?"

The boy nodded his head.

"Do you know who they were?"

"He didn't say. Indigo, who were the boys?"

He shook his head no and put his finger to his lips. Helga cut a thick slice of bread for her guest and handed it to him, along with a steaming bowl of stew.

"You don't know who they are?"

The boy shook his head again, looking down at his untouched food.

"You could tell me," Lefty said. "I could talk to them and it won't happen again."

"No," Indigo spoke for the first time, "I not say. They hurt me if I do. It is my fight." Then he started blowing on his bowl of food, eating it with the help of his piece of bread.

"You can tell me, young one. I will make it so they never hurt you again. I will tell them, and they will listen to me."

Indigo shook his head no again. "I can take care of me."

Lefty chuckled and said to Helga, "I guess it's all right then. Can't make him say who it was…But I have come to talk with you, the mother of this young warrior."

"More bread?"

"Thank you. Very good, you must teach my women how to make." He chewed slowly on a piece of meat and scooped some broth into his mouth with the bread. "Winter coming. You and your little man will have hard time if you stay living alone."

"I want to go home."

"I know you do. And my friend Abe wants that also. He told me he misses you and his oldest son. He is sad for what is happening, but he cannot change it until the woman changes. That is how he is. Not like Indian man, or Indian woman, we not stay together if one is doing what other one don't want. But I hope the old woman will do what he hope she can do, 'talk some sense to her.' We will see. But now we must take care of you and boy, and maybe you can cook for someone who does not have woman."

"What do you mean?"

"You know Carl had his wife die last winter. Sickness. He is still in sadness time. No medicine help her. Ours or white man doctor. Carl good man, work hard, but no cook, no one take care of his camp. Abe, my friend, say he no want for you to take another man, but Carl good man. He could take care of you and not try to make you his woman in married way." He handed his empty bowl back to her and she started to fill it again. "No, is good, I also eat before I come here." He pulled out his small pipe, filled and lit it. Indigo watched him carefully, and then looked at his mother. She reached out and touched his cheek.

"Mama, I like Carl, he's good to me."

Helga seemed to blush as she turned away. "Quiet, son. Let Lefty finish what he's saying."

"Well," the man said, exhaling toward the top of the lodge where the smoke-hole was, "I can finish up pretty quick here. I want you to move this lodge to be near Carl's tipi. You will cook for him and keep his camp. He will hunt for you and teach your boy. But he will vow not to take you in the wife-way. This will mean two fires in the nighttime, but this young one is strong and can bring in much wood. I will also help you when I am in the village."

Helga looked down at her hands as they twisted with each other. "I don't know. I was thinking I might be able to move to town for the winter."

"No." Lefty spoke softly, but forcefully. "I cannot let the woman and son of my brother-friend live in the white town. They will not take care of you. You have no money. You must have money to live in their way."

"I could work for somebody."

"And who can be with boy when you work?" He tapped out the ashes from his pipe on one of the circle of rocks around the fire. "Not good for you, not good for boy. You are with us now and we will be your family until you can return to Abe. Yes?" He waited for her to answer while Indigo also watched and shook his head up and down several times.

"Thank you," she said. "You don't have to do this. But I understand what you say is best for now."

"Good. We will talk with Carl when he returns from hunting. We hope he does well now he will have more mouths to feed." He got up and smiled, "and I will be coming to eat with him now because you are a good cook." Then he stooped and left the lodge, and they could hear his horse trotting away.

"Mama, I like to go to town, but don't live there, please."

"I think you heard what Mr. Lefty said. I don't think they want us to do that either. Now, how's your nose feeling, need more cold water in the rag?"

"No, make me need to sneeze. I'm tired, Mama, but I have to take care of my little beaver."

"It will be all right until morning. I'll hang it from a tree branch and nothing will take it. Now you get your bed ready while I clean up from our supper. I'm glad he came by, but I wish he would tell me more things about your Papa."

"He will. He's busy. I like him, but maybe he scare me a little bit."

"No reason for that. He's a good man and he wants to take care of us. Now you get in your bed before you fall asleep."

"Mama, can I sleep with you tonight? I might have bad dream about those boys."

"All right, but you have to help fix my bed for us."

"I will, Mama."

She gathered up the bowls while he opened up the bedding. She went out into bright moonlight and could see, in an opening between the trees, the sparkle of frost collecting on the grass. It would be getting colder from now on, she thought. And winter alone, without Abe, seemed even colder to her. If only he could come and at least visit with them...

Abe worked at their little mine whenever he could get away. Sarah was curious, but he'd decided to wait to tell her about the plan he and Lefty had come up with. He just told her he was rebuilding their water system, which was true because he had to reshape the pond so his work in the muddy vein wouldn't dirty their water. When he finished that, he found it was hard work digging into the very narrow crack with unbreakable rock on both sides. The further in he got, the harder it was to pull the hard-packed soil to where he could soak and swirl it.

Ollie had a lot of difficulty when they were up there together. It was a strain for him to work his way down among the boulders. However, his attitude stayed positive, even as his language became more vulgarly descriptive. At one point he dropped his walking stick and it slid away down an embankment. He leaned after it, but had the good sense not to fall and follow it down. Abe retrieved it and tossed it back up. Ollie then got up and moving again as he launched into a long and loud chant identifying the ancestry of the road-building engineer he blamed for the accident that took his leg. Even after all the hardships that day, he promised to return one more time if he was really needed. But only if Abe thought he didn't have enough gold for his needs.

That day came when Abe couldn't reach into the gap any further with any tool he could devise, and he was hoping he now had enough for the land purchase. As he put away his tools and once more checked to make sure the wall of the pond was holding firm, he tried to figure a better way down the slope for Ollie. If only he had a burro that could climb and descend terrain such as this.

That evening, Isaiah went to sleep early and fitfully. Sa-rah said he seemed to have a cold or something that hurt his head because he kept rubbing his neck and mussing his hair while whining and fussing.

Moon Fish brought herbs from her pack in Helga's room. "This tea will help him sleep, but we'll have to wake him up to get him to take it."

Just as the tea was ready, the little boy woke up and called out for his brother, Indigo. Sa-rah hurried to him and took him in her arms. "Quiet, now, quiet. Grandma has some good tea for you. It will make you feel better. But first it has to cool down." The boy coughed a couple of times and then let his head fall back against her shoulder. He was again rubbing his scalp and tangling his hair.

"Mama, Digo? Digo? Mama?"

"He's gone away for a while. He's with his Mama. Now sit up so you can drink this tea."

Moon Fish stirred the drink with a spoon. "It's almost cool enough," she said. "I didn't let it get too hot." She filled the spoon and placed it next to the child's lips. He made a wrinkled face, but swallowed the spoonful. Just then Abe came into the house from outside.

"How's he doing?"

"We'll see if this tea helps him," Sarah said. "It will help him sleep and maybe do more for him. We hope so. Here, little one."

She placed the cup to his lips and tipped it gently so he could drink and swallow. "You're being so good about this, Isaiah. I'm very pleased with you and I know you feel better when you wake up, I know."

Isaiah stopped drinking and pushed the cup away. He looked over at his father and held out his hands to be taken. Abe scooped him up and made his way to the rocking chair near the hearth. There was no fire, but any day now it would be time to begin that chore for the coming season. It was getting almost cold enough to frost and the garden had mostly turned brown.

The boy nestled into his father's arms and slowly rubbed his own head, and then reached up for Abe's face. Within a couple of minutes, he was fast asleep and the house was silent. Sa-rah was knitting some kind of a coverlet, and Moon Fish was back in her room. Abe dozed. After a while, Sa-rah came over and gently lifted the child to carry him to his crib in their room. When she came back, she went to stand by Abe, looking down at him, and then settled into his lap, in just the same position their baby had been in. Abe was startled and came awake. Sa-rah was stroking his hair and face with her fingertips, leaning to kiss him.

"Abe, do you want to have another child?"

"Huh? Oh, yes, I guess so. I mean…yes, of course. Why?" He covered a yawn. "You're tired, aren't you?"

"Long day."

"Do you have any energy left for us?" Her fingertips trace his eyebrows and cheekbones.

"Could be." He smiled. "Are all these questions related?"

She kissed his forehead, then his lips, "Might be."

"Well, maybe I should check the animals one more time. I don't think I closed the gate earlier. While I'm doing that, maybe I'll wake up, and then you'll have to watch out." With an effort, he stood up quickly and caught her before she fell to the floor. She straightened out her clothing and slapped him on the rear as he headed toward the door.

When they were both under the covers, their hands holding and their feet slowly moving against one another, he asked, "Is it the right time of the month?"

"Could be," she said softly.

"Don't you think it might be too soon? I mean it might be hard on you, and Isaiah still seems to need you pretty much for himself."

"I know. I won't rush it. Just wondered how you felt about it. Besides, Moon Fish says that as long as I'm nursing him, at least for another year, I probably can't get that way again."

He quickly rolled over on top of her. "Well, we could see if she's right."

Sa-rah pushed his head down between her breasts. "Oh, I think she's right, but that doesn't mean we shouldn't play a little. Every once in a while."

"Tastes good, sweet. No wonder he likes it so much."

"Don't act like you never tasted it before...Ohhh. But it's different when you do that. Now, be gentle. They're tender from him not being very hungry." Then she reached down for him and opened herself.

The next morning, Mattie and Ollie showed up. Mattie wanted to know how the baby was. Martha had been by to see Sa-rah the day before and knew he was a little bit sickly.

"He's better. He's not rubbing his head all the time."

"Good." She took the boy in her arms and sat down on the porch chairs. "Ollie says he has some kind of business with Abe. Might take all day, he said."

"Sometimes I wonder what those two are up to. Yesterday Abe was over at the Indian camp trying to find out where the original survey line is. I didn't even know there was one."

"Well, Ollie just thinks Abe is the greatest, but he also says he doesn't understand what gives you-all the right to live here and build a house and everything. He says if it's just the word of some Indians, he'd be worried."

"It's more than that, but I'm not sure I understand it all either."

Moon Fish came outside to join them and Sa-rah went to get a second chair.

Mattie smiled at Moon Fish and asked her how she was feeling.

"No worse. Maybe better than when I got here. I think I'm finding out what it is to feel old." She sat down in the chair Sa-rah placed behind her and the young woman moved to sit on the top step.

"It's almost too beautiful to do anything," Mattie said.

"That kind of day," Moon Fish agreed.

"Why don't you tell us a story," Sa-rah said, "of your childhood." Since she wasn't looking at either one of them, they asked in unison who she meant.

"Either, or both."

"I want to hear about the South and how it was to be a slave, that's always interested me, ever since I got sold from one Indian to another." Moon Fish laughed and Mattie joined in.

"Well, I don't rightly remember being sold, or bought, although I know my Momma and me was once when I was still a baby."

"Well, any story will do," Moon Fish said. Isaiah struggled himself away from Mattie's arms and went to lie in his mother's lap.

"All right then, but your turn will come along…See, there was an old, old man that lived down at the end of a bumpy, muddy lane out past the gardens. He had an old banjo he said he made himself from a small wooden box and three strings of some different sizes of wire. I used to wander down that way just to hear him sing and play that old banjo. He liked it when I came down there and he would ask me questions about what I wanted for my birthday or Christmas or whatever. The truth was we never hardly got anything, but I had an imagination, Oh Lordy, did I have an imagination and I would go on and on about the fine horse I would get for my birthday and the beautiful dress my Momma would make for me, and for Christmas… Oh my, my. I would tell him all kinds of things.

"One day, he looked at me kind of funny and asked me what I wanted when I went to Heaven. Well, I had never thought about that before, so I didn't answer right away and he said, that's all right; you can tell me next time you come to visit—now run along and I'll see you soon. With that he strummed the strings real hard and loud and pretended he was going to get up and chase me away. Oh, I say, I am getting thirsty from all this talking. Sarah Beth, can you get us some of your special tea if there is any?"

"Of course. It's on the window sill, in the sun. I'd get it, but he's asleep again and I hope he doesn't wake up for a while."

"I'll get it," Moon Fish said. "Need to move around a bit anyway."

"I know what you mean," Mattie said, standing and stretching. After the three glasses of tea were served, Mattie said, "Should I go on?"

"Of course."

"Well, now, where was I? All right, I went to our place, the little space where my Mother and all of us slept, and for the next two days I could hardly think of anything else besides the old man's question. I tried to ask my Mother about it but she was either too busy or too tired for me, so I just thought and thought all about Heaven. The next time I could go down the lane and visit him, it had rained and the red dirt of the road was muddy and slippery. I hated getting my shoes dirty even though they were falling apart anyway. We'd never even heard of stockings so the mud got inside my shoes and my toes got all squishy. I really hated that, so when I got to the shack where the old man lived, I had some new ideas about what I wanted in Heaven and when he saw me, I just went ahead and told him without waiting to be asked. 'When I go to heaven,' I said, 'I want new shoes that never wear out and I want lots and lots of pairs of them, all kinds, and I want the streets of gold going everywhere and I want to walk up and down those streets of gold in my new shoes all day, every day.'

"He looked down at me and plucked a couple of notes and asked me what I was going to do when I got tired of walking up and down the streets of gold. I said I never would and he told me right then that I certainly would and that I needed something I could never get tired of all through eternity. Well, I was a sassy little girl and so I said to him, 'Well, what do you want Mr. Knows-Everything?' He smiled kindly like and played a little tune, and then said, 'I like everything I have now. I like this muddy lane and I want the same thing in Heaven.

I like my little falling down shack, and I want the same thing in Heaven. I even like these old shoes with the holes in the bottoms and the rips in the top.' So I said to him, 'Isn't there anything different you want in Heaven?' And he smiled and played a happy little tune on the three strings of his banjo, and he said, 'I've got everything I want except for one thing.' He paused, and I saw a tear run down his cheek. He wiped it away, and said, 'I'm just hoping my dear sweet Lord will see fit to let me have a new banjo.' I waited for him to go on, but he was quiet for a long time, then he said, 'Now run along, little Miss.' I could see that he was kind of holding back the tears so I turned and ran away through the mud, and that was the last time I ever saw him because he died the next day."

Isaiah stirred in Sa-rah's arms and waved his hands around as he struggled to wake up. Sa-rah said she was about to cry herself, but thanked Mattie for the story. Moon Fish just looked over at Mattie and smiled, and then said, "I'm sure he got what he wanted."

Sa-rah got up as Isaiah came fully awake and she stood on the porch nursing him for a few minutes, then handed him to Mattie. He fussed and then began patting her hands when she started to play with his.

"Now that the sun came out, I've got laundry to hang out, and then it will be almost time to have something to eat."

Moon Fish also stood up and went down the steps, as if to go take care of her own business, but she turned and looked at Mattie, and said, "Isn't that the truth? We really do have all we need."

Around midday, they reached the flat part of the ridge where the crack was. Ollie and Abe dismounted and had their own bite to eat sitting on a couple of rocks near the split in the ground.

"I think you better plan to go at least as far as Boise to cash in what you've got, to see if it's enough. Need to go where nobody knows you."

"That's what I was thinking, but it's hard to get away now, if it means leaving Sa-rah and the boy here alone."

"Well, you don't have to do that. Mattie and I can stay here with them. I might not be able to chase down a runaway horse, but I can still shoot pretty good if it comes to that."

"I appreciate it, but I hope you didn't think I was hinting at that."

"No, but it just seems to make sense. A man can't stay in one place all the time, and maybe those women might even be able to take off for town themselves. They've done that before. Silver City ain't Boise, but it's good for them."

"We'll see."

Ollie pulled out his flask and took a short pull. "Wash down my food, y'know. Doubt you want any about now, do you?" Abe shook his head no. "Besides, maybe you could take a side trip and pay off that Indian if you owe him, and see your other wife and boy."

Abe didn't answer, but stood up and said, "Best get moving, got a lot to do here." He uncoiled the rope and began laying it out toward the crack.

"Think about it though," Ollie said. "Doubt you want that pretty young thing and your boy to forget about you."

Things moved faster this time. Ollie made it down to the bottom easily, and Abe was riding faster and took the shorter route. Soon Ollie was spreading out the piles of flake and little nuggets that Abe mined.

"How much you think you're going to need?" he asked.

"Maybe fifteen hundred, maybe more."

"Might have it here. Seems like a lot when everybody else was able to homestead for free. But that's probably why we found this stuff here, at least the way you and them Indians think about things," he laughed. "Me, I just take what comes along and don't blame nobody and don't give 'em credit either, God or no God."

Abe smiled and said, "And I imagine God thinks the same as you, probably says to Himself, 'It's all the same, Ollie or no Ollie.'"

They both laughed and then Ollie told Abe to gather the gold up into the pouch again and bring it down with them. "I could weigh it back at my place, but I'm pretty sure it's enough." Then he took off down the trail with his stick.

"Wait," Abe said, "over here. I've been clearing you a path. Bet it'll make it a lot easier. I've been working on it every time I'm up here and been using it myself."

Ollie was able to make it down to the horses without either falling or swearing, and they rode on into the stable just when it was about time for supper. When they'd finished eating, Ollie didn't wait for Abe to announce their plans, but went right on into it.

"Mattie, we're going to stay here with these ladies for a while when Abe here has to go on up to Boise to take care of some business about this here land. I told him it would be all right with you."

Mattie looked straight at him and said, "Well, you might have asked me." Then she kicked his one good leg under the table and started laughing.

He groaned and said, "You're pretty good at that with only one leg to aim at." Then he joined her laughter.

"Of course it's all right. If it's all right with Sarah Beth." Mattie said, continuing to be the only one who still used that name.

"I'd love it. But I don't want Abe to leave. When are you thinking of going?"

"Should go soon. With the way things change with the government, best get this done right away."

"What is it exactly that you have to do?" Sa-rah asked.

"Um, according to Lefty, things are getting a little tense up north there and the agreements and treaties with the tribe are being reviewed, even challenged. He thinks we need to make our claim more permanent while we can."

"Oh my, I hope there's not going to be a problem. I don't want to have to leave."

"I don't think it's that kind of a situation. Probably just more papers to sign. Now let's talk about something else." He was relieved when Moon Fish began telling what Isaiah had done in the garden that day when they were weeding and cleaning up dead corn stalks.

The next day, Sa-rah came to the stable, where Abe was trimming Bird's hooves in preparation for replacing her shoes. She watched him work. When he stopped and looked up, she said, "Kate told me just now that she's feeling well enough to go home now. She says if she doesn't get there in time to get ready for winter, she won't be able to go back until next spring. Abe, I think she's worried about not being home if her health gets worse. What do you think about taking her in our buggy?"

"I don't know. I have no idea how hard the trip is from Boise to where her family moved their village."

"Well, I don't like it. But it would be a chance for you to visit Indigo." She turned her back to him and continued, "And of course it would mean you'd have to see Helga."

"And it would mean I'd be gone longer."

"That's not the point. The point I'm making is you'll see Helga again. How does that make you feel?"

"I really don't know."

Sa-rah started to walk away and he called her to stop. "Wait, I've thought about that— maybe things are the way they should be now, but I don't think it's fair to any of us if it isn't understood and talked over. And I know I don't understand all of it."

She turned to face him. "Now you just want to hear her side of the story."

"If you want to know what I really feel, I don't want there to be sides, your side or her side. Not when it affects the boys. Didn't you tell me that Isaiah woke up when he had headaches and cried for Indigo?"

Sa-rah didn't answer and came closer to him. "Abe, how long am I going to have to pay for my mistake of letting you be with her?"

He reached out and pulled her into his arms. "It's not that way," he said, "not a mistake. It's just what happened, what your father would say is an example of God's willingness to let us live our own lives, and to learn from our acts."

"Learn from our mistakes, you mean."

He nuzzled his chin on the top of her head and then tipped her face up to kiss her. "God doesn't always make those kind of judgments. Lefty once told me that the way his people look at life is that it's all just practice."

"Practice? Practice for what?"

"He said they don't know that, but they know it's just practice because nobody's very good at it." He smiled and tipped her head back a little more so he could look into her eyes, which were now closed. "Open your eyes and smile. I love you and I always will. And I know you have always done the best you can. What comes next we never know, but don't worry about it. I'll be back and it'll be like I never left, except that then this land will be ours."

They kissed again, and then she pulled away. After a few steps, she stopped and looked back. "So should I tell Kate you'll take her with you?"

"If that's what she really wants."

CHAPTER 14

Land Deal

The winter passed without extreme storms or cold. There was plenty of hard work, but with enough firewood and food they were able to enjoy their little family and have a lot of time together. Isaiah was talking more, and he liked the days they would take him outside to play in the snow or on the hard frozen ground when the sun was shining. Finally, there came a muddy period of thawing ground and rising water in the streams and it was once again possible leave the place and to travel.

Their leave taking was emotional, with Moon Fish and Sa-rah dabbing their cheeks to dry tears. They both promised to see one another again, and Moon Fish assured Sa-rah that her stay had done wonders for her health. She was feeling both stronger and younger, and fully ready to face the next year in her own homeland. Mattie gave Moon Fish a lovely knitted shawl she'd made and the two older women hugged for a long time. Mattie mentioned that the other woman never got around to telling a story to match her own, the one about Heaven, and they both laughed and Moon Fish promised that would be the first thing they did when they saw each other the next time.

Abe had the buggy loaded and the horses ready, but he waited patiently through these goodbyes. He was anxious to get going, but wanted to be sure that Sa-rah was going to be all right and not hold anything against him for taking this opportunity to go to what she referred to as his "other family." He called Isaiah to come to him, picked him up and twirled him around, then he sat the boy up on Bird's saddle.

"You be good now, and take care of your Mama. I'll be back before you know it."

"What? Know what?" the boy said and leaned over to fall into Abe's arms.

"Don't worry about that, just be good and I'll bring you something special when I come back home."

Sa-rah came over to them and took the boy, setting him down of the ground so she could put her arms around Abe's shoulders. She pulled him close and looked up into his face, trying to memorize every detail.

"Don't forget us," she said.

"Never."

"Maybe you can arrange to see Indigo without having to see her." She looked down and away, and started to step back.

He held onto her and didn't say anything as he turned her head back into a long kiss. "I'll miss you, I really will. But it won't be long."

"Just don't forget to make sure we get to keep this land," she said and freed herself from his arms. "I'll be here when you get back." Then she picked up the boy and hurried away to the porch where she stood and watched as he helped the older woman into the buggy, mounted up, and waved to the small group that was seeing them off. He wondered where Ollie was, but it didn't matter, he knew the man would take good care of things without any final instructions.

The first night on the trip, when they'd finished eating and were sitting close to the warmth of a small fire, Moon Fish asked Abe what he felt about taking her home. "I know I didn't ask you about it first, but it was the only way I could think of to get you and Helga and the boy to be able to see each other again."

"I guess I thought you'd just been waiting for a chance to go back north."

"No, I do want to go back, but mostly I've been a little upset all along that this—what's that word? This awkwardness between these two women shouldn't go on much longer. It isn't good for anyone."

"I guess I should say thank you. It's been a long time since I've seen them. They were already gone when I returned from New Mexico, and I miss them a lot. I bet the boy has grown a lot…But are you sure this trip isn't going to be too hard on you?"

"I was serious when I said my health is improved. It was a good summer and the winter wasn't bad. Before I came to stay with you folks, I thought it might be my last one, but now I'm feeling like I'll live for a few more."

"That's good to hear."

"Well, I want to make sure Sa-rah has another child. I'm pretty sure what we did for her made a lasting change, but the second one would be a good proof and then I could feel good about passing on the knowing of these ways we used and what we did with her."

"I guess I never did thank you for all of that. It means a lot to me, and it went a long ways to help me believe in these things you have."

"Don't forget, young man. I was a white person too, you know. I had to come to believe in these ways myself. And I know what it did to us as white people, to grow up thinking there's only one true way and then we find out the only wrong way is when someone says there's only 'one way.' Old Joseph, our chief elder, said before he died, 'Don't let the white man teach my people to fight about Creator.' He told us not to let them build churches on our lands."

They were silent for a while. Coyotes howled on the other side of the river, and a horse whinnied. Abe added more wood to the fire and Moon Fish went off in the nearby bushes, then came back and rolled up in her bed.

Abe stayed awake for some time, thinking and wondering about what it would be like to see Helga and Indigo again. Certainly it would be quite a surprise to them, but there was no way to send word ahead. And he needed to remind himself, like Sa-rah said, that this trip was really about making sure they could keep the land and their home.

Abe and Moon Fish made it to Boise in good time. Before traveling, he'd found out that the big river wouldn't really rise until a bit later in the year, when the temperatures climbed in the mountains and the snow began melting. There were a couple of new ferries to choose from and one of them cut almost half a day off the route. Moon Fish held up quite well to the rigors of the journey, and proved competent at driving the buggy and Ginger while Abe roamed out ahead, keeping a look out. The weather held on to its clear, blue, and chilly air, and the bright greens of spring were painting the trees and shrubs along the way in their full intensity. Abe had packed a small tent for the older woman to use for shelter, but she preferred to be out under the stars in a bedroll of quilts and one elk hide that Sa-rah made sure she brought along with her.

When they pulled into Boise, Abe managed to find a simple rooming house that catered to travelers and had a stable for the animals. Moon Fish said she was tired and just wanted to stay in her room and nap while he went about his business. He asked if she wanted to be awakened when supper was served to the guests in the dining room. She smiled and said, "Of course. I can sleep any old time, but they probably only serve supper once and I've never been in a place like this before."

Abe got himself and then the horses settled, and went off looking for the place where land registration was managed for the Indians and the federal government. From what he knew, the states and territories didn't have authority over his kind of situation. When he was directed to the federal courthouse, he was pleased to find that the land office and the legal affairs of the U.S. Government were in the same wing of the building, but he was disappointed when he could find no one attending to the desks and offices. Finally, he noticed a small sign that informed the public that the offices were closed until later in the day.

He went back into the street and asked a marshal where he could find a bank that would exchange currency for gold. The officer looked at him with some suspicion, and asked how he came into possession of gold for sale.

"Worked a claim with an old man. He sent me. Couldn't make the trip himself." Abe made up the story to contain as much truth as possible, but wasn't ready to give out any location true or false.

"Well, I know you're not dumb enough to tell me where it is, but if I was you, I'd open an account with the Guardian Bank itself, so's you won't have to be carrying any of it around with you. This town has all kinds. Anyway, it's down this street and to the left. You want to go to them and not one of these shysters we have in these small shops. Can't miss it."

After hearing the man's estimation of his own town, Abe almost wished the marshal could accompany him and the satchel he was carrying to the bank. He looked around, trying to appear calm, and hefted the weight of the bag in a way to make it appear lighter than it was. The only incident that worried him was when a man bumped him while crossing the muddy street, but he was pretty sure that the man didn't notice anything unusual about the bag he was carrying.

Once in the bank, he waited until a teller asked him what he wanted and he spoke softly to the man, saying, "I need to turn some gold into currency."

"How much?"

"I'm not sure. Haven't weighed it."

"Well, how much money do you want?"

"Don't we have to see how much it weighs first?

"Wait here. I'll get someone to take care of you."

Abe watched as the man whispered in the ear of another gentleman who appeared to be some kind of authority within the bank. The man approached and asked Abe to come into an office. As the door closed, Abe took a seat. He noticed a couple of scales and other devices on a table next to the wall.

"Well young man, what have you brought with you today? Clem tells me you're in the gold business."

Ollie had advised him to find out what the exchange rate was before he told or showed anyone what he had. He asked about that and the man smiled and said, "Well, that would depend on the quality of the product, don't you think?"

"Well, I suppose so." He clutched the satchel on his lap a little tighter. "Is it the same everywhere?" he asked.

"Supposed to be, but I believe you're quite fortunate to have brought yourself to our establishment. Our prices are genuine and based on the market in New York City. We check with that source daily by telegraph."

"Is there any guarantee of those prices?"

"The guarantee is the reputation and well-known integrity of the Guardian Bank of Idaho, the first bank established in the Territory. If you would show me a sample, or one each of flake and nugget, if you have both, I can give you an estimate of what we're talking about."

"I've heard of safe storage in banks. Do you also have that service?"

"Certainly do."

"And how much does that cost?"

"If it's really gold, it'll be one percent of the total value per month. Now, are you ready to show me samples so we can get down to business?"

Abe couldn't help but realize that he was not an expert, not even a novice at this kind of thing. The worst thing he could think of right then was that he would be cheated and end up with less than enough to buy the land. He shook his head at his doubts, and then reached down inside the case for two small bags, one of flakes and the other with average sized stones that Ollie had polished. He carefully handed them across the desk to the banker.

"By the way, we're paying New York prices at about seventeen dollars an ounce, if it's clean quality, more if it come from the Black Hills, which I assume it did not." He loosened the string ties on the pouches and placed a monocle to his eye. He pulled out a small tray with dividers and trickled the gold flakes into one section and a couple of nuggets into the other. "Fairly clean," he said, and looked over at Abe. "Is it all like this?"

"Mostly." He knew that Ollie had worked a long time at separating all of the dirt out of the flake and rubbing the individual pieces with a rough cloth before he said it was good enough for sale. In spite of the man's friendliness, Abe was still fighting off the feeling that he might be taken advantage of due to his total lack of experience.

"Young man, you seem a bit suspicious, and I can certainly understand how it would be, were I in your position, but our tradition and reputation come from being in the Territory for the long term. To shortchange anyone at this time could lead to serious repercussions, so let's just do our business in good faith and we'll make sure you come out all right. Trust the bank, and trust me, and you'll find there's no better partner for you in your enterprise. Now, with that said, I will say that this is as high a quality as we're used to seeing...How much more is there? I mean here with you, not on your claim."

"How much is what you have there? Can you weigh it?"

"Ahhh, you're learning. Ever play poker?" Abe shook his head negatively. "Best trainingfor business I know of. Now, I will weigh this for you as you've asked. Together or separately?"

"Together is all right."

The banker got up, adjusted the scale and placed the holding tray on its arm. Then he removed it, set it back on his desk and said, "Nearly three ounces. Times seventeen dollars minus our two dollar commission for changing this into currency, gold coin or paper, that's forty-five."

Abe tried to figure out how much a pound would be worth, but his mind wouldn't work that way in this situation. "How much for a pound?"

"Your share would be two hundred and forty dollars."

Now Abe could figure what he would need if the land was going to cost about $1500, what Mike Skinner told him it would probably be worth to the government in their way of taking and selling custody of Indian land. If he had a little over six pounds that would be enough. He politely asked, "I didn't get your name, sir."

"Mr. Bartholomew, son, and yours?"

"Saunders. Now, I'm not sure how much of this I'm going to need right away, turned into money, I mean, but I would like to store it with you so we better weigh it all so you can charge me your one percent."

"Tell you what we'll do. Give you the first week of a safe deposit box gratis, that's free in banker talk. If you leave some of it here, then we start charging the rate after that first week. Up to you."

"All right, weigh it, please."

It turned out there was a bit over eight pounds, or nearly two thousand for Abe's share after the bank took theirs. That was give or take an allowance of more value for larger nuggets and less for powdery flake. Abe asked the man for a receipt and they signed some papers and shook hands. They took the gold down to an underground vault, placed it in a steel box, and locked it away. Then the banker warned Abe to be careful out on the street. Someone might have seen him come into the bank and think he was coming out with something worth stealing. Abe thanked him and left through the front doors. It was hard for him to leave all that behind, but next things next, he thought. He had to trust somebody in this situation. Now he would go on to the land office.

As it turned out, the clerk of the U.S. Office of Land, Homesteading and Mining Claims was the same person who'd helped Abe back in Silver City. The man remembered him. Abe was surprised and then somewhat worried when he realized the man might have a hunch about where Abe was getting his new wealth from, but then he smiled and remembered that he could always fall back on a partly true story about having additional income from Dr. Randall's estate.

Their conversation got right down to business after the man asked Abe if he'd seen anyone come into his office and misplace a bottle of whiskey the last time they'd met. Abe smiled when the man winked and said, "Surely not."

"Well then, let's see what's going on about that property you came to me about last time, where you're leasing from the Indians, or however the agreement is called?"

"I want to buy the land and they agree it's better that I have it than that the government holds onto it, and maybe all of a sudden gives it away to someone else."

"Sounds like a good way of looking at these things."

"How much would be asked for it?"

"Well, I'm not sure it's ever been fully surveyed. If you really wanted to know what you're getting it might be a good idea to set those lines. But here let's see if we can find it on this map. And then you can maybe draw some lines where you think they should be. As I recall, there's no neighbors out that way."

It seemed a bit of a careless way to do business, so Abe asked, "What kind of paper, or description, or deed would I get?"

"You pay good, legal money, you get back good, legal paperwork." He unrolled the map onto the table and they both leaned over it. The man traced his finger across a section of the map and said, "Right in here. Got to follow natural boundaries where we can and it'll have to add up to less than one hundred and sixty acres, then we can make you a deal for ten dollars an acre plus you get a water right if there's any springs or seeps, but the State of Oregon's going to own the water in the creeks. You got anywhere near sixteen hundred dollars, young fellow? Plus the cost of a bottle of the best, of course." He started to roll up the map, but Abe held him back.

"See this part here? There's a kind of a spring here. I'd want to make sure nobody could take that away from us. It's where we get our water for the house and garden. So I'd want this land up above it here, if I'm looking at this right."

"No problem. When I draw the lines, they tend to go where the pen goes, if you know what I mean. Then it'll be up to you to get a survey done and mark it out, if you think you need to go to all that trouble. That's for in the unlikely event that someone or other contests this."

"I see. Perhaps the line can include that part that's mostly flat up there, and we give up a little bit at the far end of the valley where nobody's going to settle anyway."

"We can do that. Now, you still have to buy this land, you know. Sixteen hundred dollars. Not a bad price if you don't take into consideration you might have had it for homesteading if the Indians gave it up."

"I don't think they would have back then. Things have changed and they seem to want to trust me to keep giving them access. And of course I will."

"Well, you never want any Indians mad at you, personally, I mean."

"Where do I pay? Who gets the money? And when?"

"I've got to trace this map and then hand carry it to the other side of this building. If I find the treasury clerk in attendance, it could happen this afternoon before closing. If you've got that much on hand. Otherwise it will be tomorrow midday at the earliest."

"Means maybe I won't get out of this town tomorrow."

"Also means you might, if you leave me alone so I can get moving on this."

"Well, thanks for your help. How will I know? I'll have to go to the bank and I sure don't want to be wandering around town with that much money."

"I understand. Guess maybe I thought it was all in that little suitcase you're carrying."

"Not exactly. Maybe I'll come by in the morning before going to the bank, just to find out how things are moving along."

"Be fine with me, long as you bring everything you're supposed to." He winked and waved Abe out the door. "Work to do."

Abe and Moon Fish had a decent supper at the rooming house, and she got along quite well with the hostess-owner. Abe decided to take a walk around downtown before turning in. The visit with the banker had made him more fearful than he would have been under more normal circumstances. As the thoughts of what he would say in the event he was recognized and accosted ran through his head, he took a few deep breaths and realized that he was making it all up and there was probably no danger to his person, with or without the bag and its weight of gold.

He passed several places that were open for nighttime revelry. Two buildings proclaimed themselves to be Dance Halls and another was honest enough to have a sign that just said Saloon. They were all three equally noisy and not very inviting to Abe. After peering inside through swinging doors, he found himself more interested in looking over the horses tied along the street's hitching rails. From what he could see in the dim light from the buildings, there were some good looking animals.

When he turned down the street toward the rooming house, he caught a glimpse of someone behind him, there for a moment and then gone. Just as he turned into the yard of the house and looked around, he saw the dark shape again, and once again it seemed to vanish. He shook off the shiver of fear and told himself that it was probably just the way things were in a town this big. It had been a long time since he'd been in a town like this and more than likely he was just feeling out of place and exaggerating the mysterious quality of the darkening street, with the only light coming from the windows of its houses.

He slept well, in spite of any nervousness, and was pleased to find a large breakfast and Moon Fish waiting for him in the dining room. They were the first ones there. She smiled and beckoned him to sit beside her. The hostess appeared almost instantly with a pot of coffee and filled his empty cup.

"Good morning, sir. Did you sleep well?"

"I did, thank you."

"I'll have your food in a few minutes."

As she bustled back out to the kitchen Abe asked his companion how she'd slept.

"I almost couldn't sleep in such a soft bed. Kept thinking I'd sink down in it and suffocate. But then I finally fell asleep and it was better than any time I can remember."

He explained to her that he didn't know how long his business would take, but hopefully if things went well they'd be able to leave early in the afternoon and see how far they could get before darkness caught them. He then handed her some coins and said she would have time to buy some gifts for her family, and he asked if she could perhaps find some things suitable for Helga and Indigo. Then he asked her how she was holding up to the journey.

"Much better than I thought I would. So don't be concerning yourself about me."

After a substantial morning meal, he went back to his room and packed his things. He carried the empty satchel and his packed bag down to the stable, and loaded the bag into the buggy, keeping the satchel with him. He fed and watered the horses, walking each animal around in a field out back. There was no grass to be had, but he still had to keep jerking Bird's head up from the ground where she was searching for something to nibble. He thought about home and Sa-rah and the boy. Recently both she and Moon Fish had brought up the subject of another child for them. He felt that they were right, but wondered how Helga would feel about it. He realized it wouldn't be that much different and somewhat the reverse of when she was the one having the baby and Sa-rah was still childless.

He put the horses back in their stalls, and checked over the buggy wheels and harness. Everything seemed in good shape. On his way to the land office, he suddenly remembered the clerk's request for the "gift" of a bottle. He wondered if that would that be classified as a bribe, and then dismissed the thought. He would just appear to have accidentally left it where the man could easily find it and it would be all right. He liked the man and remembered how helpful he'd been at preventing the outlaw men from getting the land. He rubbed his shoulder where one of them had shot him, and it brought back the memory of having to kill the other. All in all, that incident was what eventually led to the arrangement with the Indians that brought him to Boise. It had become necessary to find a way to protect the rights to that land, both for the Indians and for his family.

He had to ask someone where he could purchase a bottle at that time of day. He was told by a man on the street, who looked like he was still somewhat drunk from the night before, that next to the big hotel down the way there was a small shop that catered to what the man called, "us morning nippers." Then he gave a big wink and asked for a dollar. Abe shook his head no and walked away to find the shop. He was afraid the man would follow him, but soon lost him in the crowded street full of folks headed for their workplaces.

With the bottle in his satchel, he circled back around, taking in another part of the town's center. As he was walking along beside a park-like area near a large white church, he was struck from behind and knocked off his feet. He blinked and looked up into the distorted face and filthy beard of a man whose eyes burned with some kind of anger or hatred.

"You stole my claim, sonovabitch."

Abe pushed himself up on one elbow and started to get up when the man kicked him in the ribs. "I don't know you or what you're talking about," he said, rubbing his side.

"Seen you coming out of the bank. You took my gold in there. I'll kill you now, if you don't pay up."

"I don't know what you're saying, and I haven't taken anyone's claim. Where was it?"

"You know. Over near the line, near Montana country. Right? Right?" He pushed Abe back down just as he was starting to get up off the side of the street.

"Never been there." Abe got himself ready to roll away as a chance to get to his feet, then he kicked out, connecting with the man's shin, rolled over, and was quickly up on his feet. The man spit a wad of tobacco chew at him that missed and then charged him. Abe swung the satchel as hard as he could and heard the bottle inside break on the man's head. The man went down and didn't move. Abe emptied the glass and liquid out of the bag onto the man, and then turned to jog down the pathway through the park. One of his ribs sent sharp pains up to his neck as his breath came faster and faster.

When he got to the area with traffic and people, he spotted a marshal and went for him. He could smell the whiskey-soaked satchel and looked for a place to get rid of it. There was really nowhere. He went on and stepped up close to the marshal, who was watching the horse and buggy traffic at the busy crossroads.

"Sir, I was attacked, a drunk back in the park."

The officer looked him over and sniffed. "I'd say you might be the drunk yourself, from the smell of you."

"No, I had to break a bottle on his head to get away."

"Friend, you got a pretty good welt and some bleeding on your scalp. I'd have to say it looks to me like you hit yourself on the head, broke the bottle and now you're trying to prove to yourself that you're the victim. Move along, I've got a job to do here." As Abe slowly moved away, the marshal said to himself, loud enough for Abe to hear. "Drunks getting crazier all the time."

Abe hurried back to the rooming house, still carrying the whiskey-soaked bag, thinking how he'd need to get hold of a new one for the rest of his morning's activity. He stopped in the stable and gathered up a new set of clothes, wrapped the satchel in a piece of scrap canvas and buried it under the back floorboard of the buggy, then he went inside to try and clean himself up. He realized he had no idea how bad he looked, but he thought the marshal's treatment of him was good indication.

He tiptoed past the kitchen, not wanting to face any questions until he'd gotten cleaned up. Fortunately the washroom upstairs was empty, and a large container of water sat next to the drain. He stripped off his clothes, looked at himself in the mirror, and saw a bloody splotch in his hair, a smudge or bruise on his face that he didn't remember getting, and already a purplish bruise forming over his ribs on the left side. He grabbed a washrag from the bureau and began scrubbing and rinsing away the marks of his struggle. Combined with the smell, he could certainly understand the marshal's judgment of him and his condition. Next he was faced with a choice of using a very perfumed cleaning bar, or none at all. He chose the perfumed soap for its cleansing potential, and then rinsed as much of it off as he could. Dressing in clean clothes helped him to feel more of an upstanding citizen, and he gathered up the pile of reeking dirty clothes and shoved it into one of the leg of the pants, wadding them up. He pulled on his boots, thankful for their usefulness when he kicked the man in the shins, and then reminded himself it was time to get moving. He again snuck past the downstairs and took the filthy bundle of clothes to the buggy, and stuffed them up under the floorboards in the backend. He wondered what Moon Fish would say when he saw her again. How much would she notice?

Things went smoothly for the rest of the morning. He was able to buy a leather satchel that had the advantage of looking used. The land office paperwork was nearly complete and the clerk promised that the sale could be completed by noon because he'd already confirmed that the other official would be at work all morning.

He went to the bank and Mr. Bartholomew gave him a look of surprise. Abe told him a brief version of the encounter, and he advised Abe to leave most of his wealth with the bank. He said Abe could transfer funds from this bank to the one in Silver City; a simple telegram would suffice if he used the code number the banker would give him for the purpose. So Abe took the money for the land in the form of 32 fifty-dollar gold coins, and requested another three hundred dollars in smaller denominations to split between Hawk Man and himself. He was planning to use his share for travel expenses and purchases he would make for the ranch on the way home.

He was almost to the government office building when he remembered the whiskey. He didn't want to show up without its replacement; on the other hand, he didn't want to go back to the same store, as if he'd finished the first bottle already and was bent on drinking all day.

Just then he heard the sound of a piano coming from a dance hall. He went in, looking around for threatening or unsavory characters. He assured himself that the small number of customers looked rather respectable for such a place. He was able to purchase a bottle and stuck it into his jacket pocket.

When he did arrive at the government building and saw a guard stationed near the door he was relieved and felt a lot calmer than he'd been since the mugging. He managed to misplace the bottle in the clerk's office right behind a chair, after making sure that the clerk saw what he was doing. Next, at the treasury office he signed several documents, all in triplicate, was handed his copies and a stamped receipt for the agreed-upon sum of money, and was back out on the street within an hour, the new owner of his own land.

When he arrived at the rooming house, Moon Fish was having tea with the landlady. They both reacted to the battered condition of his face and the way that he was favoring his bruised ribs, and Moon Fish asked what happened. He explained that someone in a hurry had pushed past him on a stairway downtown and he'd fallen. He asked her where her purchases were and she pointed to the back door where there was a good-sized pile of boxes.

"And how did you get all of that here?" he asked.

"A nice young man took pity on me and hardly asked for any pay at all."

"Well, I'll get the horses ready and we can load up. Have you got your things from your room?" She nodded yes and he was about to go out when the other woman stood and motioned for him to sit.

"You're not going anywhere until you've had Mama Tessa's original lamb stew and fresh-baked bread. Sakes alive, I'd be ruined if anyone ever found out I put my guests out on the road without a decent meal to carry them along. Sit, I say."

Moon Fish covered a smile with her hand; when the woman had gone into the kitchen, she reached out and touched Abe's arm and said, "I'd say she put you in your place." Abe replied that he was glad of the invitation as he hadn't had time to eat or anything else beyond his business and cleaning up after what he called his "accident."

"But we will want to be on our way as soon as we can, and try to travel quickly. I talked to someone who said if we get to the ferry before dark we could get across and camp on the other side. Otherwise, there's so much reserved freight backed up for the morning runs that we might be stuck there until midafternoon tomorrow."

He ate one bowl of lamb stew, and turned down another. The woman wrapped some bread for them to take with them. They thanked their hostess, paid for their rooms, and hurried back to the buggy.

As they were passing near the outskirts of town, Abe caught a glimpse of the man who'd assaulted him. He was slouched down beside an abandoned wagon with no wheels. Abe considered stopping and confronting the man, who looked to be sleeping or passed out, but then he thought the man looked as if his life was hard enough without any added misery, and tried to put the incident out of his mind.

They made it to the ferry in time to catch the last evening crossing. The ferry master required Abe to unharness the horse from the buggy and tie the animal to the boat's side rail. When Abe asked why, the man told him he'd lost a horse and buggy one time when the animal spooked, reared itself overboard and pulled the buggy into the water. Although Abe was confident his horse was much calmer that that, he said he understood and did what was asked. The crossing was accomplished in good time. A steel cable stretched across the river, and two young men cranked the ferry further by turning a wheel attached to the cable. Abe was impressed by the simplicity of the machinery, and by its effectiveness. He wanted to remember this to tell Ollie about, and to see if he'd ever seen anything like it.

They re-hitched, disembarked, and asked for directions to a place where they could camp. It was nearly dark when they found a quiet opening in the willows upriver from the ferry crossing. Abe tethered Bird and hobbled the other horse and then hurried to gather firewood for the night. Moon Fish unpacked what was needed for cooking some dry meat into a stew, and had a small fire just starting when Abe returned with a large limb of cottonwood.

"It'll burn quickly, but be plenty warm enough," he said as he found his ax and began cutting off the different size branches and piling them near the small fire. When he had what seemed sufficient, he asked Moon Fish if she had any idea how far they would need to travel to find her people.

"Maybe two days and half of next day."

That evening, as they finished their meal, the woman looked across the fire at Abe and smiled, nodded her head several times, and then quietly said, "This one, this Helga. You have feelings for her?" She tapped her own heart with her finger. "Here?"

He didn't answer for a long moment, surprised at the question and needing time to sort through his own thoughts for a good enough answer. "I do," he said. "I never thought I would love anyone other than Sarah Beth, um, Sa-rah, but I guess I was wrong about that."

Moon Fish smiled and stirred the coals with a stick, added a few pieces of wood and waited until the flames made more light. "Sometimes the heart is where surprises live. You will have many difficulties, I think, until you find a way for them to be together with you, or until you make a choice of one of them."

"Either way would be hard."

"I know," she said, "but the sooner it is decided, the better it will be for the boys...I go to sleep now."

On the third morning, the woman called out to Abe who was riding ahead, "This is our old home place." She pointed at a well-worn trail leading off the dirt roadway and into the woods. "River's down there. Now, we must find the new place. We stay on this road."

After going a ways and seeing the signs of more and more horse traffic, Moon Fish halted the buggy and stood up from the seat. She shielded her eyes in the glare of the sun and pointed toward the west where there were a few ribbons of smoke connecting the trees below with the sky above. "That's where we go," she said.

It didn't take them long to reach their destination, following the well-worn track down to where it crossed a stream and then climbing up to a forested bench. The smoke of the camp's fires drifted toward them. Moon Fish urged the buggy-horse forward and Abe dropped behind to follow her. The fresh young leaves of the trees rustled in the breeze. From Bird's back, he caught a brief sight of a couple of boys who leapt out of the bushes and ran ahead of them so fast that they disappeared around a bend in the road. Suddenly the trees ended and they were looking out on a large clearing with tipis and small huts scattered around its edge. A number of horses were held in a rope corral at the center of the area and playing children ran in many directions. Moon Fish again stood up in the buggy and this time she uttered a long vibrating note followed by a series of yipping sounds. She was immediately answered by several women's voices from around the wide opening.

Abe got off Bird and led her as he followed the buggy around to one side of the open area. From where they stopped, he could see many more lodges in the forested areas near the large opening they were in. Two boys came running toward him shaking small spears as if they were going to attack and drive him away. Suddenly one of them with reddish hair stopped, dropped his spear and came running as hard as he could to leap into Abe's arms, nearly knocking both of them to the ground.

"Papa, Papa. Is this real you?"

Abe hugged the boy, who had grown much in both height and weight since he'd last seen him. "Yes, son. It's really me."

Indigo pushed himself back to the ground and turned to shout at the other boy, who was still waiting where the spear had been dropped. "This is my Papa. Come." The boy slowly came forward, keeping his eyes turned down. Indigo went and grabbed hold of his arm, pulling him toward Abe, speaking quickly in Indian and then looking up at his father, "He come for me. I knew he come for me."

Abe glanced up and saw Moon Fish's big smile as she clapped her hands together several times. He knelt down and asked the boy what his name was. Indigo said the boy didn't know white man words, but his name was like a Blue Star. The boy was still looking down at his feet when Moon Fish spoke to him in their language as she prepared to step down from the buggy seat. Abe went to help her. The boy looked up at her and smiled to hear his own language being spoken. The two of them talked back and forth for a few sentences and Moon Fish laughed and turned to speak to Abe.

"I told him who you are and he says, how can you be his friend's father when you are a white man?"

"He doesn't think of Indigo as a white boy?"

She spoke to the boy again and then said to Abe, "He says your son is a white Indian with red hair. Then he pointed to that small tree over thee with its red leaves. He says it is different than being a white boy."

"All right, I guess they've accepted him. Here, let me help you down."

When she was firmly on the ground she told Abe to go find the rest of his white Indian family and she would find out which of her family members were in camp and where they expected her to stay.

Abe tied both horses to nearby trees and asked Indigo where his Mama was. "She's down by the water, washing berries. Come." He took Abe's hand and pulled him in the direction of the soft sound of flowing water.

When they came out of the trees near the large stream, Abe immediately saw Helga's long hair and her bent back as she worked at the edge of the water. He was suddenly unsure if he was ready for this, ready to see her again and reunite in whatever that might mean. He was also surprised by the deep feeling of wanting to take care of her again, to have her with him again.

Indigo still held onto his hand as he called out, "Mama! Mama! See, see who's here."

Helga gathered up the work in front of her and used a cloth to lift and dump a batch of berries into a basket, then she raised her eyes to see what her son wanted. She gave a sharp gasp and covered her mouth with one hand. Quickly she pushed herself up to her feet and threw herself into his arms, just as Indigo had done a few minutes before.

"Abe, Abe...Oh, Abe." She was laughing and crying and she turned her face up to his and kissed him once, and then again. "You came. Thank God you came to us." She stepped back, lifting Indigo in her arms. She held him in front of herself. "What do you think of your son?"

Abe cleared his throat to get the lump out of the way of his voice. "Good. He's a strong boy, and you, you look very good. How are you?"

"We're doing all right. But I have missed you so much."

"I've missed you too. Maybe you can show me around later. I should take care of my horses and park the buggy where it's convenient for Moon Fish. She's here with me. Do you know where that would be?"

She reached out and took his hand. Indigo took the other hand and the two of them led him back to his horses and buggy. Just then he remembered that he'd never looked at the things Moon Fish had bought for him that morning. That business had completely slipped his mind after the assault in the park. He would have to ask her what she'd gotten for these two before he dispensed the gifts.

Helga walked quickly ahead and went to Bird, who nuzzled her. "She remembers me, don't you think so?" Helga asked, stroking Bird's mane.

"Of course she does. Horses have good memories, especially of people who treat them well, or those who treat them poorly." He undid the rigging on the saddle and slipped the bridle off, replacing it with a braided halter. "Where should she go?"

"We'll take her over behind my little lodge," Helga said. "Have you got hobbles?"

"Yes. And where should I put the buggy? It has Moon Fish's things. She's come back to stay for the winter."

Indigo was crawling around under the buggy, shaking the steering hardware and looking out at them through the wheel spokes. His mother told him to go find Moon Fish and ask her where she wanted her things parked and unloaded.

The boy ran off, and Helga stepped close to Abe again, looking up into his eyes. "I don't want to know anything yet. About home, about her...I just want to be happy to see you. I am so happy." She reached around his head and pulled his face to hers. "Mmmmmm," she hummed as they kissed.

That evening Hawk Man sent one of his sons to invite Abe and Helga for a meal. Helga sent Indigo to stay with Blue Star. At first he didn't want to go, but when she said he could take the small braided lasso Abe brought for him, he jumped up, grabbed the stiff coiled rope and ran away from them.

"There's still enough light for him to show your gift to his friends."

Abe said he glad the boy was so happy with his gift, but he confessed that he hadn't had time in Boise to do any shopping. Moon Fish had done it for him. Then he reached into his chest pocket and pulled out a necklace. It was made of silver beads with a large turquoise stone set in a circle of silver. He had bought it for her himself on his trip to Santa Fe. As he held it up and then slipped it over her head, he thought about how close he'd come to forgetting to bring it along. He'd put it in a secret place out in the stable because he hadn't wanted to explain it to Sa-rah. He'd also brought back a similar stone and silver bracelet for her, which he'd given her just as he was about to leave on this trip, hoping it would keep her from feeling too badly about his leaving her again this time.

Helga took the stone between her fingers and raised it to her lips. "Thank you. I will always wear this, and I will always think of you." She held it out just far enough that she could see it, and then looked up at him, blinking back tears. "I don't know how I have been able to live without you," she said.

He stepped back from her and looked around, concerned that they might be watched. He didn't know what kind of comments their behavior might bring up. He suddenly felt a shyness at the awareness that he was a guest in this place, and he didn't even know what these people knew about him, about him being the father of Indigo and Helga's man, or maybe not her man.

She took his hand and led him to a path behind her small lodge. It went down to the creek, where rushing white water gushed between boulders. Helga lifted her leather skirt to her knees, kicked off her moccasins, and stepped carefully into the water. Where the current got deeper she pulled the skirt up and tucked it into the collar of her shawl-like shirt. She motioned for Abe to come into the water and join her. He shook his head "no" but slipped off his boots and sat down, dangling his feet in the cold clear water.

Helga splashed water up and over her head and hair and then came toward him. When she stopped in front of him, the setting sun made a silhouette of her body and light sparkled in the drops of water that flew from her when she shook her hair about. She leaned over him and held his head close to her breasts. Then she spun away, and went to kneel behind him on the grassy bank.

"This is my time of the day," she said. "If I had an Indian name I would want to be Evening Sun." As they sat in silence, the last direct rays of the sun disappeared and the few clouds between them and the horizon began to glow a brilliant crimson, shot through with orange and yellow streaks. "See those colors? That's how I feel sometimes when I watch our son playing or when I remember you and me together..." She dropped the necklace stone down the back of his shirt, inside his collar. "I feel like that now, I feel like fire in the sky because you are here with me."

After a few minutes of quiet broken only by the rushing sounds of the water, Helga pushed herself back and away from him. She stood up and bent over to dangle her wet hair in front of his face. He shifted and turned to stand up, but she held him down for one long kiss, then slipped on her moccasins and began walking back to the camp. Abe watched her go and realized that he'd forgotten how the strength and grace of her movements always made him feel stronger himself. It was as if she was giving him something with the way she moved. He pulled on his boots and followed a ways behind her until they reached her lodge.

"I should take Moon Fish her things," he said, "but the boy forgot to tell me where she would be."

"I have to gather something to take to our meal. Mary Wolf will expect that. You will find the old woman through those trees and in that direction. How much is there to be carried?"

"A few bags and two large boxes."

"You can take the bags, but leave the boxes. Carl will get someone to take them." She went inside through the flap of hide covering the doorway of her tipi.

It was the first time Carl had been mentioned except when they first pulled up in the buggy. Moon Fish had pointed to the bigger lodge and said it belonged to Hawk Man's son, the one they called Carl. Abe felt an anxious twinge at this second mention of the young man's name, but he felt also that if he was worried about Helga's loyalty to him, he had no real right to that feeling. He had done nothing to change the situation between her and Sa-rah, except to make this trip to see her, and even that had not been fully his doing.

He took the bags of the buggy. He'd heard nothing about Lefty and wondered if he might be here in the camp. If so, he might be staying close to Moon Fish. As Abe struggled with the load of bags, he felt something reminiscent about the path and that time so many years ago when he'd been jumped by the boys from Lefty's camp in Missouri. He half-expected them to jump out again and run laughing away from him. But nothing happened and he arrived at a group of three large tipis and a smaller one. At first, it looked as if no one was there, then he heard Moon Fish's voice calling to him from inside the smaller tent.

"Here, over here. Thank you." Her voice came from the opening of that lodge.

He placed the bags inside and waited while she came out and thanked him.

"Is Lefty here?" he asked.

"No, but they say he should return any day. Be good if you wait for him. There are many things changing here."

CHAPTER 15

Trouble

Abe waited through two days and nights after his arrival. He was worried about Sa-rah and the home place, but felt that he needed to discuss the land transaction and the mining activity with both Hawk Man and Lefty when all three of them could be together. That first night, he and Helga went to the evening meal with Hawk Man, Mary Wolf, and others of the family who usually came to visit them in the summers.

That night, when they returned to Helga's smaller lodge, she told him that Carl would be leaving with his father the next day. She stirred up the coals of her fire and added some pitchy sticks to light up the space. Abe waited until she seemed settled to ask where he should sleep, and what would Carl know or expect him to do.

"Abe, they know I am your woman and that Indigo is your firstborn son. They don't really understand why I am here and not with you. Mary Wolf and Lefty both told me that Carl lost his wife to a sickness just over a year ago."

"So, you are expected to be with him?"

"No. Not really. They say life here is hard and a woman and child by themselves cannot make it through a hard winter, and be warm and fed. They need a man and a man needs to be taken care of as well, by a woman or women. As far as I can tell, Carl has no one, and I was told he offered to let me stay next to him and he would provide for me."

Abe felt something rising inside of himself. He tried to push it away by telling himself he had no rights to this woman, even though he wasn't the one who'd driven her away. He said quietly, "So, if they think you should become his woman? What does he want?"

"Nobody tells me I have to do anything now. And I don't know what he wants, but he is very kind to me and good to Indigo." She stopped and busied herself putting on a pot of water. "I have some mint for tea. Would you like some?"

"Thank you."

"Mary Wolf also said that in their way, a man cannot force a woman to take him, and he cannot force her to become his."

"What do you want?"

She crumbled the dried mint in her hands and dropped it into the water. She looked across the fire at him, and said, "Abe, I want you. I never stopped wanting you since before Sa-rah pushed us together… Now she's pushed us apart and I want you even if I have to share, but she's the one who doesn't want that."

"I don't know what to do."

"Of course you don't. You've never been the one to decide things."

She stirred the pot and a sharp minty odor drifted came toward him. "So, Abe, what do you want?"

"Helga, maybe I only want what I can't have."

They were quiet until the water had boiled the leaves for some time. She poured two cupfuls, passed one to him and said, "I'm sorry I don't have any sugar for you." He mumbled something about that being fine with him, and she spoke again. "Abe, maybe I am the same, maybe I only want what I cannot have as well, but I also must look out for our son." She added more sticks to the fire and it brightened the space once again.

"Would you come back if I demanded it? Of both of you?" He blew on the hot liquid.

Helga looked down into her cup, "I don't trust her anymore, and maybe I don't trust you to stay strong about that if you did. She could get angry again if something happens to your other son; even if it wasn't done by Indigo, she would blame him and we would be thrown out."

"Not if I wouldn't let that happen."

"Abe, think about yourself, who you are. What would have happened this time if you were there? Thank about that."

"I only wish this whole thing was different."

"It can't be different than it is. Ever again."

"You mean this is the way it has to be, you here, maybe with Carl or some other Indian man, and me with Sa-rah, or maybe even alone?"

"Abe, I think you are beginning to understand what this is all about. So let's not think any more about it tonight." She crawled around the fire and lay down with her head in his lap. "If this is all we're going to have, then we should be good to each other while we can. Kiss me." After a few kisses, she pushed him around so she could pull off his boots. Then she stood up and moved to place them by the door opening, and said, "If you try to get away from me I'll grab your boots and run screaming from this tipi. That's how they do it here." She laughed and came back to him, pulling on his arms so he would stand up with her.

"What about the neighbors?"

"What I told everyone, except Lefty who knew what really happened, I told them all that my man was on a long trip and I needed to be where I could be taken care of. Mary Wolf guessed what was really happening, but promised not to tell anyone."

"But won't Carl be in his lodge tonight?"

"If he is, he won't know anything because we will be very quiet. Won't we?"

"Maybe I should stay outside, or under my buggy. There's only one bed in here."

"If you want to, but then people will say that I threw you out the day you arrived," she smiled. "And if that happens they will think you must be a very bad man. And about the bed, Mr. Abe, it's larger than the little one I had when you were so lonesome I had to let you stay with me that first time."

"Maybe we need more time to get to know each other again."

"That's exactly what I think, and the best place to do that is here, under a buffalo robe."

She took his hand and eased him around the fire and onto the bed. It was made of branches all laid going the same direction, but alternating their ends with the boughs. Helga rolled out one pair of hides that were sewn together and stuffed with something, and then she threw a large buffalo skin on top of the bed and crawled under.

"It will be cold tonight, but you can sleep wherever you want to—just don't complain about it in the morning." She turned over with her back to him and pulled the robe over her head.

He had forgotten how much he enjoyed her funny ways and how she could make him feel both awkward and comfortable at the same time. "Do you want me to put more wood on?"

Her muffled voice came through the hide, "I'm warm in here. You do whatever you need to do, but I think you'd be more comfortable sleeping with me and my buffalo."

"Where did you get such a large hide?"

"Carl traded two horses for it. It's kind of on loan to me."

He removed his outer shirt and knelt down at the side of the bed. This was part of why he'd come here, and he couldn't deny it to himself. Maybe it would have been better for both of them if she'd been away somewhere and he could have just brought Moon Fish, unloaded her things, talked business with Hawk Man, and left. So maybe it seemed like it would have been better for both of them, but he knew that wasn't the truth. Nothing they did could make it better at this point. He felt her hand moving under the hide, finding his knee and softly punching it a couple of times. It would be harder every time they ever saw each other until this was resolved, if they ever did again...

He slipped under the heavy weight of the buffalo robe and found her facing him in the covered darkness. Her hands seemed to push against him, but then he realized she was just stroking his chest and undoing the buttons of his shirt.

"Maybe we should wait for this until we know what's coming next," he whispered.

"We'll never know what's coming next," she whispered back and placed one of his hands between her breasts, clasping them together. "I was so afraid I wouldn't see you again. Things here are maybe not safe for us, for the people. The men are always talking seriously, or they are working on their weapons. Abe, I have been so afraid I would never see you again."

He placed his other hand around her back, between her shoulders and felt her quivering with a soft crying.

"Don't be afraid. We will find some way to be together, at least some of the time."

"How can you promise such a thing?"

He was silent, feeling himself also on the verge of tears. It was so hopeless, or at least it seemed to be. He would just have to confront Sa-rah, tell her he could only be with the one of them who could share him, unless they both could. That would be what he would have to do. Suddenly he felt Helga push her whole body against him, taking his hand from between her breasts and moving it to the warmth between her legs. She moved her body slowly against him, again and again.

"I love you, don't you know that? I would do anything to be with you, at least some of the time. Ohhhh, Abe, touch me more, please, please."

He felt his hardness in her hand and eased himself up and on top of her, his legs between hers, the two of them beginning to move as one, seeking, finding, thrusting, and yes, even in this moment, perhaps trusting that something, somehow, could work out for them.

Abe awoke to the sound of voices outside the lodge. At least two men were talking softly and urgently in their own language. He felt a shiver of fear that he'd done something terribly wrong and would be harmed in some kind of reprisal. He eased himself up and over the sleeping Helga so that he was against the wall of the tipi. There was no way out other than through the front door-hole with its closed covering. His movements awakened Helga, and she gave him a surprised look, as if she had forgotten he was with her. He held his finger over his lips and motioned toward the voices outside.

Helga seemed to be listening, and then she smiled, and whispered, "It's all right. It's Lefty and he says he's looking for a white man who has lost his way. I can't understand much yet, but I'm learning."

The voices went further away, and she pulled him into a kiss.

"He's back now," Abe said as he pulled away from her and rolled out from under the covering hide. "I should go see him. I don't want him to leave again until we talk."

"Come back as soon as you can. I will be here or at that creek where you found me." She reached up and took his hand to keep him from leaving. "Now do you remember me?"

"Of course I do." He turned and ducked out of the doorway.

First he went and checked on the horses who were some ways from where he'd left them, but it seemed they were doing all right. He fed them grain, dumping it out on hard places in the ground. The he went to the buggy and took out the small pouch of gold pieces that he'd hidden away when they left Boise. It wasn't as much as he would have liked it to be, but since Hawk Man had said he didn't want any of it, this amount should be enough. There was no activity or fire at Carl's lodge, so he assumed that the young man and his father were already gone on their way.

He came out of the trees where Moon Fish had her new, small lodge and he stood quietly for a long moment, listening to the voices of women coming from the other tipis arranged in a semi-circle in the clearing. Two nearly grown boys saw him but kept walking to wherever they were going. He knew it was a pretty sure thing that everyone in the village knew he was there.

He heard a sound behind himself and spun around just as Lefty grabbed him in a bear hug and lifted him off the ground. "My friend, my Big Bear Happy Horse Mister Abe Man. You are here!" He set Abe back on the ground and laughed. "Maybe your new name will be, 'Man with the Long Name.' What about that?" He laughed again and took Abe's arm. "Come, we will go to my lodge and have coffee that I bring here from them Spokane people."

They found places to sit outside the lodge. Patsy seemed happy to see him and smiled shyly when he said she looked as beautiful as always. She served coffee from a new tin pot and then backed away and went into her lodge.

"My friend, thank you for returning my good Mother-woman. She tells me her heart was good with you and your wife, but she was lonely for these children here in our village. And she was curious to know where village moved. How do you think she is now?"

"Better than I've seen her since she came to be with us. I wasn't sure she should make the journey, I thought it might be too much for her, but she came through it as good as when we left. She is a strong woman."

"May she live for many years. Thank you for taking care of her. Things here would have been upsetting for her if she was not well."

"What things, if I can ask?"

"More than one year has gone by when a white man killed Indian woman and wounded husband. He was put onto a trial and the Judge say he was guilty. First time ever. Sentenced to be hanged, but nothing happen. Now more than one year later, he is gone, not in prison, not hanged. The man he wounded try to find him, to kill him for revenge. He is still looking. Some young men are helping him. The soldier chief say nothing bad must happen or he will have to take actions. Everyone is talking about this. Even our friends, even Hawk Man is angry. He say he will take a white man for hostage."

"Did the judge release him, or the soldiers?"

"We don't know, but he is gone and there will now be trouble. And for you, is not a good time to be here. I am sorry to say this. I want my friend to stay and visit with me, be here, but some of these young men crazy and only want to kill a white man, any white man."

"When does Hawk Man return?"

"He say by next night, not this night." Lefty called out, and Patsy came with more coffee.

"I must talk with him if I can. I had to buy the land. You said it might happen, and I was told by our government that if I didn't buy the land, not just homestead it, but buy it, then someone else might get it away from me, from you and Hawk Man and your people because it was not a part of any legal reservation land."

"I think that is good." Lefty smiled, "Now is even more important we keep you safe. Hawk Man say for you to wait here. But you must be ready to leave in the next morning. Carl and some other young men will take you to where the ferry can cross you to the other side of the river. You will be safe over there."

They were quiet for awhile. Suddenly a young man came hurrying up and knelt to talk into Lefty's ear. Then he got up, turned away and left. Lefty looked at Abe and motioned with his head toward the trail to the creek. They both got up and Lefty walked quickly on down that trail. They stopped when he'd looked around and made sure they were out of anyone's hearing. He took Abe's hand and shook it once.

"My friend, some of the young men are angry that you are here because they want Carl to have your young woman. They say it is his right."

"But what if she doesn't want that? She said Mary Wolf told her a woman doesn't have to do what a man wants if she doesn't want that."

"Then it will be harder for her."

"Have you talked to him about this?"

"He say it is for her to decide. But other young men want her for him or for themselves."

Abe didn't respond. Then he had another thought. "What about the boy? Is he in danger because he is also a white person? Maybe I should take him."

Lefty smiled and said quietly, "You don't have to worry about that. The old people here say he is one of us. He wears a white skin, but they say he is like Indian. He can already hunt and trap, and he can even sing some of our songs. They say he is a spirit boy and it can be seen in him having red hair. So he will be taken care of as one of our own, and his mother also…Come, I want to show you something."

When they reached the creek, Lefty knelt down and motioned for Abe to do the same. He cupped water in his hands and then held it out to Abe, "Drink from my hands." He bent his head down and tipped the hands and the water into Abe's mouth. "Now you do."

Abe cupped his hands and held them out for Lefty to drink.

"Now, we have blessed you with this living water. You will be safe on your travel. If anyone tries to harm you they will fail, and they will die in water, what you say drowning, when their time comes."

Abe thanked his friend and then reached into his vest pocket for the pouch. "My friend, I have brought this gift for you and for Hawk Man, it is from the place I told you about. I used some of that gold to buy the land and this is what is left. I only keep very small bit. You use it however it is needed." He handed over the small pouch. "I had it changed into coins."

Lefty moved his hand up and down, shaking the pouch. He smiled. "This is good. Perhaps we will be able to pay to have the white man to be hanged and then all will be quiet again." He led the way back to his own camp and then turned to Abe and said, "Even if Hawk Man not return, you must go early in morning. Maybe I go with you."

Abe nodded, turned away and hurried back to Helga's place. She wasn't there so he followed the path to the stream and saw her working to clean more berries off their branches. This time she was with several other young women. He stood quietly by the edge of the trees until one of them noticed him and said something to Helga. She came quickly to him.

"You are all right?" She asked.

"Yes, but I have to leave early in the morning tomorrow. There is some problem and they will take me to the ferry at the big river."

"I know," she said, "these girls say you are here because of me, but when I told them you are my man, they ask why I am not living with you. Why am I here? I said it is because you have another woman and she was your first and made me go away."

He looked down at the three young women kneeling at the water's edge. They were whispering to one another and glancing in his direction.

"How long will you be working?"

"It will be several hours. Maybe you could go help Moon Fish. She needs wood gathered and maybe other help. She can find Indigo for you. Spend some time with him. He'll like that." She turned away quickly and rejoined the others.

Abe backed slowly up the trail and then went over to Helga's tipi and to the buggy. He found some items in the storage box behind the seat, pots and kitchen knives Moon Fish had picked out when she was shopping for him. He took the cookware inside and put it at the edge of the fire pit where Helga would find it. He also left a jacket he hoped would fit Indigo for the winter.

When he got to the Moon Fish's lodge, he found her sitting outside, smoking her small pipe. "Good morning," she said. "Sit down."

"Hello. Are you rested from our travels?"

"Yes, I feel good. Being here is good for my breathing, and I don't cough when I smoke here." She laughed, and went on, "Lefty says you will be leaving in the morning. Says there's some who want to make trouble for you. Don't worry. He is very strong for you and I am even stronger than he is. These young men are looking for someone to make fault with for how we are losing our homes. But we tell them you are one of the white men we can trust."

They were quiet for awhile.

"There is also the problem about Helga," he said. "Being a white woman, with no man."

"This I also know. Have you talked with her?"

"I have. Last night."

"What does she want?"

He was quiet for a few long moments. "She wants to be with me again."

"What about her and Sa-rah?"

"She says she is willing to share me. But she doesn't trust Sa-rah."

The older woman knocked the ashes out of her pipe on a small stone and rubbed them into its surface. "She is right. I talked with Sa-rah, and she says it is for Isaiah that she is being like this. I think it is also about not sharing. It is the white people way. What do you want?"

He was quiet as thoughts circled through his mind. This woman was the only person who knew about their situation firsthand. She was now even closer to what was going on than Mattie.

She had lived with himself and Sa-rah, and been her teacher. She also knew the way of her adopted people and the way of a man having more than one woman. So when she asked him what he wanted, he knew she would know what he meant when he answered, or if he was being untruthful with her.

"I want what I can't have. I want it to be like it was when we were one family. None of this would have happened if I hadn't gone away to help my cousin."

"None of this would have happened if it wasn't the will of the Creator. It is not our place in this life to be the ones who can change things from how they are. It is our place in this life to do our best to be good people living with what we are given. And we aren't very good at that, so it takes a lot of practice."

"Helga says I am not strong enough to make a demand for how things should be."

"Maybe she is right about that, but it is not about being strong. More about you already know you cannot make something happen that is not on the road of your life, or of theirs." She paused, and then asked, "What are you doing right now?"

"I came to see if you needed some help with anything. Helga is busy with berries."

"Have you eaten?"

"No, I went with Lefty, but we were too busy talking to eat."

"I will feed you. You get wood for me. Here is my axe. Big dead tree down that way. But come back soon to eat."

Later, after he'd eaten, he cut most of the tree and dragged it back to her camp. Then he asked if she knew where Indigo was, or would it be all right for him to look for him. She nodded and said that he could spend time with the boy. Then she gave a shrill whistle between her cupped hands and repeated its three notes several times. Within a minute or two, the boy appeared with his friend.

"Your papa wants to see you."

"I want to see him too." The boy tipped his head back and smiled. Then he took his father's hand. The young friend hung back, but Indigo called him forward.

"This is, in our words, Blue Star. Can he be with us?"

"Of course. What do you want to do?"

"I want to show you where a bear lived in the winter. Come."

The boys led the way and followed the water upstream for quite a ways until they disappeared inside a large cave-like hole in the side of a rocky area. Then they crawled out at him growling and making big swinging arm movements. Abe pretended to be scared and tried to run away, but made himself fall down, and the boys jumped on him. After that they went for a long hike. Abe was relieved that they didn't run into anyone from the camp. When they returned, Blue Star ran off and Indigo and his father went to Helga's lodge and found her sewing on soft leather.

"I don't like you having to wear that old vest you have on," she said. "I can have this done in just a little bit more time. And we will eat when it is dark."

"Remember, I will leave in the early morning."

Indigo made a sad face when he heard this, and Abe scooped him up in his arm and swung him around. When he set the boy down, he was trying not to cry and ran off.

"See how much he misses you?" Helga said, without looking up from her work.

"And I miss both of you."

"But nothing will change, will it?"

"I don't know. We'll have to see."

Helga was quiet and motioned for Abe to sit near her. After a while she put down her sewing and looked at Abe with a soft expression and repeated his name several times. "You know I would come with you, except for her. I would go anywhere with you, you and our son… And I want another child." She was silent for a long time and Abe didn't know what to say. Finally, she spoke again, "Remember when Sa-rah was trying so hard to have a baby and she talked about when the woman needed to be with a man to make a child?"

Abe nodded. "Yes, why?"

"I think it is my time, and I hope you and I did that last night." She picked up her sewing again and said, "Now go find your son so I can finish this before we eat. I want to put some quills on it for decoration. I am learning the ways of these people. I love their beads and quills."

Abe got up and walked off. He was feeling very sad for Helga and the boy, and for himself. He found Indigo up in a tree when the boy threw some cones down. Abe thought that the worst part of all this was missing out on his first son's growing up. It just wasn't right.

Hawk Man and Carl did not return that evening so Abe spent the time with Indigo and Helga. He told the boy some of the Bible's more adventurous stories while Helga worked by firelight to finish the vest. That night Indigo fell asleep and was between the two of them until Helga eased herself over him to lie next to Abe. She whispered, "Do you love me?"

Instead of answering, he kissed her for a long, long time, knowing that this wouldn't happen again anytime soon. During the afternoon he'd realized that when he was back at his home with Sa-rah, the two of them would have to get this whole issue out in the open, so now he wasn't looking forward to being back home any more than he wanted to leave here.

Helga crawled over him and got out from under the buffalo robe. She picked up a blanket, took his hand, and gently pulled him out through the door-opening. The moon was just rising above the trees on the opposite ridge as she led him a short way away from her lodge. She found a place that seemed fairly soft and laid out the blanket. Abe stayed standing up as she arranged herself. But when he didn't move to lie beside her, she got back up on her knees and pulled him toward her. She nuzzled her face at his waist and below and then reached up and pulled him down beside her. It was awkward, and their clothing was in the way, but their urgency and common need somehow found the way to one another and they held onto each other until they were almost falling asleep.

Then she shook him, whispering, "We'll go back in now."

It was still dark outside when Abe was awakened by Lefty's voice repeating his name and shaking the tipi covering.

"All right, I'm awake," he said.

"We talk with Hawk Man and then go. Come now."

The pink edge of the sky was creeping higher where the eastern horizon could be seen at the mouth of the valley. The two men hurried across the camp. Behind some trees, a fire was blazing outside the largest tipi Abe had yet seen. Hawk Man was squatting near the flames rubbing his hands together. When he saw them arriving he stood and held out one hand to Abe.

"We shake," he said. "I happy see you."

"Good. It is good to be in your camp."

The man spoke quickly in his own language and Lefty translated, "He says he sorry not to be here when you visit to him. He say, many things calling to him to go here, to go there. People not happy with white men now. But I tell them you are our friend. He say he know this." Hawk Man called toward the tent and Mary Wolf appeared with a pot of hot coffee. When she'd poured Abe's cup full, she handed him a small pouch.

"For your son at home."

She gave him a quick smile in the flickering firelight, and he thanked her as she turned away and left them to their business.

Again Hawk Man began speaking in his language with Lefty translating, "He say I tell him you buy land now. He say you are a good white man to be the one own land. It is good because he cannot be there on that land all the time to keep it. He say it must be taken care of and you can do that for his People. Other way is some other white man who does not let Hawk Man and his family be there. Now is time of many quarrels between whites and the people. We do not know what will happen. But if it is war, it will be bad for everyone. What do you think, he say?"

Abe thought for a moment, "I don't know about all of this. Some of my cows have been stolen, but no fighting. When I went to Boise to buy the land they talked about Indians trying to keep the land that the white man needs. The government man told me I was lucky to buy this land before other people, rich people from far away. They are buying much of the land."

"And this?" The man held up the small pouch of gold coins that Abe had given Lefty, who translated, "There is more on that land?"

"That and the money to buy the land is all that we could get without explosives, but there may not be any more and we have told no one where it came from. I do not want any more mining on that land. I do not want explosives and machinery and destruction of the land. I want cattle and I want you and your family to come back often and spend time with me."

"Ho!" Hawk man said, making a flat gesture with his hands. Lefty translated, "Is good. Is what we want. Is why I know you are a good man. Is why we let your blood go into the land, so you can be relatives with us and with that land. And when I return to be with you I bring young stallion we get from that Bird-horse and my horse. He is good animal and now will be making good colts, one for you I bring.'"

"And I thank you. I will always do what is needed to give back to you for what you have done for me and for my family, but I'm not sure I can take care of a stallion. Maybe you keep him and I take next one if it's a female."

"That's good...This woman of yours, she stay or go with you?"

"It just isn't time yet for her to return with me. There is a problem between the two women. I will do what I can, but I am so thankful to you for taking her into your camp."

Lefty smiled and translated, "He say it is Lefty bring her here, and Carl take care of her now. Maybe you not have problem anymore. He says, white women do not know what is good for them. Indian women do not want one man for only one woman. One man is too much trouble. Woman need her sisters, other wives, to help take care of man." Hawk Man laughed and pointed to himself. "Look at me,"

Lefty said for him, "I am too much trouble for three women." Then he got to his feet and motioned for Abe to get up and come close. He spoke very softly and Lefty whispered what he said to Abe. "He says, you must not return here again soon. There are some who do not believe Hawk Man when he says you are our relative. He says, he will get word to you when is safe for you to come visit. Now go." Hawk Man held out his hand, but this time he gripped Abe's forearm and brought him close, face to face, and he said, "Peace. Must have peace, you, me. Peace." Then he let go and turned away, hurrying off into the growing light of the dawn.

"Come," Lefty said, "we move quickly. Get your horses and wagon ready. I come for you." Then he too, moved off into the shadows.

Helga came to the doorway of her lodge. She was wrapped in a blanket and came to stand next to him. "What's going on?"

"They came for me. I talked about the land with Hawk Man. Now Lefty has to escort me as far as the ferry. There are young men who are upset with me being here. I must quickly get ready to leave."

She reached out and took his arm, holding onto him as he tried to move away. "Abe, a friend of mine here, she said her man wanted to capture you because some white man killed someone. I didn't tell you because I was being selfish. Abe, I didn't want you to leave, but maybe I made it more dangerous for you. Abe, I'm so sorry, but my love and my loneliness make me crazy."

He took her in his arms. "Be strong. You'll be all right here. They promised me, and they say Indigo is a spirit-child. You will both be safe here."

He moved away, but she held onto his arm and came along with him. "I don't want to be safe here. I don't want to be here. I want to be with you, I only want to be with you." Her voice rose and she held on, trying to stop him.

"I must go. It will be worse for both of us if I don't leave now. I want you to be with me. I do. But I have to go home and try and work it out. I'll come back when I can."

Helga let go of him and dropped her arms at her sides, "Go," she was crying, "and if I never see you again, know that no one will ever love you as much as I do, not her, not anybody." She turned away, and hurried back into her lodge.

Abe caught the horses and harnessed Ginger to the buggy. He saddled Bird, even though he was planning to tie her to the buggy to follow after. He led both of them down the path to Helga's place. The sun was close to rising now and coming more quickly. He dropped Bird's reins. She would stay there that way. He walked quickly back to Helga's tipi.

His things were set outside. The new vest was on top of the small pile of his bag and coat. He called softly for her and then looked inside. Indigo was sleeping in the bed, but the woman wasn't there. He pulled his head back outside. He wanted to call for her, but knew he should remain quiet. Just then he heard a low whistle coming from where he'd left the horses and buggy. He grabbed his things, put them back down and pulled on the vest. It fit well.

Lefty was waiting with his own horse. "We will meet others by creek crossing. Come. I see your woman on my way here. She say she not want to say good-bye. We go." He mounted and went in front as Abe led Bird and the horse and buggy.

When they reached the large creek, he tied Bird to the back of the rig and climbed in. He took one more look around for Helga, but she was nowhere to be seen. They moved into the water and crossed to the other side where there was a rough road, but it was passable. Lefty put his horse into a trot and Abe followed after. It was almost morning and the sun behind the ridge cast its glow across the sky. Now that he was moving, the feeling of loss from having to leave Helga and Indigo behind seemed to be growing inside of him and he, too, felt like crying.

Two young men came along came out of the woods and escorted Abe, one in front of him and one behind. Both men had their faces painted, one yellow, the other black. Lefty looked to be his usual self, white man clothing and dark skin. All three of them carried rifles across their saddles. Taking a warning from the others, Abe reached behind the seat of the buggy to make sure that his own gun was easily accessible.

Several hours passed before they stopped to water the horses and eat some dried meat pounded together with berries into a food designed for travelling. Lefty showed Abe how he should break off pieces and soak them in his mouth for a short time before trying to chew. They rested there for awhile, letting the horses browse on the roadside vegetation. Lefty commented to Abe, "Looks like they don't want you so much. I thought those angry ones might follow."

"Who are they?"

"Young men from Wallawa land. Our people, but not our group, not our families. They came to try to get our old men to help them. To give agreement for them to take revenge for the woman who was killed and the white man who was let go free. That is what I know. One of them say they should keep you until white man is hanged, then let you go. But Hawk Man very strong to say you are relative and cannot be our prisoner or he will fight them himself."

"I'm sorry for this. I only wanted to bring Moon Fish back to her home."

Lefty looked at him for a long moment, "And to see your younger woman and son."

"Yes. But now perhaps I have made it worse for them."

"We go. River not far. You take ferry across big river and these ones will not follow. We will wait there after you go, until it is late in the day. You will be safe. Come."

Abe went to catch the hobbled horses and hitch up. Just as he caught hold of Ginger's halter, he was suddenly surrounded by three Indians with guns. He had just time enough to notice that these men also wore face paint and that the guns looked to be older. One of the men grabbed for the horse's halter and yanked it away from him. Another motioned at him with his handgun and pointed in a direction away from where Lefty and the others were supposedly waiting for him. His mind raced through several things he should or should not do, and yelling was the only possibility he could think of.

He let out a loud yell and was immediately hit on the side of the head by the third man's rifle. As he went to his knees he saw one of his two escorts dodge behind a tree and then disappear backward. His head was throbbing, though when he wiped at his hair there was no blood on his hand. The pain was terrible, but he couldn't tell if he was badly hurt.

Then he heard a loud shout from behind. He struggled to turn and saw Lefty standing with his legs spread apart and his hands holding a rifle pointed at the nearest stranger. Lefty spoke rapidly in Indian. That man spoke to the one who'd hit Abe and was standing over him. All three of them began talking to one another at once. Lefty's two helpers now stepped out from behind the trees where they'd been concealed, each of them pointing rifles at one of the ambushers.

Lefty spoke again, but this time he laughed and dropped his gun. He sat down on the ground and rolled himself a cigarette. Then he said to Abe, "I told them you are powerful man with evil spirit helpers. I told them we are trying to get you away from our village and away from our country, because your woman ran from you. You are very angry and can do much evil."

Abe struggled to try and stand up, but his guard pushed him back down.

Lefty spoke again to them, and then to Abe, speaking as if he were very angry, but he gave a quick look, almost a smile when he said, "Big Bear Man, get up fast, spread your arms wide and high and spit in his face." Abe wasn't sure he wanted to do that, but Lefty said it again, "Arms up, spit in his eyes. Now!"

He did it and the man's hand instantly went to his face. A shot rang out and the man dropped his gun and slumped to his knees, then fell over. Lefty began singing in a low voice. The other two men were talking to one another in low voices. They still had their guns pointed at Abe, but they were backing away.

The one on the ground moaned and tried to stand.

Lefty yelled at the other two and gave them orders to point their guns to the ground and pick up their companion. "Drag him away, before he dies from the poison," Lefty said in Indian and then translated for Abe. "I'm telling them to leave before he will die from your poison, your bad medicine. I say, we will have to kill them if they don't leave right away."

The two men dragged the third into the trees, followed by the two who'd been escorting Abe to the ferry. Lefty got up and came to look at Abe's head.

"You will have big head," he smiled, "Big Bear head."

Abe rubbed his head where he'd been hit and felt the large swollen knot that was already forming there. "What happened? I don't understand."

"I told them who I am. I said, 'Do you know me?' They said no so I said my name in our language. I told them I was the only one of our people who would dare to take you away from our village. Because you are very bad man and have medicine from the white man's Devil. And then I told them that you have rattlesnake power and that if he spits on you, you will die."

"Did they know who you are after you told them?"

"They said they thought I was a white man with dark skin, from the south country, maybe a Mexican. They are those ones I told you about, our relatives from Wallawa, but they never saw me before. I'm glad of that because if they knew me from before and knew Bird was once my horse, they would know you and I are friends. But now you are the evil one." He laughed, and went on, "Even your spit is poison. They believe that now. Come, we must keep moving, if you can. I will drive your wagon, you will rest until it is time to cross big river."

Once he crossed the big river, the rest of his trip was uneventful, even almost relaxing after all the stress of the rest of the journey. He was tired but relieved when he pulled up at the Skinner place. It was a good feeling. He'd already decided on the way back that he wouldn't say anything about the troubles going on with the Indians, then remembering the incident in Boise, he thought he shouldn't mention that either. He knew Sa-rah would be very upset if she knew about either one of those things.

Martha was churning butter under a shade tree. She called out to him that it was good to have him back.

"I'm glad to be back. Is Mike here?"

"No, but he should be here soon. Are you hungry?"

"I'd be lying if I said no, but I'm almost home."

"Get down. I'll feed you something to take you the rest of the way. Can't have you going faint between here and there." She got up and worked the paddle of the churn from a standing position, and then stopped. "There, that should be done now."

She took off her apron, shook it out, and went quickly to the house. It seemed like only a minute before she was back with a thick slice of bread and roasted meat.

As he took his first bite, she asked, "How was it? A good trip? Did the old lady make it there all right? Oh Abe, I'm sorry your mouth is full and I'm asking you all these questions. I'll just wait and let you take your time eating. You look famished."

He finished the food and told her that the trip had gone as well as could be expected, and that Moon Fish seemed to gain strength rather than to get weaker as they got closer to her home and her own people.

"I saw Helga and Indigo, only briefly, but they are doing well. The boy seems happy with his new friends. It made me realize he never had anyone to play with around here, except Isaiah, who was just a baby."

"It's hard for children to understand that difference between their ages and size," Martha said, "and it's not my business, but I don't think Sa-rah understood that very well. I'm glad to hear they're doing well, but I do miss Helga. She was always so helpful and friendly."

Abe thanked her for the food and excused himself to hurry on the rest of the way home. When he arrived at the stable area and was unharnessing Ginger, he heard a high-pitched scream and turned around to see Isaiah on the ground, having fallen. He went to him, picked him up and then saw Sa-rah hurrying to catch up with the boy.

They all gathered into a hug and then Sa-rah wiped the tears from Isaiah's face and looked up into Abe's eyes. "You're all right? I'm so glad you're back safe. I have to tell you I couldn't help worrying."

Isaiah was rubbing his face with his little hands and Abe turned his own head to hide the still-sore bump. Sa-rah held the little one's head off to the side and was able to reach up for a kiss from him.

"It's good to be home," he said.

"Well, you'll have to tell me all about it, but I should let Mattie know you're back. She's been staying here and Ollie's been away somewhere, but I know she's eager to get back to her own place. Come, Isaiah, we'll let Papa put the horses away." Isaiah hung onto Abe, but then let go and went with his mother, who led him by the hand back to the house.

He gave both horses some grain, hung up the harness, and pushed the buggy under its shelter. He thought he would wait to unpack. He wondered what Sa-rah meant when she said she'd had to worry about him. Had she dreamed something?

That evening after a celebratory supper, Abe sat with Isaiah until the boy fell asleep. He was himself dozing off when Sa-rah came to take the child to his bed. Abe shook his head no and said softly, "I like having him right here for now."

Sa-rah smiled and said, "He missed you. Every day I had to tell him that you would be back soon. He didn't like it with you gone… Of course, neither did I."

"I know. I came back as soon as I could. I needed to see Hawk Man on some business and he wasn't there for almost two days."

She had taken the chair next to him and moved it even closer. "So you had to wait and be with your other son?"

"Yes."

"How is he?"

"Seems very well. Growing fast. And he has other boys to play with. Lefty told me he is welcome there. His reddish hair is considered a sign of a good-spirit person."

"And his mother?"

"She is also doing well. Has her own small tipi and is working with others to gather food for the coming winter."

"I won't ask any more than that."

They were quiet with only the sound of her rocking chair to intrude on the silence. Isaiah shifted in Abe's arms and struggled, waving his arms.

"Here," she said, and got up to take him. "I'll take him to bed. There's a fresh pie on the warming rack if you want some now."

"I'll wait for you. I've got to get some things from the buggy."

When he came back inside, she'd dished out one large piece of pie and a much smaller one for herself. "Berries," she said, "just now ripening."

He handed her a package and sat down next to the small table with his pie. Sa-rah carefully unwrapped the bundle and took out a bolt of blue fabric. "It's thick," she said shaking it out across her lap.

"It's that denim they have now in the mercantile stores."

She stood and let it hang down from her waist. "It's perfect."

"When I saw it in the store on my way home, I knew it was just the kind of thing you could sew into pant-legs. Remember?"

"Of course, I was the scandal of the wagon train. A girl in pants. I'll bet those Mormon women never did stop talking about it."

"Well, the outfit you made from your own clothes did look a lot better on you than the ones you took from my clothes and shortened." He laughed at the memory.

"But they're so practical for working and especially for riding."

"Maybe that's why women aren't supposed to wear pants: to keep them where they belong. In the house."

She gave him a sharp look and he laughed.

"Well," she said, folding the skirt and setting it on another chair. "I might not be able to wear anything like that much longer."

"Why not, I promise not to laugh at you again. About that, I mean."

She stepped across the space between them and fell into his lap. "Abe, I think we need to have another baby." She put her arms around him. "Are you ready?"

CHAPTER 16

Baby

There was already over a foot of snow on the ground when Christmas came that year, and Abe brought the cattle down from the upper lands where he'd moved them for the months of the fall. He was now running over fifty mother cows with their calves, and four breeding bulls. No one had settled further up the valley above them and he was able to let the herd roam as far as they would go. The valley narrowed and the side hills formed a kind of natural enclosure, with several narrow draws where the animals could escape the wind during storms. But now, with the grass covered up and frozen, he was worried that there wouldn't be enough for the next few months down near the house and where the Indians camped. Mike no longer kept his own stock, and was always glad to have Abe's herd move through his place to keep the brush and grass from becoming a fire hazard during the summer heat.

Mattie had taken ill and was now living in Silver City with Ollie. Abe and he had made one more entry into the crevices of the rock and found a bit more gold, just about enough to pay for the house in town. In addition to it being a good thing for Ollie and Mattie, it was also good for when Sa-rah, Isaiah and Abe came into town and needed a place to stay over before heading back. Although there were no specific symptoms to Mattie's illness, she was getting weaker, and the local doctor said it was something to do with her lungs, that she needed to stay out of the cold and the wind. As Mattie said, "Well what do you expect from a southern belle?"

The biggest change that was happening to them all was that Sa-rah was with child again, and feeling especially grateful after trying for the past year. They had seen none of their Indians, and Sa-rah was anxious to get a message to Moon Fish with the news. Abe knew better than to suggest that he take word to the older woman; things had been going along quite peacefully ever since he'd returned from the trip to see Helga and Indigo. Now this new baby would make it even harder for him to get away.

By this time, Isaiah seemed almost as big as Indigo had been when he and his mother moved away. So often, when watching the boy playing with the dog or making toys out of sticks and string, Abe wished that his sons could be growing up together. It was the one great regret of his life, and although he'd been praying regularly for some kind of answer or shift in the situation, nothing seemed to change as far as all of it. The last thing he'd heard was that Helga was now moved in with Carl, but there was no way to confirm what that meant. It was news passed on to him by one of Lefty's friends, a French trapper travelling south. He stopped by to tell Abe that things were all right with his Indian friends, and that Moon Fish was hanging on. His remark about Helga and Carl seemed like an afterthought. It wasn't clear if Helga still had her own tipi, or if she really had moved into Carl's to be with him. When Abe pressed the man about it, he only said that he didn't know them himself, and didn't know any more than that.

The road was another new development. Ollie had helped Mike Skinner and Abe to design a better route from the main road up the trail in their valley. They'd worked hard to straighten some parts, and build two log bridges that cut off quite a bit of the distance and difficulty. Ollie was frustrated that he didn't have a team of horses with a blade for digging and levelling, because as he said several times during the job, "Can't seem to get good help these days." He was, however, still able to find ways to show them how to remove boulders and support the side-cast waste dirt to build a fairly safe and much more comfortable road. His flask was also more in evidence, but since neither of his two coworkers wanted to share with him, it stayed out of sight most of the time.

Late in the fall, just as the last leaves were beginning to flutter from the trees to the ground, the small group held a ribbon-cutting ceremony out in front of the Skinner place, and they christened the road, "Mattie's Way," at Ollie's insistence. The only concern was that they might get more visitors, both wanted and unwanted, now that it was easier to get to them. Mike brushed that off by saying that he'd be happy to sit on his porch with a shotgun and charge tolls from anyone they didn't want to deal with.

Mattie came out for the celebration, but needed to be taken back to the Skinner place early to rest. She and Ollie had borrowed a buggy from one of their neighbors in town, but it wasn't all that sheltered, so Abe loaned them a buffalo robe. Mattie protested and said she wouldn't need it, but Abe said he'd get it back sometime. It had been a gift from Lefty and his woman Patsy, and he wanted her to be well taken care of by its warmth and the friendship that was in the work that went into it. When Abe told her that, Mattie gave him a strange look, and said, "How did you know that?"

"What?"

"What you said about friendship being put in a blanket or something."

"I don't know. I guess I somehow remember that stuffed horsehair blanket that couple gave us on the trail. They thanked me for saving their little girl in a river accident, and told us that the quilt was very special to them and they wanted us to have because it would help us have children. They said it was a friendship blanket."

"Well, I declare, my Momma told me the exact same thing when I was a little girl, only the way she said it, you can put either good or bad in a blanket by how you feel about the people who's going to sleep under it. And those feelings are very powerful and last a long time because, and she said it very seriously, 'People spend more time under their blankets than they do anywhere else.' And I do believe she was right, so I know I'll be well taken care of by this buffalo. Thank you." Then she called Sa-rah to come close to her and spoke softly to her, "I wish I could be here with you. But there isn't much I can do these days. Just know how much I love you, and as long as you can still make the trip to town, please, please come see me and plan to stay over with us."

"Oh, I will, and I'll miss you every day, but this is what's best for you, and baby and me will be just fine," she said, patting her growing curve.

New Year's Day dawned bright and chilly. The sun climbed out of its bed as late as it ever did all year long and the mist along the streams took a few hours to burn off. Now that Isaiah was four years old, he had some idea of what a birthday meant, and he woke up excited. He immediately spotted two wrapped presents and wanted to open them right away. Abe stopped him and said, "Open the small one now, but the big one will have to wait until our friends get here later."

The boy pouted for a moment, but then grabbed up the smaller package and tore the paper away from a book about wild creatures. It had pictures of birds, as well as bears, fish, and snakes. He looked up at his parents with a kind of wonder in his eyes and asked if he could look at it all right then. Sa-rah asked him if his hands were clean and he held them out for inspection. She told him they were all right, but that he should always remember it was a special book and he should never look at it with dirty hands. Then she went to the kitchen to prepare a birthday breakfast of corncakes and jelly with smoked dry meat and potatoes, all favorites of his.

Later, when the Skinners arrived, they brought a surprise. Martha's niece and her husband showed up with them. There was also a young girl only a little older than Isaiah. The niece, named Abigail, brought in pumpkin and apple pies in a lovely basket and said the basket was a gift to the family of the house. The young man, who looked to be about the same age as Abe, asked where he could put the team and carriage he'd rented to bring them from Silver City. They'd taken the stage that far from their hometown further north, and had been able to get this small buggy and team from the Silver City livery.

Abe grabbed a coat and hat and went out to show the man around and get the horses settled in. "Didn't catch your name in all that excitement," he said.

"Roland, Roland Alexander. Two first names, I guess, so you can call me either one." He removed his glove and held out his hand.

They shook and Abe said, "Abraham Saunders, Abe. Pleased to meet you."

While they unharnessed and turned out the team of horses, Roland told Abe a little about his family's story, at least the recent part of it. They'd had a run of bad luck and were just now beginning to sort things out. Their place, a good-sized ranch, was up near the little village of Three Forks on the South Palouse River. He paused to ask Abe if he knew where that was. Abe said he'd been as far as the southern edge of the Lapwai Reservation area, but not further north.

"Well, there's not a lot going on where we come from, or at least there wasn't much before some fool killed an Indian woman a few years ago. She was chasing a horse out of her garden and the owner of the horse, a white man, shot her. After he got picked up for the shooting, he claimed she'd stolen the horse. They let him go. Ever since then, it's been hard to feel safe up there. The Indians are causing trouble."

Abe waited for the young man to go on, curious but too polite to force the conversation.

"Where can we push this here wagon?" he asked, looking up into the clear sky. "Doesn't look like it needs to be under cover."

"Is Mike coming horseback, or on a buggy?"

"He said he'd ride over in a little bit, so I assume he won't bring another set of wheels." He smiled and then said, "Mike spoke highly of you folks. Said my aunt never would have stuck it out with a codger like himself if it wasn't for the neighbors." He grabbed a bag from behind the seat of the wagon and then looked over at Abe again, saying, "Anyway, ever since that happened, there's been trouble between the whites and the Indians. When my father came into that country twenty years ago, everything was peaceful, but now there're some bad traders who give whiskey to the young Indians, and there's some crazy Indians that want a war with the whites. We got kind of in the middle of it all and our barn got burnt down with all the hay we'd put up. That was in October. Then my father passed away a little over a month ago. Mom's been gone a few years, so me and Abby just didn't know what to do with ourselves. I sold the cattle cheap and came on down here like Aunt Martha invited us to do. Problem is, not sure if we can get back up there and make another start. Just have to see how the weather and things turn out."

Abe spoke softly, "Sorry to hear this. I was up there at one of the Indian villages, have some relatives near them. These troubles you talk about were getting started there as well. What you say makes it sounds worse now, though. Guess I was hoping it would settle down, been wanting to get back up there again."

"There is a fort near where we were,' Roland said, "and a small garrison, but they're not near enough soldiers to make peace or war. It's all wait and see now."

"And what's your little girl's name?

"Her name, well it sounds like the word 'name.' It's Naomi, after my grandmother."

As they walked back to the house, Abe had the feeling that this young man didn't get much of a chance to talk with anyone very often, because he had a lot to say. Sort of like myself, he thought.

The New Year's dinner was a great success with plenty left over and folks having to wait on dessert because they were too full from the main courses. Isaiah was acting shy with the guests, but he was also eager for his second present. He went to where his father was sitting and tried to wait patiently while the two men talked about cattle, but after a while he couldn't keep himself from pulling on Abe's sleeve to get his attention.

"What is it?" Abe asked.

"You said, you said I could have it when they got here."

"Oh, that's right. I guess I forgot. Can you bring it to me?"

The boy hurried across the room and began pulling on the big bundle. When he got it to the middle of the room. Abe told him to stop there with it. "You have to guess what it is," he said as the others gathered around.

"Don't know, Papa."

"What does it feel like?"

Isaiah rubbed his hands over the feed sacks the present was wrapped in. "A cow head-bone," the boy guessed.

"Nooo. Guess again."

"Can't know. Have to see inside. Now, Papa?"

"All right. Go ahead."

Isaiah pulled on the string, and the sack fell away to reveal a perfectly made half-size saddle.

"Papa, Papa, I like, I like." He pulled it around so it was upright on the floor and then climbed onto the seat. Everyone clapped and he pretended to be riding.

"It's just right for you," Sa-rah said, laughing. "Don't get thrown off."

He rocked back and forth a few times and then stopped and looked up at his parents with a serious expression. "Mama, Papa, where's the horse for me?"

Abe laughed and said, "One thing at a time. We'll get the horse, maybe next year."

Isaiah rocked back and forth faster and said loudly, "Need horse, need horse, need horse."

Sa-rah bent down and put her hand on his should and shook him gently, "That's enough of that now. Say thank you to Papa, and we'll talk about the horse later."

"Thank you, Papa."

"Now why don't you and this little girl, Naomi, just sit quietly and look at your books. I'm sure she'd like that." Sarah cleared a place on the floor near the fire and put a couple of pillows there for the two of them. They were shy about it, but as soon as Naomi saw that one of the books was one she had at home, she said she could tell it to him and they settled into it.

Sa-rah and Abby went into the kitchen where Martha was cleaning up the last of the supper dishes, and they made some fresh hot tea. Soon they were talking about their different birthing experiences, and Abby confessed that she'd been trying hard to have another child. Martha came over to stand beside her chair and put her arm around the young woman.

"Maybe Sa-rah can help you, She's had some treatments from the Indians that seem to have helped her."

"Oh really, I'd try anything at this point."

Sa-rah admitted that she herself didn't have the power to give the treatments, but there were some things she could share, like what kind of herbs to make tea out of and what foods to avoid. She pointed at her own belly and said, "If I really knew how to make it happen this one would actually have come a lot sooner."

The month of January was filled with more than the usual amount of snow, and there wasn't much chance for travel. Roland and his family stayed in the small house Ollie and Mattie had built, and the young man proved his worth as a good hand, helping both Mike and Abe.

When the weather did take an almost balmy break, the snow blew off the road and the three women decided to make a trip into Silver City for supplies, and just to get away for a couple of days. Abe was all right with the expedition, but warned them to keep an eye on the weather and head back right away if there was any threat of another storm.

Fortunately, the clouds stayed mostly white and travelled quickly overhead on an easterly wind. The weather got colder, but remained dry. Sa-rah stayed with Mattie, and Martha and Abby found a comfortable room at a lodging establishment. The shopping didn't take that long, but they found other things to keep them busy and for two days enjoyed long midday meals at the lodging house dining room, strolling in the park where waterfowl inhabited a large pond, and other diversions of what they were calling their "winter break." When they got ready to head back, there wasn't enough room in the wagon for the load of goods and all three of them. Abby said she would have no problem riding, but they didn't have an extra horse. Sa-rah got an idea to fix that and asked Ollie to track down a friend who had a small horse for sale. The friend loaned them a saddle and tack and agreed to return Sa-rah's money if the horse didn't work out.

The horse was named Copper after the color of his mane and tail, which shone nicely against the duller brown of the rest of his coat. Abby gave him a ride and pronounced him gentle and manageable. So they got ready to leave early the next morning.

Martha, her eyes twinkling with laughter, asked in a mysterious tone of voice, "And my dear, whatever are you going to do with another horse, especially one this small?"

Sa-rah laughed back and said, "I bet you could never guess."

When they reached home with all the things they'd collected, they spent a whole day in sorting and dropping things off, first at Martha's and Abby's places, and then taking the rest to Sa-rah's. Roland helped her make the short trip between the two places, leading Copper behind him as he rode his own horse. Sa-rah drove the wagon and team.

Abe was chopping wood when they arrived, but he stopped when he saw her coming. She slowed and then halted the horse so the wagon was lined up with the back entrance of their house. Abe came hurrying to help her down from the wagon.

He felt her belly and said, "You got bigger in just these few days." Then he saw the horse, Copper. Roland was tying him to the back of the wagon. "What's that?" Abe asked.

Sa-rah spoke gently, "Abe, that's a horse."

"Well, I know it's a horse, but what's it doing here?"

"Shhh...Where's Isaiah?"

"He's taking a little nap. He ran around so hard all morning, he's just tuckered."

"Good. I think you should hide this horse for now. I think it's going to be perfect for him. His name is Copper. Isn't he pretty?"

"Yes, but I didn't think we were ready for this yet."

"He may not be ready to ride by himself, but you can teach him and he'll have a friend. The man we got him from is someone Ollie knows, and promised to take him back if it didn't work out. But he seems so well-behaved. Besides, while we were coming home, I thought about that thing you said about Indigo and how good it was for him to have friends. Isaiah has no one to be with except Happy, and the he's getting too old to want to play."

"We'll have to see. I just wasn't ready for this, although I know he'll be excited."

"Abe, I'll be so busy with the new baby I can't spend as much time with him as I have."

Abe gave her a hug and said quickly, "I better say hello to Roland and get this wagon unloaded. Is he taking it back to Mike today?"

"I think that would be best. Just bring everything in but your things for the animals. I do need to sit down and get my feet up." She got a few small bundles from under the seat of the wagon, and slowly climbed the stairs to the house.

"Roland!" Abe called out.

The young man was standing over by one of the corrals looking at a young bull. He turned and waved, "What're you doing with this one?"

"Not sure yet. Saved him in case he looks good enough to breed, otherwise we'll butcher him soon, before he loses too much of that weight waiting for spring."

"Makes me miss my herd."

Abe leaned against the top rail next to him. "Depends on what happens with you. Stay around here, maybe you could run some of these on Mike's place. Take care of them and I could go shares with you. I do need help these days."

"We've been talking about it, Abby and me, and Mike's getting to where he can't do everything anymore. But we're just not sure. My aunt says she'd like us to stay."

That evening, when everything was unloaded and at least protected from the weather or put away inside, Abe settled back with a newspaper he'd asked Sa-rah to bring home for him. It was from

Boise and several weeks old, but he smiled when he thought that old news was news to him. They'd decided to wait until morning to show Isaiah the horse, and he was happily playing with the ceramic farm animals his mother had brought home for him.

It had been a while since Abe looked at a newspaper. The Boise paper didn't carry many articles about the rest of the U.S., but he liked to keep up with the news from this part of the country. A headline caught his eye talking about an "Indian Outbreak" up near the Salmon River in the Idaho Territory. That was not far from the camp where Moon Fish and Helga had been living. He quickly read through the article and was bothered by references to "drunken savages" and to the death of at least one of the four Indians accused of stealing horses from a white settler. The article went on to say that the horses had been found one week later near where they'd come from, and there was no way to tell if they'd wandered back on their own or been returned by the horse thieves. The story went on to say that this was an unusual incident, but could be a sign of things to come since the president revoked the creation of additional reservation lands, and that at the same time additional white settlement was being allowed on land claimed by the tribe. An Indian leader by the name of Joseph was quoted as saying, he would "do his best to keep his men from doing anything to cause bad trouble, but it would be difficult if any more incidents occurred..."

Abe had heard of this Joseph from Lefty, about how he'd been given some authority by the white government agencies, but that he and his band from the Wallawa area refused to settle on the reservation up near Fort Lapwai, close to the border between the Idaho and Washington Territories. Joseph had told Lefty there were too many whites selling alcohol to the Indians in that area, and he was afraid of what would happen if someone provoked any of them. Most of Joseph's group was angry because they had to leave the land in their own ancestors' country, and now that the settlers could see that it was not good land for farming they wanted to leave and have other land. That night Abe had trouble falling asleep as he worried about his friends, his son, and Helga.

By the end of January, the snow was almost too deep for anyone to ride a horse except in the low-flowing or frozen creek beds. Helga had never been so cold in her life, and the daily struggle to find broken tree branches to drag back to the camp was almost harder than she could bear. Some days she and Indigo would stay in bed under the buffalo hide as long as possible before lighting a fire. Even the Indians were calling this the "Hard Winter" in their language.

Carl kept making sure that she at least had enough wood to get by on, using one of his horses to drag nearly rotten wood back from the riverbanks. One day when it had snowed heavily during the night, he spoke with her and tried to make himself understood in a mixture of both languages. His hands talked as fast as he did, and he made it clear that she needed to move into his tipi so they would only need one fire. He made gestures, pointing to his hands and to her, that seemed to be saying he wouldn't touch her, and he took her inside his lodge and showed her that one half of the space was vacant of any objects or bedding. He pointed to her and to that half of the space and said as best he could that this part was her place now. Helga had learned enough words that she could understand him, but was still not ready to make the move. Although there was no doubt that she was his woman in all ways but in the way of being a wife, she didn't want the other people to think that she had given in and taken the final step. No matter how impossible it seemed because of the weather, she was most concerned that such news not get back to Abe. She was still hoping, no matter how hopeless it seemed now, that he would show up in the spring to tell her everything was worked out, and he could take her home with him.

The next morning Hawk Man came for his son and called Carl out of his lodge.

Helga was working inside of her own lodge, trying hard not to give in to the cold and just crawl back under the hides and blankets with Indigo. In spite of a fire there was no warmth in her tipi. Hawk Man saw her looking out the doorway, waved, and then turned to leave. Carl went back inside his lodge, and then his father turned back and came over to Helga.

"Son, him, good man. Take care," he pointed with his chin at her. "Not bad to you. Go in to that one." He again gestured with his chin, this time at the nearby lodge. "Best for you now. Only way, I say." Then he turned and shuffled away on the hard-packed path.

Carl came out again and this time he was heavily bundled against the cold. He signed to her that he would be gone, riding to a nearby village for a ceremony. "I help my father," he said. "You, here," he said, tapping on the skin of his tipi, "boy, here." He pointed behind her to her smaller lodge and said, "Much cold, not good." Then he said in his own language that he would return in three days, and turned away, crunching through the snow, striding after his father.

The fire was burning inside the larger dwelling. She hurriedly gathered up her necessary things. Indigo protested at being pulled out from under the covers, but she told him to be quiet, they were moving into Carl's.

"With him?"

"No he is going away for a few days, with his father."

"I wish Papa was here to take me somewhere."

"Shush. Now help me move these things."

She was careful with the fire and went out the next day for all the wood she could carry back, but Carl's tipi was warmer than hers had ever been since the hard cold spell began. That night she was even able to do some sewing when the boy went to sleep. She looked up and around at the poles and the skins as she placed her stitches in tight lines across the saddle bag she was making from a soft-tanned elk skin. It required a punch and mallet for the holes, but the greased sinew thread slipped easily through them. Carl's headdress, the one for dances and she didn't know what else, hung from one of the poles. It was made with a ridge of quills standing up along its center and feathers hanging down from the headband that would flutter and wave with his movements. She'd seen him dancing once before during some kind of summer feast. He was quite graceful and seemed to lose himself in the sounds of the drum and singing and his own movements in rhythm with them. Thinking of summer brought back good memories of a time when even a light store-bought dress seemed to be too heavy during the heat of the day.

Her eyelids became heavy, and she had trouble focusing on her work in the erratic light of the fire. She put the project away, rubbed her face, and got up to go out for more wood and one last look at the night sky. She made her way down the short path to where they had a small pit for their basic needs, lifted up her dress and squatted down. The moon was halfway across the sky and it was half full. The only sound in the night air was the frozen snapping of twigs high up in the nearby trees. Suddenly she heard a louder snap and then another. She stood up quickly, and turned back toward the tipi, moving in that direction, not thinking about bringing in wood now.

Suddenly a dark shape appeared in front of her. She was unable to make out anything but shadows in the silhouette caused by the moon behind it. She heard a loud grunt, and then a belching sound as a hand reached out and grabbed for her. She jumped back, but not soon enough to avoid being grabbed by the arm. The voice of a man spoke with a growling sound and muttered something in Indian words. She struggled, but couldn't free herself as she was spun around and the man grabbed her from behind. At that moment she remembered her woman's knife. Mary Wolf had showed her how to fasten it under her skirts and she'd never been without it since. But now it was tied to her leg on the opposite side from her free arm. The man belched again and the sickly smell of alcohol surrounded her head like a fog. She felt his knee driving between her legs and he tried to trip her. She stomped down as hard as she could on his foot, and at the same moment her shrill scream reverberated through the trees in the silence of the night. The man grunted as she spun away and grabbed under her leather skirt for the knife. Thank God it was there! She twisted the blade loose from its sheath and as he pushed her down to the snow-covered ground, she thrust the knife backward as hard as she possibly could. The man screamed and stepped backward, nearly falling.

Just then Helga heard Indigo from a few feet away, "Mama, Mama, what is it? A bear? You hurt, Mama?"

She freed her shawl from the man's grip and ran to the boy, "Come," she said, "Hurry." She pulled him with her. She still had the knife, nothing could have made her drop it. She ran past their lodges and out along the path that led to the next camp.

She slapped on the covering, whispering loudly, not wanting to be heard at any distance. She was friends with the woman of the camp and said her name over and over, and finally louder. There was a sound of movement inside and then the covering flew open. The woman's man stuck his head out and asked what was wrong. She couldn't answer and began to cry. Indigo spoke up, more able to speak the language than his mother, and he told the man his mother was attacked in the dark near their camp. She was quickly pulled inside with Indigo where she could see her woman friend building up the fire.

As soon as there was enough light, she looked down at the knife still clenched in her hand. It was bloody on its blade and the woman held out a rawhide container and motioned for her to drop it in. Helga was fighting back the tears and sobbing that came from deep inside of her terrified self. She turned to Indigo's touch as he stroked her hair and began crying himself.

The woman, whose name in white man talk was New Leaf, heated water in a pot. When it was warm, she placed a clean rag in it and set it in front of Helga, motioning her to wash her stained hands. She remembered the Indian word for "drunk" and said it softly and then again, louder. The man grabbed a fur coat and wrapped it around himself, stuffing an old pistol in the coat's pocket on his way out through the opening.

As her sobbing slowed and stopped, Helga flattened out her skirt and inspected it for damage or blood. It seemed to have come through all right. She could hardly believe that this was important to her right then, but the clothing was a gift from Mary Wolf and this was the first winter she'd had anything that could begin to keep her warm when she was working outdoors. It was made from two pieces of hide with the hair left on one of them, and sewn so that the hair was in between the two layers.

The woman of the lodge was as young as Helga, but had no child as yet. She made signs to ask if her guest wanted her to make a bed for herself and the boy, but Helga was still too upset and shaken to be able to decide anything and just shook her head and held her hands palms up. Indigo was curled up with his head in her lap and was now sleeping. Suddenly she realized she might have killed the man. Her hand went to her mouth and she gagged at the thought of him lying in the snow bleeding from a gash in his belly. No matter how frightened and angry she was at the attacker, she didn't want to have killed him. She signed that she would wait until New Leaf's man returned so she would know what had happened.

She had no idea how much time passed as she dozed on and off near the warmth of the fire. Then she was awakened by the sound of feet stamping and voices outside the tipi. The door flap opened and the man of the lodge came inside, followed by Lefty. Helga gasped and eased Indigo from her lap and stood up. She hadn't known he was even in the camp, having heard that he was gone on a journey past the buffalo country to the east. She stepped toward him and then tripped on something, falling so he had to catch her.

"You are all right?" he asked.

"Yes. I didn't know you were here."

"Could not get over pass, turn back, too much snow." He held her at arm's length and looked her over. "All right. Good. We are very sorry. We not like this to happen in our camp to you or nobody. It is alcohol, making our young men crazy."

"How is he. Is he…?"

"He is alive, but hurt. Old man look at him, say he will get better, but you hurt him deep. He will be taken away. Not one of ours. From Wallawa, same one try make trouble for Abe."

"Why," she said, "why did he do this to me?"

Lefty helped her sit back down beside Indigo and himself sat on a rolled hide. The younger man was sitting by New Leaf, and talking very softly to her.

"You will be safe now." Lefty took out his small pipe and pouch, loaded the tobacco and lit it. He inhaled and then blew the smoke up toward the hole at the top of the tipi. "His friends are with him. Take him to Lapwai, to fort there, see white doctor maybe. He say you are nobody's woman, so he going to have you. But he must have known Carl gone now." He smoked some more, then knocked the ashes out of his pipe and put it away. "You stay here or back to Carl's tipi?"

"I would stay there if it is safe. This is too small for us to be with them."

"You will be safe. Come, I take you and put my war-shield on your door flap. Even a drunk know he will die badly if he pass by my power. Come."

He took her back to Carl's tipi and stoked up the fire for her. Then he told her to stay inside until morning, but not to be afraid of anything, because she was being protected both by his spirits and by the camp soldiers who felt very bad that they let this thing happen to her.

The next morning, three young women who were her acquaintances showed up and brought warm food for her. They waited outside while she woke Indigo and gave him some of the food. Then she went out to join the women who started dancing together and making slashing motions with their arms. They giggled and then made some more gestures with their imaginary knives and ended up trilling out a bird-like call and clapping. They kept saying one word in their language over and over, and pointing at her. Then they presented her with a shawl made of trading post fabric with quilted designs of different colors and fabrics.

Later in the day, Lefty came by to retrieve his shield and to ask how she was doing. She told him she was all right and feeling pretty good. Then she repeated the word the women had chanted and asked him what it meant. He smiled and said, "They say you are now go by name of Brave Knife."

"I don't know if I want that to be my name."

"Don't worry, they cannot give you your real name, but this is how people will call you among themselves." He paused and then said, "Oh, Carl has returned. He is at his father's camp. When he heard what happened to you he jumped up and grab spear. We had to stop him from going to kill that one. He is very angry."

"I don't want anybody to die, but I guess it shows Carl is a good man and cares for me."

"I go now. I will follow those young men. Make sure they stay away."

"Thank you, Mr. Lefty."

Lefty started to leave and turned back to face her. "Carl is good man. Take care of you. Maybe time now you have your own man." Then he turned quickly and trudged down the trail toward his own camp.

When Carl returned an hour or so later, he brought with him a horse blanket for Indigo, one that would strap on and clasp around a horse's belly. Indigo took it and immediately threw it over a snow-covered log and jumped on it, pretending to ride away. Helga laughed and watched him from the doorway of Carl's lodge. He also watched Indigo for a minute and then came toward her with a bundle under his arm. He held it out to her and motioned for her to untie it. She got the tie loosened and then shook out a beautiful mountain sheep hide with long white hair. She held it up in front of herself and pretended it was a dress as she twirled around once with it. Then she remembered he was right there and she was embarrassed and wouldn't look at him as she thanked him for his gift.

Carl tried to talk, but only a few of the words were in English and she could hardly understand very many in his language. But she got the idea that he was very, very sorry for going away and leaving her to be hurt. She tried to show him that she wasn't hurt, but she realized she was feeling badly that he might think something worse had happened to her as she brushed her hands over herself, trying to say she was clean. He only smiled, seeming to understand, and said, "Good, good." And then he said very quietly, "You hurt, I kill."

"No, no. Is all right. I am all right and Indigo good too."

Then Carl stooped down and looked inside past the door-flap. He pulled his head back out and said "Good," and he made a sign with his hands that meant sleeping. He nodded to her and toward the inside of the lodge. Then he surprised her by saying, "For you, here, I there," and he pointed at her smaller lodge.

Even if that might be what she wanted in her heart, her mind told her that it was unfair to him. If he was willing to take her in, she would have to go ahead and stay in his lodge. She was almost shocked that he would kill someone because of her, for her. And now he was offering to leave his own home for her. She would stay with him, but be her own person, and it wouldn't matter what others thought.

"No," she said, and pointed to herself. "Me here." And then pointed to the side of the lodge where her bedding was set up. "You here." And then pointed to his side.

He shook his head as if he was in doubt, but then said, "Good," and walked away, going somewhere. She went into her own tipi and realized just how small it was. Half of Carl's space was as much as hers, or more. She gathered and folded the clothes she and Indigo had hanging on ropes tied between the poles, carrying them out into their new place. Another trip and she had most of the personal and craft things she'd need, and then it was one more trip for her cooking things.

Later that afternoon Carl returned and called her outside. She'd never heard him say her name before and it sounded like "Hoga." He was standing in the fresh falling snow with a large bird that looked like a turkey without its feathers. She reached for it and said she would be happy to cook it. He handed it over to her and then motioned that the boy should come with him.

"Indigo!" He appeared at the opening. "Carl wants you." The man motioned for the boy to follow and they went off together. Helga was glad that Indigo was still bundled up from the last time he'd been outside, because Carl seemed to be in a hurry.

She went inside and began arranging his and her cooking things to suit herself. There was no question in her mind that this new situation would require her to do the cooking for him and themselves, but that was fine with her. She realized she didn't have any idea how or what the man had been eating those night when she didn't bring food over to him. She went out and got the bag of potato-like roots, skinned them, and set them to soaking. She cut the turkey into pieces and began boiling it into a soup. One of the things that she missed with this way of living was a stove and an oven. Everything here had to be either boiled or roasted over the open flames. Maybe she could get herself one of those iron pots with legs that served as an oven when set over the coals. She smiled at the reality of having no money, but then something might change.

After they ate and she sewed for a while, she crawled into her bedding with Indigo. Carl went outside and she soon heard him singing softly beside the tipi. She would be flattered, she thought, if he were singing to her, but she knew that most of the men had songs they sang at the end of their waking days. When he came back inside, he added wood to the fire and got it going again. If this was how he kept his fire, life here going to be much warmer than in her little lodge.

That night she dreamed that a man was in her bed with her, but she wasn't at all afraid because it was Abe and it felt good to have him close to her. Then he turned over and in her dream she realized the man was Carl, but she still wasn't afraid.

As the days grew longer and the sky brighter, Isaiah became more and more impatient to ride "his" horse. He'd polished the leather of the saddle almost to the point of being able to see his reflection in it. Abe had convinced him that if he was a pest about it, it would just be a longer wait, but it was getting so hard for him that he often went out to the pen and hollered at the horse as if it were the animal's fault. Abe and Sa-rah would see and hear that going on and laugh together about it, but Sa-rah also would always ask Abe what he was waiting for.

Abe would rub her belly and ask the same thing, "What are you waiting for?" And they would kiss and he would go to the pen and help the boy catch the horse to brush it and clean its hooves. Finally one day he just swooped the boy off his feet and onto the horse's back. He didn't let go in case Copper got skittish. However, the opposite happened and the little horse seemed to freeze when he felt the boy on his back. Abe was holding tightly to the halter and rope, and when he looked past the head to check on his son, he was surprised by how serious the boy looked. No smile, no sign of happiness, just an almost stern look of pure determination. Then they both heard Sa-rah call out from the house some distance away. The horse's ears pricked forward, but still he didn't move. Then Abe gently eased some tension into the lead rope and nodded to Isaiah.

The horse resisted and then took one step and then another. After a couple of these single steps, Abe had him moving very slowly, but with no stopping. Now Isaiah let a smile come across his face. Just as quickly, it was gone as he knotted the horse's long mane around one of his fists and began to slowly move his small body in rhythm with the walking motion.

After several circuits of the pen, Abe handed the lead rope to Isaiah, but kept hold on the horse's mane. This went on for several more circles and then Abe let go and just stood still. The horse also stopped, so Abe stepped in from of him and started walking. Copper followed. Twice more around the pen and Abe stopped again and took the rope from the boy.

"Good. You did really good. Do you like it?"

"Yes, Papa. I like it." And then he suddenly lifted one of his legs over the neck of the horse and slid to the ground. He caught his balance and reached for the rope. "Can I let him out now? He might be very hungry after all that hard work."

Abe smiled and nodded yes. He was relieved and glad the horse behaved so well and the boy also. He closed his mind's eye and tried to picture what it would be like to ride out after the cattle with the boy when he was more grown up. The only thing missing in that picture was his other son.

When May came and the wildflowers burst into colors across the valley floor, Sa-rah also felt like she couldn't get any bigger and was ready to burst. This time she planned to try and make it to town to stay with Mattie until she could have the baby with the doctor and nurse Carla in attendance. Abe was disappointed in this plan. He was afraid he would spend too much time in town waiting around and getting behind on his spring work. He wanted to cut and brand the calves, and move the herd further out the valley, where he might need to run off predators.

Then one night when they were going through the preparations for the trip to town, Sa-rah's water broke and she fell against the bed. Abe quickly got a piece of canvas from the porch, laid it on the bed with a flannel cover, and helped her to lie down.

"How much time do we have, do you think?" he asked her.

She looked up at him with tears in her eyes, and said, "If I were someone I was helping do this, I might be able to tell you, but for myself, I have no idea."

"What should I do?"

"Go for Abby and Martha as fast as you can, and don't wait for them, just turn around and come right back." She clutched at her belly. "That was a real pain. You must hurry, please."

Abe saddled Bird as fast as he ever had and leaped on her back, thankful the waning moon was rising, giving enough light for the horse to see where she was going. They galloped on the new road, and this was another thing he could give thanks for. Still, it seemed like the familiar ride was taking hours, even though he knew he'd never done it so fast. He started yelling when he got within sight of the lights of the house. As he pulled the horse to a stop at the front steps, Mike appeared in his long underwear with a shotgun.

"Hell, Abe, thought it might be savages, way you was yelling."

"No time to talk. Get the women and have them come to us as fast as possible. Sa-rah's water broke out and she's having pains. Got to get back to her." He wheeled the horse around and took off again.

When he got back, Sa-rah was thrashing her legs every few minutes and then dropping off as if unconscious. Abe stoked up the fire and heated water. He felt under her and found that the covering over the canvas was soaked. He got another blanket and waited until her legs were raised again and slipped it under. She moaned, then screamed, and called his name several times, her eyes staring at the ceiling.

"I'm back, I'm here. They're on their way. What can I do?"

She pushed herself down the bed a ways and patted the pillow behind her head. "Sit here, behind me and hold on my arms when I, when I..." she screamed again as he kicked off his boots and crawled onto the bed, arranging himself between her and the headboard. She kicked again and he caught her arms to keep her from rolling off the bed. "Somebody hold my legs," she cried.

"There's no one else here," he said, taking a cloth from the table beside the bed and wiping the sweat from her forehead. "What do I do?"

He worked himself back off the bed and went to kneel by her feet. She was quiet, motionless, then a tremor passed through her body, and she moaned long, and louder and louder.

"Where is she? Where? Where is she?" her voice was raspy and he reached up to raise her head and offer her a drink of water. She swallowed a couple of times and then spit the water off to the side of the bed.

"They're coming. They'll be here. Martha and Abby will be here very soon."

"Helga, I want Helga, she knows what to do...Aieeee, uhh, uhh..." She kicked again and he had to struggle to catch and hold her legs.

"She's not here," he said.

Her back arched and then she collapsed back onto the bed, then arched, collapsed, and with one long scream, her legs pulled away from him so her knees went up by her face. She was sobbing and groaning and he barely heard the sound of the wagon pulling up outside.

"I see the top of the head," he said, unable to contain his excitement.

"Then do some...thing...when I push..."

Again her knees went to her face and she screamed and pushed and pushed harder and more of the head showed and the others came into the house, stomping their feet from the snow.

"In here," he called as Sarah fell back and then bent forward trying to reach both of her hands between her legs. There was no way for her to help herself with the bulky belly in the way, even though it was now lower down than it had been.

Martha came to Abe's side, and quickly washed her hands in the pail of warm water. "I've never had a baby," she said. "But it has to come out."

"I've pulled calves, but never a baby," he said.

Abby came to the other side of the bed just as Sa-rah gave out with a piercing scream. Abe fought to hold her legs, afraid that she might squeeze the baby's head if it came out now. "Easy, easy, easy," he kept saying.

"God, God, God, God, God help me!"

Slowly the head emerged as Martha eased the constricting tissues past the ears and then held the baby's head in her hands. Sa-rah was weeping. Abby was helping Abe wipe away the messy puddle of blood and mucous that was forming between the mother's legs.

Martha reached and pulled Abe's hand under the baby's head. She said loudly to Sa-rah, "Next time push as hard as you can." Sa-rah did and suddenly the baby slid out and flopped out into their hands as Sa-rah doubled over and reached for it. They let her take the baby, and she immediately cuddled it to her breast.

"Girl!" Abe said as Sa-rah struggled to hold the baby upside down by her feet. Abby and Martha moved to her sides and helped her. The baby coughed, once, twice, and gave a soft cry that grew louder. Her mother quickly brought her back against herself and asked for a soft blanket which she wrapped over both of them.

"I can't believe she can even move like this," Abby said. "I don't think I was even awake after my baby finally came."

Just then, Isaiah appeared at the doorway, rubbing his eyes, and asked what was wrong. "Why is everybody here?"

Abe went to him and picked him up in his arms. He realized they'd forgotten all about the boy and wondered how he'd slept through all of his mother's screaming and the arrival of the visitors. Then he also heard men's voices on the porch.

"You have a baby sister," he said. "Just born." He carried the boy to his mother's side and leaned over.

Sa-rah pulled the blanket away from the tiny face and smiled up at the two of them. "Our new baby girl," she said.

Isaiah turned away while still in Abe's arms. He was frightened by the streaks of blood on the wrinkled face of the baby girl.

A while later, when the afterbirth was out and they'd cleaned up the mess, and washed and dried Sa-rah and the baby, Martha and Abby went outside to tell their husbands that everything was all right. Abe and Isaiah sat at the side of the bed as Sa-rah gave the baby a chance to nurse.

Nothing happened right away, but she nuzzled and moved her lips.

"She's just fine," Sa-rah said.

Abe smiled and asked, "So what's her name?"

"I thought we said if it was a girl, we could name her after my mother, Dora. Did you forget? Or did you have another name for her?"

"I only had a name for a boy. I would have wanted to name him after my General, Lee."

"Oh Abe, that's perfect, DoraLee."

"You think so?"

"Yes, oh yes. Isn't that right, little DoraLee?" she said kissing the baby's forehead. "Oh, I'm suddenly sooo tired. Did I do all right?"

"You did great, really great. Thank you so much."

Part V

FLIGHT

1877

CHAPTER 17

Disruption

The winter had been what the old people were calling "the hard one," but thanks to Carl's generosity and patience with her, she and Indigo made it through in good health. One night Indigo stayed across the camp with his friend, and Helga cooked a fish stew with two fresh trout Carl had caught on his way back down the river from a visit to Fort Lapwai. Hawk Man and Carl had gone along with other leaders, including Joseph, White Bird, and an Umatilla visiting chief named Grass on Fire. They'd been summoned at the request of the soldier chief. His reasons were not clear to them before they went, and after they returned Carl wouldn't say much to her about it. All she knew was that there had been more trouble with some of the young warriors and alcohol, and that the army was stating that the chiefs must restrain their young men or they would be taken to prison. Further, if any white settlers died, the killers would be taken to prison and hanged. The whole situation took her back to her terrifying experience with the drunken young man who attacked her and was now reported to have recovered from the knife wound she'd given him.

The fish soup was excellent, and when she'd finished cleaning up from their meal, the young man motioned for her to come and sit by him on his side of the fire. When she settled next to him, he drew a small box out of his shirt pocket and handed it to her. When she opened it, she saw a simple beautiful ring.

"Is you." The man said. "White man say, 'ring' for you."

"Carl, I don't know…I don't know what to say," she said in Indian.

"For you. I give it you."

"Yes, I know, but this means…What does this mean?" she said mostly to herself.

She let her thoughts tumble without control as the years past flashed by in her memory. With no sight of or word from Abe, the hardship of living here alone and then being taken in by this gentle warrior, the way he took care of Indigo, teaching him and making him the tools he needed to become a strong youngster in this place… She looked up from the ring and into this friend's eyes, and what she saw there gave her happiness, gave her feelings of being taken care of when she had no one else in this world. She slipped the ring from the box and onto her finger. Its band was gold and reflected the light of the fire, its dark blue stone seeming to absorb light and hide it away. She held her hand out to Carl and he took it in his. Then she leaned toward him and kissed his fingertips.

He pulled away and got up to go outside for a few minutes, returning with more brush wood, needed more for light than for heat in this warming time of the year. Then she went out herself and stopped at the edge of the wooded area to look up into the millions of stars that crowded the heavens, and she gave thanks and whispered a prayer for help to do what was right.

When she went back inside their lodge, he was already lying under the single elk hide he used for his bed. He motioned for her to come sit beside him and then when she sat down, he slowly leaned her back and held her in his arms. He was so gentle, and his fingertips as they explored her shoulders, neck, and breasts, were like tiny creatures moving across her body. Neither one of them removed their clothes, but she, too, began to stroke his arms with her own hands. She turned to him and they kissed. He pulled away with a soft laugh.

"I like," he said. They kissed again.

She waited, apprehensive of what would come next, but after a while he turned aside, and still moving his hand gently back and forth along her leg, he seemed to fall asleep. Helga lay there quietly for some time, waiting for sleep, thinking of her life, her past, and now this future. If there was a God who really cared about her, she thought, He would have given her a simpler life and not this one of hardship and all the complications with the different men she'd been around. That Bishop and his boys, the fear and the pain of their roughness, never having known her own father, and then there was Abe, the one she'd learned to love and to be loving with, then to have it end because he wouldn't stand up to his wife. Now this, a man she could hardly talk with, a man who had done everything she needed from him and never required anything from her that she hadn't wanted to give, right up to this moment. She glanced over at his face, his striking Indian profile flickering in the dying light of the fire, and she wondered what it would take for her to feel love for this man, or whether she did already. Whatever it was, it wasn't a flood of feelings, more like a soft rain of goodness, falling gently into her mind and maybe even into her heart…If only she didn't miss Abe so much she knew she should be happy with this one.

In the morning there was a clamor toward the center of the camp. Carl pushed up out of the bed, grabbed his rifle, and slipped on his moccasins to run out through the small doorway. Helga followed, joining the women from the nearest tipis. They were talking rapidly, so she couldn't understand anything they said except to know that they were alarmed by what was going on. Just then four young men on horseback road through that part of the camp. They were followed by another man, much older, but someone Helga thought she'd seen before.

Before long Carl and their neighboring men returned. He gestured to her to begin taking down their lodge and packing things into the leather boxes they used for moving. He was able to tell her not to take her smaller structure down, but to gather her things and be ready to leave soon. He signed that he would be gathering his horses and soon be back to load, and to help her with the work. As he ran down the trail toward the horses, she went inside and quickly began folding up the hides and blankets, and also gathering her cooking things into a pile. Then she began removing the pegs that held the hide-cover door above the entry. Just then Indigo appeared and she was able to lift him up to remove the highest ones that she couldn't reach.

"Mama, what's happening? What?"

"I don't know. We have to move away from here, quickly. I don't know why. Help me pull up all the stakes in the ground." They both started around the bottom in different directions. She grabbed a canvas bag for the sharpened sticks and had Indigo place his inside with hers. One of the nearby women came over and helped her remove the cover and then roll it into a bundle that she tied up with a horsehair rope. The sounds of the camp-village coming apart, coming down, grew louder as the men returned bringing horses.

Carl caught three of his best animals and led them to his lodge. Then he started pulling down the poles and lining them out so they could be fastened to the rigging he attached to the horses. He fastened short cross-pieces between them and then he and Helga began lashing the hides and hide-boxes onto the poles.

Helga stopped him and asked "What happened?"

"Army," he said and hurried on with his efforts to get their things ready to move.

She stuffed clothing into a bag and loaded it next to Carl's bag. He had fastened his spear and bow to a pole alongside the back of a horse and filled his pockets with ammunition for his rifle. He looked around, motioning they would leave anything else behind, and ran to bring in two more horses. He ran over to help another group with their poles, and then came back, lifted Indigo onto one of the pulling horses, and helped Helga onto another animal. He took the lead rope of the horse Indigo rode, and they started off toward the road.

A crowd of shouting people and neighing horses milled at the junction between that pathway and the road there. Carl saw Hawk Man, and ran through the people toward his father.

"Mama, Mama, will we be all right?" Indigo asked.

"Yes, son. Just be ready to ride and stay on good."

"But my traps. I didn't get my traps by the river. Maybe they have animals in them."

"That's all right. We can get more traps."

"But who will kill the animals in the traps?"

"I'm sorry Indigo, but we can't worry about that now."

When the people began to move out, order was quickly restored to the chaotic scene. Although it was a long time since this band had made a real move, the order of families and the work of managing livestock was familiar and quickly organized. A space was made for Carl and his small group just behind the large number of horses and people that made up his father's contingent. Behind them came Lefty and his wives, children, and mother. They moved slowly along the wide trail and she kept looking over her shoulder to make sure that Indigo was there right behind her. Each time she caught his eyes he gave a quick smile, and then went back to looking as serious and grown-up as he could.

The last thing she'd done before they left their own campsite was to put dried meat and berry patties into a small pack that now rode on her back. It also contained spare moccasins and over-shirts for all three of them. Although the sun was shining and it was getting warm, she knew that dusk would bring a chill no matter where they ended the day. As they came to more straight lengths of road she tried to raise herself up to see how long of a procession they all made, looking forward and then back. There was no way to count, but it was a larger number of horses pulling poles and loads than she had thought would be needed for all of the camps in their small village. This made her think that they'd fallen in behind and merged with other groups at some point along the way.

Finally, when the sun was overhead and they'd entered a canyon with steeps sides, a halt was called and people quickly dismounted. Carl unharnessed their horses from the pole-sleds and led them down to the edge of the small river. All up and down the caravan, children shouted and ran in circles while their mothers and big sisters set out food. Now Helga could see that there were at least fifty horses being allowed to drink along the stream and eat the lush grass along the banks. She glanced up at the walls of the canyon and was struck by the beauty of the shadow-patterns and sunlit rock formations, ranging in color from deep gray to shining reds and yellows. Indigo found two friends and they were excitedly chattering about what they were going to do when they got to their new camp. Carl slipped hobbles onto the front legs of his own horse and tied the lead ropes of two others to that one and then came back for the two Helga and Indigo had been riding, taking them for water and then linking them together with one rope between them so they could graze.

Helga called softly to him and motioned to the food she'd set out. As he came and sat on the ground beside her where she knelt, she realized that this was the first time all day she'd been able to just look at him when he wasn't in motion and busy. He truly was a handsome man, she thought, and she found herself hoping he thought her pretty. After a few moments, she said she would like to go back and see Moon Fish or Lefty, just for a short time. Carl wiped his mouth and nodded it would be all right.

Lefty and Moon Fish were sitting together off the trail, leaning against two trees, both smoking their pipes. Helga announced herself and they beckoned for her to join them.

"How is it with you?" the older woman asked.

"It's all right. I think we've got everything we really need. Had to leave things behind."

The woman smiled and said, "Not much time to get ready."

Lefty tapped the ashes out of his pipe and stood up to move away. "You are doing good," he said and walked away to find something or someone.

Helga looked at Moon Fish with a question ready, but the woman started talking before she could ask it. "This will be hard. We don't know where we go, but it may be that we are in a war with the soldiers."

"Why, what happened?"

"I don't know much," she replied, "but some of the young men got crazy with drink and killed some whites, ones who made them angry. Our chiefs could not make talk with the Army and now we must leave."

"Are you all right?" Helga asked because she could see that the woman already looked tired.

"It would be better if I was a younger woman, but it is too late for that now." She gave Helga a quick smile and then said seriously, "This could be bad for our people. No matter what happens you must try and stay away from any white man seeing you. Do you have some of your white woman's clothing?"

"Only one good skirt, a shirtwaist, and a shawl. I couldn't bear to leave them behind."

"That's good. Take them and be ready if you need to run away from us. You will be safer as a lost white woman than with us if it gets bad."

"Thank you for telling me that, but I would be so afraid by myself with my boy out there," she motioned with her head toward the land surrounding them and the tall cliffs.

"You will know if that time comes. Just be ready."

Indigo ran up to her and said quickly, "Carl says come now."

"All right, son, but mind your manners and say hello to Moon Fish here."

"Hello, Grandma," he said, addressing her in the Indian way of all children when speaking to an elder. "Come now, Mama."

"Help me up, dear," the woman said, and Helga helped her to her feet. "I'll see you again, later," she said hobbling off toward her family.

That evening the large group, now numbering some seventy warriors and their families, made a temporary camp at the top of the ridge sloping down into that part of the canyon that led to a confluence with the big river. Known as Non-Treaty Indians by the army and the white people, this group led by Joseph and his brother Ollokut, had been close to giving in and moving onto the reservation at the time the outbreak had begun, just two days before. Now they were in flight because of rash and revenge-motivated actions of a small group, and they were being joined by others who also sympathized with resistance to being crowded into one small part of their ancestral homelands. As the cook-fires were lit and the children fed, the talk was all about how large a force of soldiers was in pursuit, and could they escape across the big river before they were overtaken. Scouts were coming and going, and by the time full darkness came at this time of the longest days of the year, word was that the soldiers were now close behind them.

Helga arranged a bed for them in a sheltered area among some cottonwood trees, along with several other families. Carl picketed their horses and then sat by the fire checking and cleaning his rifle. Indigo fell asleep with his head in his mother's lap. He was exhausted from all of the excitement of the past two days, and she carefully slipped out from under him, half-carrying and half-dragging him to the bed. He had gotten so much bigger, just in the last few months. She then went back to ask Carl what, if anything, he could say that she could understand about what was going to happen next.

"We fight," he said.

Mary Wolf appeared in the shadows at the edge of the fire. "Helga," she said, "It's good to find you." She squatted down and began speaking both with her hands and her voice. "First early light. There may be fight. Maybe we cross river. Must be ready. If fight, send boy to me," she pointed with her chin to the opening where a larger fire could be seen through the woods. "Carl will ride horse to fight. You must follow with his other horse. When he need second horse, you give, come back for another horse. Is way women help the fighting. You understand?"

Helga nodded her head, and asked, "Do you really think there will be a fight?"

"If not here, somewhere. Not tomorrow, next day or next day." She stood up and turned speaking rapidly to Carl. "I tell him what I told you."

"Wait." Helga took a couple of steps toward her and then reached out to give her a hug. "Thank you for taking care of me, for everything."

"We are sisters," Mary Wolf said and then hurried away.

Helga quickly got herself ready for bed, packing anything that was loose and making sure that she could leave this place suddenly when and if they had to. Then she crawled in next to Indigo, leaving the space next to her for Carl. Sometime later, he lay down next to her and she pressed against him, needing his strength as her fear couldn't be avoided any longer. He wrapped his arms around her and held her tightly as she fought against the tears and the fright. He hummed softly and then she listened as he spoke a prayer in his own language. The sounds of the camp had diminished and now the silence of the star-filled night covered everything.

Before light, she felt Carl untangle himself from her and rise up, quickly pulling on his special shirt and taking up his gun. Then he knelt down and, for the first time, he kissed her. And then he was gone and the camp came alive with the sounds of low voices and horses neighing. Long wavering coyote calls came from behind them on the way they'd come down to this site. She woke Indigo and shook him to get his attention.

"Go to Mary Wolf. That way." Even as recently as a year ago, she wouldn't have thought he could take care of himself even that much, but now she watched with a mixture of worry and pride as he picked his way through the woods, no questions asked.

The dim gray of dawn filtered down from the layer of light that was now arching over the camp. Women leading horses were moving back up the wide trail that brought them to this place. Suddenly the whooping of many male voices and the thunder of hooves sounded out that way. Shots rang out and the fight had begun. Helga tried to calm the horse she was leading and saw a woman she'd often gathered food with a few steps away from her. She called the woman's name and the response was a smile and then a motion to follow her, following others who had taken a side trail. More shots rang out, and Helga realized that only the women stood between the fighting men and the children and old people in the camp. She wanted to pray, but her thoughts stumbled over the question of which god to pray to. The white men, she knew, were fighting and claiming the protection of their God, and the Indians were likely to be equally assured that they, too were doing the will of the Spirit. In spite of the sounds of battle and horses, she couldn't stop her thoughts about her own role as a kind of orphan all her life. This seemed ever more true now that she was this nearly helpless woman on both sides or neither side in this battle. She looked around at the other women holding onto their men's horses and felt somehow reassured that these were her people now, Carl's people, but terribly anxious that being with them could get her killed. She sucked in her breath and then joined as best she could into the trilling of women's voices as they gave forth with their support for their men.

She hadn't noticed before, but there was a small bag tied to the horse's mane. She touched it and could feel the rifle shells inside. Just then one of the warriors appeared nearby and slid from his horse, running to another one, climbing on and disappearing back up the slope toward where sound of the fighting. Just then she saw Carl and Lefty riding toward her. She hadn't noticed that Patsy was also in her group of women, and she was now pulling the horse she held toward the two men. She carried a skin pouch of water and offered it to them. Helga joined her and took the lead rope from Carl's heavy-breathing animal.

Lefty said loudly enough for her to her. "They are running away. We go after them."

Carl gave her a look that said thank you, touched her hand that held the rope on the fresh horse, leaped on its back and trotted after Lefty.

Helga and the other women led the battle-tired horses back toward the temporary camp, stopping to let them drink from a small creek that crossed their path. She so wished that the horse could tell her what all had happened out there, but since it couldn't, she stroked his mane as they walked along and wondered about what would come next. The painted hand-print on the animal's neck was smeared some from the animal's foamy sweat so she knew that the battle had been strenuous, and from Carl's smile as he rode away, that it must have so far been successful. She could only hope that they would continue to be protected and safe.

When they reached the camping area, some of the older men were giving instructions in loud voices and moving about through the temporary piles of goods and poles. Helga looked for Mary Wolf and saw her some distance away. She also saw that Indigo was near the woman and hurried to them. The boy saw her coming and ran to her.

"Mama, they say is a big fight with Army. I wish I could be there."

"Well, I'm glad you're not. It's dangerous." She waved to Mary Wolf and called out, "What are they saying?"

"To get pack. We must cross big river." She turned away to get back to her work.

"Come, Indigo. I need you to help."

When everyone and everything was ready for the move, they waited anxiously for the men to return and lash up the horses to the pole-sleds, and a sudden and nearly complete silence settled over the large group of women, children and elders. In the silence they could hear the continual sound of shots echoing off the canyon walls.

"Mama," Indigo spoke softly, "why are they fighting?"

"I don't know. I mean I don't know for sure. There have been some small fights, and now the white people's government wants the Indians to give up all their land and live in one place."

"Who is government?"

Just then a warrior galloped into the camping area, whooping loudly and making his horse rear and prance around. He shouted to the old ones who were gathered near the center of the crowded area. Then he slid off his horse and led it to one of the piles of belongings. The woman beside them took his hands in her own, bowed to him, and hurried away, returning moments later with a horse that the man hitched to their poles. Now more warriors rode into the camp, shouting and making raucous wild animal calls. Helga kept looking for Carl, but couldn't see him.

Lefty rode up to her and leaned down to say. "Some are chasing soldiers away. He is with them. I send my nephew to help you."

Within a few minutes, most of the pole-sleds were lashed to horses and Helga had returned with one of theirs. Lefty's young man helped her connect the leather ropes and rigging, and led the animal into the line forming at the edge of the area. Within minutes the cavalcade was moving out, in something akin to a celebration or parade. Helga helped Indigo onto another horse and mounted one herself.

They hadn't gone very far when they heard the sound of the river. As they neared it, the leaders turned and led everyone away from the afternoon sun and through openings in the mixed woodland and grassy areas. From horseback, Helga tried to count the people who were walking, running or riding along. It was impossible to even guess at the number, but someone had told her that there were about 70 fighting warriors, so she counted the ones who looked like they'd been in the battle. She was able to see at least 40 on horseback, now leading or moving with horses pulling the belongings. Then the trees ended as if they'd all been cut down or taken away, and the view of the river opened up. A long broad stretch of water curved away from them and seemed calm and even quiet in this place. From downriver, however, came the roar of what sounded like a large, long set of rapids.

Shouts came from the some of the men who were called the Dog-men in their own language. They were a kind of police force and kept order among the people in any disrupting situation. All around her people began unloading their bundles from the pole-sleds and re-tying or tightening the ropes around them. Men began tying the bundles onto the horses. The youth who'd been helping Helga called out to someone and another man came running. The two of them grabbed the bundles from her pile, fastened them together and situated them over a horse's back. She ran to get Indigo's horse and then her own. Although six of her bundles were loaded onto three horses, there were still two left on the ground. The horse that she'd been riding stood as calmly as could be expected amidst the chaos, and the young man helped her climb on and then boosted Indigo up behind her. Then he tied the last two bundles on the horse Indigo had been riding. Ahead of her she could see horses gathering in a mob at the edge of the river as the Dog-men lashed at them with short whips.

Riding-horses and pack animals collided and scrambled for footing as the river became crowded. There was no time for her to think about what she was doing, of what was happening to her. Just follow, she thought, and don't fall off and get trampled.

"Hold on to me," she yelled over her shoulder at Indigo and felt his arms tighten around her waist.

All around her, horses with bundled packs or riders were plunging into the cold waters of the river. Dog-men whipped or pushed any horse that hesitated. Never had she ridden across anything like this river. She could only hope that it didn't get any deeper than the water that was now up around her hips. Her horse seemed to know what it was doing and she didn't try to direct him in any way. Midway across, she saw the horses in front drop suddenly and nearly disappear as they struggled and began swimming and tossing their heads. The strangest thing amid all the thrashing of the animals and the splashing of the water was the silence of the people. Very few times did she hear a voice cry out or yell at a horse or another rider. The thought raced through her mind that as strange as all this was to her, most likely everyone else had done this many times before.

Through the melee in front of her she caught sight of Lefty, with Moon Fish hanging on behind him. Then Hawk Man appeared alongside her with two boys hanging onto him, one in front and one behind. Indigo yelled at them and they yelled back. The swimming part lasted only a short ways. When the horses found footing once again, they floundered briefly and some bucked to get even better balance on the rocks beneath. She saw a young woman with a baby strapped onto her suddenly slide off of her rearing horse and slip into the water. Helga tried to get in the way to block the floating woman, but her horse shied away and fought onward. Two Dog-men whipped their horses into place on either side of the woman and dragged her back up. Helga could only hope that the baby was all right, please, dear God or Spirit or Whoever.

They finally reached the opposite bank, but rather than dismounting and resting they were rushed forward into the wooded area along the river. She followed the others as they dodged trees and hurried up the sloped land, away from the sound of the water. She had no idea how far they'd come in the mad rush from the riverbank. When at last they stopped she saw almost everyone slide or fall from their horses. They had reached a long inclined space of grass and shrubs, and the sun's comforting warmth sliced through the fast-moving clouds above to welcome them to this place. She saw the pack animals being gathered into one large group and allowed to graze. She still held onto the rope that was looped around her horse's nose and neck. She sank to the ground, shaking from shock and shivering from the cold wetness of her clothing. She put her arm around Indigo and pulled him close.

DoraLee's arrival had changed all of them. Sa-rah seemed happier than she'd been for a long time and often mentioned that they lived in the only place on earth that was good enough for their family. Though she worried about the quantity and quality of her milk, the baby girl grew quickly enough, and although a bit frail compared to the two boys they'd had in the family, the infant seemed healthy, with good color in her cheeks. Before her first month had gone by, she would stare directly into someone's eyes with an unwavering intensity that seemed to be trying to communicate something beyond language.

Abe found himself delaying leaving the house for his outdoor work, especially if it took him away from their main compound. He told Sa-rah that it wasn't laziness, but that he could hardly make himself go look after calves and momma cows if it meant she and the baby had to be left behind for the day. In the evening he would often sit for a long time with the child cradled in his lap, whether she was sleeping or just being peaceful. Of course he would have to give her up and hand her over to her mother when she got fussy from hunger. But he did learn to change her messed under-clothing, something he'd never done with Isaiah, and, without being asked, he sometimes stayed around the house to help wring out and hang up clean laundry on sunny days.

The biggest change seemed to have come over Isaiah. In spite of his mother's concern that he might not be gentle enough with his little sister, he was always very careful and quiet around her, and he could sit for long periods of time just watching her or singing softly. He asked his parents countless questions about her: "Why can't she talk to us?", "Was I that little?", "When can she play with me?" Many of the questions didn't have an answer or couldn't be answered in a way that satisfied his curiosity. When she was napping he would go outside and gather small flowers, or little stones, or bring her long strands of hair from Copper's mane. Sa-rah collected these things from him, and said that they would be saved until she was old enough to appreciate them.

"What's preshiate Mama?"

When the baby was a little over a month old she developed a hacking cough. Sa-rah decided that she needed to be taken to town to see the doctor; it would be good to get a check-up anyway, since they'd had no real medical attention at the birth or since.

Abe had been very pleased to have Roland as an occasional helper and was showing him pretty much everything there was to know about the operation. When Abe asked the young man if he could watch the place for a few days while the family went off to Silver City, Roland was completely willing and said he was confident there wasn't much he couldn't handle until they returned. As a part of the same conversation, he did bring up his need to return back north and see what was happening to the place they'd owned, whether there was anything worth returning to or of enough value to sell off.

They loaded up and left in the buggy with Ginger pulling. Even though she was getting much older now, she was still the steadiest of their horses and Sa-rah made that a priority with the baby coming along. Abe had set up a soft cradle, lashed behind the main seat. Isaiah was excited about the trip and kept asking Abe if he could drive the horse.

They left soon after daybreak, and stopped for a bite to eat at the Skinner place. Martha insisted on it and said she'd lie down in the road to stop them if they didn't come inside for the sweet rolls she'd just taken out of the oven. She also had some of Mattie's things that the woman had requested. They were on the move again after a short stay, and Sa-rah settled herself and DoraLee into the small area set up for them. The baby continued to have fits of coughing, but they weren't lasting as long or coming as often.

As the horse trotted down the improved roadway, Abe allowed Isaiah to sit between his legs and handle the reins. The sun rose behind the distant range of mountains, and then seemed to jump into the sky all at once, bringing warmth as well as light. It was certain to become a hot day, but one that would be long enough to allow them to make it to Silver City by dark or soon thereafter.

The trip proved mostly uneventful, especially as the baby slept most of the way. Sa-rah commented that she would then probably be awake a lot of the night, but it was better this way. When they stopped for a mid-day meal, they found a shady spot near a small creek, and Isaiah had his clothes off and was splashing about in the water before anyone could stop him. Once he came out of the water and dressed again, he devoured the bread and meat Sa-rah fixed for him. DoraLee was awake, but didn't seem hungry and Sa-rah complained to Abe that her breasts were beginning to hurt. He smiled and offered to take care of that problem for her, but she scowled and said it wasn't funny. Abe apologized and thought about how during the past few days, since the baby got a little sick, Sa-rah's mood had changed and she seemed more easily upset. He hoped they'd get reassurance from the doctor so she could get back to her easygoing happiness of the previous few weeks.

At one point during the afternoon, they rounded a bend in the main road and met a herd of cattle coming toward them. Abe steered Ginger off to the side of the road as far as he could and then waved to the cowboys to show he couldn't get any further off the road. They'd have to go past him like that. As the dust from the animals came closer, he turned to urge Sa-rah to be sure to cover DoraLee, but she was already taking care of it. The sounds of the cattle and their closeness as they moved on by was somewhat alarming, especially when one of the cows stumbled against the wheel of their buggy. Abe extended his whip and flicked against the necks and flanks of any other cows that came close. Isaiah jumped up and down on the seat until Abe reprimanded him. He stopped jumping, but kept on yelling and laughing at the cows.

As soon as the cattle mob had passed, Abe hurried Ginger forward to get down the road and past the cloud of dust that was still hanging over it. The baby did have a coughing spell, but it didn't seem to have been unusually affected by the situation and they were soon out from under the dust. The cows all had the same brand, but it was one that Abe didn't recognize and he made a mental note to ask about it. He didn't expect any neighbors, but didn't know where they might be driving to if it wasn't in the direction of their place.

It was dark by the time they pulled up in front of Mattie and Ollie's house. Isaiah was sleeping and had to be disturbed so Abe could get himself down. He walked up to the door and knocked. Ollie opened it and stepped out onto the porch, giving Abe a big hug, and laughing softly.

"Great to see you, young man. Glad you made it."

"Same for me. Sorry to arrive so late, but the day was long enough to make it the whole way and that seemed best. The baby's got a cough and we came to get her looked at."

"Don't worry about that. Mattie's asleep already, but I better wake her up. She'll have my skin in the morning if I don't. We didn't know when you'd come around, but she's been waiting for you-all any and every day." He lowered his voice, "She hasn't been doing so good."

Abe wanted to know more, but Sa-rah was holding out the baby bundle to him. He took the little one and Ollie held out his arm for her to use climbing down. They hugged and Ollie said, "We've got the room for you-all."

He led Sa-rah into the house and Abe followed, carrying a drowsy Isaiah and dropping him onto a pallet on the floor of the guest room. He went back out for the things they would need for the night.

"Where do I put the horse?" he asked.

"I keep forgetting you haven't been here before."

"Yeah, Sa-rah has, but not me."

"Well, there's a small stable out back, you just lead her around that side of the house and park the buggy right back there as well.

Damn, I'm sure glad to see you, son." He handed Abe a lantern, and Abe lit it when they went out to the porch. He found his way out back, stabled Ginger, then gathered up the last of their bags. It crossed his mind that he'd brought along the least amount of baggage and was the biggest person in the family. The smallest of the four of them, DoraLee, brought the most.

The baby surprised them by sleeping soundly during the night, with only a couple of coughing fits that woke Abe and Sa-rah, but didn't seem to affect Isaiah in the least. When morning came, Abe got himself up and out early enough to get water for the horse, something that had worried him during the night. Ginger was thirsty but not unusually so. When he checked her feet and legs, she was no worse for the wear of the trip, and she was excited with her portion of the grain he'd brought along. Have to get more of that this time, he remembered.

When he slipped quietly back into the house, he found Mattie sitting near the stove. She shook herself to alertness when he walked in and gave him a big smile, holding out her arms to him. He gave her a gentle hug and then squatted down beside her.

"Pull over a chair for yourself," she said softly, and when he'd settled himself, she went on, "I just cannot hardly wait to see this little one. I'm so happy you came to see me."

"It just worked out, Mattie. We'd have come sooner, but it's only been a month and I wanted to be sure both of them were strong enough."

"Well, that's right. And are they?"

"As it is, part of the reason we came in is to have a check-up and find out if this cough the baby has is anything to worry about."

"Most likely not. Oh here they are."

Sa-rah had just appeared at the doorway with the baby in a blanket, one that Mattie had sewn for her.

"Good Morning, Mattie."

"Oh my sweet, sweet girl. And what's that in your arms?"

"It's our little DoraLee," she said as she pulled back the covering hiding the baby's face. "But she does have a cough and I wouldn't want you to catch it."

"Don't you worry about that, dear girl. It'll take more than a baby's cough to get to me."

Abe stood and helped Sa-rah to sit as she bent forward to hold the little one out to Mattie.

"Oh my, my. How pretty, and how pinkish." She looked up and said, "I'm always surprised by how pink little white babies are when they're this small. DoraLee, isn't it? DoraLee. Well, that's so fine." She settled the small bundle in her lap and began slowly rocking.

Just then Ollie came into the room from upstairs. "Now we're all together again," he said, running his fingers through his tousled hair and then tucking in his shirt. "Almost forgot you-all were here. Anybody make coffee yet?"

Nobody answered so he went on through to the kitchen and was heard rustling among the pots and pans. Abe followed him. "How's Mattie doing? She seems a little slower, but still sharp."

Ollie gave him a quick look while running water into the coffeepot. "Doctor won't tell me nothin'. Acts like he doesn't know what's wrong, but I'm feared it's more and he doesn't want me to know whatever there is to know. Goddammit, Abe, I wish there was another sawbones in this town. I'm about to find one of those Indian doctors, like old Moon Fish. Couldn't hurt Mattie, that's for sure."

"Can she still move about all right?"

"Still up and down those stairs once or twice a day. Won't move the bed down here."

"And what about you, you doing all right? You look same as ever."

"Ugly as ever, huh? I'm doing fine. Except for being worried about her." He pointed down at his replacement leg. "Queer thing though, sometimes that damn old foot starts to itch and feel like it's twitching down there. Like it used to when it was still there. You wouldn't think that could happen."

"Ever happen with that missing hand of yours?"

Ollie raised his stump above his head. "Used to, but now it's just the opposite. I can't feel a damn thing from the elbow down. Not cold, hot or wet or dry. Nothin' there," he smiled, and asked, "What do you want for breakfast? I'll be doing the cooking 'less Sarah Beth wants to."

"I'll ask her."

"Well, tell Mattie the water's hot enough for her tea. And ask her which kind she wants this time."

Later that morning when they stopped by the doctor's office they found a sign on the door that said he would be gone for the day, it being Independence Day, but that he'd be back the next day. Abe looked at Sa-rah and said, "Forgot all about that."

"But what if there was an emergency?"

"I imagine he could be found. Nothing for it but to stay over. What do you want to do with the rest of the day?"

Just then they heard the sounds of a brass band tuning up down the street at a bandstand in the park. A group of young boys went running past them, and a couple of wagons decorated in red, white and blue bunting drove past. Abe crossed the street to ask an old man on a bench what was planned for the day.

"Be a parade, band concert, and some squawking from the mayor and maybe a state politician or two. Fireworks at night, though, best part, and a fiddlin' dance later on."

"Well thanks." He went back to his little family and reported the information. "I think I'd like to see some of all that," he said.

"Do you think it'll get very dusty with all that going on?"

"I'm not sure."

"Well maybe you could walk me back and then you and Isaiah could come back when it all gets started."

After they'd returned to the house, Ollie told them what time things were supposed to get going, but said that he, himself, wasn't much for going to all that hypocritical stuff. Besides," he said, "a friend of mine's coming by, take me down to the river for a little fishing. Wish me luck and maybe we'll have a fish fry."

When Abe and Isaiah got back down into the town, a man had set up a small corral in the park and was offering pony rides. A newsboy sold papers at the entrance and Abe bought a copy of the *Lewiston Teller*. There were two headlines. One said, "America the Greatest," and in smaller type on the bottom half of the page, the other said "Savages on the Warpath." He paid for Isaiah's ride and waited with the boy until his turn came up, then found a shady spot under a big tree.

He hurriedly read through the article about the "outbreak near Lapwai" and the Army's response. It seemed that the Indians in the area, Nez Perce, had been ordered onto a reservation area set aside for them and they'd only had until June 15th to comply. He looked for the date of the newspaper and saw that it was two weeks old, from June 20th. Around the same time, a small group of young warriors went on a killing spree and some seven or eight white settlers were killed. Alcohol was suspected as a contributing factor, but nothing was proven. The region's army commander, a General Howard, was quoted as saying that he had ordered a mobilization of troops, was calling for local militias to stand by, and that he thought "we'll make short work of this." That was the end of the article.

Abe waved to Isaiah who was grinning widely, whooping and urging his pony to go faster. Abe quickly went to find the newsboy to see if he didn't have a later edition. The boy looked a little embarrassed and admitted he did, but that he wanted to sell all the oldest ones first. Abe paid him again and got a copy of the weekly's most recent news, June 27th.

The headline in this newspaper read: "Hostiles Wipe out Army Detachment." That battle occurred at the mouth of White Bird Canyon on the 16th and 17th and the report said the military contingent was outnumbered three to one. One of the civilian militia volunteers interviewed by a reporter from the Portland newspaper, *The Oregonian*, and quoted in the Lewiston paper, said there were not anywhere near that many Indians, that they were poorly armed, and that the soldiers were surrounded and thirty-three of them were reported killed. This number of casualties was not ascertained until more than a week after the skirmish, which was how long it took to find and bury the bodies. Abe read both of the articles twice and then sat back to let his thoughts tumble through his mind, foremost among them his fear that something could have happened to Helga and Indigo.

He looked over to the pony corral, where Isaiah was still riding. With a big smile and loud shouts, the boy stood up in the stirrups, waving one arm around his head.

Abe wondered if the local telegraph office would have any more recent dispatches from the conflict. If necessary, he thought he could still pass himself off as a reporter and see if he could get any more updates. Then he realized the office would most likely be closed for the holiday. Once again the band began to play a marching tune as they seemed to be warming up, or perhaps from the number of mistakes and the shouting of the conductor, to be practicing together for the first or second time.

Abe noticed that Isaiah's time was up, and went to meet him at the corral and lead him out of the park. "We need to go back to Mattie's house to eat so we'll be able to come back when the parade starts."

When they were back inside the house, Mattie called Isaiah over to where she was sitting and began asking him questions about what he'd been doing, his little sister, and anything he wanted to tell her. Abe took the newspapers into the guest room where he didn't know Sa-rah was putting the baby down for a nap. He backed out quietly, and went to the porch. He realized he would have to be a little careful in how he shared this news, but he was worried enough that he couldn't keep it to himself.

When Sa-rah came out to join him, he showed her the headlines in the two papers, and she immediately asked if this had anything to do with their friends, and with Helga.

"I don't know, but it's near where she's been living, and the same area where Lefty and Hawk Man had their village."

"And my dear friend Kate, Moon Fish," she said softly. "Oh Abe, is there anything we can do to find out more? What else does it say?"

"Not much, just that there have been a couple of small battles between the army and the Indians, and it sounds like the Indians have the upper hand. At the very end, though, the latest one quotes the general as saying when he gets his request for a large number of additional troops, it won't be much of a problem to put down the insurrection of what he calls the Non-treaty Hostiles."

A bit later, it turned out that the parade went right down the street past Mattie and Ollie's house as it headed for Main Street and the park. Abe and Isaiah had already left to go watch it in the center of town, and Ollie was off fishing, but the two women enjoyed their vantage from the porch. The only problem was that the loud noise seemed to frighten DoraLee so much she started crying and coughing. Then they all went inside and watched through a window.

After the parade, there were awards and prizes given out to leading citizens, a couple of students read essays they'd written, a drama about Paul Revere's ride was enacted, and there were speeches by local or visiting political dignitaries. The last speaker, an assistant to the governor, gave a rousing and long-winded address on the consequences of allowing savages to be treated as if they were the same as human beings.

He finished by saying, "Just look at what is happening this very day, only a short distance to our north. We are engaged in war with these red-skinned savages. Our white brothers and sisters, their children and babies have been murdered in their sleep. Why? Because we have allowed stupidity and ignorance to determine how we deal with heathen infidels whose whole and entire despicable history here in this land has never, to this day, produced a single accomplishment worth noting. Why has God brought us to this land? My friends and neighbors, all of us, civilized people, you and I, have been brought here for one purpose only, and that mission, given by God Himself, is the supreme purpose of taming this land and making it as productive as any in the world. We have been brought here by God Almighty to rid this earth of such savagery and idolatry and blasphemy, and to bring peace and enlightenment to this land. Pray for our soldiers engaged in these battles for holiness and freedom, pray for our innocent victims of the atrocities brought about because we have failed to understand that one is only expected to 'turn the other cheek' to a civilized enemy. These vermin, this plague on the land, the red man and his spawn must be eliminated. We will and we must, each and every one of us, pledge our support and our allegiance to the cause of exterminating once and for all these heathen savages, and we must be prepared to die if need be protecting our children, our women, and our dreams, now and forever. Amen. God bless America."

The people responded with loud and prolonged cheering, and the band struck up a military march. Abe suddenly wondered if there was anyone standing nearby who might recognize him as the rancher who lived with the Indians a day's ride south of town. He took Isaiah's hand and quickly moved through and away from the crowd, back to the house.

CHAPTER 18

Fighting

They made camp near the Clearwater River after a short day of travel. There was much shouting of instructions and women were loudly deciding where they would place their lodges. The young boys were moving the horses away from the camp area and up the long slope to where there was abundant grass. As soon as Helga had removed the packs, Indigo begged to be able to take their horses to join the rest, but she told him to stay with her because she needed his help. She'd lost some of her poles in the rush to leave and then had to leave most of them by the riverbank in order to cross. A few days later, when they stopped for two nights in one place, she and many others had cut more and although they were still green and oozing pitch in the summer heat, it was a relief to once again have the privacy and the shelter of their lodge.

Two nights and days had passed since she'd seen Carl. He was assigned to scouting the movements of the army behind them. Since there were no reports of soldier movements, a hopeful feeling was spreading throughout the camp that perhaps they would be left alone to travel over the mountains to buffalo country beyond. This changed suddenly when the people of Chief Looking Glass's band appeared unexpectedly, still frightened and nursing their wounded from an attack on their peaceful village. This group had pledged peace with the whites and avoided any fighting until that attack happened. Their village was often used as an example of good practices and relationships when the missionaries and government agency people talked to other Indian groups, trying to persuade them to settle on the reservation. These people's success in raising gardens and even beginning to build some cabins was seen by their chief and leaders as a kind of shielding protection against the turmoil launched against the "non-treaty" or rebellious groups of the other chiefs, Joseph and White Bird. Now, however, they too were having to flee and join with their tribal relations in an attempt to avoid the flames of conflict being fanned by white settlers demanding action by the military and forming their own militias.

Two of these refugee families set up their lodges near Helga; when she went to see what they might need help with, she was pleased to find that one of the women spoke some English. Indigo quickly made friends with her two sons and took them with him to get water in their hide buckets.

That evening when they had a chance to talk, the woman said her name was Ellen Standing Horse, and she'd been placed in a school with the missionaries after her own parents died from a sickness she didn't know the name of. She married a man who was some years older than she was, but confided in Helga that, as an orphan, she had no choice because this was the only way to get away from the whites. The man was able to convince the churchmen he would take care of her, and she was not unhappy with her situation. As far as what was happening now, she only knew that their village was blamed for attacks on whites, and although their chief told the government and soldiers this was untrue, and "there was no white people's blood on his or any of his people's hands," he was not believed. Suddenly one morning, their village had been awakened by gunshots aimed at their lodges and they'd run for their lives. When the attackers were gone, some of her people were able to sneak back for the belongings they needed for traveling, and to gather some of their horses, but many of her people had been forced to walk a long distance with heavy loads on their backs before they caught up with these relatives of theirs.

That night when Helga was preparing for bed, Carl showed up and came quietly into the small tipi they'd been able to save and carry with them. It was dark and Helga couldn't help being frightened by the sound of someone coming inside. Then he spoke his name and found the edge of the bedding with one of his hands. Indigo was sleeping outside near his friend's lodge with the boys and their uncle. As soon as she knew it was Carl she was relieved and so glad he'd returned that she got up to her knees and took his hands in hers and pulled him down to the bed.

"You all right?" she asked, using the Indian words.

"I am good. But I must sleep."

"Please be here," she said, and he lay down with her, still fully dressed in what she could feel was his battle-wear.

"You?" he asked.

"I am good now. I'm just so relieved that you came back. I was afraid for you and nobody had seen you, none of them who came back. I have been waiting."

He sat up and slipped his leather shirt off and slid under the elk-skin cover she'd managed to hang on to through all the haste and panic of the past few weeks. Then he lay down on his back and slipped his arm under her shoulders, pulling her close and then easing her over on top of him, keeping both arms around her. There was some awkwardness with their clothing, which they both pushed out of the way. Suddenly he was inside, and they were moving together, moving slowly, his hands around her waist, pulling her and sliding her body against his. When he finished and she could feel his whole body relax, she thought how this was their first time, a beginning when she'd been so afraid it was the end, that he might not return to her. She'd been so anxious when he didn't come back during the past few days, and now she was so relieved, now that this had happened and she was feeling very good about it.

When he awoke in the morning, he was proud to show her his trophy from the fighting. He held up a shiny bugle and pointed to himself and made the sign of a rifle which he pretended to fire, and then he dropped the instrument and mimed the death of the bugler.

Her first thought was that she had just spent the night as wife to a killer, but this quickly evaporated as she felt a rush of pride that he'd helped to save all of them from the soldiers.

While Helga was stirring the coals of her cook-fire outside the tipi, Indigo and the two boys showed up. Carl held up the bugle so the boys could see it. Their eyes lit up and they all wanted to hold it, so he handed it to Indigo, who immediately tried to make a sound by blowing through it. Nothing happened except the sound of his hard-blown breath. Carl took it back and he tried to make a sound come out of it, but only got a kind of a squawk. Then he hung it over his shoulder and walked away, going somewhere in a hurry.

Helga ran after him and asked if he didn't have time to eat something, but he shook his head and pointed across the camp, then signed he would be back. She touched his hand and he smiled at her, and then took off again, this time trotting across the open space between their side of the camp circle and the other side. The boys were playing at being buglers by holding sticks of wood to their mouths and making loud tooting noises. Ellen Standing Horse appeared and asked what was going on with the boys. Helga explained what happened in Carl's part of the battle.

"That is good," she said. "My man Talking Bear say that horn is how their chief gives orders in fighting. That chief tells man with horn what he want soldiers do, and man makes the right noise on horn."

"Then that's why this man is so proud of killing that soldier with the bugle."

"You his woman?"

"Yes," she answered slowly. "It's a long story, but he took care of me when I had no one. I ended up with his family. They knew me from before."

"Maybe we talk more later. Your story and my story. They say we move again today."

"Oh no," Helga stood up from the soup she was cooking. "Are soldiers coming again?"

"I don't know, my man say this place not good for us now. I go, maybe help you soon."

Helga fed the boys and then walked into the open space between all the lodges, looking for Carl across the camp. A large group of warriors was standing around over there and some of them were waving their arms and speaking quite loudly. She wished she could hear what they were saying. Then they all went quiet and she could hear White Bird's voice as he pointed toward the low line of mountains to their north. Another man spoke for a while and kept pointing to the east, where the sun was already a ways above the horizon. Suddenly, it was over and all the men headed off in different directions toward their own camps. Carl hurried toward her.

"We go." He pointed to the east and made a motion that signed the river and people crossing it. She handed him a bowl of the soup and he drank it without letting it cool. He ducked into the lodge and came out with his personal battle dress and weapons, which he wrapped in a blanket and tied into a bundle. He left it there on the ground near her and called for Indigo, who came running from the neighboring campsite. Carl motioned to him and the two of them went running off toward the hillside where the horses were being guarded. Other men and boys were catching their own animals and leading or riding them back into the camp.

Once they were on the move, they only stopped for a temporary overnight camp, then late the next morning they were on the trail again. The whole caravan stretched out along the well-used trail for over a quarter mile, and the mood among the people was happy. They were still celebrating the victory at the Clearwater. The weather had also improved and was gaining heat with each day of the new summer. When they stopped in the early afternoon to rest the horses and people, the warriors, who must have captured a store of ammunition, practiced shooting at some distance from the rest of the tribe. For Helga this was unpleasant, even frightful, because she couldn't help thinking about the battles and skirmishes they'd been through, wondering about what was coming next. Her new friend,

Ellen, said she'd heard the soldiers would probably leave them alone if they kept moving away from where they'd started from.

Several days of this slow movement and temporary camping gave the Indians time to repair and repack their equipment and supplies, and for their hunters to bring in a good store of meat that could be dried in very thin strips during the heat of the day when they weren't on the move. This would be kept on hand in case a time came when they wouldn't have time to hunt or to do the drying. Things seemed peaceful and the chiefs spread the word that once they made it over the LoLo Pass and down the other side, there would be no trouble with the whites, who were much different than the ones in Idaho.

When they reached the Warm Springs on the descent into Montana, they stopped and took time for healthy doses of the healing waters and for socializing, almost as if it were a normal summer such as those that had always come before this one. At one camping place the women were able to gather the leaves of a shrub that made a healthful and good-tasting tea. Helga was unable to find out the name of this bush, but she very much liked the sweet flavor of the tea and collected enough of it for them to use for many weeks.

As they started down the rest of the mountainous trail toward the Bitterroot Valley, they came to an open flat place with room for all to camp and to hold a dance of thanksgiving and blessing. The festivities went on for two days and nights. Although the large ceremonial drums had been left behind when the journey started, there were enough hand drums and flutes to make accompaniment for the groups of singers who took turns motivating and inspiring the dancers. At one point Helga was standing near the outside of the large circle of dancers and watchers when Carl surprised her by coming up behind her and pulling her into the parade of couples who were shuffling and spinning to the sound of the drums. When the song was finally over, he led her back to a different place on the circle and there were Lefty and Moon Fish. She was very glad because he hadn't seen them since before the last skirmish and flight. The old woman was seated on a bundle of blankets and didn't try to get up as she reached out her hands to Helga, pulling her down to kneel in front of her.

"Oh, my dear," she exclaimed. "I am so pleased to see you again. Is it good with you now?"

"Yes, and for you?"

"I never thought I would do this kind of thing ever again. At my age."

"But she's the best of us," Lefty said as he reached out to shake Helga's hand. "Always first one wake, ready to go."

"Only because I have trouble staying asleep when the sun is waking so early." Then she pulled Helga closer to herself and spoke softly, "I see you with the young man. Is he good for you?"

"Yes, he is very kind and takes good care of my boy."

"I remember when I was a young woman, the only white woman in the camp, and I felt like everyone was whispering about me. Now it is you that is that one among the many, but I have heard no whispering about you."

"They have been good to me. But I am so afraid when I am alone at night. I am afraid he won't come back. What would I do then?"

"You will always be taken care of among these people. You are one of us now, and someday when we are able to sit in quiet and not have to be running this way and that, I will be able to tell you how important it is to be one of these people and to be so different at the same time. You will have important things to do when the time comes that white people and Indians begin to talk to one another about the future. They will listen to you. I will help you be ready."

In the morning, a small group of soldiers appeared with a white flag asking to talk with the chiefs. They met together on the opposite sides of a small creek that passed close to the Indian camp. They had to talk loudly, but not so loud that any of the rest of the people could make out what they were saying. Chief White Bird was especially demonstrative, waving his arms and walking back and forth. After a short while the Indians came back single file. The soldiers folded their white flag and rode away.

Ellen was able to tell Helga that they would be staying in this camp for another night, and then she invited her over to her own lodge for the evening meal. When the two boys came to get her and

Indigo, Carl showed up and she asked him to come with them. He
nodded his acceptance. When Carl and Talking Bear had eaten and
began to talk, Ellen leaned over and spoke softly, telling her guest
bits and pieces of what the men were saying. Apparently, a large
group of soldiers were blocking the Lolo Trail down the mountain
where they planned to go, and the chiefs and the soldier-chief were
arguing about this. The soldier-chief wanted the Indians to give up
their guns and go peacefully down into the valley where the warriors
would be taken to Fort Missoula and kept there until the Big Man of
the soldiers would come to say what would be done with them. The
chiefs refused, saying that was surrender. The soldiers said it was not
surrender, but was now the only way for peace. They all agreed to
meet again the next morning.

When they were getting ready to go back to their own lodge,
the two boys asked their mother to have Indigo stay the night with
them again. She repeated this to Helga and gave a look that said it
was all right with her. Helga said yes, and she and Carl went back to
their lodge. Carl built up the fire so he could see to clean and oil his
rifle, and sharpen his knives. This was upsetting to Helga because
she was afraid it meant more fighting, but she knew it was necessary
to be prepared. She tried to convince herself he had more chance of
not being hurt if he could fight well, if that was what had to happen.
When he'd finished his work, he put his things away and silently got
up and walked away into the growing darkness.

She knew better than to call out or ask if he would be coming
back, that was not the way of these people. It was the same when she
was growing up among the Mormons, as it was never allowed for the
women to interfere with the men. She thought how different it was
between Sa-rah and Abe, and even herself. They were always either
informing one another or asking what was going on. Thinking about
all of that was enough to send deep feelings of loneliness into her
heart and she had to fight back the hurt it brought on. It just wasn't
fair, there was nothing that she'd done that wasn't permitted and even
encouraged by Sa-rah. Helga couldn't help feeling that she was equal
as Abe's woman to that one who was his wife. Now, here she was

alone, among a people running for their lives from the government of the white people, her people really. Helga fought back the tears and crawled into bed, pulling the hide up around her eyes. It would be cold again this night, up here in the mountains.

She didn't know how long she'd been asleep when she woke up to feel Carl crawling into bed beside her. She was relieved and grateful and lay against him, thinking that it was only his strength that kept her alive now, and that he seemed to need her as much as she needed him. His hands found their way across her breast and she felt the gentleness of his touching and stroking. It was the only comfort left in all of this fear and fighting, and she tried to lose herself in his caring and need.

There were two more mornings of negotiations between the two sides. After the impasse of the second meeting, the whole camp was alerted to be prepared to move when daylight came. This was accomplished with a minimum of sound for such a large group; even the horses seemed to know that they weren't allowed their usual neighing and jostling. In the early light of dawn, the long procession began the steep, rocky climb up and away from the main trail. Only the faintest of glimmer of daylight showed the way over the treacherous ground.

Once the orderly crowd of people, horses, and dogs reached the ridge top, they found bare rock and easier going than on the climb up. At one place they could look down and see the work of soldiers where they attempted to block the main trail with fallen trees and piles of brush. Below the barricade, some few hundred yards down the twisting roadway, was the military camp with its white tents and wagons and the first stirrings of its own daybreak activity. Fires were being kindled and horses rounded up to be brought close in to the camp. The line of Indians moved back from the edge of the ridge where they might be seen from below and increased their hurry. Within a few hours, the leaders turned and headed down though a long slope of grass to rejoin the trail once again. They halted when all of the approximately 300 people and their animals were safely regrouped and the army's blockade had been bypassed. The call went out for a brief stop for food and a short rest, but they were warned that this was no more than a temporary break and that they would have to remain ready to move quickly if needed.

The chiefs worked their way to the back of the crowd and waited at the trail, anticipating another confrontation with the soldier-chief. Soon, he and several of his men appeared as expected, and once again there was a lot of arm-waving and loud talking. Helga was able to watch this exchange from her place near the rear of the procession. Soon Talking Bear returned and spoke rapidly to Ellen. When he moved off toward the front of the crowd, Helga asked Ellen if she could say what was going on.

"The soldier-chief is very angry," she said. "He say we should still be waiting on trail where we sleep, to have talk with him. Not to go around him. Our chiefs say they change minds, not want to wait for him to clear trees from trail so we can pass by."

"Will we keep going today?"

"Yes, we go to make good camp at Big Hole River."

It took a few days to reach the place where the chiefs wanted to have a camp where they could stay for some time. They were now on their way to the Yellowstone area. As they left the mountains, they began seeing large open prairies with isolated patches of forest. They made camp in the evening and next day, following a brilliant orange and purple sunrise, the women went upslope to gather new tipi poles and berries, while many of the men went to hunt. Helga felt a relaxed atmosphere in the camp as evening came and the dance leaders announced a celebration beginning with darkness.

The drumming began with the fading of the sun's light and by dark there were many young couples and a few elders circling in the grassy circle that was cleared for this. Carl and Helga arrived together, and Indigo quickly found some friends to have mock-battles with beyond the circle of light from the large central fire. When the opening dance of the main event began, the couple joined the parade of people swaying and moving in rhythmic steps around and around the great ring of seated onlookers. Helga couldn't help thinking that even if many of these people didn't know them, this would be more than enough to show them that there was a white woman living with an Indian man within the camp among the bands of the tribe. She was very shy about the movements and the footwork that everyone else seemed to be so used to. Carl, who may have himself been reacting shyly to the scrutiny they were attracting, was good enough to help her and correct her when she lost track of either the rhythm or the steps.

After what seemed like a very long time, that opening dance ended and many of the people left the ring to stand in small groups, talking and watching. Next came a series of performances by men or women who showed incredible skill and endurance in what almost seemed like a contest between the dancers and the drummers. Helga saw Moon Fish sitting across the circle, and excused herself from Carl to go visit the elder woman.

"Ah, my dear child," the woman said when she saw Helga beside her. "You are doing well, and your boy?"

"We are doing well. It is hard, but it must be much harder for you."

"I'm still here, still moving along, but not for much longer."

"I wish I could help you more, but I don't have much choice where I find myself in the line of the people," Helga said.

"I have help."

The drums grew louder and it became difficult to hear and speak. Helga bent down and gave the old woman a kiss on the top of her head, and then stood quietly next to her for a few more moments. Across the circle she saw Carl and many others of the warriors stripping off their shirts and brandishing their clubs and axes. They shouted loudly, and then one after another they stomped and whirled into the dance area.

Moon Fish reached up and took Helga's hand and pulled the young woman down so she could say something, "War Dance now. Bad time coming for our people. Be safe, my child."

Helga felt the urge to cry a little because of the sadness she felt for this woman, who should be living in a restful place with her family around her to take care of her instead of being among all of these people fleeing for their lives. She kissed the woman's hand, let it go and then walked quickly away.

The fire burned higher and the pace of the drum sped up. Shouts and whoops resounded across the camp and everyone seemed to be moving to the sound and energy of the dance. The youngsters, including Indigo, were leaping and jumping around the edges, shouting and shrieking in imitation of the warriors, practicing for who they would someday become.

When that dance finally ended, the people moved away to their camps, and because it had been a difficult day of travel, hard work making camp, and now this dancing, almost everyone was quietly making for bed and sleep.

As the short night ended and the first inkling of light in the east came forth, only a few of the women were stirring the coals and re-kindling their fires. Suddenly there was the sound of a single shot echoing through the darkness, followed by the crash of gunfire and loud shouting coming from across the small creek. A surprise attack by the army roared toward the nearly one hundred lodges arranged peacefully alongside the river. They were three deep in three long lines. There had been no warning, and the troops were concentrated and rushing toward one end of the camp. The rain of bullets on the tipi covers was reported later to have almost been mistaken by some for the sound of heavy hailstones. Men awakening to this completely unexpected attack grabbed for their weapons and tried to crawl out to get away from the shooting while they recovered from the shock of the assault. The women and children inside tipis under attack tried to stay as low as possible, but to little avail as soldiers ripped open the coverings with knives and bayonets and continued firing, making no attempt to see who they were shooting at. A few women were able to grab guns from the fallen men who'd been unable to get away. These women fired at the soldiers, but were all killed before they could reload.

At the other end of the camp, men were fighting their way toward the main group of soldiers while their women and children made for the creek and hid among the willows or in the water. Helga and Indigo rushed into the water behind a sand bar of shrubs; Helga pushed to where Indigo could hang onto the brush to keep his head up, and she squatted down so only her face was above the water. Next to her were two women with babies, and beyond them another woman and a young girl tried to support an old woman who was gasping and choking.

With no warning three soldiers splashed toward them, swinging the butts of their rifles across the surface of the water and shouting, coming closer and closer. The mothers held their babies out toward the soldiers, shrieking for mercy. A soldier hit one woman in the head with the butt of his gun and she went down under the water, her baby screaming and flailing until her friend grabbed it out of the current. The other two men shouted at the soldier, pushing him back toward the stream bank. Helga could hear them yelling about not killing women and babies.

The one who'd swung his gun shouted, "Varmints all the same" and fired his rifle at the women, charging again. He stopped when he saw Helga's face, shouted an obscenity and began screaming "White woman? What the hell! You die." He raised his gun and pointed it at her.

Helga ducked underwater, pushing Indigo away, moving as low and fast as she could, reaching for the man's legs. She couldn't see anything, couldn't think or breathe. Then she felt the boots, clutched his ankles, and pulled the man over on top of her as she struggled to the surface for air. She pulled out her knife just as the man spun around and grabbed her by the hair. Indigo screamed and leaped on the soldier's back, trying to grab his head. Helga drove the knife as deep as she could into the soft place above the man's belt, and felt him collapse, doubling over. The water around them turned red as one of the other women snatched the rifle. Although the gun had been partially submerged, she was able to fire it at the other two soldiers who were now backing away on the stream-bank. The woman's shot hit one man in the face, the other man fired once and ran away. That wild shot hit Helga in the shoulder and she doubled over with sudden and terrible pain.

Indigo thrashed his way toward her, his head bobbing through the water. He grabbed onto her and pulled toward the opposite bank. The body of the soldier she'd stabbed was jerking, but he was face down in the water. She had a crazy thought to try and help him, but instantly dismissed it. She struggled to move, with the boy pulling her across to the other side of the creek, until he grabbed her wounded arm and she screamed, pushing him toward the bank with her good arm, yelling at him to get out of the water and into the bushes. When she reached the edge of the creek and was standing knee deep in the water, Helga looked back and saw the woman with the two babies fighting to get to where she was. She turned and took a couple of steps, holding out her good arm and taking a baby. The two women then held on to one another to keep from slipping and falling.

They reached the bushes beside the water and Indigo pushed branches out of the way so they could get into a kind of sheltered space. Helga looked back and saw that the woman with the gun must have managed to reload it and was aiming at a white man on a horse who was swinging a whip at her. She fired and the man screamed and whipped his horse to get away. The soldier Helga had stabbed was still floating face down in the water across the creek, and the woman whose skull was smashed was only partially out of the water, lying on the slope of the bank, not moving. The old woman and her young companion were nowhere to be seen. Helga fell and nearly fainted, but she struggled to stay conscious, handing the baby up to the other woman, and telling herself she would die if she didn't stop the bleeding from her shoulder. She sat up and stripped the torn shirt from her torso, wadded it and pushed it hard against the wound. Indigo was curled up in a ball and sobbing hard. She tried to comfort him by thanking him for his help, saying how brave he was, and telling him it was going to be all right, but she was thinking to herself that the situation seemed hopeless.

Some older warriors appeared on the far side of the creek, one of them on horseback. The woman with the babies yelled to them and the horseman crossed over. He called to her to come with him, get on the horse, but she spoke loudly and gestured with her chin toward Helga, who was now hardly conscious at all. The man slid down from his horse and swiftly reached into the bushes where she had collapsed. He pulled on Helga's legs, then lifted her up and laid her across his horse's back. He led them through the creek and past the dead soldier on the bank. The camp was quieter now and the gunfire had moved off toward a low hillside some distance away. The man who'd rescued her called out for help and lowered Helga to the ground. Two older women came running to him, and he showed them the shoulder wound, then turned back and headed for the creek where the other man was helping the woman with the babies. Indigo was by now midstream and struggling with the current, trying to keep his head above water and splash his way across. The horseman jumped off, threw the boy on the horse and slapped its rump to drive it back across.

Several of the tipis in the line of camps were now burning and women were pulling the flaming hides or canvas away from those that were still untouched. Loose horses galloped through the camp and women lashed loads of belongings onto pole-sled travois, hastening to rig them onto horses. Many elders moved through the clearing, administering to the screaming wounded. As her vision came clearer and she was able to sit up, Helga could even see some people near the edge of the woods, frantically trying to dig holes for burying the dead. Then she fell back and lost all of her senses in the darkness of the pain that came from someone shoving something into the bullet-hole that went clear through her shoulder, but that had miraculously avoided any bones.

By the time darkness fell, the entire camp was on the move. Only a small band of warriors was left behind to keep the remaining soldiers pinned down behind their hastily-made barricades and shallow trenches. White Bird and Joseph hurried up and down the lines of the people, encouraging them to move quickly, but not to panic and cause confusion. "Keep your horses quiet, stay in the line," they called out. Looking Glass remained behind with the young warriors who were being led by Ollokut, Joseph's younger brother, who was known as the bravest of the young men.

When Helga regained consciousness, she found her arm strapped to her chest and the chaos of the escape going on all around her. Ellen relayed the chiefs' words and the details of the plan. She'd strapped her white friend to a travois, and was leading that horse and another with her own bundles and one of Helga's that she'd found near the knife-slashed tipi. To keep from screaming as the rough trail jostled and shook her, Helga bit her lips until they bled. She knew Indigo was riding on the horse that was pulling her, but couldn't turn her head to look at him. She was trying to think, to think what was missing, what they'd lost beside the tipi and she realized she didn't know where Carl was, or even if he was still alive. Suddenly, with a shock, she remembered she'd killed that soldier in the water. She shivered in spite of the heat, but it wasn't from shock or fever. It was from the overwhelming awareness that she'd killed a man, a white man trying to kill her because she was with Indians. She choked and coughed from the dust of their procession until finally Ellen appeared, walking beside her, placing a wet rag over Helga's mouth and face. It felt so good and she could breathe more easily.

Ellen asked if she could tell if she was still bleeding. "Don't think so but it hurts me. I'm so sorry I can't help you."

"Don't care about that, woman say you save babies" the woman said. "I think we camp not too far from here."

After they returned home from their Fourth of July town visit, Abe grew more and more concerned about the whereabouts and circumstances of Helga and his son, Indigo. The newspapers and the word of mouth he'd heard in Silver City were old news, and now back at the ranch there was no way for him to find out what was happening to them. If it really was a war, it would still be going on, but where and what was happening?

Sa-rah couldn't help noticing his anxiousness and asked if it was caused by the news he'd gotten in town.

"Where did the people go?"

"I don't know," he said. "And I can't find out unless I get another newspaper or some kind of message."

"I'm so sorry, but there's probably nothing you can do for them."

"I know, and that's what makes me so upset."

Later that night when Sa-rah was asleep, Abe eased out of their bed and found his way in the darkness to the outdoors. He hadn't been able to get to sleep, and couldn't seem to think clearly. Part of him wanted to tell Sa-rah that this was all her fault so she would have to let him go look for them, even if that was only partly true. What would have happened to Helga and Indigo if they hadn't had the Indians to go to? He looked up into the star-filled heavens, and the logical part of his mind told him that there was nothing he could do for them now. He could only hope and pray that they would be safe, that all of his friends would be protected from harm and from the guns of the soldiers. Another war to go through. As if that last one hadn't been enough to show anyone that these wars never solve anything. The losers will always seek revenge on the winners, no matter how long it takes. He remembered some of the conversations he overheard when he was in President Davis's camp retreating from the final Union offensives. There were many officers swearing oaths that they would never accept defeat, that surrender was only a tactic to be used to buy time for the Southern states to regroup and revive. This was being said in spite of the loss of most of the able-bodied young men of the Confederacy to death, wounds, or insanity. Abe knew very little about history, but what he thought he knew now was that no one ever wins any war.

There was only one thing he could do about it and that was to go himself to where this was happening. He approached the stable and whistled for Bird to come closer. She came to the pole fence and nuzzled the hand he held out to her. What he needed was a reason to go away and someone to take his place here while he was gone. Where was cousin Louis when he was needed? Ollie couldn't do much anymore and Mattie needed him to do what he could for her. This young man Roland was a possibility, but lately he was talking about going away himself.

"Bird," he said softly to the horse, "you really are my best friend. Help me if you can. You have helped me out so many times. Help me now, if you can." Then he prayed in his heart, prayed to God for an answer to his fears and loneliness for his son and the boy's mother. He sat down on a pile of hay and was very quickly asleep, not waking until first light when he went back into the house and started the morning cook-fire.

He heard the baby crying and went into the bedroom, bent over and picked her up. She quieted quickly as Sa-rah rubbed her eyes and turned over toward them.

"Where were you?" she asked, yawning and reaching out for DoraLee.

"I couldn't sleep, so I went out and walked around. Then I fell asleep on the hay."

"You really are worried, aren't you?"

"There's nothing I can do about it. I'll go heat some water. You want tea or coffee?"

He hurried through his breakfast preparations and eating, mumbled something to Sa-rah about wanting to get an early start. A short time later, he was saddling Bird and packing food into his tool bag. He was headed out to his current project of cutting and hauling poles from the nearby forest. He was planning to build a fence to keep his cattle from wandering into a dangerous draw with unstable rocky sides. Although the work wasn't so far away that he really needed to stay over nights, he'd lately been using this job as an excuse to avoid talking about his anxiety and frustration regarding Helga and Indigo. As he re-tightened the cinch and was preparing to leave, he heard Sa-rah calling his name and turned to see her hurrying across the open space between him and the house.

She stopped in front of him with her hands on her hips and said flatly, "You're going off again but we need to talk, don't you think?"

He didn't answer, but held out his arms to her for the hug he wanted to have given her before he left.

She backed away saying, "I know how worried you are, and I'm sorry. And I know why you won't talk about it with me. You think it's all my fault. You're blaming me for what might have happened to them, or might be happening."

"I'm just concerned, that's all, and there doesn't seem to be anything I can do. Even if I knew what was going on."

"Well maybe you should just go off and find out what's going on. I'll be fine here with the work and the kids by myself. Don't worry about me."

"I wouldn't do that and you know it. Not unless I could find someone to take care of everything."

"What about Edwin, he knows this place?"

"He's busy with his own place now, and helping out his Dad as well."

"I suppose you've already tried asking him." Just then the baby started crying from her little pen on the porch and Sa-rah turned to go to her.

He took a few steps following her, and said, "I'll be back tomorrow afternoon." He caught up and reached for her shoulder. She shrugged his hand away and then faced him.

"It is all my fault, I know that. But what was I supposed to do? It wasn't my fault that you gave me away to your Indian friend. Maybe none of this would have happened if you hadn't done that. Now go, be alone with your thoughts." She went quickly to pick up the crying baby. "I'll be here when you get back. I always am." Then she turned and went inside, letting the screened door fall shut behind her.

When he got out to where the job was waiting for him, he found Ginger grazing near the cattle. He easily caught the old mare and led her to the tree where he kept the harness hanging when it wasn't in use. He hooked her up and led the horses upslope with him. He tied them both to trees while he felled a dozen small pine trees, and lopped off the branches. Then he and Ginger began hauling the poles back down the hill in sets of three. He repeated that process three times, zig-zagging down the long slope and stacking the logs. By then the heat of the day was catching up with him and the animals. He led them to the small creek, turned them out on a grassy area, unpacked his mid-day food, and settled himself into some shade, leaning against a boulder.

As he was finishing off his food, the thought came to him that none of this was anyone's fault. They had all had good intentions, even Hawk Man had only been trying to help them fit into their Indian ways. Helga was still at the stage where she was doing what she was told to do, and Sa-rah had been doing whatever her emotions told her to do to give them a child. He was the only one of them he couldn't completely justify, and maybe Sa-rah was right about him giving in to the Indian and his ways, and not having the courage to risk their place on this land. Maybe if he'd been stronger, none of this would have happened like it did. He had the sudden and powerful wish that right now he could talk to Sa-rah's father, the good and wise Dr. Randall. But what about? He looked up to see three vultures spinning circles in the empty blue sky above him, and wondered if they were a sign of something dead below, one of his cattle or calves perhaps. Their spirals moved away from him and they were gone over the next ridge, seeking but not yet finding what they were looking for.

And what about himself? What did this situation tell him about his own faith? How weak was his belief in the ways of God for their family and for their needs being met? If this was a test of his faith, how could he be sure that whatever happened to Helga and Indigo was for the best? And where was the confidence he had always shown in Dr. Randall's teaching? If we truly have a need and express that need in prayer and thought and are unswerving in our beliefs, then when it is right for us and we deserve it, we will be met with an opportunity that fulfills our need. Right now, he knew he was assuming his biggest need was to be able to go away, go now and find the woman and his firstborn son, to find what was happening to them in this conflict between the government and the Indians, and to help in whatever way was needed. He was convinced this was his need, but there no one showing up to take his work and take care of these members of his family. This need wasn't being met like the time that stranger, Sam, showed up unexpectedly with news from his cousin and then offered to watch the place while Abe went to help Louis.

He pushed himself up off the ground, got a drink from the creek, caught the horses, and went back to work. It wasn't until darkness fell and the flickering light of his small campfire illuminated the tree branches nearby, that he got some sort of answer to his doubts and questions. Maybe, just maybe there was nothing he could do for them right now. Taking off without a plan could be some kind of misuse of his time and energy. He knew that if he could find out what was going on he'd have a lot more peace of mind, but if they were going through serious hardships and danger, his peace of mind was certainly less important than theirs, and if he had any faith at all, it was that he would see them both again, that they would be taken care of, and that somehow things would get straightened out.

With these thoughts in his mind he made his bed on the ground and lay down to look straight up into what seemed to be hundreds of thousands of stars in the crystal clear night air. To straighten things out, he would first need to apologize to Sa-rah, and admit that his anxiety led him to pass judgment on her actions, but to explain that there really was no blame and all he wanted at this time was to get back on the path of making her and his children happy and secure. Then, when he'd taken care of that, if she accepted it, he could go for a two-day run to Silver City for the latest news, just to settle his mind, or at least to give him something tangible to be concerned about. No more making up things that he couldn't know were either true or false. He was sure she could understand and support the need to learn more about what was happening.

CHAPTER 19

Deaths

The people never stopped that first night after they left the valley of the Big Hole River. The wounded screamed, children cried, women and men yelled at their horses, and some of those hurt the worst died or begged to be left behind. Helga had nothing to compare her pain and discomfort to, other than giving birth to Indigo. All that night as she tried to fall asleep on the rocking, clattering travois, she focused her thoughts on the joy that he'd brought into her life. He was now riding with Ellen's boys and she hadn't seen him since darkness fell. Since she couldn't do anything for him in her condition, she was very grateful he was being taken care of.

Finally, with the first streaks of light above the far off horizon, the chiefs called a halt to the caravan and word was sent down the line that this would be only a short stop to eat and re-pack the loads that had loosened. Helga realized she was very thirsty and hadn't had any water all night. She'd never even gotten up to leave the trail to relieve herself. Now, with the sudden stopping of the horse and her pole bed, she tried to climb off and stand up. Instantly, she went down, falling to her knees, reaching out to support herself with the one good arm. Indigo came to her at that moment.

"Mama, I help you. I was so scared all night."

"Just let me catch my breath for a moment. Then I'll be able to stand up." She pulled him close to herself and held him tightly. "It's going to be all right. I know we'll be all right."

"I wish Papa was here. He could take care of you. I don't want you to die."

"Of course not, why do you say that?"

"Other ones are died. I see them fall over and not come with us anymore."

"Well, that's not going to happen to me. Your Papa was hurt just like this one time and he is all healed up from it, and so will I be. Now help me stand and walk over to that bush."

As daylight filled the sky, Ellen came to give food to them, some dried meat and hard bread her man stole from an Army mule he'd captured. "We'll be moving again soon," she said, and hurried back to her own horses.

Just then Helga heard her name called out and turned to see Lefty coming toward her. "Oh," she said, and began crying immediately on seeing him. "Oh, you are alive."

"And so are you," he said. "Let me see that wound. I heard what you did. You are a brave woman, but we already know that." She turned toward him with the bloody, patched place and felt his fingers quickly and gently remove the crusty cloth dressing. "It looks bad, worse than it really is, and it will heal. I go find Moon Fish. We will not move it now, only later."

After what seemed like a long time, he was back with the older woman. She carried a bag over her shoulder and looked tired.

"My girl, my girl. You have suffered much to come this far like that."

"Yes, but not as much as many others."

The older woman looked around, saying, "I need some water, do you have?"

"No, but my friend Ellen might, over there."

Moon Fish came back with a small container of water, took a clean cloth from her bag and very carefully worked it around the area of the bullet wound, which was now closing up.

"You are fortunate," Moon Fish said. "It could have smashed the bones. Now, I'm going to put some of this plant into the hole to keep it from going bad, to make it better." She took a handful of leaves from a pouch and chewed them vigorously, then spit out a pulpy mass which she pushed into the wound as gently as she could. "This will hurt because I have to force the wound to open again. Here, bite hard on this and don't look at what I'm doing."

Helga bit down on a bitter tasting twig, and then felt a pain worse than anything she'd felt since the bullet went through her shoulder. She fought herself to keep from screaming, to keep from spitting out the stick, and then it passed and a cool, wet cloth was placed over the throbbing of the pain.

"We will wrap this with some grease to keep the air away from it, and you will have to be careful not to move your arm. I will tie it to your chest. Do you think you can ride a horse now?"

"I don't know. I can try."

"I will send Lefty with one of our horses. A quiet one. He can tie you on her. Better for you than being thrown about on the rocky road. I go now. Others need my help." She bent down and gave Helga a kiss on the forehead, and then said "You are Brave Knife. Strong medicine."

When the word came down the line to move on, Lefty showed up leading a small black horse with a very long tail. Helga struggled to stand up, and put one foot in his clasped hands, letting him lift her up onto the animal's back. The horse stood quietly while he took a long strip of old blanket material and wrapped it around her, tying it to the old saddle. He checked for its tightness and handed her the single nose-rein.

"She will be good for you," he said and started to walk away.

"What's her name?" she asked.

"You give her one in your language." He smiled and again turned away.

"Lefty, sir. Have you seen Carl?"

"No. I don't want to say about that."

"What? Tell me. What?" The feeling of dread almost caused her to choke. "He's dead, isn't he? He's dead."

Lefty turned back and reached up to take her hand in his. He held it to his face and let her feel the tears that came from his eyes. "Yes. So sorry. He fight good. I did not want to tell you now. He kill soldiers with big gun, cannon gun that could kill many of our people. He break gun before he be killed. Brave man. One of best. I'm sorry."

Helga fought back the tears and then gave up and let them come. Lefty hurried away, and she was left alone in the midst of the crowded chaos, maybe more alone than she'd ever felt in her life. "Oh God," she said softly, breathing hard through her sobbing. "Not fair, God, not good, not fair." The horses in front of her began to move forward and hers started moving as well. The sounds of the people and animals was almost deafening as they surged forward. Within a few minutes, even though the sun had barely risen, the omnipresent dust cloud surrounded them. All of this went unnoticed by her as she tried to breathe and wiped her eyes to see. Oh God, she thought. Oh God, I'm beginning to hate you...

The scouts guarding the passage of the people stayed behind, watching the movements of the military force, and reported they were taking a rest stop and falling behind. The chiefs gave the people a rest as well, for a day and a night, and then led them up and over a very difficult mountain pass. Each night when they stopped Helga was untied from the horse. She'd named the mare "Nurse" because without this animal she felt she would be dying alongside the trail, like so many others. Lefty had explained this to her, when she asked about the old ones she saw sitting and watching the procession of the people pass them by. He said that in their way, when one became a burden to their family, to the people, then he or she would request to be left behind, or if they still had strength, to walk away to die alone. She said that seemed cruel, but he replied it was everyone's duty to the whole tribe to give way to the younger ones, those who still had strength to go on, and needed what there was left to eat for their own survival. In this way the people would go on into many more generations.

After that, during the heat of the next few days, Helga even felt that way herself. She wasn't sure how much longer she could go on, and she felt some guilt every time they stopped and others had to take care of her needs. This was especially true every day when she saw Moon Fish, who came to treat her wound. She looked older and more exhausted, and Helga was afraid that one day she would just not show up. This fear wasn't only for her own sake, but out of caring for this special person and all of her knowledge and her loving ways. It was also because the elder woman was the only other white person in the whole crowd of fleeing people, and that was coming to mean even more to Helga now that she was alone without Carl, and especially because she had now killed a white man herself.

Then there came a day when the caravan of people suffered under the heat of a day without relief. They were crossing open country and only those in the very front of the procession were free of the choking dust stirred up by so many hooves and feet. Helga became so thirsty that she began to try to untie the torn strip of blanket that held her on the horse. She no longer cared what happened to her. If only she could get into some shade somewhere. Even sitting under her horse would be enough. Far ahead through the fine particles of the blowing clouds, there came the sight of some trees on a ridge. But how far, she wondered, and was it even real? Just then, as she was swaying back and forth and close to fainting in her saddle, she thought of Indigo. She hadn't seen him for over a day, and she knew she had to go on, and on, if only for his sake. She wiped the dust from her eyes and looked up into heaven, begging forgiveness from God for her lack of faith and for even thinking that she could hate the One who made and gave all that is.

A hand touched her leg and she shielded her eyes from the glaring sun. She found herself looking down into face of a man who was holding up a bucket made of hard leather. He said only one word, but she could understand it. He said, "Drink."

She took the vessel in her free hand, tucked the nose-rein under her trussed-up arm, lifted and tipped it to her mouth. The taste of the water, the feeling of it filling her mouth kept her from swallowing.

She thought she would never again go anywhere without water in her mouth. She swallowed and took another mouthful. Then, knowing there probably was not much more anywhere, she held out the container and said softly, "Thank you." He motioned for her to take another drink, and then took back the pouch with the rest of its water.

As the man turned to pass behind her to the next ones down the line, she recognized him as Joseph, the one she'd been told was the chief whose job it was to take care of the people. Now as she licked her parched, but freshly moistened lips, she knew he came to her from God, and she heard her own voice softly asking for forgiveness again.

Roland rode into the yard and looked around, not seeing anyone. He tied his horse to a post and went to the house, calling out, "Sa-rah, Abe, anyone home?"

Sa-rah came to the door with the baby in her arms, and just then Isaiah came running around the corner. "Hello," she said. "Abe's not here right now, he's out that way," she nodded her head in the direction of his work project. "Can I get you something cool to drink?"

"That would be fine, but it doesn't have to be cool, long as it's wet."

"Yes, it certainly is hot." She turned and went back inside.

Roland went to the porch steps and sat down in the welcoming shade. Isaiah stood back a ways, until the man waved to him and called him over. The boy came slowly and then pulled a rope from behind his back and quickly twirled it a couple of times over and around his head. He let it drop and coiled it back up.

"Getting pretty with good with that, aren't you?"

"I want to get really good," Isaiah said and came close enough to sit on the lowest step. "I have a horse now, and I want to ride and rope at the same time."

"Well now, that's kind of a tall order, I'd say. But if you get good at both of those things separately, it won't be any problem to put 'em together. That's what I did."

"Can you rope good?"

"Well, I used to win prizes at the fair, when I was younger."

"Maybe you can show me."

"Maybe I can."

Sa-rah came back outside and handed the man a glass of cool tea. "I keep it in a cold box in the dark after I make it in the sun. Isaiah, if you want some, you can get your own. It's on the kitchen counter." He ran up the stairs and into the house.

Sa-rah sat down in the porch chair she favored and excused herself for nursing DoraLee under a shawl. "So how are you, how's your family?"

"I'm doing well. Been pretty busy helping Mike with an addition on his shop. Got more business than he can handle these days. People coming all the way out here. Says he's going to train me to be his helper."

"Does that mean you're going to stay around here?"

"We'll see. I've still got to get back up to our old home place, see what's happened, straighten it out, and see if maybe I can get something for selling it?"

"And Abby, Naomi?"

"Naomi is doing really well here. I just wish we could get them," he motioned to Isaiah who'd just come back out, "together more often. I think they both need it."

"We'll work on that. Besides, come fall they need to start learning. Just because there's no school out here doesn't mean they don't need it."

"That's for sure right...Big news is, we think Abby is expecting again, thanks to you."

"Oh, my. That's wonderful, but no thanks to me. If anyone, it's my old teacher, Moon Fish, and her medicines."

"Well, Abby thinks otherwise. She says when she found out how long you had to wait and how hard you tried, she was inspired, that's the word she uses, inspired."

"That's great news. I'm so happy for you." DoraLee stopped nursing and struggled to sit up in her Mama's lap, making what seemed like random sounds. "She'd almost talking, don't you think?" she asked.

"If you say, so," Roland smiled and then looked serious. "There's other news, as well, not so good, I guess. Ollie sent a message by one of Mike's customers. Mattie's not doing so well and has been asking for you."

"Ohhh. I knew I should have been back to see her. When did you hear this?"

"Just yesterday. I came soon as I could. Martha's probably coming over later today or maybe tomorrow. Wanted me to let you know. And she has something for you."

"All right. Oh, I wonder if she could go with me. I'll have to tell Abe. We'll see what works best."

"I can help too, you know," he said. "I think maybe I'll ride out and find Abe. Need to talk cattle with him, and if it's all right I'll tell him about this news."

"Certainly, please do. And thank you so much for coming by."

"No problem. Thanks for the drink. Sure was good." He set the glass down and started for his horse, then turned and pointed at Isaiah, who'd come back out on the porch. "Keep practicing with that rope, kid. It's got to be like it's part of your arm, a really long arm."

After about half an hour of hot riding, he found Abe notching and lashing trees into a fence at the mouth of a small canyon. He didn't see any cows, but knew they must be nearby.

Abe said it was a good time for him to take a break, so they went to a small patch of shade and settled onto the soft needle litter under the trees. After some small talk about the heat and the chances of a drought catching them this fall, Roland dropped his news about Mattie.

"So, she sent word she'd sure like to see your wife."

"Well then, got to make it happen."

"Martha would go along if you can't make it yourself. She said that they got pretty close, her and Mattie."

"Don't think I could not go myself, just worry about this place and all."

Roland took off his hat and wiped the sweat from inside the band, and said, "Guess I'd be available. If I'm going to stick around here, and it seems more likely all the time, then I'd like to work with you and see if we couldn't add something to each other's outfit."

"That'd be what I'd like, but what about your place up north?" Abe asked.

"Well, come to that, I've got to head up there fairly soon, see if I could sell it. Y'see, Abby's pretty sure she's going to have another baby, and she wants to have it here and stay away from the troubles going on where we come from."

"Hey, congratulations, bet that'll make you proud, huh?"

"Yeah, it will. Tell the truth, I was beginning to think might be something wrong with me. Or her. We're both pretty relieved now."

"I know how that goes."

"She says Sa-rah had a lot to do with it," he paused when Abe gave him a funny smile, and chuckled. Roland responded, "No, I don't mean like that. I'm the father, we know that."

"Just struck me funny way you said it. I know Sa-rah was helping with the teas and exercises, whatever women do for each other, so I'm happy for you."

"We are too. Brings me to another subject. Say I was to sell off that place and come back with some change in my pockets. Who'd a guy buy cows from around here?"

"Besides me?"

"Thought you were trying to build up."

"I am, but sometimes money talks louder than a fella's ideas of his own business. Not saying I'm ready to sell any but a few for meat, those that shouldn't probably breed with their bull grandfather."

Roland thought for a minute and then said, "And if we were partnered up on this, we'd best share bulls as well. Maybe I'd best bring in some new blood."

They talked on for a few more minutes about prices and availability and whether a drive from the sale up in Boise would be worth it. Then Roland promised to come by the next day and get lined out on what Abe would need if he took his family to town. Then when he'd mounted up, he turned his horse around, and said, "Forgot to tell you Mike's starting to train and put me to work in the black-smithin' business. Got more work than he can handle. See ya tomorrow. I'm getting a little excited about how things seem to be falling into place."

Abe watched him ride off and had a good feeling for the young man, and he was pleased that things did seem to be working out for the couple after their spell of hard luck. He also couldn't help but think that for all the unknowns in the situation, this might be the missing piece of the puzzle for himself in terms of being able to get away and go check on Helga and his son.

Next day, Roland returned and the men went over some of the items that needed looking after. The young man asked for some work that needed attention if everything went along well and he didn't have much to do. Abe took him back out to the fencing project and showed him how he wanted the logs cut and connected. Roland promised to show up again the next day bright and early so the family could get started on their trip to town.

It was nearly dark when Abe pulled the buggy to a stop in front of Mattie and Ollie's house. He took the baby from Sa-rah while she climbed down, and then gave her back so he could carry the sleeping Isaiah. The house was nearly dark inside and when he knocked there was no answer.

"Maybe we should just go in," Sa-rah said.

Abe pushed the door open, and Sa-rah called out Mattie's name. She was answered by a thumping from the downstairs bedroom. It was Mattie hitting the floor with her cane, and calling out "Who is it? Who's there? I've got a gun in here."

Sa-rah identified herself and went quickly into the room. Abe laid Isaiah down on some cushions and followed her in with the one lamp that was lit. Mattie was lying in bed surrounded by a pile of pillows and holding out her arms for little DoraLee.

"Oh, my dears, my dears, I'm so glad you've come. And you, my little sweetie." She cuddled the baby in her arms and began softly humming.

Sa-rah sat down on the edge of the bed, moved some pillows, and reached for the woman's hand. "Your hand is cold. Do we need to make a fire for you?"

"It's still summer dear. I've never had a fire in the summer and won't start now. I'm not cold at all, only my hands are cold and that's their problem. Besides, now I've got this sweet baby here to warm me up. How are you all, my dears?"

"We're all fine, Mattie. But what about you? We got a message you wanted to see us, and and we were worried, so we came right away."

"Oh everyone exaggerates these days," Mattie said. "Probably some ne'er-do-well friend of Ollie's. He has the strangest friends, you know. It was just that I told him if he ever knew anyone going out your way to have them tell Martha and Mike that I'd like to see you." She paused, and went on, "There are a few things we ought to talk about." DoraLee began fussing and Sa-rah reached out to take her, slipping the baby under her shawl to feed her.

"Well, I'd best carry in our things and stable the horse. All right to do the same as we've done before?" Abe asked.

"Of course," Mattie laughed, "it's not like either of us old folks has taken up horse-riding lately."

All of them were tired and went to bed soon after eating a small supper. Mattie told them to settle into the biggest of the two upstairs rooms. She didn't know when Ollie would be coming in, probably late, and he was using the other room.

"I'm sorry to be taking up this room. It would be best for you, I know, but those stairs."

Sometime in the middle of the night Abe was awakened by a crashing sound downstairs. He pushed himself out of bed and lit the lamp, carried it out into the hallway and looked down into the space below. Ollie was sprawled out on the floor. Abe hurried down the stairs and went to him, kneeling down to see if the man was hurt.

"I'm not hurt," Ollie said. "Goddam leg give out again."

Abe could smell the whiskey on his breath and had to say twice who he was and what he was doing there.

"Damn good to see you partner. Want to help me up them damn stairs? I'm done in, down and out for the count."

"Sure. Here, grab hold of my arm and we'll get you up."

It was a struggle but they got up the stairway and Abe helped Ollie onto the bed in the smaller room. "See you in the morning, partner."

"Good. Glad to be here, now sleep well," Abe said.

The next day began with rain, but soon the sun broke through. Abe waited for Ollie to wake up and then they had coffee and went out to the stable to talk and exercise Abe's new buggy horse, a replacement for Ginger, who was getting too old for work anymore. Sa-rah stayed with Mattie after feeding the children and setting them to play with the toys she'd brought for them.

"She's not doing so good," Ollie said when they were out in the back paddock. "Can't hardly get out of bed to use the pot we got for her. Sometimes I'm not much better off. Don't get old, son."

"Who was that you sent with the message?"

"Fella named Mercer. Worked with him on the roads before I got blowed up. Had some work for Mike to do, and said he wanted to check out that area. Did he come to your place?"

"Not that I noticed. That young man, Martha's relation, came over to give me the word."

"Well, Mattie's probably happy to see you, but not so happy with me. Didn't want me calling for any help, or nothing."

"Proud woman."

"Damn right. And she's getting worse instead of better. I figure she needs to talk to someone besides me about what she's going to do. Still got a little money put away from Sa-rah's father, and we got this house clear of debt now. I don't need much, and still have a little left from the road department for their screw-up on my leg, what used to be my leg." He pulled his flask out and offered it to Abe who was brushing the horse.

"Too early for me, my friend."

"Never too early for me these days. Sometimes seems it's too late. So how are you folks fixed these days, if you don't mind my asking?

"We're doing all right. Starting to be able to sell a few head. I'm just worried about Helga and the boy. They were with the Indians, and I've been hearing about warfare going on where they were. I need to find out what's happened to them."

"I haven't heard much about all that business. Some folks around here are pretty down on the Indians, but there's some just as pissed at the army." He paused. "Say, listen, you ever get any more shiny stuff from that outcropping?"

"No I didn't. I thought you said it was pretty well played out, and I sure don't want that mountainside blown up."

"Well, you change your mind, I'm pretty good with a bore hole and we could do some precision tests. Not saying either of us needs it, but it's curiosity much as anything on my part."

Abe smiled and said, "I'll keep that in mind, but some of it depends on what happens with the Indians. I'm hoping I can get away to head up there and find out."

Ollie looked into his eyes and said, "Sure hope that girl and kid is all right." Then he turned to go back to the house, "Hey, I've got to meet someone down in town, but be back in a couple of hours. I'll take you down to the stockyards, introduce you to someone who might help you with the buying and selling part of your business."

"Good, we might be in the market."

They spent the day with Mattie, and Ollie when he came back. Abe made a quick trip downtown for newspapers, Sa-rah made supper and they all went to sleep at dark. They were ready to head home early the next morning. As they were saying goodbye, Mattie called Abe over to her side and whispered in his ear, "I've told her what I think now, and I hope she'll listen. That sweet girl Helga didn't deserve to be chased off. She is family."

Abe thanked her and then went back downstairs to help Sa-rah gather up their things and move the children out to the buggy. Once they were packed up, Sa-rah went back inside, saying she needed one more goodbye with Mattie. Ollie came outside carrying what looked to be a brand-new rifle.

"Don't hunt no more myself," he said. "You might as well have this." He handed it over to Abe. It was one of the new Winchesters, and Abe was impressed.

"Are you sure?" he asked.

"Won it on a bet. You'll get more use out of it than I ever will. And keep me in mind if anything changes about the 'mother lode' up there."

"I will, and thanks for the introduction to MacCallister. Could be a useful contact when I get more into the cattle market."

On the way back home, Sa-rah said she wanted to talk with Abe about Mattie and some of what was on her mind, and she went right ahead into it, "She started off by saying she's ready to die, but there's a few things still left to tidy up. Those were her words."

"Have they said what's wrong with her?"

"Her Doctor said it's nothing specific. She says she was both a slave and a free woman here on earth, but now she's ready to be truly free. And she says she's tired all the time, even when she's sleeping. Oh, Mattie."

"Did she say what those things are, that have to be taken care of?" He reined hard to the right to avoid a small boulder in the roadway. Sa-rah and DoraLee fell against him and the baby started to wake up, but Sa-rah made soft sounds and she went on sleeping.

"Funny how similar babies and old people are," she said. "Anyway, yes, she said she wants to be buried out on our place, wherever we choose."

She was quiet for awhile.

"That would be all right," Abe said. "We can find a good place, somewhere we can dig and there's not many rocks. I'm sure Hawk Man and Lefty wouldn't mind, long as it's out of the way."

"She also said she's still got some money put away from my Father. She wants Ollie to have that house and a little of the money, but most of it is for these children. 'Never did get to know any of my own grandchildren,' she said, 'so I want to make up for that.' Then she stopped talking for a long time and I didn't know if she'd dozed off or was just thinking."

"Maybe she can do both at the same time," Abe smiled. "She's pretty special."

"Oh, I know. I don't know what I'll do without her. Even though I don't see her very much anymore, at least I've known she's there if I need her."

They rode on in silence for a ways, and then Abe asked, "Was there anything else?"

"Yes. She's quite worried about Ollie. Doesn't like some of his friends, says he's drinking most of the time now, and won't admit it to her."

"I noticed that myself, but he's always been a drinker."

"She said she's afraid he'll get beat up and robbed someday, especially if he doesn't have to come home and look in on her."

"Did she ask for us to do anything?"

"Not really. Oh, and she thinks it's wonderful that Martha's young relations have the place she and Ollie built. One more thing about Ollie, and she apologized for even bringing it up. Doesn't want us to do anything about it, just try to keep track of him somehow, when we come to town or however."

They drove on in silence for awhile. Isaiah woke up from his short nap in the space behind them and said he was hungry. They stopped for a break and some mid-day food, and Abe got out the newspapers he'd gotten in town, and read them over again. The news from the Indian struggle was vague and not especially favorable to the Army. A couple of correspondent reporters blamed the General for being too slow in the chase and for needlessly losing one battle and some skirmishes. One big headline even said, "SAVAGES EMBARRASS ARMY".

Helga was unable to keep track of the days, and although her pain was lessening, the constant difficulties of travel and movement kept causing the wound to drain. Moon Fish came back from their place in the caravan as often as she could, but it was clear to both of them that the older woman was suffering from the strain of the journey almost as much as Helga. Indigo was a big help, washing out her dressings and clothing at every chance they had when camping or moving slowly beside any waterway.

There were occasionally other skirmishes, and every time she heard gunfire, Helga was overcome with the grief and loneliness caused by losing Carl. The rumor among the women was that they would soon be moving through the Stinking Waters area, in the place the white man called Yellowstone. How far it was to the buffalo country, nobody seemed to know, and now there was talk that the only safety for all of them was to try and make it to Grandmother's Land in the north, where there were already other Indians who could take them in and help them prepare for winter. The name of Sitting Bull was mentioned to her more than once, and Lefty told her that the warrior had led the Lakota people to safety from the army after some big battles to the east of where they now were.

A time came when they were told they could stop and rest for a couple of days, and during this resting time, Helga found herself feeling much better. On the second day of this stop-over, Lefty came to her and said one of the chiefs wished to speak with her. He said if she felt strong enough, he would come back toward evening and take her to eat at the man's camp. She agreed and asked "What about Indigo?"

"This man, he is Joseph, and he likes all children. He is their guard on this travelling. I'm sure it would be all right to bring the boy."

When the sun was dropping toward the mountains in the west, he came after her and the boy. By supporting her carefully, he was able to help her to cross the camp area until they reached a tipi with canvas patches where the hides had been torn, probably in the same battle when she was wounded. Lefty said, "You are welcome here." He motioned to give them places to sit between himself and the Chief. He held out his hand to Indigo and they clasped each other's forearms in the Indian way of greeting. The man spoke softly, and Lefty translated, "I hope you are doing well and healing from your wound. I know you are weak so I will not keep you long and you may speak in your own language if it is easier for you. You are a very brave woman and your story will be told around many campfires among out people."

"Thank you, but I didn't know what I was doing. I was so afraid."

"Bravery often comes from fear, they are like brothers who strengthen one another."

A young woman brought in bowls of meat for Helga and Indigo. Then she left and quickly came back with servings for Lefty and the chief. When they were all taken care of, she again went out. The chief blessed the food and they all ate in silence. When they finished, the woman was called and the bowls taken away. The chief took out a pipe, filled it and passed it to Lefty who lit it, offering it to the directions, the Earth and Creator, then he passed it to Helga who took it in her one strong hand.

"You don't need to smoke, but touch it with your mouth."

Helga did that and handed it to Indigo, who very seriously did the same thing. Joseph spoke quietly and Lefty said, "He say this young one is strong and will grow to be great."

Helga smiled and Indigo just looked down at his hands.

"Are you healing now?" Joseph asked.

"Yes. You are the one who gave me water when I was very thirsty, very dry. I thank you so much for that."

"He say he remember you. Tied on horse, very dry."

"Best water I have ever tasted."

"He say, good, water is life. He want you to know he is very sad for losing your young man. Says young man very brave, save many lives by breaking Army big gun."

"I am very sad also. He was good to me." There was a pause and silence.

"Chief say he has question for you if you can talk with him now."

"Yes, say I will try to answer him." Indigo leaned against her good arm and nestled there.

Joseph spoke slowly for a long time. Lefty waited until the man was quiet, then he translated. "He say, you are white woman, now live with his people. It may be you can tell him answer to his question. He ask why white man's God allow them take his home, kill his people, make us run from fighting. Make us have to kill white people. Why?"

Almost without knowing it was happening, Helga began crying. She tried to hold back the tears and Indigo looked up into her face and started crying as well. She mumbled to the Chief that she was all right, not hurting, just very sad. Indigo wiped his face on her sleeve and buried his face in her shawl. Joseph made a sign with his hands.

Lefty said, "He say you don't have to answer."

"Tell him, I don't know the answer and I want to know the same thing. It's horrible. I hate this fighting and all these poor people being chased, hurt, and killed. I hate it." She wiped her face and looked over at Joseph who was sitting still, with a kindly expression on his motionless face. She lowered her head and said in a quiet but strong voice, "I hate all this, and I almost hate God."

Lefty translated. Joseph replied. "Joseph say, maybe the white man God is not God." He raised his voice and called a name, and a young woman came inside. "This is his daughter," Lefty said. "He's asking her to bring you something he has for you." The young woman went out, and the two men talked in their own language. When she returned she was carrying something wrapped in a black cloth. She handed it to her father.

Joseph unwrapped what was revealed to be a Bible. He held it carefully in his hands and then began speaking, with Lefty softly translating, "The white man want us to live on one of his reservations. He want to give us what we need to farm. He want to give cows that make milk. He say he will give us place to learn how to read his books. All of this good. If we can no longer live in our homeland where our fathers and our fathers' fathers always live, we will need these things, we will need help to live in new way. If we do not live in new way, we always be running away. This how I see things now. But there is one thing the white man want to give to us that Joseph not want, not good for us, and we must say no to this one thing. He want to give us churches, missions, but these we not want, these we no need, because they will make us fight about Creator, fight about God. This is what I see the white man do, he fights about his God is better than any other man's God."

"Indians all have One Creator, and all Indians can talk to Creator in own way. Nothing to fight about, but already some of our people becoming like the white man, believing in his God and fighting other

Indians about this God." He paused, and then said. "I want you to tell all the white people you know that we do not hate them, even when they take our homes and kill our women and children. And tell them we do not want to fight anymore."

Helga lifted her head and looked into Joseph's eyes. "If I go to live among my own people again, I will tell them what you say," she said in their Indian language.

He handed the Bible and its cloth wrapping to her and said for Lefty to say to her, "Now, this book is yours. You can understand it. Someday may help you. I cannot use. You take."

Helga held the Bible in her good hand, trying not to disturb Indigo who was now asleep.

"Thank you. I will care for this. It is a very special gift...One more thing," she said, "that day you gave me water, I thought I was going to die...When you gave me the water, I knew that you came from God, from the real God, whoever that is. I know you are a man of God, and I will always remember you for your kindness."

Lefty translated and Joseph nodded his head. Then he said "We are relatives."

Two days later the procession of wounded and exhausted people wound their way through the strange landscape of the Yellowstone basin. At one point, gunshots echoed off the walls of a canyon they were passing through. It was difficult to tell which direction they came from, but sometime later, Helga saw a few white people being escorted toward the front of the caravan of Indians, and she wondered what would happen to them.

That night, Lefty came to where she was camping with Ellen and her family. He came alone and asked to speak with her privately. The two of them walked a ways away and Lefty helped her down a short rocky place to a log they could sit on. When they were settled, he asked, "How is it for you, traveling? Are you stronger now?"

"Yes, it's getting much easier, but I so wish this was all over with, that we could just stop and stay somewhere."

"That may happen for you. Now that you are alone among us, again with no man. It could be very hard in the next few moons and who knows what will happen in the wintertime. I am also worried about my mother, Moon Fish. I don't think she can live this way much longer. She is beginning to talk of being left behind so she will not be a burden to us. It is our way, but I don't want that."

"I wish I could help more."

"It may be you will. I must tell you some hard new things we have learned. We have two white women and one man as prisoners, but we don't want them. Chiefs say we should not hurt them, have told young men that anymore who harms a captive will be left behind for the army. The chiefs say they will let these three white people go, leave them to find their way back to where they came from. That is one thing…"

"It is generous, with everything that has happened," Helga said.

"We do not kill women who are not fighting us." He paused. "One other thing. Today we capture half-Indian who we know. He is scout for army. He tell Joseph army is very angry about white woman who killed a soldier."

Helga quickly covered her mouth with her hand, catching her breath and holding it. She motioned for him to go on.

"We do not know what will happen to us, if we will be able to fight our way to Grandmother's Land in the north, or if we must surrender to protect our women and children and old people. This scout-man say army want to hang this white woman if they get her…"

Helga felt herself beginning to tremble. "That's terrible," was all she could say.

"I was there when chiefs were arguing about what to do with white prisoners, and also what to do with you. I asked if I could speak. They say yes. I tell them about my mother and her weakness. I ask them if they could put you and Moon Fish on horses and let you go away from us. When they let other white people free, you find each other. You say this old woman need help, she is your grandmother. Your home many, many days travel, long ways back was burned, your man killed and two of you been with us. You hurt and we not leave you to die."

"I would have to lie."

"You would lie to live and to return to your people, even to Abe and Sa-rah. You have white woman clothing?"

"Yes, I've kept some."

"Moon Fish also have. I don't want to see you and her try to go any farther with us. When this over, I find you. Is only way you to be safe."

"But it is also dangerous. What if someone, a soldier, recognizes me?"

"Cut your hair, and wear hat covers face. You think about all of this. I come back in morning." Then he stood and helped her up. "You will be safe only in this way. I know."

"What will become of you?"

"I will go with these people where they go. I will live."

The next morning, Lefty came to get her and Indigo. He was leading three horses. One of them carried an older white woman wearing a sunbonnet and riding side-saddle. When they came closer, Helga could see that the white woman was Moon Fish, but she was barely recognizable without her usual native clothing. Helga had cut her hair as suggested and was wearing a man's narrow-brim hat, a long green skirt and a shirtwaist that didn't match, but was also a shade of green. Indigo was wearing a denim overall with pant legs that had obviously been clumsily cut off. His braid was tucked into his shirt collar and didn't show.

"Moon Fish, that is you, isn't it?" Helga asked.

"Yes," the woman said, looking down from horseback. Then she smiled her familiar smile, "But don't tell anyone. Now I am Kate again."

Lefty somewhat unpacked a set of bags that carried food, and blankets, and showed what was in them to Helga, asking if she had anything else to add. She handed him Joseph's Bible and a small bag with her hairbrush and a mirror. These she had carefully taken care of throughout the time they were fleeing the Army, and she was pleased to have protected them.

Indigo walked up the one of the horses and asked Lefty, "Name?"

"Whatever you want to be." He reached around the boy and lifted him up and on.

"I want to take my bow and arrows," he said.

"Sorry, but that way know you are red-hair Indian. You must be white boy now." He then eased Helga up onto a horse, helping her adjust the reins and stirrups to make her as secure and comfortable as possible.

Lefty led them out of the camp and down the trail. He gave directions to Helga as to how far to follow the stream they were alongside and where to cross over. He said that the prisoners the chiefs would free later in the day would have the same directions.

"Stay ahead of them if you can, but not so far that you don't know where they are from their fire at night or the sound of their horses calling to yours. I now tell them we seen other white people. Remember your farm was burned out, your man killed by Indians, and you do not know where you are. The Indians kept you with them until you could ride with your wounded shoulder. I will tell them these thing. They will take you. I tell them to do this."

A week after their return from Silver City, Ollie showed up driving a wagon pulled by a matched team of black horses. Isaiah was the first to see him coming and ran down the road to meet him. The man reached down, pulled the boy up beside himself and handed him the reins.

"Not too fast now, just easy."

Isaiah sat very straight and carefully wrapped the reins around his wrists as he'd seen his father do. Then he said "Giddap," and the horses moved ahead.

Abe was unloading some lengths of metal he brought over from Mike's shop. They were to be fitted together to make a gate across the road. In the back of his mind he was preparing for when he would go away the next time, seeking Helga and his other son. He wanted to fashion a swinging gate across the road between two fence lines. The gate would have a bell attached so Sa-rah or anyone else at the house could hear it if someone came through.

"Stop'em here, young fellow." Ollie said and waited for Abe to walk over to the wagon.

"Hello, Ollie, what's up?"

"The old lady, she's in back here." He gestured into the back of the wagon at a long narrow box.

Abe stepped to where he could see the coffin in the back. It was simply made of polished planks and had a wooden cross lashed to it. Abe let out a large sigh and said, "She's gone?"

"Yeah, three days back. I couldn't get here no faster."

"How'd she go?"

"I think it was good...I wasn't there, found her when I come in. She looked peaceful and the bed wasn't mussed or nothing."

"Sa-rah will be hurt. But we have to tell her. Pull over into the shade there."

Ollie took the reins from the boy and guided the team under the one tree in the yard. Isaiah climbed down and ran to tell his mother to come out. The man slid down and was able to reach the ground by landing on his one good leg. He reached out his hand and Abe took it. They held together that way for a good long time until Ollie wiped his nose and face and pulled away to begin walking toward the house.

Sa-rah came outside with the baby. "Oh no, please, it isn't so," she said. "No!"

Abe reached out for her and she handed DoraLee to him and climbed up into the wagon, kneeling beside the box. The men moved away and left her alone with her grief.

Isaiah climbed up to be beside her and asked. "Mama, what's wrong? Where's Mattie?"

Sa-rah just put her arm around him and fell forward onto the box.

Ollie asked Abe, "Where shall we take it, or should I unhook the team for now?"

"Not sure. She did talk to Sa-rah about being buried here, but we haven't really had time to think about it."

"I think she always liked to walk down by the creek, over that way. Not where it'll flood, but where she can hear the water running."

"Sounds all right. It's getting late though. How about you unhook and turn them out over near that paddock. Not a lot for them to eat, but some."

"I brought grain."

"I'll take a walk over there and look for a place to dig." Abe started off and then stopped. "Unless you want to come, too."

"No, that's all right. It's your place," Ollie said. "Besides, I'm beat."

"Then tell Sa-rah where I went when you can. I won't be long."

He walked down the slope toward the creek and then beside it, where Isaiah and he made a trail some time ago. He couldn't help thinking how hard this would be for Sa-rah. Mattie was her last relative besides him and the children. For himself, it was a reminder of just how much he missed her father and the friendship they'd had. He turned back upslope at an opening in the willows and walked to a piece of flat ground. If it wasn't too rocky, it would be a good place. The space could even be made big enough that it would be a good place for their family's cemetery. He looked around and then paced out the area that could be cleared of brush and still be fairly level. Probably enough for six or seven plots. Then he suddenly realized that Sa-rah would want to spend time out here, and he added room for a bench or two in his design ideas. Suddenly he was overcome with a wave of sadness. Mattie was gone, and after all she'd done for him, for them, there was no more time, no more chance to thank her, to be with her and feel the strength and warmth that came from the set of her chin and the gleam in her eyes. Gone, and now this life was one person smaller.

He picked up a broken stick and traced the outline of a hole large enough to take the box. Then he drew the shape of a cross in the dirt and laid the stick down where the head would go. He started for the house, wondering what, if anything, he could say to Sa-rah. Was there anything that could help her through a time like this? Then he again felt the tightness in his own throat and sensed the warmth of a few tears sliding down his cheeks.

The next morning, Abe and Ollie walked out to the site carrying shovels and a pick-ax. Isaiah clamored to come along. At first Abe turned him down, but then Martha rode into the yard and climbed down to run and embrace Sa-rah. Abe told Isaiah to come along with the men.

The day warmed quickly and the work went slowly. Ollie insisted on digging by standing on his metal leg and pushing the shovel blade into the ground with his good one. Isaiah also begged for turns to dig. Abe was left to pry and twist the pick to dislodge the few large rocks that showed up. With a lot of hard work, the hole got deeper.

Back at the house, Martha took a jar of dried apples and some other ingredients out of her bag and, after she and Sa-rah had a good cry together, she began to work on an apple pie. "Always was her favorite," she said.

Sa-rah sat slowly rocking as she nursed DoraLee. Martha said she thought they should be singing something, like Mattie always did when working in the kitchen. She was quiet for a long moment and then led off with the first verse of "Rock of Ages." Sa-rah hesitantly joined in, singing softly so as not to disturb the baby who was falling into sleep for her morning nap.

When the men returned, they ate and then went back outside to shift the box onto a small cart that the two of them could maneuver to the gravesite. Abe and Ollie managed to slide the box out of the cart and tug on ropes enough to get it to the hole. Isaiah helped keep the ropes from tangling. There were two planks laid crosswise that they shoved the box onto and Ollie planted the temporary wooden cross. They were wiping their sweat away when the two women appeared. Just then they heard a holler from back near the house.

"Where are you-all? Be right there."

It was Mike, who must have just arrived. Ollie yelled back to let him know where they were, and in a couple of minutes, Mike, Roland, Abby, and their little girl appeared pushing through some brush. There was an exchange of hellos, hugs, and handshakes, and then the solemnity of the moment brought a deep silence upon the group. Sa-rah was wiping her tears away with a corner of the baby's blanket and motioning to Abe to say something.

"I'll say something," Ollie said as he stepped close to the hole and box, and put his one hand on it. "She was the best. Took in a bum like me and tried to make me into something good. I tried, but I must be too set in my ways to get good at this stage. But God knows she tried and she always forgave me for every time I messed up. She had a rough life and nobody could have blamed her if she was mean and selfish, but she was good as gold and twice as nice, like they say. I'm going to love her always." He stepped back and pulled a handkerchief from his pocket, wiped a couple of tears away and blew his nose.

Martha spoke next, saying, "I loved her too, still do. We used to talk together a lot, mostly about how strange it was to have ended up clear out here where most of what we'd known back in the east didn't exist. And she said, didn't do any good to miss what you don't have. That was so like her. Always looking for the good in life, in people, and trusting in God to work things out." She covered her face with her hands and stepped back further.

Isaiah spoke up, "Can I say something?" He was standing next to his Papa who patted him on the head and nodded yes. "I like Mattie because she played with me." He looked down and then turned his back on the box and his shoulders shook with his crying. Sa-rah came close to him and put her free arm around him and drew him close to her waist.

"I can't say much, because there's too much to say," she said. "She was better than a mother to me, and my best friend, and I'm going to…" She gasped and then began weeping. Abe moved to be next to her and looked away into the distance.

Then he spoke softly, "The valley of the shadow of death, we are always passing through that valley in this life. Mattie taught me that. And she taught me that we don't know what God's plans are for any of us, but He always has a plan. She often told me, 'If you can build a house, you can build a life.' She was the first one to tell me that Sa-rah, we called her Sarah Beth then, she told me that this girl was waiting for me to notice her." He coughed and cleared his throat.

"There's nobody can ever take her place, but I know the angels in Heaven are rejoicing to have her up there among them now..." he paused, then asked if anyone had anything more to say. There was silence, so he said, "Dust to dust, ashes to ashes, from this life into the next."

After a long silence Martha began softly singing "Amazing Grace," and the others joined in. When the last words of the hymn drifted away into the great emptiness of the sky above them, Ollie stepped forward and took hold of the end of one of the ropes under the box, and the other three men took hold of the other rope ends. Abe told Isaiah to pull out the planks when they lifted up the box and when he'd done that, they lowered it into the hole. The first clods of dirt hit the box with a hollow sound, almost like a drum, almost like thunder, but really not like any other sound in this world.

CHAPTER 20

Crises

The sun was just coming up as Lefty helped both of the women into their white-man saddles, and boosted Indigo up to his. He walked along in front of them for quite some time. Then when he was sure they were headed in the right direction, he stopped and stood by them, reaching up to take their hands in his, one after another.

"Can you ride?" he asked each of them. Moon Fish nodded yes, patted him on his cheek, and looked away so he wouldn't see the tears on her cheeks. Indigo nodded yes and sat up straight, holding the reins of this new horse in both hands.

Helga replied as she hitched up her skirt above her knees, "I'm all right for riding, if it wasn't for this white woman skirt."

The man held her hand for a long time, his lips moving in time with the nodding of his head. "You go now. You will be safe. I can take care of you with song and spirit helpers, you take care of boy and my mother." Then he turned quickly and trotted back toward the camp.

They took several breaks during the day and had to figure out how to get one another mounted again each time after they rested. Moon Fish was too weak to pull herself up alone, so she was put on her horse first, putting one foot on Helga's bent knee. Helga would find a log or boulder to use since she couldn't use her injured shoulder for pulling herself up. This usually worked, but once she had to have Indigo get down on all fours so she could stand on his back and throw one leg over the saddle. Indigo was the only one who could pull up by himself, but it was quite a struggle.

When evening time came into the woods, it began to rain. They sought shelter under a thick spreading pine tree and made a small camping area by cleaning away the branches and stones. They tethered the horses and sent Indigo to gather armfuls of grass for feed. Moon Fish lit a small fire of broken branches and Helga sharpened sticks for holding pieces of meat over the fire.

While they were eating, Helga kept looking at Moon Fish, now Kate, she reminded herself, thinking how different she looked now. "You look so much like a white woman," she said.

"Well I am, you know."

"I see that now. Never thought about it before."

"And you," the older woman said, "you look more like an Indian, even though you're wearing white woman clothes. And you know your chopped off hair, that's the custom for these Indian women. When they have a death in their family, they cut their hair, and most of them do it themselves, so it looks like yours does now. But I doubt the white people we run into will know about that. If they ask, we'll tell them that I cut it because you couldn't take care of your long hair with only one arm."

"Unless it's the soldiers, and we don't want them to remember how I looked."

"Mama, I'm tired and I want to go back with my friends."

"I'm sorry, son. I miss our friends too. Now you just crawl under this blanket and we'll try to keep you dry in close to the trunk of the tree."

It stopped raining, and the next day they were off again with first light. The drizzle started again, but none of them had gotten very wet during the night. They continued to follow the creek flowing downstream as Lefty instructed, wondering when or if they would encounter anyone else. Then Helga heard voices. They were coming from up ahead and sounded like they came from the other side of the creek. Kate held up her hand to signal a stop.

When Helga pulled her horse up beside her, the other woman spoke very softly, saying, "Let me do the talking. I'll tell them I'm your mother and that you're still somewhat in shock for the wound and the whole experience of getting captured by the Indians." Then she gave a loud "halloo" and urged her horse forward. It took only a couple of minutes before they saw the small group of people across the creek. There was a man leading two horses, and on those were a grown woman and someone who looked much younger. Kate waved her arm and shouted that they were friendly and needed help.

The man spoke to the other two and dropped the reins of the horses. He came down to the edge of the water. "Who are you? What are you doing out here like that?"

"Can we come across so I don't have to shout?" Kate asked.

"Sure, go back up a ways, better footing where there's sand." He walked upstream and then pointed to a good place to cross. Once they were on his side, he motioned for them to follow him back to the others, who had dismounted and were waiting.

"Like I said, who are you, and what are you doing out here?" he repeated his earlier questions, and moved to stand protectively between the two women.

Kate brushed her hair from her face and re-made the bun on top of her head, replacing her bonnet, and said, "So glad to find someone out here, and white people even. We've been captives of those Indians until yesterday when they gave us these horses and let us leave. We had no idea where to go. It was just by chance and the grace of God that we found you. This is my daughter and her son."

The woman spoke, "What do you need, where do you want go?"

Kate said, "We need someone to travel with who can take us to civilization. We've been with these savages for over a month. About two weeks ago, their camp was over-run by some soldiers and my girl was wounded in the shoulder. She's still so afraid that she doesn't talk much."

"I noticed the wound dressing. Is it painful?" The other woman said. She addressed this to Helga, who shook her head up and down and mumbled something.

Kate said, "Only some of the time now. It's when she's riding the horse that's the worst. But she's not been complaining."

The man led their horses to some brush where he could tie them, and then came back. He reached up to help Indigo down and then Kate. When he went to help Helga, she pulled back and then let herself slide off on the other side of the horse. The man took their horses and tied them in the same area as his own.

The older woman told the younger one to get some food out of their saddlebags, and went on to say, "Ida, be sure to get a cloth to set things on." She turned to Kate and said, "I'm Emma Cowan. Frank Carpenter there is my brother and the girl is Ida, his daughter. And you are?"

"Oh, well, I'm Kate Simpson and my daughter is Helen Rogers. The boy is Charles. She lost her husband in a raid on the place they were homesteading back in that Idaho country. I had just arrived to visit. Terrible things happening in this part of the country. I do believe in the last days and if this isn't the beginning, I don't want to be around for worse days."

"Are you trying to get somewhere in particular?"

Kate looked at the woman with a cautious smile, "Anywhere in particular will do."

"Well, we're from a place called Radersburg, but right now we're just trying to get to Bozeman. A friendly savage who could speak a little to us told us which way to head, and we'll keep going until we find our way out of this awful wilderness."

"Might we join you for a little ways? We have provisions of our own that we could share, or we can just follow along separate."

"Oh, my dear, we're good Christian folk and we wouldn't think of leaving you on your own, you'll be with us now." She called out. "Frank, can you get us some water in a pot for some mush?" She confided to Kate, "We haven't eaten yet today."

While they were sharing the mush and some hard bread Kate pulled out, Emma asked her brother to tell these folks how they'd been released by the Indians.

"They gave us these two horses, but told me I would have to walk. The one who could talk English was called Poker Joe, and he was supposed to take us on our way. He had his own horse and when we got out of the main camp, he pulled me up behind him and we all moved along pretty good. That was yesterday. We come to a place where he said he was going back. He gave us directions and said three days would get us to Bozeman and then we could go where we wanted to, but he said move right along. Don't stop, even at night, otherwise some Indians might find us and not know we'd been let go by their chiefs."

Emma then asked Kate where she was headed.

"Well, since we don't have a home to go back to, I suppose any place will do, but I'd like to get to Idaho where I have some relatives who could take us in for a while."

"I think you should come on to Bozeman with us and then we'll see if there isn't a way to do what you said." She looked over at Helga, whose face was in her hands. "Is there anything we can do for her? I have some healing ointment here somewhere but it might burn too much."

"No, she's all right, she's healing. Those Indians had some poultice medicine they made out of plants and it seemed to do wonders. It's just going to take a while to get over the shock of losing her husband and the hard times we had with those Indians. Not that they didn't treat us the same as they were doing for themselves, but you were with them, it was pretty awful."

"Oh, I know, don't know what I would have done if we had to go on like that. Ida here was beside herself not being able to get clean."

"That's not true, Auntie." It was the first time she'd spoken since they'd all joined up. "I just didn't want to wash with all those savages down at the water with me."

Kate smiled and said, "I know the feeling."

The rain was stopping and the clouds seemed to have moved on away overhead. As they traveled north they came to and passed by the Mammoth Hot Springs as indicated by a sign beside the boiling, stinking pools. They kept on heading north. They did stop to rest some during the nights, but not much. Helga became concerned about Kate's health, but the old woman told her she was doing as well as could be expected and that she was going to make it to that town, Bozeman, no matter what.

The second night when they laid down for a short sleep, Indigo, who'd been so quiet ever since they left the Indians, whispered to his mother, "I don't like the way they talk about our friends, about the savages."

She told him to keep quiet and not to let it bother him. After all, she said, that man lost his wife and the woman lost her husband in the fighting.

The boy replied, "My friends told me that all the white people are the same, they're all our enemies."

"But that's not true," she whispered back. "We're white people again, you and me, and we're not enemies to the Indians. Now go to sleep. We have to get up and go again very soon."

After three days with no incidents other than the discomfort of the trail ride and one of the horses coming up lame, they could see the smoke of town ahead of them. Indigo chose to walk and let Ida have his horse when hers started limping, and he walked along leading that animal just as Mr. Carpenter was walking and leading Emma's horse.

At one point in the early hours of the third day since they'd been together, they were discovered by a patrol of troopers, also headed back to Bozeman from a scouting mission. Helga quickly pulled her hat down more to cover her face, and Kate put herself and her horse between the younger women and the soldiers. Nothing came of the encounter except that they were escorted toward the town in what was probably a more direct route than what they'd been taking.

When they reached the outskirts of the settlement, and the soldiers turned off to return to their barracks, Emma leaned back and told Kate that they were going to get rooms for the next day or so, and she didn't know if Kate could pay for that. They, themselves, were going to have to use some kind of credit from the local bank to pay because they didn't have any money with them. Kate told her not to worry, they had a little money they could use. Later when she and Helga were settled in their room, the younger woman asked her where she got any money.

"I've had it for a long time, for something like this. Now why don't we ask the host for a tub and a kettle so we can take some baths?" She smiled and said, "Without any savages looking." Helga smiled back, and then laughed for the first time in a long time.

"What is it?" Kate asked.

"Just thinking what those women would've done when we would all go down to the river and bathe, and some of the women would be nursing their babies, and others without their dresses, and the men shouting and laughing from somewhere nearby."

"Well, I daresay, my dear, I'll wager it took you a bit of getting used to yourself."

"They were always nice to us though, I'll say that for them."

Indigo was looking out of their second-floor window that faced onto a busy street. "I think the army's coming back down the street."

The two women joined him at the window and watched as a double line of mounted troops and a pack train of mules passed below them.

"Maybe that's a good thing," Helga said. "Less chance of a problem for me with that many of them gone."

"Better for us, maybe, but probably worse for our people out there. I'll go arrange for a tub to be brought up, and a lot of water to heat up. You put some more of that coal in the stove, and Indigo, you can just keep watching out there for us."

The boy stood up straight and gave a salute, imitating a soldier.

"Where'd you learn that?" his mama asked.

"Lefty showed me. He said white army men do that when someone tells them to do something."

The next morning, Helga was sick to her stomach and stayed in bed while the other two went down to the dining room for a morning meal. As she lay there with the chamber pot within reach for the spasms of dry vomiting she was going through, she was convinced that this was not sickness, or food poisoning. It had to be the sign of new life growing inside of her. Although she'd experienced hardly any of this with Indigo, she'd heard enough about it to be aware that this was not at all uncommon. She would ask Moon Fish, or Kate, when she returned from downstairs, but combined with the absence of her last two moon-times, this was enough to make her feel quite certain. She began staying with Carl some time even before the people broke camp and began their flight from the Army, but by counting backwards, she realized that this change likely could have had its beginning around the time of the first battles, when they still had their own tipi, and some small amount of privacy.

She gagged again, but nothing came up. This was to be somewhat expected, given that the small amount of food they'd had along the way had been suddenly followed by the big dinner of the night before. She could only hope that it would pass quickly, and she would regain the appetite she remembered so well from her first pregnancy.

As she lay there waiting and hoping for the nausea to leave her, she thought of Carl and his surprising gentleness with her. It was in such contrast with the things she heard around the camps about his bravery and exploits in battle, the ferocity with which he fought and the great things he'd done to try to save the people. Now there would be this, something he left behind in death, something she would do everything in her power to protect and raise in his honor, and in gratitude for all that he'd done for her when he'd hadn't needed to. She thought how easily he could have just taken her into his lodge and made her his servant, and neglected her while treating her like a slave as some others of the tribe might have done, her being nothing more than a helpless and somewhat useless "white woman."

She heard Indigo's voice through the door, and then they were back in the room. The boy came quickly to her side, but then saw the pot and its contents and quickly turned away from the embrace he'd been about to give.

"Mama, are you all right? That smell bad."

"Yes, I'm all right. Do you think you could be a big boy and carry it down to where it can be emptied and cleaned out? I think I won't need it for that anymore."

"Yes, Mama. But I don't know where."

Kate interrupted and said, "You know where that door was open to the back of this house? That's where it goes, there's a barrel out there. I saw it when I emptied it early this morning."

He picked up the pot and held it out away from his face. "All right. Ugh."

As soon as he was gone and Kate closed the door behind him, Helga said, "I'm not sick, I mean not with an illness. I haven't had my monthlies and I think this is why."

"I thought so," the older woman said. "You've been standing differently, so I'm happy for you. It's almost a miracle that you could keep it with what we've been through. It will be a strong child."

"And a brave one, like his father."

"Or her father," the woman smiled and poured some water from the pitcher into the basin. "Are you ready to get up and wash yourself, and get that taste out of your mouth?"

"I think so."

As she was cleaning herself up, Kate told her that she'd met someone at the breakfast table who was hauling goods on a wagon to Boise. "He said there would be room in the wagon for one person and if the other two of us would take turns riding horseback, he would take us along. He said he'd do it in exchange for us cooking along the way."

"That sounds fine. But I hope we can stop at night and sleep, not like it was with Mr. Carpenter."

"I think the man was scared and only doing what he'd been told to do by the Indian, that one they call Poker Joe."

Helga wiped her face and hands and said she was feeling much better already. Kate unwrapped food she'd brought back from the dining hall and Helga tried to eat. Then she said, "You know you speak white man talk really well. Especially since you haven't been speaking it, for how long now?"

"Nearly thirty-five years. Lefty and I would practice every once in a while, and I did talk with Abe and Sa-rah, but you're right. I've surprised myself, but it seemed to come right back almost like it was never gone."

Roland had gone north to check on his property, and to see if he could find out more about what the news articles were calling the Nez Pierce War. Abe was getting impatient to find out anything at all. When Mike needed some iron-work pieces delivered to a new bank being built in Silver City, Abe jumped at the chance.

Sa-rah baked sweet rolls from Mattie's recipe and packed them up for Ollie. The memories associated with the recipe brought tears to her eyes, and she knew it would be a long time before she would get over this loss. Even losing her own real mother hadn't been this sad for her, but then maybe that was because she had been so much younger then. A few days after the burial, Isaiah was the one who found the best stone for marking the grave, and was very excited when he and his father were able to shove it onto a sled and have Ginger drag it down the hill and over to the site. Now he was all eagerness to start carving her name and whatever else would go on it. Sa-rah told him he'd have to wait until they had a chance to talk to Ollie about that, since at the time of the burial they'd all forgotten to ask if she had any last words she wanted put on her stone. Abe promised to remember to find out when he saw the man.

He got an early start on his trip to town, but with a heavily loaded wagon he wasn't able to make it all the way before he needed to rest both himself and the horse for the night. He was able to pull into town next day before noon, find the new bank's construction site, and park the wagon so it could be unloaded. He waited there long enough to hear the admiring comments of the building's architect when he saw the first of the grill-work teller's cages being unloaded. Mike had outdone himself with some very fancy scrolling between the bars, and had confided to Abe that he hoped this would bring additional clients to him so he could afford to employ Roland more of the time when the young man returned. From the look on this client's face and the comments he made, that would seem to be a pretty sure thing, and Abe was glad for them, even if it meant that he might not get as much help from Roland.

He led the horse back through the outskirts of the growing downtown to the house. He tied the horse in the yard and knocked on the door, but Ollie didn't answer. He put the horse away, fed it some of the grain he'd left there on the last visit, and settled himself on the porch. It wasn't long before he was dozing off, still tired from two short nights in a row. It was a warm day and there was very little traffic or activity on the street in front of the house.

Sometime later, he jerked awake to a hand grabbing one of his legs and nearly pulling him out of the chair. He fought his way through the grogginess of his nap and laughed out loud when he saw that it was Ollie yanking on his leg. "Thought you was sleeping sound enough I could hack of your leg here and try it on for size. The doc down the way might be able to stitch it onto me."

Abe shook his leg free, and said, "I'm still using it or I'd consider it. How are you?"

"I'm all right, what about you?"

"Doing fine. Brought a load of ironwork in for your brother-in-law. Needed to check on you anyway."

Ollie pulled up another chair and sat down, pulled his flask out of his vest pocket and offered it to Abe.

"No thanks. Rather have something to eat first. Fell asleep without thinking about that."

"Well then come on, we'll take a short walk here and I'll buy you lunch, breakfast or whatever you want."

When they settled into their places at the little restaurant, it seemed that everyone there knew Ollie and had something to say to him. He gave up trying to introduce Abe to them all and shooed them away, saying, "Me and my partner here have got some things to talk over, so leave us be, if you don't mind."

While they waited for their food orders, he leaned over the table confidentially and said quietly, "Price of gold going steady up."

"Really."

"Could be the right time for you."

"No, Ollie, I told you, we don't need to cause all the trouble that would come of something like that. You and I know what it does to men. And I've got things pretty good now, building up the herd and all."

"I know; just thought I'd let you know. I know some folks that might be pretty interested, and would keep it under their hats."

Their food arrived and they didn't talk much while they ate. When they settled back for some more coffee, Ollie asked, "How's the family?"

"Doing well. Baby's growing fast and Isaiah is getting to the place where I think he can take care of himself pretty well. Sa-rah seems to be doing all right, too, just still missing Mattie."

"Me too. Nobody to take care of, and nobody to take care of me," he paused. "Heard anything from your young woman?"

"No. Part of the reason I wanted to come up this way, try and check the newspapers, or any other information. I have to say, I worry about her and the boy all the time."

"Well that business sure ain't made any new friends for the Indians. Are your friends on the run with the rest of that bunch?"

"I think so, but no way to know for sure. Roland went off to check on his old place, see if maybe he can sell it off, or some of the equipment, tools, whatever. When he comes back, he said he'd watch after my place and stock, so I could get away and go check on them."

"Well, I wish you luck. I always did fancy that young lady."

Ollie paid the bill and they split up. Abe went into the main part of town and collected every newspaper he could, went to the library and read whatever he could find, and then made his way back to Ollie's house. Most of the articles were just copies of army dispatches and when he scanned them they didn't tell him much about the Indians. From all reports, it seemed they were on their way to the Yellowstone country, and some reports even had them heading for Canada. If Helga was still all right, and still with them, there was no way he could find them now.

He did some shopping, following a list Sa-rah had given him, picked out a few little gifts for the family, and decided to get started home right away rather than wait for another early morning. This way, he figured even if he didn't get very far before dark, he should be able to reach home by late afternoon of the next day.

He'd left the harness with the wagon, and when he found the house unoccupied and locked up again, he put his shopping goods into a large feed bag and led the horse back down through town. He was passing a saloon when he heard a man shouting a lot of cusswords interspersed with the name, "Ollie." He tied the horse to a rail and crossed over to look inside the building where the sounds of trouble were coming from.

Just as he reached the swinging doors, a man came stumbling through them, and nearly knocked him down. He jumped out of the way and the man went down on his face in the street. Ollie followed him out the doorway and stood over the man in the street, who rolled over and tried to pull a gun. Ollie kicked it out of his hand with his artificial leg and spit a stream of tobacco juice into the fallen man's face. By this time several other men had come outside and were forming a circle around Ollie and his victim. Ollie was breathing hard and leaned over with his metal arm held above his head.

"You take it back, say you're goddam sorry, or you might not ever get up again."

The man cursed, kicked at Ollie's leg, missed, and rolled over on his frontside again. That was when Ollie noticed Abe, bent down, picked up the gun and flipped it to him. "Here, my young friend, take care of this." Then he staggered a few steps back and repeated what he'd told the man lying in the street about taking it back, and then started counting after saying, "You got 'till I say five. One... Two...Three... Four..."

"All right, I take it back."

"Say you're sorry."

"I'm not, but I'll say it, I'm sorry."

Ollie stepped forward and kicked the man in the shin. "Think about what that's going to do to your head next time I swing it."

"All right, I'm sorry."

"All right," he looked around. "You hear that boys, says he's sorry. But I should've killed the sonofabitch. Drinks are on me, fellas."

Abe stepped forward and helped him turn and climb the two steps up to the porch and then pass into the dark space inside. Ollie fell into the first chair they came to, and from his heavy breathing Abe couldn't be sure whether he was drunk or just weary.

"Drinks around," Ollie called out, "and especially for my young friend here." Abe tried to refuse, but Ollie wouldn't have it. "You have to drink with me. It was partly about you."

"What do you mean?"

"I beat his hand four times in a row. Took his money every time. Sonofabitch called Mattie a nigger, me a nigger-lover, and went on saying he heard the young fella I was with this morning was a goddam Indian-lover. I couldn't let him get away with it."

The bartender delivered their drinks. Ollie raised his glass and Abe did the same. "To you, son. And to the love of Indians and Negroes." He tipped his shot glass back and downed it. Abe took a careful sip of his.

"Who is he?"

"Some cow puncher from Nevada, been trying to get me drunk for a couple days now."

"He might look familiar to me."

"How's that?"

"Well," Abe spoke slowly, "I didn't think of it before, but when you said Nevada I remembered he stumbled away with a pretty good limp in his leg, not the one you kicked either."

Ollie yelled for another shot for himself and Abe covered his own glass with his hand.

"So what's all that mean?" the man asked when he got his drink.

"It means he could be the same one I shot when we were first building the house. Two of them showed up, claimed the land was theirs and tried to force us off. Set fire to the house when it was only half-built, and when I chased after them, I had to shoot one of them in the leg and then finally kill the other one or he'd have got me, self-defense."

"And you think this might be the one that got away with the bum leg?"

"Didn't get away. Helga kept a gun on him, and had him under control until I got back to her. I'd been shot in the shoulder, same arm I got wounded at the end of the War, but it wasn't as bad. No bones this time. Anyhow, we kept him trussed up until the law came and took him away. If I ever thought about him since, I just figured he'd still be behind bars."

Somebody at the bar gave a toast to Ollie and he downed his glass. "Well, that might explain something. Other night he asked me a lot of questions about the country out your way. Said he knew a blacksmith in those parts. Nice land, he said, except for the Indians. I let it go and he got me pretty drunk. Didn't think I'd see him again, until he showed up at this here card game today."

"Then it is him. What'd he ask you? What'd you say?"

"Don't rightly remember now, but it must have been something about Mattie and about your friendship with the Indians used to own that land. Nothing more than that, but that's where he must have got that stuff he was saying today when I had to call him out and kick his butt."

"Here," Abe said and pulled out the gun from behind his back in the chair. "Guess this is yours now."

"You keep it. I've got plenty of 'em. Sounds like he owes you something anyway."

"Thanks, I guess. Anyway, I'm headed back, soon as I hitch up. Get home by tomorrow dark if I leave now. Oh, one more thing. Mattie ever say what she'd want on her grave marker?"

"Said she didn't want nothing, but if it had to have something, should be 'God Is Love.' Nothing else." Ollie stood up, unsteady, and leaned on the table to grasp Abe's forearm with his one hand. "Son, you take care now, and give my best to your folks and to Mike and my sister. Next time you come into town, I'll take a ride back out there with you. Gets a bit lonely in here."

"I'll do that. And you take it easy. No more fights." He turned and left, looking back at the doorway and waving.

Abe got back next afternoon as he'd hoped. He dropped the wagon and Mike's delivery paperwork at their place, and borrowed a saddle horse for the rest of the ride home. When he reached his place, he was met with a noisy greeting. Bird nickered from her corral, Happy barked and jumped around the strange horse he was on, and Isaiah came running out of the house yelling, and took the reins of the horse when his Papa climbed down. Abe told the boy to lead the animal over to the hitch by the stable, and went on up to the house where Sa-rah and DoraLee were waiting on the porch.

"You made good time," she said as he took the little girl from her and he kissed his wife.

"Yes, went well. I'll tell you all about it when I've fed the horse, she's a good one." He turned and went back out to help Isaiah with the chores.

"Papa, I took my horse for a ride today. All the way to the hillside by where the creeks meet up, you know, by the Indian camp."

"That's good, but I thought I told you not to ride out of sight of the house."

"I wasn't. If I stood up in my stirrups, I could still see the chimney."

"Well, that's stretching it, son. From now on that's as far as you go. No further than where you can see the chimney, and I don't mean the smoke, but the chimney itself. Now get me a can of that grain in the barrel." He handed the boy the horse's nosebag. "Only half full."

That night when he told Sa-rah about his encounter with Ollie, he left out the part about the fight and the gunman from Nevada. On the way home, he'd gone back over his memory of the incident with the man and his partner, how he'd killed the one and wounded this one, but also how all that happened when Sa-rah was gone away with Hawk Man. It was Helga who went through that time with him. The memory left him sad and even more concerned for her since the news reports and the conversation he was able to have at the telegraph office all described failures on the part of the army to bring the chase to a rapid finish. However, the key message seemed to him to be the near-hysterical attacks on the Indians in the press and the calls for the army to seek maximum revenge for the deaths of whites at the hands of the "savages" and their "evil heathen ways." It was all a sharp reminder of some of the articles he'd read in clippings from northern papers when he was on President Davis's staff just before the end of that War. Part of his job was to read and select news items for the chief of staff and the president to read, and he was always somewhat shocked by the language that described the troops of the Confederacy as subhuman or less, and the same characteristics applied to the Union Army by the southern press.

What was surprising, as well, was that some of the officers quoted here, in this case, who were leading the pursuit of the Indians, were singled out as veterans of the War Between the States. It made him remember and think about something that Sa-rah's minister father had said to him about how he'd been nearly thrown out of his pulpit in western Virginia because he prayed for peace rather than for victory. Now these Indian Wars, as they were called, seemed to prove again that humans didn't want to learn from the past. Abe had tried to shake off those thoughts as the wagon rolled through the beauty of the landscape in this isolated part of what was being called Oregon, but it was hard, and the fight and its causes between Ollie and the Nevadan was another confirmation of this truth.

When Sa-rah asked him what he'd learned from the newspapers, about what was going on with Helga and Indigo, he didn't answer right away. After a long pause while he sorted through what he'd learned and how and what it was best to tell her, he decided to just come out with it.

"The army has chased the Indians as far as the Yellowstone country. Some of the papers are calling for the general and his officers to be dismissed and new people put in charge, because, as they say, let me read it to you. 'It is an embarrassment to the United States of America, that a poorly armed mob of stone-age savages burdened down with women, children, and old people, driving hundreds of horses ahead, can escape and even prevent the pursuit of the world's greatest Army. Shame on you, General Howard.' And that's one of the more polite statements here," he patted the small pile of newspapers.

"So what do you think is happening with them?"

"Unless they stayed behind in Idaho, they are as desperate as any of the Indians, and I'm sure that Hawk Man, and possibly even Lefty, are right there in the middle of it all."

"And Moon Fish?"

"Maybe they left her behind. We can only hope so, because I don't see how she could survive the hardships of them all running for their lives."

"Oh, I feel so terrible. It's all my fault this has happened to our family. I feel bad, so bad I can't even pray about it, it hurts me so much. Abe, I'm truly sorry..."

He stood and moved over behind her. He put one hand on her head and with the other he reached down to lightly touch the baby's sparse light-colored hair. "Father in Heaven, we come to you in our hour of need. We ask for protection for those of our family whose lives may be in danger, and who are probably living every moment in fear. We ask for your protection and comfort for them, and we know that there is no blame for the things we do if we are truly asking you for forgiveness. And to the Earth, in the way we've been taught by our friends, dear Mother, we are so grateful for this home and this land, and we ask we will be shown what we can do to bring this land into fruitfulness, and to bring our family together once again. Amen."

When he finished his prayer, he felt Sa-rah's warm tears falling on his hand, and he hoped that he hadn't been too judging in his prayer. He didn't mean to be; above all now, he needed her to be the strongest mother she could be for all of them now.

"Sa-rah, my dearest. What has happened is free of blame because we all shared in it, and now we are all forgiven and we can and will move on. I'm tired now, and I'd like you to come and lay down beside me. We have so much to be thankful for."

"I know, I know. But I've hurt you and who knows what's happened to them because of my selfishness."

"I don't think it's selfish when a mother is protecting her child. Here, I'll lay her down." He took the little one in his arms and rocked her gently when she stirred as he went to place her in the crib. "Goodnight, baby girl."

It was still dark and the people were already beginning to move about and begin packing up for another move. Scouts had reported that more army was moving toward them, and the other chiefs were certain the general's plan was to trap the People between the two forces, his from the northwest and the others from the south. The only chance the People had to avoid this was to move quickly, heading northeast, and hoping to escape by crossing the white man's border into Grandmother's Land.

Chief Joseph sent for Lefty to come to his camp in the pre-dawn hours.

"What is it?" Lefty said in their language, as he came through the covering of the shelter.

"My friend, we are weak, and it is getting colder every night now. I have had no dreams, but I know we may not be able to escape. If we cannot go on, I will surrender. I cannot let these ones go on and die with no hope in fighting. We can no longer fight. We have few young men, and even the horses can no longer carry us. The other chiefs say they will fight if they have to, but I will only try to get away from fighting. Pray for us, my friend."

"I will not leave you."

"You must. You are the only one who can tell the story of what has happened to us. The only one who can tell it in the white man words to make them understand. You are more important as our messenger than to be here with us, no matter what happens."

"But I and my family cannot leave you and make our own way. We will be caught."

Joseph looked down at his hands and then raised them over his head. "With these hands, with my heart, I will save your family if anyone can do this. You can do no more for them here than I can. But you can do much for our people by going back where we came from and making the whites understand what they have done to us. You tell them this is what Joseph says. Tell them they have betrayed their own Jesus-God. You tell them we only want our homeland. Tell them we are dying. Tell them I will fight no more." He stood and pulled Lefty toward himself, grasping the other man's arms, and saying. "We will meet again. Take my best horse. Go!"

A week passed peacefully as the days shortened and the first crisp nights of fall threatened frost. Although Abe was still very worried about Helga and Indigo, he tried to put that out of his mind, since there didn't seem to be anything he could do about it. Perhaps when Roland returned. He thought that should be any day now.

Isaiah was a big help to his mother as they gathered the late berries that grew near the creek. He worked hard because his parents had promised that if he worked a certain amount each day, he could go riding alone, but still never out of sight of the chimney. He'd worked out quite a route down to the creek going one way, crossing it and working his way back up the other side until he was past Mattie's grave, and then riding up the hillside above the road where he could see the chimney from quite a distance. When Abe or Sa-rah asked where he'd been, he'd usually answer, "Oh, you know," and gesture in some direction. One day Abe saddled up and followed him at a distance and found that even though the boy really went quite a distance, he was careful to always find a way to be able to see the house or chimney.

Then one day the boy didn't return before it was beginning to get dark. Abe came home from working on some firewood over by the Indian camp where he could get it with his wagon, and Sa-rah came running toward him yelling "Isaiah's gone. Isaiah, he's not here! Oh Abe!" She fell into his arms.

"What do you mean, gone?"

"Copper came back, but Isaiah's not with him. He must be hurt somewhere."

Abe jumped back on his horse and took off along the boy's usual route. He rode quickly, but stopped from time to time to yell the boy's name and listen. Nothing, no answer. He began riding back and forth through the middle of the large oval bounded by the creeks. Still nothing. Each time he got near the house Sa-rah was there waiting and he had to tell her he hadn't found any sign. It was almost dark, so after one final ride through the area, he put Bird away and grabbed a lantern from the stable and set off on foot, still calling every few steps.

Finally, after a couple more hours of futile searching, he stopped at the house and gave Sa-rah the bad news that he'd found nothing. She made him sit down and eat something, but he was soon off again. She called after him that it wouldn't do any good to keep looking in the dark, but he plunged out into the brush, thinking only that he couldn't begin to accept it if he were to lose both his sons.

At one point during his search, probably around midnight, he had the idea to light a fire near the middle of the area. Perhaps the boy would see the flames and find a way to come toward them, even if he were hurt. But what if he wasn't nearby? What if he'd broken the rule and gone off some other direction, out of sight of the house, out where they would have no way to even guess? Abe tried to stay awake by the fire he'd built, but at some point he knew that if he didn't get moving again he'd fall asleep, so he kicked dirt on the fire and headed back for the house. When he passed Mattie's burial place and reached the trail they'd made back to the house, he asked for her help, asked for any sign, anything at all.

Sa-rah was dozing with the baby in her arms, rocking in the chair. She woke with a startled look and then cried out, "You find something? Anything?"

"No," he said. "And it won't do any good to keep looking now. I've tried everything. I'll start looking again before dawn, and I'll take the dog with me."

He lay down on the couch and felt her hands removing his boots. He knew how upset she was, but right then there was nothing more he could do. It was as if it was out of their hands. Sa-rah wiped her tears away and sat down on the floor beside him. Now it came into her mind that no matter how hard this was for her, it must be even more terrible for her dear Abe, now with both of his sons missing.

"If you wake up early, wake me," he mumbled through his exhaustion. "I'll go…"

Early, even before there was light in the sky, DoraLee woke up crying and wanted her mother. Sa-rah woke, gathered the baby from her crib and crawled back into bed. She suddenly heard the sound of a running horse outside the house. Then there was a crash against one of the windows.

"Abe," she screamed as she got up and hurried toward him. "Abe, someone was out there and something hit the window!"

"What, what?" he said sitting up. "What happened?"

"Abe, I heard a horse running by the house and something crashed into the big window."

"Did it break?"

"No, whatever it was must be out there."

He pushed himself up and away from the couch, and stumbled over to grab his rifle.

"Be careful," she said as he moved to the door and opened it a crack.

"Can you get me a lantern?" he asked.

"Yes." She went to the kitchen and lit a lamp, bringing it back to him. He reached through the narrow opening of the door and set the lamp on the porch floor. Then he moved around inside to another window and pulled aside the curtain. The glow of the light lit up the yard, but he couldn't see anything out there. He went back and eased himself out the door, crouching low. There was only silence, silence and darkness. He reached behind him, picking up the lamp, and carried it around to the window she said had been hit. There was a small bundle on the ground by the foundation stones of the house. He set down the lamp and picked it up. It was an old sock and inside was what felt like a rock. He gripped it in his free hand, cradled the rifle with his elbow, and looked carefully around the yard. He picked up the lamp again, and worked his way back into the house.

Sa-rah and the baby were waiting for him when he came back inside. He ejected the cartridge from his gun, leaned it against the wall, and held up the knotted sock for her to see.

"This is what it was."

"That's Isaiah's sock?"

"There's a rock inside," he said, untying the knot that held it closed at its top. "Stand back. Who knows what it could be, a snake or spider, whatever." He shook it to get the contents to fall out onto the floor. There was nothing but the rock and a crumpled piece of paper.

"What is it?" she asked.

"I don't know. There's writing on it."

"Well, read it. Hurry." Sa-rah leaned closer.

Abe unrolled the paper and glanced through the note, took a sudden intake of breath and slammed his fist to the floor. "Damn it!"

"What? Let me see."

"I'll read it… *'I know about your gold mine. I got kid - you owe me – want $500 in gold or never see boy again. Want my gun too. Put on big rock in creek where road crosses. You get boy - no tricks or he dead.'* That's all it says."

Sa-rah had fallen back into a chair and was gasping for breath. DoraLee began crying loudly, and she quieted the baby by nursing. At last she said, "What do you think it means?"

Abe looked at the paper again and then folded it in his hands. "It means Ollie told our secret, got drunk. He told me he got drunk with this man. Then he had to fight him the day I was leaving town, smashed the side of his head with his metal hand and kicked him with his metal leg. The fellow tried to draw on Ollie so he kicked the gun out of his hand, then gave it to me to take when I left town."

"Who is it? What does it mean you owe him?"

"When you were gone with the Indians that time, I had to kill one of the men who tried to burn down our new house. They said this was their land. This is the one I wounded and who wounded me, and then they took him off to prison."

"I remember all that. You told me, but what's this gold mine?"

"I never really told you the whole story, but the money I got to buy this land from the government came from gold we found up near where our water comes out. Ollie and I found it and we only took enough to pay for the land and give a little to Hawk Man. Ollie said if there was any more in those rocks we'd have to use explosives to get it. The Indians don't want us to take any more. And I don't want to either because I thought we could keep it secret. Anyone who finds out could bring all kinds of people here. They'd overrun the place. Ollie told me after the fight, that the gunslinger got him drunk and he doesn't remember what he might have told him."

"Why didn't you ever tell me about all this?"

"I thought it was best to just forget it altogether, once I decided we'd never try to take anymore."

"Abe! What do we do now?" She was pacing back and forth. "Do we still have that much gold? Or that much money? What he wants. Do you?"

"No," he said quietly, and buried his face in his hands.

Sa-rah moaned and said softly, "God is taking my son from me," then louder, "God is taking him away from me for what I've done."

Abe looked up at her and said, "No, that's not right, because he's been taken away from me too…I've got to find him." He got up off the couch and grabbed his rifle, loading it. "I will find him."

End of Book II

Edwards Brothers Malloy
Thorofare, NJ USA
May 13, 2016